Summer People

Brian Groh

AN ecco BOOK

HARPER PERENNIAL

NEW YORK • LONDON • TORONTO • SYDNEY

PRAISE FOR

Summer People

"This is an introspective tragicomedy about depression, class, and finding a mooring in life. . . . 3 out of 4 stars."

—*People*

"There's a little of F. Scott Fitzgerald's Nick Carraway (of *The Great Gatsby*) in the 'outsider' Nathan's cautious evaluations of the bright world into which he is almost, if not quite fully, welcomed. And I was reminded more than once of Thornton Wilder's novels (such as his unfinished *Theophilus North*), in which intuitive young men find their own sensibilities opening to new possibilities within the confines of essentially closed societies. . . . An agreeably thoughtful and provocative novel."

—*Down East*

"Funny and fast-paced . . . believable banter is definitely one of Groh's strengths. . . . Grade: A."

—*Cincinnati CityBeat*

"Groh's dry social observation, his wicked ear for dialogue, and flashes of ironic humor transmute [*Summer People*] into something more philosophical, as Nathan moves through a tragicomic landscape, coming to grips with class, money, Aristotelian precepts, mortality, the essential loneliness of the human condition, and the possibility that the pursuit of happiness might not be all that it's cracked up to be. . . . [A] beguiling tale full of wit and wisdom."

—*Kirkus Reviews* (starred review)

"No one knows quite how to act toward Nathan: Is he a driver? A nephew? A companion? Throw in a love interest . . . plus a set of local rich kids, and watch the classic tension between the wealthy and the hired help unfold. Groh's novel is strong . . . and Nathan's character, like the lead in [Nick Hornby's] *High Fidelity*, ultimately charms."

—*Booklist*

"*Summer People* captures so well the balancing act one must perform when struggling between unignorable duty and overwhelming desire. Startlingly humorous and affecting, the author's debut novel provides a window into a rarefied, cloistered world, filled with characters who still go through my heart—just a delight to read."

—Elizabeth Strout, bestselling author of *Amy and Isabelle* and *Abide With Me*

"Please be careful if you're taking Brian Groh's *Summer People* to the beach. Once you've started this fine and funny novel, it will take a strong-willed effort indeed to put it down again. But if you must, be sure and wear plenty of sunblock, and be prepared for a few looks from your neighbors—they're going to want to know why you're laughing so much."

—Owen King, author of *We're All in This Together*

A NOVEL

Summer People

HARPER PERENNIAL

P.S.™ is a trademark of HarperCollins Publishers.

A hardcover edition of this book was published in 2007 by Ecco, an imprint of HarperCollins Publishers.

HarperCollins books may be purchased for educational, business, or sales promotional use. For information please write: Special Markets Department, HarperCollins Publishers, 10 East 53rd Street, New York, NY 10022.

FIRST HARPER PERENNIAL EDITION PUBLISHED 2007.

Designed by Jessica Shatan Heslin

Library of Congress Cataloging-in-Publication Data is available upon request.

ISBN: 978-0-06-120997-0
ISBN-10: 0-06-120997-X

07 08 09 10 11 WBC/RRD 10 9 8 7 6 5 4 3 2 1

For Jeff and Steven

One

Ellen Goes Missing ~ A Visit to St. Michael's ~ An Unconventional Sermon ~ An Apparition Becomes Real

In the morning, Nathan awoke and discovered Ellen was not in her room. Her bed was clumsily made, the blue comforter pulled over rumpled white sheets, and her closet door stood wide open. Downstairs, sunlight poured through first-floor windows, and on his way through the living room, Nathan still registered mild surprise at his surroundings. The house, a sprawling, white clapboard manse, with three chimneys and a wraparound porch, sat on top of a grassy slope with a breathtaking view of Albans Bay. Yet where Nathan had expected an interior expensively understated, he'd encountered only a kind of rundown rusticity. Couches and chairs didn't look much different than the faded department-store variety in the shared house where he'd been living, the dull hardwood floors hadn't been polished in decades, and his bed upstairs was so old that its creaking had occasionally interrupted his sleep. In the kitchen, he shouted, "Hellooooo!" and went to the window. The sun flashed between the distant islands and anchored sailboats of Albans Bay, and staring down at the pale crescent of Parson's Beach, Nathan saw for the first time what he would see repeatedly that summer: wealthy New England parents and their children, relaxing on unfolded chairs and blankets, with the sound of silvery laughter filling the air. Nathan thought, Sweet Jesus, it exists, the scene I've been seeing in Lands' End catalogs all my life. As he stepped onto the porch, the screen door slapped behind him and he cupped his hand above his eyes. Besides the few clusters of families, a man in a fishing hat was walking his dachshund, but that was all.

Backtracking through the house and upstairs, Nathan peered into the three extra bedrooms, where white sheets were still draped over much of the furniture. He called her name but heard only distant voices on the beach and the barking of a neighbor's dog. In his bedroom, he pulled on his shoes then wandered back down to the kitchen. He opened the door to the cellar and peered into the musty shadows.

"Ellen?"

He waited.

"Ellen?"

With a sigh, Nathan tramped down the stairs. A dust-smeared window let in only a cloudy beam of light at the back of the room, and although a lightbulb dangled from an old, fraying cord, Nathan was too afraid of electrocution to touch it. In a near corner lay bags of mulch that the yardman must have recently purchased, but near the back wall, old paint cans, bags of cement, and wooden lobster cages looked as if they had been moldering down there for decades. As Nathan turned, a spiderweb pulled gently across his forehead and he scrambled back up the staircase like a smothered man desperate for air.

In the living room, he stood staring out the French doors that led onto the porch and offered a view of the harbor. Was she down on Parson's Beach, somewhere he couldn't see? The back lawn sloped steeply toward the water, and Nathan took long, purposeful strides, stopping once to survey the grounds, before continuing down to the shore. He nodded and smiled at the parents who watched him as he weaved in between the massive rocks.

"Did you lose something?" asked a man, squinting through sunglasses, his children laboring in the sand beside him. Nathan had recently attended college, but looked younger, and he suspected the older man was trying to find out if he was trespassing.

Nathan didn't look at him long, not wanting to satisfy him. "I just lost my watch."

"You want some help?"

"No. Thank you, though. I don't want to bother you."

"It's no bother."

The father set his book down on his chair, and Nathan wasted several minutes walking back and forth over a stretch of sand that was the one place on earth he now knew Ellen was not.

"Are you visiting someone here?" The man had a long, patrician face and unnaturally white teeth.

Nathan admitted, "I'm kind of helping out for Ellen Broderick this summer."

"Is that right? So she made it back. Well, good for her. She's doing okay?"

There was more in the man's question than a casual inquiry. But, distracted, Nathan answered, "Yeah, she seems like she's doing all right."

When he hastened back to the house, and entered the kitchen, he patted the pockets of his shorts and felt the car keys against his thigh. There was no reason for him to be worried, he thought. She had seemed in good health around him, if a little quiet, and it was her first morning back in her summer home, so she had probably gone next door to visit friends. Nathan made a piece of toast and ate it as he walked around the first floor, sipping orange juice, occasionally glancing out windows. He decided to retrieve from the car the bag of art books and comics he'd brought with him from home. Outside, in the warmth of the sun, he was crossing the well-manicured lawn toward the driveway when he noticed Ellen. She was sitting in the passenger seat of her maroon Volkswagen Passat. Her head was resting against the closed window, and although she was only seventy-two, according to his father, Nathan immediately feared the worst while hurrying toward her. Her once petite frame, now slackened into a huskier solidity, sat slumped in its seat, but her face still held the high cheekbones of a once classically beautiful woman. Her eyes were closed, her lips barely parted, and Nathan's heart pulsed in his ears as he rapped hard on the glass. Ellen's head jerked from the window, her blue eyes wide.

Nathan waited to see if her heart would fail, then opened the door. "My God, I'm sorry, are you all right?"

Clearing her throat and blinking, Ellen's eyes narrowed in recognition. "I suppose so," she answered. She wore a blue, calf-length dress, and an unbuttoned white cardigan that nearly matched the hair, pulled into a bun, which rested against the base of her neck. Pushing a loose strand from her face, she sighed and looked Nathan over. In addition to the same pair of shorts he'd worn to pick her up from the airport the previous evening, Nathan was wearing old running shoes, a wrinkled T-shirt, and his hair, still uncombed, looked as if someone had rubbed it vigorously with a balloon.

Nathan asked, "Why were you sitting out here?"

"I was just thinking." Ellen turned to look through the front windshield at nothing in particular in a neighbor's yard. "This is Sunday?"

"Yeah, I think so."

"Well," she said. "Would you like to take me to church?"

Nathan hurried back to his room, changed clothes and combed his hair, then hustled back to the car. "All right, can you tell me how to get there?" he asked, helping Ellen fasten her seat belt. Ellen flashed a more wrinkled version of the flat-lipped smile Nathan had first seen in an old photograph while interviewing to be her escort to Maine. In the photo, positioned on top of the grand piano at her home in Cleveland, she was a slender, elegant young woman, sitting by herself on the beach, her chin over her shoulder as she smiled amusedly through windswept hair.

"I've been coming here since I was a little girl," Ellen said.

"Okay," Nathan said, nodding. "Well, do you know if we're on time for a service? It's a little bit after eleven."

"I think we'll be fine," Ellen said. She guided Nathan up the gravel road onto Birch Hill Boulevard, a broad, tree-canopied street that was the central corridor of Brightonfield Cove. On the far side of picket fences and spacious lawns, large homes of brick and clapboard sat with robust contentment. Bicycles and beach toys lay waiting on porches for children to finish breakfast or return from church, while cheery flowers waved from windowsills and modest, well-tended gardens. In the fresh morning light, the neighborhood glowed like the America of Norman Rockwell's sweetest dreams, and with one arm draped outside the window, Nathan sighed and settled into what he was starting to hope would be a long drive.

"Here we are," Ellen said, gesturing toward a narrow blacktop road that cut through the trees and sloping grass of a golf course on the left. Nathan sat up straight and glanced at Ellen—doubtful now of her directions—but as they turned and ascended the sloping hill, a steeple rose above the horizon. The stone Episcopal church sat beside a small graveyard in the very center of the Alnombak club golf course. St. Michael's in the Field was the church's proper name, but it was not uncommon during the summer to hear it called St. Michael's in the Way. Wire mesh protected the stained glass, and there was no parking lot, so parishioners, most of them golfers, parked their cars gingerly on the fairway. Women in pastel dresses and men in summer blazers congregated near the stone walkway, and only when Nathan noticed a slow trickle of parishioners into the church did he stop hoping he could escape attending the service. Other stragglers greeted Ellen with warmth—and occasionally questioning expressions, Nathan noticed—as everyone filed through the arched doors. While they sat toward the back on an uncushioned, hardwood pew and a few people stole furtive glances at her, Ellen sat with almost perfect posture, head erect, her chin tilted slightly up. Her deepening laugh lines and crow's-feet, Nathan knew, were the result of a lifetime of summer tennis and golf, but she seemed to be aging naturally, without tucks or lifts, and she held herself with a kind of dignity that—although he couldn't determine if she was oblivious to others' glances, or just ignoring them—made Nathan strangely proud to be with her. She stared ahead as the pastor rose to the pulpit and cleared his throat.

" 'Let no man seek his own, but every man another's wealth,' " the man began, reading from Corinthians I. The sentence hung in the stony-smelling church air as he raised his head and peered out at the congregation from behind round, wire-rimmed glasses. Hefty and broad shouldered, black hair prematurely flecked with gray, Eldwin Lowell had ashen crescents beneath his blue eyes and looked more like an overworked professor than the eager boy-man ministers Nathan had known.

The story he told, about how his son had recently started school and acquired new friends, eventually led into an exploration of Aristotle's writings on friendship, provoking Nathan to glance around him at the surprisingly impassive reactions of the congregation. Growing up in suburban Cleveland, he had attended church almost every Sunday with his mother, but he had never heard any minister quote Aristotle.

"Perfect friendship is the friendship of people who love one another not because they are useful to one another, and not because they are entertaining to one another, but for themselves," Eldwin continued. "Aristotle says that such friends wish the best for one another by reason of their own natures, and such friendships last as long as they are good—because goodness is an enduring thing." Eldwin had been looking down at his notes, but now he looked out into the faces of a few of the people seated before him. "Because goodness is an enduring thing.

"I'm sure that this morning, looking around at people you have known for many years, some of you are lucky enough to have such friends here. But it seems to me, as I'm sure it seems to you, that even these perfect friendships aren't perfect. Even with those select few—or select one—with whom you speak freely of your hopes and feelings, you know you're always speaking with a limit. There is a limit to our trust and understanding of one another that cannot be helped. Nevertheless, this longing, this hunger for understanding, propels us toward nobler, higher friendships, which give our lives meaning and joy, and provide us with glimpses of the joy of heaven and of communion with God. When you feel yourself weakening, tempted toward sins of cowardice, or self-indulgence, be strong in knowing that there are others who are also working for good, and that if we persevere in God's work, we will join their company, and the longing in our hearts will be answered."

Eldwin asked the congregation to join him in prayer, and everyone bowed their heads. Nathan bowed his also but kept his eyes open. Late the previous evening, while preparing for bed, he'd pressed his face to the screen of his bedroom window to watch a young woman stride through the moonlit grass of the yard below. She seemed a kind of apparition. But now a young woman who looked very much like her was sitting just a few pews ahead of him, with two small children on her left. When the prayer ended and she rose to sing with the congregation, Nathan saw she wore a dark green summer dress. She tucked a lock of hair behind her ear as she reached down for her hymnal.

"Aren't we going to sing?" Ellen asked.

Nathan pulled out the hymnal in front of them, but by the time he'd found the right hymn they only had time to sing the last chorus. He glanced sidelong at Ellen to see if she was disappointed, but she just smiled expectantly at him, waiting for him to lead them out of the aisle. On the way out, old couples crossed over pews to chat with Ellen, and although their inquiries about her health were often delivered with faces pinched by concern, Ellen assured them she was fine and thereby encouraged the conversation to hurry along to something else. She seemed pleased to see her friends, but she addressed very few people by name. She nodded, smiling, saying, "Oh, yes," and "Oh, fine," and "It's great to see you, too," but she spoke very little about herself. Those who approached filled in the silences by speaking about grandchildren recently born, a son's admission to Exeter, a husband's long hours at his firm ("He's planning to come up sometime next month and he'll be so pleased to know you're here"). Outside, along the stone walkway, Eldwin Lowell shook hands with Ellen and Nathan and explained how he was the replacement for Pastor Russell, who had returned to Boston for cancer treatment. Eldwin said to Nathan, "You should introduce yourself to Leah, our nanny. She's with Meghan and Eliot around here someplace."

Nathan's face reddened. He knew the young woman he'd been admiring was walking with Eldwin's children on the fairway.

"All right, I will," Nathan said, extending his hand for the pastor to shake although they'd already shaken hands a moment earlier. Surprisingly, for a woman of otherwise erect bearing, Ellen employed a gold-handled cane, and as she said good-bye, balancing between the cane and Nathan's arm, her white, toothy smile closed into tight-lipped determination. Together they shuffled down the stone walkway, onto the grass, while Nathan tried to set a pace that would allow her to keep her balance but put them inside the car as soon as possible. He wanted to go back to the house, sit on the porch, maybe draw a sketch of Leah as he remembered her from last night, walking up from the beach. He did not want to talk to her now. He wanted time to think about what he would say when he met her, and he wanted to be wearing something other than this short-sleeved, button-down navy shirt. It made his pale, unmuscled arms look even more pale and thin than they were. As they inched closer to the car, Nathan tried to seem preoccupied with Ellen—turning his head only between her and the ground—but he could feel the young woman approaching.

The two children had broken away from her, racing back toward the church, and she was following unhurriedly after them, strolling between the parked cars, just a few yards from Nathan. Her cotton dress curved over full breasts, but she walked with a teenager's slouching posture. Pushing a lock of loose brown curls from her face, she confirmed Nathan's hopes and anxieties. Warmly knowing dark eyes, puffy roseate lips. Her attractiveness was of the no-makeup, slightly oily hair variety, and although a moment earlier he had hoped she would pass by without noticing him, he felt the lovely pull of her upon him.

"Leah?" he asked. The young woman turned and raked her hand through her hair to keep it from blowing into her face. Nathan introduced himself without moving and said, "I was just talking to the pastor and he said you were nannying for his kids this summer?"

Leah glanced back at the church where the children were hanging on to their father as he spoke with parishioners. "Well, I'm trying," she said, a lock of hair escaping from her grasp and falling into her eyes.

She laughed at the futility of the battle she was waging with the wind, and Nathan returned her smile. He gestured through the back window at Ellen, who was staring straight ahead at the church. "I'm kind of Mrs. Broderick's chauffeur for the summer. We just got here yesterday. I think I might have seen you taking a walk last night."

Leah said, "Oh?"

"How long have you been here?" Nathan asked.

"Two weeks."

"How's it been?"

"It's been okay. I was making plans to run away in the beginning," Leah said, grinning as she glanced out to where the golf course ended in a steep cliff overlooking the ocean. "I'm not used to taking care of kids, but I'm better now." She looked a few years younger than Nathan, as if she was perhaps still in college, or had recently graduated.

Nathan said, "I haven't seen many people up here our age."

"No, I know," Leah said. "I've seen a few people on the beach, but I haven't met anybody."

Nathan walked over to the driver's side with studied casualness and said, "Well, I think I'm probably free most evenings if you want to take a walk sometime. I live in that big white house with the front porch that's just as you're coming up from Parson's Beach."

Leah's eyebrows rose and her voice seemed to resonate with possibility. "Oh! Well, I live two houses up the same street. It's a smaller house, with a little deck out front?"

Nathan managed to say only, "Okay. Great." Opening the car door, he raised his palm in farewell. "Well, feel free to come by or maybe I'll try and stop over at your place sometime."

Inside the car, hot, stifling air settled around him, but Nathan took a deep breath. He put on his seat belt and watched through the windshield as Leah walked the rest of the way across the grass.

"It's very warm," Ellen said, her right hand on her neck.

"Sorry," Nathan said, inserting the keys to start the car. "I forgot it was so stuffy in here."

The direct sunlight on the car's upholstery seemed to be releasing the smell of Ellen's golden retriever, back home in Cleveland, and Nathan immediately pressed the automatic windows down. But perhaps because the breeze was blowing from behind them, off the ocean, much of the stale air remained as they waited for the car ahead of them to move. When Nathan eventually pulled out of the church driveway, onto Birch Hill, he pushed the gas pedal down hard. The car filled with a sudden rush of fresh air, and inhaling it felt like a kind of triumph.

Two

A Portentous Moment at Gilman's ~ The First Supper ~ Carl Buchanan Vents His Frustration ~ Nathan Interrogates His Father

Light mist thickened into heavy rain that afternoon, and instead of going to the Alnombak club as planned, Nathan and Ellen took seats in front of the TV. Nathan read a comic book on the couch and later pulled out his sketch pad to draw a profile of Ellen in her lounge chair watching golf. He worried that he had not picked up enough groceries for dinner that evening and he was concerned about leaving Ellen. But it was raining too hard for her to go with him, and an hour later—the rain still pouring in blurry waves—he told her where he was going and drove the quarter-mile into town.

Gilman's was a one-room clapboard store that sat on the far west end of Birch Hill Boulevard, across the street from the post office and near the narrow strait leading out from the inlet, or cove, into Albans Bay. Beneath Nathan's tennis shoes, grains of sand scraped against the hardwood floor. The near corner offered a rack of rental movies, and farther along the same wall, the butcher's glass case contained an iced arrangement of gourmet seafood and meat. In back, a sandwich counter stood in front of a few tables with windows overlooking the water.

Nathan grabbed a cart and wandered the store's three narrow aisles, searching for things he could cook. In addition to steak, corn, and potatoes, he picked up assorted breakfast food and sandwich meat, a two-liter of soda, and a bottle of Captain Morgan Spiced Rum.

"That all you need?" the cashier asked. She was a thickset woman in jeans and an untucked shirt, with long, charcoal gray hair piled somewhat carelessly on her head. Her thick New England accent, coarsened by decades of smoking, surprised Nathan, and it occurred to him that this was the first time since his arrival in Brightonfield Cove that he'd met someone native to Maine.

"That's it for now," Nathan said, his own Midwestern accent sounding strangely flat to his ears.

The woman picked up the items from the counter and punched their prices into the register. "Who you here with?"

For an instant, Nathan was too startled by her perception to answer, but the woman knew a stranger buying groceries was very likely a summer resident's guest.

"Ellen Broderick?"

"Oh, how is she?" The woman pulled off her bifocals to turn toward Nathan with softening eyes.

"Okay."

"Oh, that's such good news. We were so afraid that after her accident last summer she—" The woman raised her chin to peer over the aisles. "Frank, Mrs. Broderick is here this summer. She made it back."

A balding man with thick glasses approached from down the far aisle, wiping his hands on his apron. "Aw, that's great news. She seems okay?"

"Yeah, she seems all right. What accident?"

The woman's smile fell a little as she glanced back at Frank. "Her accident with the car."

Nathan nodded, and said, "Oh." The parishioners at St. Michael's had seemed so surprised by Ellen's attendance, and so concerned about her health, that Nathan was relieved to learn she wasn't suffering from some death-sentence illness.

"Tell her to stop by and see us," the woman said as she stacked Nathan's groceries in paper bags. "So this'll go on her tab?"

"Her tab?"

"Mrs. Broderick runs a tab and then we send the bill to her at the end of the summer."

"Oh, right, on her tab."

The woman pulled out a pen and paper to record the amount. It began to feel odd to Nathan that he had not heard of this car accident earlier, perhaps during his interview, and he wanted to ask for more details, but it seemed too late. The cashier and her coworker were beaming at him in a manner so warm and familial that Nathan could not bring himself to shatter their misconception that he shared their relief. Outside, the rain had stopped and the sun was breaking up the dense gray clouds overhead. Men and women in the street pulled back the hoods of their Patagonia and L.L. Bean raincoats to glance up approvingly at the sky. In addition to brooding over the news of Ellen's accident, Nathan was also contemplating the fact that he had just paid for something *on a tab*—something he had only seen done in old movies. Brightonfield Cove seemed imbued with this strangely anachronistic quality. The white picket fences of Birch Hill Boulevard that morning had reminded him of Rockwell's paintings, and now, talking with this folksy old couple in this quaint, old-fashioned store, Nathan felt nostalgic for a time he had never known. He drove down the gravel road toward Ellen's house and spotted a rainbow that arced over her roof and dissipated somewhere above the Atlantic. The town was almost movie-set picturesque. And because it was doubtful that he would ever have the money to own a house in such a place, Nathan assured himself that his hardships would later be transformed into great works of art.

On the rain-washed back porch, Nathan grilled two steaks and ears of corn, then carried them into the house. This was the first real meal he'd prepared—the others had been cereal or sandwiches—and as they ate, he watched Ellen with a growing sense of having failed her. She chewed the corn in careful, diminutive bites but left the thick steak untouched.

A tall row of windows surrounded the dining room on two sides, and the fading sun painted the white walls a luminous peach. Ellen wiped her mouth with her napkin and watched the seagulls glide over the harbor.

"Have you done much sailing?" Nathan asked.

"No," Ellen said. She tilted from side to side in her chair to indicate the roll of the sea, her nose wrinkling with mock nausea, before flashing him an impish grin. "It makes me sick."

"Did your husband?"

"Mmm, he had a boat called the *Proud Rooster.*"

"Where did he get that name?"

"Well, that's what he was."

Nathan smiled and took a long sip of his water. He thought it would seem impertinent to ask her to elaborate, but he wished he knew more about her life. From conversations with his father and during the interview for this job, Nathan had learned some things about her: He knew, for instance, that she had been born into money (her grandfather had been governor of Ohio and her father had owned a radio station in Cleveland), so she'd never held a real job. At her massive Federal style Cleveland home, Ellen employed a chauffeur, a gardener, and a live-in cook. On the living room walls there were photographs of her as a debutante waltzing with a bow-tied young man; then, as the years passed, as a birder grinning through leafy branches, binoculars dangling from her neck; and in khaki pants and a photographer's vest hiking the misty mountains of Peru. By world standards, Nathan supposed his own middle-class existence was a life of comfort and opportunity enjoyed by only a fortunate minority, and he did not dislike Ellen. The way she sometimes scrunched up her face in good-natured distaste, or absently stroked her long hair, reminded him that the young woman he'd seen in photos was still somewhere beneath that slackening skin. But Ellen had lived a life of comfort and opportunity enjoyed by a still smaller minority—a minority in which Nathan was not included—and in his gut he could not help but carry a dark kernel of resentment toward her.

After a while, Nathan said, "The people who work down at Gilman's seemed glad to know you were back here this summer. They said you had some kind of accident last summer?"

"Mmm-hmm."

Nathan waited. "Did you get in a car accident or something?"

Ellen's eyebrows bunched together as she finished chewing. "Mmm . . . it was a car accident . . . but I'm okeydokey now." There was an aggressive singsong quality to her voice that Nathan sensed was intended to put an end to his inquiry.

"Was anyone else hurt?"

"No."

Nathan stared at Ellen, but she did not elaborate. "Well, that's good," he said.

As Ellen continued to eat, Nathan gazed behind her at the glass-fronted liquor cabinet built into the wall. His eyes slid over bottles of Maker's Mark bourbon and Meier's sherry and finally rested on an old bottle of Wray & Nephew white rum.

"Do you mind if I have some of this?" he asked as he rose to open the cabinet. Because he had already drunk a tumbler of the rum he'd bought at Gilman's, Nathan knew he shouldn't drink any more. It often made him sulk for his ex-girlfriend. Pale and willowy, with closely cropped, mussed blond hair, Sophie Hurst liked to read, drink lots of wine, and make short, impressionistic films he occasionally thought were rather beautiful. They had dated for two years before she'd abandoned him a few months ago for someone else.

Ellen looked at the bottle Nathan was holding and frowned. "Only you?"

"Oh, well, would you like the rum or would you prefer the sherry?"

Ellen nodded at the wisdom of the question until she'd swallowed a bite of her steak. "Sherry."

Nathan poured their drinks and slumped back into his chair. He draped one arm across the back of the chair beside him and watched the sun burn into the horizon, slowly gilding the White Mountains of New Hampshire.

Ellen said, "If I die, don't bury me at all. Just pickle my bones in alcohol. Put a bottle of booze at my feet and head. If I don't drink, you'll know I'm dead."

"Hear, hear," Nathan said, raising his glass.

In the living room, they watched *The Philadelphia Story.* After a late-night party, Cary Grant slid into Katharine Hepburn's parked car to rouse her softly from a drunken slumber. With both of them cloaked in shadow, heads resting against the bench seat, it was almost as if they were lying in bed. Hepburn had heavy-lidded, bedroom eyes, a voice like dark honey, and even though her words were coy and elusive, you could tell that she loved him. Nathan felt a dull longing for movie-style romance and glanced at the clock on the mantel. In her lounge chair, Ellen's head bobbed and swayed in an ongoing effort to stay awake. Nathan wished she'd stop trying. He was on his third rum and Coke, and as soon as Ellen went to bed, he planned to walk up the street to see if Leah felt like taking a stroll.

Ellen's eyes had been closed for several minutes when a woman's reedy voice called through the partly open front door, "Anybody home?"

Nathan stood, but the woman and her husband were already stepping inside the house. "Oh, Eleanor, don't get up," the woman pleaded, hurrying over to clasp her hand. "It's so good to see you again." The husband, a jowly, sad-eyed man in khaki pants and a green V-neck sweater, followed his wife with the slow, cumbersome movements of an old Saint Bernard.

"Well," Ellen said, blinking at everyone with surprise. "It's wonderful to see you, too."

The husband reached over to shake her hand. "I'm sorry if we're barging in on you. We were just on Parson's Beach and Franny saw the lights on, so—" He rubbed the back of his neck and stepped back, glancing behind him, as if afraid he might knock something over.

"Oh, you're not barging in," Ellen said, and smiled. Her reassurance sounded a little tired, but then she tilted her head to one side and seemed to eye the man in front of her with greater fondness. "How are you, Carl?"

"I'm all right, I guess," he said, the corner of his mouth hooking upward with pleasure.

"Oh, but how are *you*?" Franny asked, grasping Ellen's forearm affectionately before she took a seat on the couch. Franny's round glasses reflected the light from a nearby lamp and she touched her helmetlike gray coiffure. Nathan asked for drink requests and led Carl into the dining room to let him choose his own wine. Meanwhile, Franny carried on about the exciting Alnombak centennial. Next year the hundredth anniversary of the tennis and golf club would be celebrated with an enormous party and the publication of a limited-edition, leather-bound photo album. They needed additional photographs from the 1920s—and as Franny talked more about it, Nathan slipped into the kitchen. The coffee-machine clock read 9:14 P.M. He exited out the back door to where, in the gathering darkness, he could see the luminous windows of the pastor's two-story house.

Nathan wanted to walk over and ask for Leah, but he wasn't sure if leaving would mean shirking his responsibilities with Ellen. For the first time, he saw the dilemma that would plague him for much of the summer: Was he a caregiver, in which case he could soon walk back inside and suggest that perhaps it was time for Ellen to go to bed? Or was he just a chauffeur/cook, in which case he could just leave her talking with her friends? Neither job description seemed accurate, and as much as Nathan blamed himself for not nailing down his summer duties, he also blamed his father.

When the older man had called from his office last week to ask if Nathan would be interested in escorting a client to Maine, Nathan's instinct had been to tell him no. The call had come at seven thirty in the morning, for one thing. Nathan didn't normally wake up until noon. He'd tried to explain how inconvenient it would be to leave his part-time job at the Cleveland library and sublet his room in the house he was sharing, but his father had not been persuaded. He'd said the job lasted eight weeks and paid eight thousand dollars, tax free. Or, as he'd later phrased it to Nathan,

"Two months of doing nothing to earn half of what you make in a year." Nathan had bristled at this condescension and almost refused; but over the next several days, after receiving another bill from the dentist for his emergency root canal, a Visa bill for the new timing belt on his Civic, and a note slipped under his door asking for the previous month's rent and utilities, he'd begun to see the logic of his father's argument.

Now Nathan wasn't so sure. Eight grand for eight weeks still seemed like a lot of cash, but he had already spent twelve hours tied to Ellen, and the day still wasn't over. Wandering down the fragrant, freshly cut lawn, he stopped to stare at the blinking yacht lights reflecting off the dark waters of the bay. Voices and laughter wafted from the boat decks across the water, but Nathan was unable to make out what they were saying. A few minutes later, he turned back toward the house and noticed Carl behind the porch railing.

Nathan raised his hand and called hello as he ascended the porch stairs. Carl sipped from his wine and settled onto the swing. In the summer breeze, strands of hair rose and fell around his forehead, his unruly gray eyebrows looking like the bristles of an old toothbrush. "So what did you and Ellen do today?" Carl asked, his voice a low rumble.

Nathan told him about attending St. Michael's and explained how the rain had kept them housebound for the rest of the afternoon. Carl said that when the weather was better, he should take Ellen to the Point, a short, jutting plateau, not far from the golf course, which she apparently loved for its incredible view of the Atlantic. Then he asked, "Have you met many people up here yet?"

"Just a couple people at church."

"I was here for three years before anyone would talk to me," Carl said, smiling with wan satisfaction. He had been staring down at his glass, which he held gingerly with both hands, but he glanced up to see Nathan's reaction.

"Why wouldn't they talk to you?"

Carl pushed out his lower lip and shrugged. "Well, I was from Oregon, an accountant at Boston College when I met Franny. I don't think

I'd even been to Maine. I think it's a little more open now, but maybe it just seems that way because I've been here so long. What's funny is that most of these people don't even have that much money. Their parents or grandparents bought the house and put a couple million in the bank, and now they just live off the interest."

Nathan wondered how much money Carl must have married into for a couple million not to seem like genuine wealth, but he was more interested in taking a walk with Leah. He tried glancing down at Carl's watch, but there was not enough light from the house to see the time. Carl adjusted himself in the swing, clumsily moving his fat hand over the age-spotted crown of his balding head, and something about the gesture made Nathan wonder if Carl had been drinking before he arrived. The heavy man tilted his head back to finish off the last of his wine while Franny's nasal voice bleated from the other side of the French doors.

Carl glanced up at Nathan as if noticing him for the first time, and said, "Ellen seems like she's doing all right, though?"

"I think so."

"How confused is she?"

Nathan searched Carl's face before answering. "She seems a little absentminded, I guess. Why do you think she's confused?"

"Well, that's just what I'd heard—from people who see more of her in Cleveland. But we haven't seen so much of her lately. A few summers ago, she was back home taking care of Harry before he died, so . . ."

"Harry," Nathan said.

"Her husband."

Nathan knew that Ellen's husband was dead, but he did not know that he had died so recently. A moment passed wherein Nathan considered how little he knew about the woman with whom he'd be spending the rest of the summer.

Carl said, "Then last summer she had to leave early because of her accident."

"Yeah, everybody seems kind of surprised that she's back this summer."

"Well, there's the rock," Carl said, gesturing down at Parson's Beach as if pushing something away from him. "Imagine hitting that, going thirty or forty miles an hour without a seat belt, at her age."

Nathan stepped away from the porch column where he'd been leaning to approach the railing for a better view. Eyes narrowed, he glanced back at Carl. "What rock?"

"The big one there on the right, by itself."

Parson's Beach was littered with seaweed-covered rocks of various sizes, but on the eastern rim, moonlight struck the pale barnacles of a single boulder roughly the size of a tank.

"She just drove into it?" Nathan asked.

In Carl's dark, recessed eyes it was possible to see him process the information: Nathan did not know the story of what had happened. The recognition seemed to tire him, and he sighed. "It was at night, and she got into the car and drove down through the yard until she hit it head-on."

Nathan scanned the grounds for what Ellen might have been trying to do when she slammed her car into the boulder, but he could think of no explanation. On the other side of the house, Harbor Avenue dead-ended into her driveway, and on this side there was only the steeply sloping lawn and a rocky beach, where no sane person would attempt to drive.

"What was she trying to do?"

Carl shrugged.

When it was evident Carl was not going to say more, Nathan asked, "How bad was she hurt?"

"She messed up her hip, I remember. She's using a cane now to walk?"

"Yeah, she has when I've been with her."

"That's what I heard," Carl said, nodding. He glanced down at the empty space beside him as if gauging whether the swing would accommodate him lying down. "She hit her head pretty badly, too," he said. "Totaled the car. She might have died if Bill McAlister hadn't found her when he was out walking that morning. They took her to the hospital here for a few days, but then her son Glen came and flew her back to Cleveland."

Nathan stared out at the rock with arms folded across his chest, biting his thumbnail.

Carl said, "I'm sure she's doing okay now. I don't think Glen would have let her come back up otherwise."

The older man's sad, faintly smiling face made him such a sympathetic figure that Nathan told him what had happened that morning—about waking up to find Ellen sitting in the hothouse atmosphere of the car—but he watched Carl absorb the information as if each word were a blow, pushing him further and further into himself. Carl inhaled deeply, leaning back on the swing. "Well, I had heard she was having some problems. It might be a good idea to keep a special eye on her, then."

"I will," Nathan murmured. He shook his head, almost laughing with sudden nervousness. "I'm just having a hard time believing that they sent me up here with her alone."

"She wasn't always like this, you know," Carl said, his eyes suddenly flinty, as if Nathan had suggested otherwise. "Did you know this bay, Albans Bay, would be filled with shit right now if it weren't for her? They were going to pump waste from South Albans," he said, gesturing vaguely down the coastline. "They were going to pump it right *here,* but Ellen started a petition and was able to stop it. This was before environmentalism was so popular, so she had to be tenacious to convince those people. She was charming and smart and very beautiful . . . but . . . ah hell, how do you explain how somebody was?"

Nathan nodded in sympathy and stared down at the cracks in the wooden floorboards.

"Have you seen pictures of her when she was younger?" Carl asked.

"I've seen a couple."

"I never met a more beautiful woman in my life."

Nathan glanced through the French doors at the two dimly lit women still in the living room.

"I tried to tell her that once, and she said . . . she said I had a high fructose content," Carl said, his smile fading as he rubbed his thumb along the rim of his glass. "I don't know if it's a stroke, or Alzheimer's, or whatever it is going on, but you won't know what it's like until you get old like me, to see something like this happen to someone who was so beautiful and lovely to be around that you—" Carl's voice grew hoarse with emotion and he clamped his mouth shut.

Wind rustled the branches of honeysuckle bushes beneath them, and a bell rang out on a yacht, followed by distant laughter, across the harbor. Nathan was afraid to look at Carl, but after enough time had passed, he nodded as if to affirm something already agreed upon, and said, "I guess I should probably go in and check on her."

As he started toward the French doors, Carl pulled himself up from the swing. His bulky frame swayed back and forth like an old sea captain not yet used to solid ground. Then he reached back with surprising quickness and flung his glass in a high arc across the lawn. The glass somersaulted across the moonlit sky and landed almost soundlessly in the tall grass and shrubbery along the shore. Nathan's body tensed, and he pretended not to have noticed as he grabbed the handle of the French door. He half-expected to be slapped in back of the head or hear one of the chairs over-turned. But Carl just mumbled, "Sorry, I shouldn't have done that," and followed Nathan into the house.

They waited as Franny finished chatting about a friend's equestrian daughter, then pushed her hands from her lap to her knees. Her feline eyes flickering at Carl with irritation, she said, "Well, maybe we should let Eleanor get her sleep."

"It was a pleasure seeing you again, Ellen," Carl whispered. He held her hand a moment longer than necessary, eyeing her blearily. Then Franny reached for his arm.

By the time Nathan closed the door behind them, Ellen was already shuffling toward the front stairs.

"Are you heading to bed?"

Ellen frowned. "Oh, I think so."

Near the base of the stairs, she turned and outstretched her arm in an apparent invitation to hug good night. Hesitating, Nathan leaned closer—leaving a foot of space between them—and patted her back. Struggling to escape the awkwardness of the moment, he said, "Was it good seeing your friends again?"

Ellen looked away, sighing, as if taking a moment to consider whether it really had been good to see them. She shrugged. "It was okay," she said, beginning a slow ascent of the stairs.

In the kitchen, the clock read 9:55 P.M.—too late to head over to see Leah—so Nathan cursed and sat down at the kitchen table. Outside the window, the colors of the sailboat lights streamed like melted crayon across the water. Living in Cleveland, Nathan had not often dreamed of the sea. But now he found himself yearning for a sailboat and everything a long sea voyage would mean: freedom from this job, from his father. Maybe part of it was the age difference. Nathan's parents hadn't had him until they were in their late thirties, but his father had never been a great communicator, and Nathan's mother had been crucial to the maintenance of their adult father-son relationship: sorting out misunderstandings, soothing egos, helping each to see how much the two men had in common. Now they were trying to get along without her, and Nathan wondered if it was possible. He cradled his head in both hands for several minutes, then picked up the phone.

"Hello?" his father answered, a note of concern in his voice, undoubtedly wondering why someone would be calling him so late. Nathan could picture him downstairs, in front of the television, tilted back on the old couch that reclined and propped up his legs like a La-Z-Boy chair.

"Hey, Dad."

"Hey, Nathan," his father said, but then there was a rustling on the other end of the line. Nathan listened to what he suspected was his father losing control of the phone as he searched the couch for the remote to turn down the volume of the television. When Nathan could no longer hear the exchange of TV voices, he heard his father fumbling again with the receiver.

"Hello?"

"I'm here."

"How're you doing?"

Nathan said he was fine, but then told him about his conversation with Carl. He asked, "Ellen's son, Glen, didn't tell you about any of this?"

"No . . . not that I can think of . . . not anything about her trying to kill herself."

"Jesus, I don't know if she was actually *trying* to kill herself. But Glen never breathed a word to you about her wrecking her car up here last summer?"

"I don't think so," his father said, but in the silence that followed, Nathan could hear his father trying to remember if perhaps he had known and forgotten. His thick, graying eyebrows would knot together as he stared across the darkened room and worked his tongue across the cigarette stains of his teeth. When Nathan was still in junior high, his father had stopped smoking and, with Nathan's mother's encouragement, started a regular workout routine. Every other evening the two of them had gone to the local YMCA to stretch, walk the track, and mildly exert themselves lifting weights. But since her death three years ago, his father had let his membership expire and resumed his old habit, his teeth turning the color of old newspaper.

"I think maybe he did say something about his mother having an accident last summer," his father admitted. "But I don't remember him saying she drove the car into a rock."

"You didn't ask him what happened?"

"I manage their estate, Nathan. I'm not their friend."

Nathan leaned forward and clutched the back of his neck. "I'm just trying to figure out if I should be up here."

"Why do you say that?"

"You mean in addition to her driving her car into a boulder?"

"I wouldn't worry too much about . . . She's an older woman, Nathan. You knew that before you went up there. It sounds like she just probably lost control of her car. Don't let yourself get worked up over it."

"How about this morning when I woke up and couldn't find her anywhere in the house? I looked around for half an hour and finally found her asleep in the car with the windows up, in the broiling sun."

His father did not respond immediately. "What did she say she was doing there?"

"She didn't say. She just said she wanted me to take her to church."

"Well," his father said. "Why don't you just see how it goes for a little while?"

"I think I'm going to call Glen. I just want to know if there's anything else I should have been told about her condition."

"You can't reach him now. He's on vacation with his wife until next week. Why don't you try someone at the house? Like her nephew?"

"You mean her grandnephew Ralph?"

"I'm sure he can tell you if there are things you need to be aware of about her."

Nathan snorted. "Okay."

"What?"

"Nothing. It's just that that guy isn't right."

"Well, we're all a little not right," his father said, in a way that made it easy to imagine his sad smile. "How else are things up there?"

Nathan exhaled. "Wonderful. How are things there?"

"I'm doing all right," his father said, grunting as he reached for something. Nathan knew he wasn't doing all right, though, and he listened to the older man shaking a cigarette from a pack of Camel Lights. Nathan might have tried to say something to him again about smoking, but the last time he'd tried, his father had muttered bitterly, "Give me a break here, okay?" So Nathan answered questions about his drive up from Cleveland on Friday, and the weather, but afterward there did not seem much to say. He was tired of talking with his father, frustrated by the weariness in the man's voice, which always reminded Nathan of his dead mother. When he hung up, he stared out at the glimmering bay, fighting his urge to hurl the phone against the far wall.

Three

A Letter to Sophie ~ Visiting the Alnombak Club ~ Kendra Garfield Requests the Pleasure of Nathan's Company ~ In a Black Bikini Leah Speaks of Love

The next morning, Ellen sat in the living room, watching television, while Nathan washed the breakfast dishes then went upstairs to search for something to occupy his time. He masturbated to a seminude photo of Geena Davis he found in an old *Rolling Stone* on his closet shelf. Then he wrote a letter to his ex-girlfriend.

Dear Sophie,

Greetings from the rarefied world of Brightonfield Cove, Maine. I tried calling you before I left, but I guess things have been pretty hectic, between work and moving into your new apartment (I don't know your new address, so I'm going to mail this to your mom).

Yesterday was my first day here, and while driving around in the afternoon, Ellen and I passed a church where a young bride and groom were walking down the front steps. Watching them made me think of you, and of us, and I couldn't help feeling a little hope.

I think it was good for me to leave Cleveland, though, and it seems like it's going to be a great summer. Ellen is much cooler than I expected, and the beach just in front of her estate is kind of the local hotspot for a lot of people our age. I met most of them last night when they flocked onto our porch after a clambake. They were friendly and interesting and one of them—a girl who recently graduated from NYU film school—reminded me a little of you. I showed her my graphic novel and the drawings in my sketchbook and she said she'd like to use some of the images in a documentary she's making about graphic novelists! I'm not sure the documentary would be shown in theaters, and I doubt I would make any money from it, but she says she loves the stories I've drawn and it may be hard to resist her.

Best regards,
Nathan

Later that afternoon, Ellen asked to be taken to watch tennis, and on the way to the club, Nathan brooded over the letter. Had it been too much to make the girl an NYU film student when Sophie, a graduate of the Cleveland Institute of Art now working full-time at Dugan Florist, spoke longingly of film school? And what about the arrangement of those last two paragraphs? The soul-sickening fiction of it notwithstanding, was it better to remind Sophie he might want to marry her before attempting to pique her jealousy? Or was it better to pique her jealousy and then remind her that there might still be time for her to win him back? Pondering these questions exhausted him, and pulling beside the blue mailbox across from Gilman's, he fed the letter into its mouth.

The Alnombak club was so close to most members' homes that they did not need to drive there, and there was no parking lot anyway. Nathan parked Ellen's car on the quiet, shady street off Birch Hill Boulevard, and stared out at the kind of club where he could envision a plucky, aristocratic Katharine Hepburn character striding across the green lawn. An immaculately manicured, waist-high hedgerow separated the road from the grounds, and on the far side men and women in white were playing tennis on four flawless clay courts. High wooden fences kept balls from bouncing off of the clay, and on the near side, viewers sat on wooden benches or chairs, in the shade of a modest green-and-white-striped canopy. Everyone seemed to be talking and laughing in the easy, confident way Nathan associated with having bankfuls of money.

When he escorted Ellen to a chair, a gaggle of older women in white visors greeted her warmly, until, finding her as politely uncommunicative as she'd been at church, they gradually turned to watch the tennis matches and resume their earlier conversations. A few of them had introduced themselves to Nathan, but none of them asked him any questions about himself. He stared out beyond the tennis courts where the golf course stretched out in verdant, rolling hills to a horizon broken only by St. Michael's church. Sitting there was reminiscent of junior high dances when his date wouldn't talk to him and he couldn't see anyone else around he knew.

"Would you like something to drink?" Nathan asked Ellen.

"How about a half-and-half?" Ellen said, smiling up at him from beneath her visor.

"What's that?"

"Half tea, half lemonade."

Nathan frowned contemplatively, but nodded, and stood up from his chair.

Something about the rugged gentility of the clubhouse, with its roomy wraparound porch and wicker chairs, gave Nathan the feeling that the place had enjoyed a past life in colonial Africa. Inside, after he ordered at the counter, the mousy woman said, "Name?"

"My name? Oh, Broderick," Nathan said. He pushed his wallet back into his pocket and grabbed the two drinks.

Turning toward the door, he noticed affixed to the wall, between the ancient wooden tennis rackets and golf clubs, a collage of old photographs representing the club's nearly 100-year history. Time marched backward from color to black-and-white and finally to a sepia photo of the "First Alnombak Club Golf Tournament," dated 1899. The shot had been taken from almost the exact location where Nathan had parked the car. Dressed in suits and corseted dresses, everyone in the photo was blurry, as if shivering, and Nathan's eyes settled on a young couple standing in front of the clubhouse porch. The woman wore a pale and lacy long-sleeved dress, and held a parasol, while the young man beside her wore a closely fitting suit that accentuated his gangly frame. His arm hooked around her waist, but he stood a few feet away, as if this was the first time he was reaching for her. For an instant Nathan wondered where they were now, but they were all dead, of course—even the little girl dashing around the corner of the clubhouse so quickly in her fluttering dress that she appeared little more than a haze of light.

On his way down the front steps, Nathan tried to see the people gathered outside as figures in a photograph that would be seen a hundred years in the future. But the melancholy detachment he'd cultivated was blown away by the sea-smelling air, the blue sky, and the cheerful vitality of the people surrounding him. One of these cheerfully vital people—a thirtysomething woman Nathan found rather attractive—had taken a seat in his chair. Nathan handed Ellen her drink, and after learning that the woman was Ellen's niece, Kendra Garfield, he pulled over another chair to sit beside them.

"So, you're Ben's son, right?" Kendra asked, leaning forward so that Nathan could see the constellation of freckles stretching beneath her brown, attentive eyes. When she talked she focused on one of Nathan's pupils, then the other, so that although her voice sounded calm, if a little abrupt, Nathan sensed it belied an inner tension. He was also surprised by the question. His father had lots of wealthy clients, but the fact that his reputation had preceded him at this club left Nathan feeling an unfamiliar, muted pride.

Kendra said, "We were going to stop by and see him and Regina when

Lucien—my husband—and I were in Cleveland last month for a wedding, but you know how those things go, the whole weekend was over before it had even begun."

"Yeah, I wouldn't worry about it," Nathan said. He had no idea who Regina was, but he assumed she was someone at Varclow and Powell, his father's firm. The last time he had visited his father's workplace was in grade school when his father had been a financial manager at Parker Fasteners. Nathan remembered little about the visit except the photograph of himself and his mother on the desk and the otherwise depressing lifelessness of the bare, neon-lit room. His father's new office at Varclow and Powell at least had windows—he had mentioned this one evening at dinner soon after taking the job—but, perhaps guessing his son would not be interested, he had not invited him downtown for a tour.

"Do you go to college there, in Cleveland?" Kendra asked.

"No, now I work at the Cleveland Public Library."

"Oh, they let you have the summer off?"

"Yeah, pretty much. It's like an unpaid sabbatical kind of thing," Nathan said. Not because this was true, exactly, but because he was embarrassed to say he had dropped out of college and didn't have a real job and because taking a "sabbatical" was how he had pitched it to his supervisor. Nathan had explained that he'd be gone for two months, and that he would return to his part-time job at the end of the summer, but his supervisor had only frowned at him. She would, of course, accept Nathan's application when he returned. But she could make him no guarantees.

When Nathan asked Kendra about herself, her face brightened. Wrinkles appeared in the corners of her eyes when she smiled, but her button nose, which resembled Ellen's, made her appear spry and youthful despite the primness of her lips. She said she'd been born in Cleveland but after college had moved to Boston, where she was now married, with a child, pursuing her graduate degree in architecture. What she wanted to do with her degree was restore old homes in the Boston area, making them as beautiful as they once had been. Nathan sensed within her a lust for order and immaculate furnishings that made him want to have rough, messy sex with her.

Despite her flirtatiousness—the occasional touching of his arm, the disbelieving look she gave him when he mentioned he didn't currently have a girlfriend—Nathan knew it was in his interests not to brood over his attraction to her. She was wealthy, married, and a mother—i.e., unlikely to be interested in him. Yet, as she stood up to leave, she asked Nathan if he had any free time.

"Yeah, I think so. I'm usually free in the afternoons, when Ellen takes a nap, or sometimes in the evenings when she's gone to bed."

Kendra pulled a pair of Jackie O. sunglasses from out of her ponytailed strawberry blond hair, so that Nathan could no longer see her eyes. "Well, I'm inviting some people to take the yacht out tomorrow afternoon, if you'd like to come." Kendra bent down to kiss Ellen's cheek. "You're welcome to come along too, Aunt Ellen, but I know how much you like sailing."

"Is that all right, Ellen?" Nathan asked.

Ellen affected a pout and said, "No." But then she laughed and glanced at both of them.

Nathan flashed a charitable smile and asked Kendra how long she thought they'd be gone.

"Oh, not too long. Maybe a couple hours."

Nathan knew that Ellen's naps only lasted about an hour and a half, but he could not help seeing himself as a young JFK, sailing the blue waters of New England, surrounded by elegant women. Kendra said they were meeting tomorrow at one o'clock at the yacht club, near Gilman's, and Nathan told her he'd be there.

On the way to the yacht club the following afternoon, Nathan felt more welcomed and respected by the people he smiled at along the road. It was true that members of the Alnombak club hadn't been particularly friendly toward him yesterday, but after all, they didn't know him, and maybe once they did get to know him, their attitude would change. Kendra had gotten to know him, and now she was inviting him on her boat, wasn't she? That meant she saw him not just as hired help, but as the type of person you'd want sailing with you, and he wondered what he would do if her husband wasn't there and she continued flirting with him that afternoon. He imagined scenes in which Kendra asked him to free her of her clothing and inhibitions in some darkened hold of the yacht.

A quarter-mile past Gilman's, Birch Hill Boulevard bent sharply south, and beside a gravel driveway a posted sign read:

BRIGHTONFIELD COVE YACHT CLUB

NO TRESPASSING

Members and Guests Only

Nathan walked down the driveway until he reached a small parking lot where he saw, with some disappointment, that except for a single Alfa Romeo Spider, the cars were no more expensive or exotic than those parked on his father's street back home. Directly ahead, an embankment sloped down to the inlet where three narrow boarding docks held dinghies roped to each side. The dinghies, Nathan realized, were used to ferry club members to and from their yachts, which were anchored behind him in the deeper waters of Albans Bay. Yet no one was on the docks. It was still shy of one o'clock, but he could not help wondering if perhaps Kendra and her friends had left without him. On the far west side of the parking lot, a two-story, white stucco clubhouse sat beside the channel or "gut" connecting the cove to the bay, and as Nathan walked over, he noticed a small cluster of people, including Eldwin Lowell, the pastor, standing on the pavement near the water's edge. He was an even heftier man than he appeared in his black robe, and was wearing dark sunglasses, his arms folded across his black polo shirt. His blond son was crouched beside him, picking at something in the lawn.

Seeing them made Nathan think of Leah and compounded the uneasiness he was already feeling. It had been nearly two whole days since he had seen her. Last night, after waiting for Ellen to go to sleep, he had walked over to see if Leah might be interested in taking a walk. Eldwin's wife, Rachel, had answered the door. She was a pallid, angular woman whose loose-fitting shirt and sweatpants hung from her like clothes on a rack. Frowning in the porch light, she'd told him that Leah had taken the kids to Brightonfield to see a movie.

"Oh, do you know what time you expect them back?"

"Not too long from now," Rachel had said, struggling to push back a panting black Labrador behind her. "Do you want me to tell her you stopped by?"

Nathan had said yes, but Leah hadn't come over to the house that evening, and the memory increased his self-consciousness as he stood in the sun-blasted parking lot, his hand shielding his eyes from the glare. He turned in place, surveying the grounds for signs of Kendra, and wishing that someone would approach him to tell him where to go. Walking toward the clubhouse, he hoped she would be inside, and if not, perhaps he could use the restroom to sit and think about what he should do. He was halfway up the porch steps, glancing through the glass doors, when Kendra appeared beneath him, rounding the corner of the building. Nathan called her name and she turned to squint through her sunglasses.

"Hey, Nathan, it's good to see you. I was wondering if you were going to come."

She paused to grab the railing, but as Nathan came down the stairs, she started walking again.

"Yeah, no, I wouldn't miss it. Is everybody else here?"

"Almost everybody. Do you mind walking to the car with me? I just need to get a few more life jackets out of the back." She looked purposeful and radiant, dressed in khaki shorts and a white blouse that allowed Nathan to see the faint outlines of her bra. As she glanced down at her watch, a roll of flesh appeared beneath her chin, making her look momentarily older than Nathan remembered, and he felt an erotic tenderness for her. As they walked, Kendra said, "It's supposed to be beautiful all day, thank God, and a decent wind, finally, too. Have you been sailing much this summer?"

"No, I haven't. This is actually going to be my first time on a sailboat."

Kendra glanced at him, and said, "Oh, you're kidding."

"Nope. It's been a lean life."

After a pause, Kendra said, "Well, I think you're going to love it. You know, Lucien and I were just talking about how it's too bad that your parents weren't able to come up this summer; we would have loved to have taken them out with us."

"My parents?"

Kendra tilted her head and peered over the top of her sunglasses. "Don't tell me they didn't mention going sailing with us last summer."

"No," Nathan said, laughing through an uncertain smile.

Kendra laughed also. "Well, maybe they didn't, but we had such a good time with them. Your father is hilarious."

"Yeah?"

"Oh, God, yes. You'll have to ask Lucien about the night your father tried cooking swordfish."

"I'm not so sure my father was up here last summer."

Kendra tucked in her chin and frowned, "No, I think you're mixed up. I know they were here because the Carlisles were with us, and they had just gotten back from their trip to Ireland with your parents."

Nathan said, "My mother passed away a few years ago, so she wouldn't have been here last summer."

"Regina?"

"No, her name was Carol."

By now they'd stopped walking and Kendra's pale cheeks were flushed a warm, mottled pink. "So who's your father?"

"My father is Ben Empson."

Kendra lifted her sunglasses until they rested in her hair. "Then why did you . . . Well, who are *you*?" she asked, her eyes darting back and forth from each of his pupils.

"You don't know my father?"

"No!"

Nathan smiled uneasily. He explained to her who his father was, and how he'd gotten the job taking care of Ellen for the summer, and as he talked, he waited for the softening of her face: for the recognition that it was all a simple misunderstanding and that they could laugh about it and go sailing and maybe even refer to it jokingly, every once in a while, for the rest of the summer. But Kendra only stared at him until she glanced back at the gathering of people beside the clubhouse and shook her head.

"I thought you were Ben Darrow's son."

"Well, I'm not." Nathan smiled, not knowing what else to say.

"Will you excuse me for just a minute?" Kendra said, moving through a few rows of cars to where a light blue Volvo station wagon was parked. She opened the hatchback and pulled out several life jackets, draping them over her arm without glancing back. After locking the car, she stayed two rows of cars apart from Nathan as she walked back toward the clubhouse. Maybe she was planning to talk with her friends about the confusion, to make sure that they were comfortable with the situation before inviting Nathan onto the boat, but Nathan was embarrassed by that idea, and couldn't help calling her name. Kendra stopped and raised her eyebrows as if surprised to see him still standing there.

Nathan took a few steps closer to her and said, "Listen, I'm sorry if there's been a mix-up. If you invited me thinking that I was someone else, and now want to . . . you know . . . if you don't feel comfortable having me on your boat, I guess I can understand that."

Despite squinting into the sun, Kendra's face softened. Nathan thought she looked disarmed by his maturity, and she tilted her head, almost smiling. "Well, thank you, Nathan," she said. "I think that is the case."

Walking home, Nathan entertained visions of a rogue wave that would wrench the yacht to the ocean floor, but allow Kendra to escape and flail for hours before being torn apart by a shark. In the end, he was relieved not to be on the yacht with people who did not want his company, but replaying the humiliating episode in his head led to depressing thoughts about his father, who was, at that moment, most likely at his desk at the office, sifting through papers, taking off his glasses to wipe his eyes. Soon he would be home and then . . . what? Eating his takeout alone in the fading light of the living room, watching some sitcom? Lumbering out into the yard with his little hand shovel to inspect for weeds among his landscaped shrubs? Nathan felt imprisoned by his father's suffering, and a dark coil of hostility compressed within him as he considered the older man's lonely routine.

The front porch of Eldwin's rented two-story house was surrounded by a waist-high, loosely latticed railing, and Nathan was so preoccupied with thoughts of his father that he almost didn't notice Leah. She was on the other side of the railing, in a low, canvas beach chair, dressed in a black bikini, reading a book. Nathan hesitated, wondering if he could handle the possibility of two humiliations in one day, but he was wearing his favorite gray T-shirt, and he could not stand waiting any longer.

"Hey there," she said, squinting up at him. "Are you taking a walk?"

Nathan glanced back up the road and shrugged. "Yeah, more or less." He smiled, but she just smiled back at him. So he said, "I stopped by last night to see if you might want to take a walk with me, but I think I just missed you. The pastor's wife said you had taken the kids into Brightonfield to see a movie."

"Oh, she didn't tell me." Leah glanced back at the house and leaned forward, whispering, "You can't trust her to give me messages; she doesn't even tell me when my mom calls."

"All right," Nathan whispered. He enjoyed the intimacy of whispering with her and continued to speak quietly. "So, how did you end up here for the summer, anyway?"

"Oh, my mom goes to the same church where Eldwin is the pastor—or co-pastor, or whatever—in Cambridge," Leah said, resuming a normal conversational tone. "I graduated from college in June and didn't have a job lined up, so my mom heard they were looking for somebody to come up here for the summer, and they were willing to pay pretty well. So, here I am." She laid the book on her stomach and sipped from the straw in her Coke bottle. "How about you?"

With an air of resignation, Nathan explained how his father had hooked him up with the job without telling him about Ellen's accident, and how he'd awakened on Sunday morning to find her waiting for him in the car.

Leah said, "Nobody told you she was like this?"

"No."

"Well, what are you going to do?"

"I think I'm just going to keep doing what I'm doing, for the time being," Nathan said. "I mean, I can't be with her every minute we're up here, and she seems all right most of the time, but I'm just going to try and keep more of a watch over her."

"Where is she now?"

"She's napping, and she usually sleeps pretty soundly for like an hour or two." Nathan glanced down at Ellen's house and then back at Leah. "Do you have some time off?"

Leah shook her head. "No, I'm lucky I was able to come out here for a few hours. Meghan's upstairs taking a nap, so I can't go anywhere."

Nathan nodded. "What are you reading?"

The hardback resting on Leah's stomach looked like the kind of book restaurants placed on mantels to lend the place an air of sophistication.

"Well, I was reading *Cosmo,*" she said, gesturing beneath her beach chair to the glossy, opened pages of the magazine. Nathan saw a photograph of a slender woman on her back, legs raised above her in a V. "But I got tired of reading about exercises that would make me a better lover, so I picked this up in the house." She held the book open in front of her. Nathan glanced at the faded spine, distracted by the smoothness of Leah's stomach and her now half-opened legs.

"What do you think of this?" she asked, flipping through a few pages then raising the book to read aloud: " 'I came to realize that when you are in love, then in all your judgments about love you should start from something higher and more important than happiness or unhappiness, virtue and sin in all their accepted meanings, or you should make no judgments at all.' "

"Who wrote it?"

"It's Chekhov—why?"

"It just kind of sounded like a man."

Leah ran her tongue behind her upper lip. "Why do you say that?"

"I don't know," Nathan said. His nervousness had faded briefly, while they were talking about their jobs, but all of her talk about sexual exercises and love had made his breath quicken. Turning his head to hide his discomfort, he stammered, "I think he sounds haunted . . . and a lot of guys I know are haunted in a way I don't think women are as easily."

"Are you haunted?"

"No," Nathan said, though he couldn't help thinking of Sophie. "Are you?"

"No, but I think that's because women are much better at *processing* the things that happen to them."

"Processing," Nathan said.

"Yes, we cry and talk to our friends about what's happened until we've gone through it—*processed*—and can move on. Do you know what time it is?"

Nathan said, "I think it's probably a little after one o'clock."

"Yikes," Leah said, frowning, as she stood up from the chair. "I have to go. I'm supposed to take Meghan to go sailing."

"You're going down to the yacht club?"

Pulling the navy blue towel from the beach chair, Leah said, "Yeah, and I think I have to watch the kids tonight, but do you want to try and do something this weekend?"

"Yeah, sure," Nathan said.

"So you agree with the quote then?"

"Read it to me again."

Leah held the towel and bottle, but she reopened the book, reading so that he could see her full lips shaping themselves around words that were no longer making any sense to him. He knew only that the words were romantic and that he wanted romantic things to be true.

"I've felt that way," he said.

"Do you feel that way now?"

"I do."

"I don't." Leah sighed, shutting the book. "He writes like someone who's never had his heart broken."

As she crouched to grab her *Cosmo* from beneath her chair, there was plenty of time to respond, but Nathan had no idea what to say. He thought it troubling that she would say such a thing about someone who was supposed to be as great a writer as Chekhov, but Nathan had not read anything by him.

"I'll have to think more about that," he said lamely.

Reaching for the front door, Leah smirked and said, "Do."

"All right," Nathan said, pulling his hand from his pocket to wave good-bye. "I'll talk to you soon."

I'll talk to you soon? For God's sake, it had taken two days to have one brief conversation with her—and this had happened purely by accident. The magnitude of the lost opportunity seemed to compound with each step away from her. Why hadn't he made a definite plan to meet up with her on Friday, or Saturday even? He glanced back to see if perhaps she had returned to the porch, but she was gone.

Four

Reflections on a Dead Husband ~ An Invitation and a Rejection ~ Ellen Wakes in the Night ~ Nathan Interrupts Ralph's Party

At dinner that evening, Ellen didn't ask a single question about his experience on the yacht, and Nathan felt in no hurry to talk about what had happened. After clearing their plates, he poured drinks and carried them onto the porch. Ellen brought with her a dog-eared novel, a multigenerational saga about the rise and fall of an aristocratic New England family, and Nathan was pleasantly surprised to see her peering down through bifocals, reading. He brought his pencils and sketchbook from his room and sat down in a chair as Ellen rocked gently beside him on the swing. Normally, sketching worked as a kind of meditation, forcing Nathan to focus on the drawing of a line, forming the lines into an illustration, and forging the sequence of illustrations into a coherent story. It was a way out of the disorder of his life and the riot of memory. That evening he worked on a drawing of himself and Ellen on the porch, staring out over the rocky shoreline of Parson's Beach, the small islands, and the glassy tranquility of the harbor. After an hour had passed, however, he grew impatient with what he'd drawn. Above the illustration of himself he hastily sketched a thought balloon that contained the image of Leah, open armed, gazing down at him with pietà eyes. Nathan sighed and looked up from the drawing at a small sailboat tacking across the sun-streaked water. After a few minutes, he asked, "Did you and your husband used to sit out here a lot?"

Ellen squinted over her bifocals at Nathan before gazing out at the ocean. "No, not a lot."

"He didn't like the porch that much?"

"He and his friends liked to go yachting, so he wasn't here that much in the summer."

"That's no fun."

"I think he was having fun."

"Well, I mean for you."

Ellen pulled a strand of hair back from her face in a gesture that made her seem younger. "Oh, it wasn't fun for a while, but then I decided I would try to have my fun, too."

Nathan nodded and pretended to focus on his illustration. "What would you be doing if I wasn't here?" he asked. He wondered if it was an insensitive question—accentuating the fact that she now needed a caretaker—but he was curious about the life Ellen had led and about the lives of other people in the community. Kendra's invitation had awakened him to the fact that not everyone in Brightonfield Cove stayed at home, watching television, with occasional trips to the Alnombak club and St. Michael's. These were affluent people, certainly the most affluent people Nathan had ever known, and he couldn't help wondering about the fun and interesting things they must be doing without him.

Ellen said, "Maybe going to a cocktail party, but I'd probably be right here."

"I'm going to walk down to the beach," Nathan said, made more restless by the possibility that there was a party going on somewhere without them. But after setting down his sketchbook, he walked only down into the yard. He didn't know what he wanted to do, so he poked around in the tall grass, searching for Carl's wineglass. Bored after a while, he tramped back up the hill to the porch. He tried sketching again for a few minutes and then stared out at the bay a long while before announcing he was headed inside to watch TV. When the sky turned the pinkish purple of a clamshell, Ellen stepped inside and told him she was going to bed. Nathan said good night without getting up from the couch. In the flickering light of the room, he was bothered by a nagging resentment that they had not been invited to any parties. He hoped it had more to do with Ellen's condition than the possibility that he would tag along with her. On television a woman was on her front porch, talking with an old, smiling postman, and the scene was like sunlight breaking through the stratus clouds of Nathan's thoughts. He had not been doing his job. He had not picked up Ellen's mail.

Ten minutes later, Ellen's post office box revealed what looked like three invitations. Two had sealed envelopes, but a third, from Bill McAlister, was not sealed, and was for a party the following evening. On the back side of the cream-colored invitation, the man had written a short note:

Dear Ellen,

Wanted to send this to you in case you come up this summer. I hope you do. Hannah and Eugene say they saw you a few weeks ago in Cleveland and that you look like your old self. Don't know if you've been getting my letters, but I would like to see you again.

Love,
Bill

Sifting through the other mail—including advertisements and flyers for Fourth of July parades and craft fairs—Nathan saw an envelope that stopped him. It was light pink, with his name written in large, cursive letters, so that even without a return address, he knew who it was from. He read it once while in the post office, and then, back at home, he read it again with a stiff drink while seated in Ellen's living room chair.

> Nathan,
>
> I am beginning to remember the dear things you have been telling me these past few months. I am so sorry to have been as cold as I was, but I was stubborn and refused to listen. I was so afraid you were attempting to manipulate me and I thought you would only reject me if I came back to you. Now it doesn't matter. Once I loved you so much I could cry at the thought of a hangnail on your finger. But please—no more phone calls and no letters. Don't make me doubt myself now. And don't dismiss me as one of the others. My name is Sophie Hurst, remember? And you are still the voice I talk to in my heart and in my mind.
>
> Love,
> Sophie

In the dimly lit living room, Nathan crumpled the letter into his fist and held it beneath his chin. Then he peeled it open again and flattened it across the wooden end table. *Now it doesn't matter.* When Nathan could finally take his eyes from her beautiful handwriting, he stared into the empty fireplace. The handyman who had prepared the house for their arrival—turning on the water, making sure the stove was functional—had also left a stack of wood in a metal container outside the front door. Nathan got up and retrieved a few of the logs. He found some old newspaper, opened the flue, and while sitting Indian style, started a fire. He listened to the crackling of the logs and the melancholy whisper of wind across the top of the chimney. In a little while, a door creaked open on the second floor. The ceiling groaned above him and he saw Ellen at the top of the stairs, wearing her aged blue bathrobe, her hair hanging in loose strands around her shoulders.

"What's going on, Ellen?" Nathan asked.

"Well, I can't sleep."

"You got a lot on your mind?"

Ellen wrinkled her nose and shrugged. "I suppose so."

She shuffled downstairs through the living room and into the dining room, where Nathan turned on the light. As she grabbed the tops of chairs and the side of the table for balance, Nathan ran upstairs to her room to get her cane. When he returned, she was sitting at the kitchen table in a narrow wedge of light from the hallway.

Nathan flicked on the kitchen light and asked if she wanted anything to eat.

"Not especially."

"Is there anything I can get for you?"

"Oh, I don't think so," she said.

An old *New York Times* lay on the table, and she pulled it toward her, narrowing her eyes at the print.

"Well, all right. I'll be in the living room," Nathan said.

Returning to the tile in front of the fireplace, he poked the logs and blew, making the flames leap and flutter higher. After a few minutes, he sat back on the couch, his mind searching for things to stave off depression, and thought about the invitation for tomorrow's cocktail party. He wondered why the name Bill McAlister sounded so familiar. He wasn't sure if it was the name of someone he knew in Cleveland or maybe a character in a book he'd once read. His drink needed refreshing, but he didn't want to go back into the kitchen with Ellen, so he stared out the French doors at the glittering lights of the coastline. In a little while he heard her push her chair back from the table, the legs scraping across the linoleum floor, then the *whshh, whshh* of slippers across the hardwood toward him.

Propping herself up with one arm in the doorway, she smiled and asked, "What's going on in here?"

"Not a lot," Nathan said. He raised his nearly empty glass to finish it off and gestured at the badly wrinkled letter on the end table. "Just reading some mail."

"Anything interesting?" Ellen used her cane for support as she moved to sit in the old recliner.

Nathan stood and gathered her invitations. As he was handing them to her, however, he noticed that the one on the bottom—from Mr. McAlister—still had the envelope open. Ellen withdrew that invitation first and held the opened envelope in her hand. She looked up at Nathan as if awaiting an explanation, then glanced down to turn the invitation over. Nathan's face flushed with prickling shame. In his uncertain role as chauffeur/ caregiver, he had crossed a line by reading her mail. She continued to stare at the card while Nathan returned to the couch and sat down.

"Were those invitations?" he asked.

"Mmm."

Nathan raised his empty glass to his lips, swallowed dryly, and then let it rest between his legs. He waited until she'd opened the other two envelopes, and then said, "I noticed one of the letters was from Bill McAlister. Do you know him very well?"

Ellen looked up from the invitation she was holding. After a moment's hesitation, she shrugged, sighing, and stared into the fire. "Oh, yes, we've spent a lot of time together."

Something about the sad tilt of Ellen's head and the way she sighed made Nathan realize where he had heard the man's name. On the night Carl hurled his wineglass at the ocean, he'd mentioned that a man named McAlister had possibly saved Ellen's life by discovering her the morning she'd driven her car into the rock. Nathan wanted to ask Ellen about the incident, but she had already demonstrated that she did not want to tell him the story. Looking down into his glass, Nathan asked, "Do you think you'll want to go to the parties?"

"Two of the invitations are old," Ellen said, resting her head on the back of the chair.

"Do you think you'll want to go to the one that isn't?"

"Oh, I might like to."

Nathan waited for what seemed a long time, then cleared his throat. "Do you think you might like me to go with you?"

He felt as if he was asking for her forgiveness. But Ellen allowed only a trace of a smile and did not turn to face him. She grunted indecipherably. Her blue bathrobe looked gray in the flickering shadows of the fire, and with one hand resting regally on her cane, she reminded Nathan of a dying queen.

He wanted to know how many of her brain cells had burned out. Or rather: How much did she understand, and how much was pretending? His father had suggested he call Ellen's grandnephew Ralph. But Nathan half-suspected Ralph suffered from something like Tourette's syndrome. Last Wednesday, during Nathan's informal interview at Ellen's mansion in Cleveland, Ralph had acted as master of ceremonies and had done most of the talking. He wore cut-off khaki shorts and a faded Social Distortion concert T-shirt, sported a frizzy tangle of dark, rust-colored hair, and looked like he hadn't shaven in days. He said he was a student at Case Western and wanted to be a professional photographer. Did Nathan know Walker Evans? Henri Cartier-Bresson? Ralph admired their work and thought that cropping your photographs was cheating. Roaming downtown streets for scenes to shoot, he often carried one of the guns he kept upstairs. On the old Zenith television in front of them, Venus Williams and Martina Hingis hustled from side to side across a tennis court, and Ralph occasionally halted his monologue to comment on Hingis's supposed ability to give great blow jobs. Enough that Ellen eventually turned, confused, and asked, "You think she smokes a pipe?"

Now Nathan wondered if it was too late to ask the questions he should have asked during that meeting. Pouring himself another drink, he watched a TV movie about the blossoming friendship between a deadbeat grandpa and his retarded grandson. But his interest in the movie was overwhelmed by thoughts of Ellen. He walked onto the porch and stared at the boulder a long time before he walked back into the kitchen. Opening his address book, he finished the last half of his drink and dialed.

"Chateau Hassett," a man answered. His voice was barely distinguishable over the roar of music and people talking.

For an instant, Nathan wondered if he had dialed the wrong number. "Ralph? This is Nathan—"

"Heeey, Nathan!" Ralph shouted, sounding like Nathan was an old friend he hadn't heard from in years. "How's the monkey?"

"Monkey? Ellen?"

Ralph ignored him to tell someone at the party that people who had parked their cars in the yard should move them to the church parking lot down the street.

"Actually, that's what I wanted to ask you about," Nathan said. He took a deep breath and explained about his conversation with Carl.

Ralph said he didn't know much more about the accident than Nathan, although he seemed to remember that Ellen and a couple of other people had gone out to eat, then back to the house for drinks. Eventually everyone went home, and the next time anyone saw Ellen was when what's his name found her lying on the ground beside her car.

"How do you know about all this?"

"Glen told me, I guess," Ralph said, moving into a quieter room where he no longer had to shout into the phone. "But I think my mom told me, too."

"Do you know why she did it?"

Ralph laughed. "I don't know. Why does anybody drive their car into a rock? Her brain just farted or something."

Nathan waited a moment, wondering if Ralph was drunk. "Have you asked her?"

"Yeah, I'm sure I did. She's not big on long conversations anymore, though. I'm sure if I did, she just looked at me or something."

"Why didn't you come up here with her?"

"Because I'm working on my photographs. I've got my own shit to do here."

Nathan paused. "Well, why didn't Dora come up here?"

Dora was Ellen's live-in cook in Cleveland. She had interrupted Nathan's meeting with Ralph and Ellen by screaming so shrilly the hair stood up on the back of his neck. When Ralph and Nathan had raced toward the kitchen, they found that Ralph's pet boa constrictor had escaped from his bedroom, coiling itself behind the refrigerator.

Ralph said, "She's a middle-aged black woman with kids."

Nathan listened to Ralph turning on a television and changing the channels. "Well, I just wish somebody had told me about this before I came up here."

"About the deal with the car?" Ralph asked. "Yeah. How come your dad didn't tell you about it?"

"Well, because he's her estate planner. He doesn't know that much about her personal life."

A silence followed, and Nathan couldn't tell if Ralph was still mulling the situation over or was just engrossed by something on television.

"Yeah, you know what, though?" Ralph said, suddenly. "It's not even that big of a deal. She just kind of forgets things every once in a while. I think that's what happened with the car, you know? She just forgot where she was going, or how to drive it, or something. But with you driving, I don't think you have anything to worry about."

Nathan wondered whether there was any point in asking the questions he wanted to ask. What if she forgets that red coils on the stove mean they're hot, for instance? Or takes a walk and forgets the way home? What if Nathan was a former part-time librarian and deep sleeper, not a goddamned registered nurse?

Instead he listened to Ralph inviting himself up to Brightonfield Cove. "It won't be for a while," he said, his voice increasing in volume as he moved back into the room where people were attempting to shout over the music. "Like in a couple of weeks or something. Just for a few days. I've got to visit a friend in Portland, and I figured why not spend a few days in the Cove just relaxing, you know?"

Five

Hope at the Post Office ~ Eldwin Gives Nathan a Lift ~ An Old Video Conjures the Past ~ Glen's Request ~ The Cocktail Party ~ A Marriage Proposal

In the morning, Nathan awoke to the sound of pounding on the front door. He pulled on a pair of shorts, stumbled down the front stairs, and opened the door to find a sinewy woman in cargo pants and a yellow T-shirt carrying a bucket and sponge. She smiled primly as she entered, pretending not to notice Nathan's bed head, and in return Nathan pretended not to notice that she'd nearly beaten the door off its frame.

"You called Monday saying," she looked down at her clipboard, "Eleanor Broderick wanted a bath this morning."

Nathan noticed the nurse's badge clipped to the woman's pocket, nodded, and said, "That's right." Back home, Ralph had told him that Ellen employed a nursing service in Cleveland to help her bathe, so Nathan had scanned the local yellow pages to find someone to do the same for her here.

After introducing the nurse to Ellen, he guided them upstairs to the bathroom, then told them he'd be back in half an hour. The sky was a threatening concrete slab, but Nathan wanted a little exercise, so he decided to walk the quarter-mile to Gilman's grocery. Since the weather would likely keep them from the club, Nathan picked up a few videos and another two-liter bottle of soda. On his way out, he glanced over at the people trickling in and out of the post office.

There was no urgent reason to check the mail that morning, except that Nathan was hoping for another letter from Sophie. It was possible, after all, that after mailing her last letter she'd been stricken with regret and self-doubt. Maybe her new, knuckle-dragging boyfriend had come over afterward and compelled her to wonder—as Nathan did—why she'd ever started dating him. Later that night, she might have cried and pulled out her pink stationery to write a new letter. A letter asking Nathan to love her again and pleading with him to return.

That was the welcome missive that could be waiting in Ellen's post office box. Except that it wasn't. And Nathan knew it wasn't. And going over there to find the box empty except for Pizza Hut and grocery coupons would only plunge him deeper into his current gloom.

Unless, of course, the letter was there.

Nathan ambled across the street, assuring himself that he was only going to check the box for Ellen's mail. He'd been neglectful of this part of his job and now he was going to be more conscientious. An attractive, freckle-faced young woman smiled at Nathan as he opened the post office door, and he felt a surge of optimism about finding a letter from Sophie. Then he got himself under control. He forced himself to confront the fact that no letter from her would be there, and when he opened the box, finding it barren, he was for the most part prepared for the hollow tightening inside him.

Rain spat against Nathan's face. A few women chirped happily on the front porch of Gilman's, and a handsome thirtysomething couple, huddled beneath an umbrella, seemed amused by the weather and laughingly wished Nathan a good morning. Nathan nodded almost imperceptibly. He debated whether it was worth the trouble of setting down his bag of groceries to unzip the hood of his windbreaker and prevent the rain from dripping down the back of his neck. But he did not stop. The windy rain lashed against his eyes while, behind him, a car's tires hissed against the wet pavement.

"You want a ride?" said a man, speaking through a narrow opening in the window of his rusty station wagon. Squinting to see through the rain, Nathan could make out a wide, big-boned face that took him a moment to recognize. Instead of a pastoral robe, Eldwin was wearing an army green sweater, and although Nathan hesitated, fearful of being trapped in a dully pious conversation, he accepted the offer and trudged to the other side of the car.

"I'm probably getting your seat a little wet," Nathan said, arranging his bag of groceries on top of the heap of old mail and newspapers beneath his feet. But the more he took in his surroundings, the more his concern seemed superfluous. Cottony stuffing pushed out between the seams of stained, tan upholstery, and the air was acrid with the smell of cigarette butts overflowing their tray.

Eldwin said, "Ah, don't worry about it." He wasn't wearing his round, wire-rimmed glasses, but indentations remained along his temple where the sides of the frames normally squeezed his broad head. "How are things going with Mrs. . . ."

"Broderick?"

"Yeah."

"Things are going all right, I guess."

"That's good. I'd heard she wasn't doing so well lately."

"Where did you hear that?"

Eldwin tilted his chin up to scratch his neck. "I think that was on the boat yesterday, people were saying that. I saw you down there, didn't I? At the yacht club?"

Nathan gave a grim smile and said, "Well, someone invited me to go sailing, but it turned out she thought I was somebody else, so I didn't go."

"Who invited you?"

"Ellen's niece, Kendra . . . Garfield, I think."

Eldwin drove the car down to Ellen's driveway and parked behind the nurse's black Escort. A dimpled smile crept across his unshaven face as he stared out the window at the dense, brainlike clouds now looming over the ocean.

"Do you know her?" Nathan asked.

"No, I *didn't* know her, but she invited my kids and me to go out sailing with them yesterday, so I guess you would have been with us. Who did she think you were?"

"I don't know. The son of a family friend or something." Nathan shrugged. "Anyway, you went with them? How was it?"

"Well . . . actually . . . it was pretty nice." Eldwin inhaled deeply and exhaled with an embarrassed laugh.

Nathan stared out the window at the leafy tree boughs bending away from the ocean. He was enjoying the unexpected company and was in no hurry to go back into the house. Eldwin removed a pack of American Spirits from above the visor and pushed in the car lighter. "So you don't have much time off with this job?"

"Well, the job description's kind of vague," Nathan explained. "I had some stressful stuff going on back home, and I kind of thought I would come up here and just drive Ellen around and stuff, but also kind of relax and clear my head and . . ." Nathan stared out the window. "I don't know. You're right that she's not in the best shape, so I might have my hands full."

Eldwin nodded as he slapped the pack of cigarettes against his palm.

"So what's your arrangement here?" Nathan asked.

"My arrangement? Well, St. Michael's provides the house and in return I'm supposed to be the pastor there until Labor Day."

"I liked your sermon on Sunday."

"Yeah? I wasn't sure whether to give that one."

"How come?"

"I don't know. I borrowed from Emerson, which should have appealed to some of their New England sensibilities, but it was a little heavy on the Aristotle. I just doubt it was the kind of sermon they were expecting."

Eldwin stuck a cigarette in his mouth and shrugged as he reached for the lighter. "Who knows?"

"Well, I thought it was better than a lot of sermons I hear."

"Do you hear a lot of sermons?" Eldwin asked. He lit his cigarette and exhaled a thin stream of smoke through the open window.

"I used to," Nathan said. "But I imagine I'll be hearing your sermons fairly regularly."

"We'll see. They might tell me to get lost."

Nathan said, "Seems like a pretty good gig if you can keep it."

"Yeah," Eldwin said, slowly, as if uncertain whether to affirm that this was true. "Giving one sermon a week, a lot of them sermons I've already given, is not a heavy workload. But we have Meghan and Eliot, with none of their friends around or normal places to take them. And we have to figure out how to deal with having a nanny living with us."

"You've never had a nanny before?"

Eldwin shook his head, coughing without opening his mouth, a few bursts of smoke escaping his bulbous nose. "No, have you?"

"No, but yours makes me think it might be nice to have one."

Eldwin glanced at Nathan, chuckled, then sighed. "Yeah. She's attractive."

Lightning stabbed across the charcoal sky, and the sudden crack and roar of thunder made the car tremble.

"Whoa," Nathan said.

The wind keened louder through the window and rain began to fall in dull plunks against the windshield, blurring the gray waves of the ocean. "All right, I should probably head in here," Nathan said, reaching down for his grocery bag. "Thanks for the ride."

"Hey, do you know if Ellen got an invitation to a party tonight?" Eldwin asked.

"She's invited to Bill McAlister's party."

"Are you going to go?"

"Ellen may, but I don't know. I may end up dropping her off or something."

Eldwin's brow furrowed, but the rain drummed on the car's roof like thousands of impatient fingers. Flicking his cigarette out the window, he called, "Try and come. I'll bring Leah along."

Nathan nodded, then got out of the car and hurried across the puddled lawn. He clamped the newspaper over his head, but by the time he reached the porch, his windbreaker was soaked and hanging from him like an old person's skin.

"Do you know what this is, Ellen?" Nathan was crouching beside the TV stand. He'd planned to pop the movie *Chariots of Fire* into the VCR but had noticed an old shoe box on the bottom shelf. Ellen was distracted by the view outside the French doors, so Nathan opened the box and found within it an old Audubon bird guide, a pair of binoculars, and a videocassette entitled "1936–1957." Nathan held the cassette up for her to see and read the title aloud.

"Old movies?" she said. She was sitting with her feet up in her lounge chair, looking more vital since her bath. Her hair was pulled back in a ponytail and she was dressed in a cotton khaki-colored dress.

"Do you want to check it out?"

Ellen looked down at the tape. "I don't see why not."

The video slid into the machine with a series of rough clicks, as if something had broken inside, but after a moment, the static screen was replaced by darkness and funky, seventies music that Nathan associated with old porno films. Seized with the sudden dread that Ralph might have left an old X-rated movie among Ellen's birdwatching materials, Nathan kept his hand close to the stop button of the VCR. He waited, half expecting to see a well-muscled and mustachioed man bumping behind a chesty blonde, but as the screen brightened, Nathan sat back and relaxed.

It was an old black-and-white film, perhaps shot in sixteen millimeter, because the gray snow was falling more quickly than it does in real life. Occasionally mottled with dark splotches and squiggles, the screen showed an imposing brick house sitting on top of a snow-covered hill.

"Isn't that your place in Cleveland?" Nathan asked.

Ellen's right hand fumbled against the side of the recliner, searching for the lever to push her upright and make it easier for her to see. Nathan scooted over to assist her as a boy appeared onscreen, running and diving headfirst onto his rail sled to careen the rest of the way down the hill.

"That's Tommy, my brother," Ellen said.

"Oh, does he still live in Cleveland, too?"

"No, he was hit by a car."

"Oh."

The boy stood up from his sled. He grinned through crooked teeth and licked at the snow accumulated around the woolen collar of his coat. Crouching to paw at the ground, he found the rope attached to his sled, then ran in short, high-stepping strides back up the hill. Near the rear porch of the house, he flopped down on his back, lying motionless, his tongue lolling out in mock death. Then he opened his laughing eyes and waved his arms and legs against the snow. When he finished, he rolled over to view the angel shape he'd made, then packed a few snowballs to hurl at the round-faced girl on the porch. The girl turned, wearing a shapeless dark coat that barely trembled as the white clumps hit her back and fell away.

"Is that you?" Nathan asked.

Ellen didn't hear him, but when the girl faced her brother, her nose wrinkling in amused protest, Nathan did not need to ask the question again.

Moments later, decades passed into a world of color, and Ellen appeared in the style that she would settle into for the rest of her life. Her hair was parted on the side and pulled back, and she was dressed in a button-down, calf-length summer dress. She stood with arms crossed amid dozens of others on the grass bank of the cove that connected through a narrow strait with Albans Bay. A banner flapping between two poles on the shore read "1957 Father-Son Dinghy Derby," and a row of dinghies in the water huddled along the embankment, a man and boy in each one. The young Ellen took a few steps down the sloping grass and crouched beside a red-and-black dinghy named the *Little Red Hen.* On the seat, a towheaded boy sat running his hand through the water beside his father. The little boy continued to stare down at the water, answering his mother's questions until he looked up and smiled as she backed away.

"Is that your son, Glen?" Nathan asked.

"Yes, and his father, Harold."

Dressed in white pants and a short-sleeved oxford shirt, Harold seemed not to have noticed that his wife had knelt down beside the boat. He was a slender, athletic-looking man, with the kind of square jaw and closely cropped hair that Nathan thought of as classic 1950s handsome. He was talking with a husky man onshore whose facial expressions seemed overeager. The man had thinning blond hair and laughed at moments when Harold only smiled.

"Is that what's his name . . . Carl?"

"I think so."

Farther up the shore, an old, barrel-chested man in suspenders held a pistol above his head. He shouted something before the gun jerked and a wisp of smoke curled and vanished into the air.

The men in the dinghies began to row, while the boys waved to the crowd. The Ellen in the movie walked a few feet closer to the water's edge, waving, as strands of sandy blond hair fluttered across her blue eyes. Nathan could see how beautiful and elegant she'd been. He wondered, if he had been born earlier, in her time, whether she would have had anything to do with him, and how much of himself to see in Carl. The already balding man now stood only a few feet from Ellen, arms folded, smiling as he looked out at the boats, perhaps unsure of what to say to her. In front of them, the dinghies began to blur into one another along the horizon as the screen faded to black.

There was no shower in the house, so after dinner Nathan took a bath, then dug out from his suitcase clothes he thought might be appropriate for the evening's party. He pulled on a pair of khaki pants, a dress shirt, and a navy blue sport coat he'd noticed in the room's closet. After shaking the musty sport coat out the window, Nathan slid his arms through the silk-lined sleeves and was surprised to see how well it fit. There was probably more room in the chest than Nathan needed, but it was certainly wearable. He moved several yards back from the mirror into a partially shadowed area of the room where he thought he looked the most handsome. When the phone rang, he hustled into Ellen's bedroom to answer.

"Hello, is this Nathan?" a man asked.

"Yeah?"

"This is Glen Broderick."

Nathan imagined the pensive, blond boy, idly stroking the water, then he remembered a more recent photo of Glen he'd seen on top of Ellen's piano in Cleveland. In the photo he was a hearty, middle-aged man with a dark, mountain-man beard, standing with his arm around his mother's shoulder in a field of waist-high wildflowers.

"I wish we could have talked sooner," Glen said, speaking in a hushed, gently masculine manner, as if reading Nathan a bedtime story. "But things got kind of hectic here toward the end of June. We thought Ralph was going to take my mother, and then when he couldn't make it, we hoped one of my cousin's sons was going to go with her. And when that fell through, and your father mentioned you, by that time it was just a few days before Allison—my wife—and I were getting ready to take this trip to Alaska."

Nathan said, "Oh, well, I'm glad things worked out the way they did."

"You and Mother have been having a good time?"

"I think so."

"What have you been doing since you arrived?"

"Well, we've been down to the Alnombak club to watch tennis, and we've taken some drives, sat out on the porch. We're supposed to go to a cocktail party this evening."

"Oh, that's great. Whose party?"

"Bill McAlister's," Nathan said.

There was a low grunt of acknowledgment. "Mother asked you to take her to this party?"

"Well, I showed her the invitation and she expressed an interest in going." Nathan waited, but there was a deafening silence on the other end of the line. "Is that a bad idea?"

"It's not a . . ." Glen took a deep breath. "Yes, I think it probably is a bad idea."

"Oh."

"Do you think you could find something else for you and my mother to do this evening?"

"Well . . . I don't know," Nathan said, with an awful, nervous laugh. "I mean, I think she kind of thinks she's going to this party."

"Well, just see what you can do, Nathan. My mother has had a pretty rough go of it these last couple of years, and I'd like to see this summer . . . I'd like this summer to be relaxing for her."

"Okay," Nathan said slowly, glancing down at the sport coat he'd begun to think made him look gallant. Not attending the party would mean he would have to take it off, tell Ellen she'd changed dresses for nothing, and probably settle down with her for several more hours in front of the television. "So this guy Bill is not a good person?" Nathan asked. "Somebody told me he was the one who rescued Ellen when she had her accident with the car last year."

"He was, but he was also . . . He and my mother got to know each other pretty well after my father died, but my impression is that Bill is just kind of a roguish character. I think he and his wife are estranged, but they're still married, for one thing, and I just think it would probably be a lot more peaceful and enjoyable for Mother—and for you too, I would guess—if we could limit the number of upsetting things she has to contend with this summer."

Nathan sighed, "Okay." He wanted to ask Glen more about the car accident and the relationship between his mother and Bill, but it was clear Glen did not want to give him more details, and Nathan did not want to pry. He had a vague understanding of the conversational etiquette of the affluent—based mostly on Victorian costume dramas he'd seen on television—and he knew that in genteel society, you were supposed to let the unspoken remain unspoken.

"Great," Glen said, evidently relieved not to have to talk about the subject any longer. They spoke briefly about phone numbers to call in the event of an emergency, then Glen said, "I don't know if my mother is nearby, but do you think you could get her on the phone?"

After Ellen picked up the phone downstairs, Nathan lay back on his bed and imagined Eldwin, Leah, and other stylishly dressed men and women drinking and laughing on the veranda of a palatial home while he languished in his room. He loathed the idea of telling Ellen they weren't going and he wondered what he would say. *Ellen, your son and I have decided that it's not in your best interest to attend Bill McAlister's party.* Those words would never come out of his mouth. He supposed he could lie and tell her he was suddenly feeling too sick to go. But the thought of missing an opportunity to talk with Leah compelled him to fling one of his pillows across the room. Even given Ellen's uncertain mental condition, what right did Glen have to try to influence who his mother could and couldn't see? Nathan returned to the shadowed corner of the bedroom, where he checked himself in the mirror, running his palm down the front of his jacket, before exiting into the hallway. At the top of the stairs, he peered down through the banister to where Ellen was still talking with Glen on the phone.

"Oh, I know that, Glen," she was saying. She was seated on her recliner, staring up at the ceiling. "No, I won't," she said. "Oh it *is* good to know that you are thinking of me."

She brought her thumb and forefinger to the bridge of her nose as she tilted her head down and closed her eyes. She listened and nodded and then listened some more. "Oh, that would be wonderful," she said suddenly, her eyes opening as her face brightened. "Oh, Glen, I will so be looking forward to it."

When she finally said good-bye and hung up, Nathan didn't go downstairs immediately for fear she'd think he'd been listening in on her conversation. He walked stealthily back into his bedroom and dropped into the wicker chair beside the window. Watching the seagulls glide serenely above the water, Nathan considered the fragments of conversation he'd heard and whether Ellen had perhaps agreed to follow her son's suggestion. Nathan chewed his thumbnail and muttered profanities. Yes, he was being paid to take care of Ellen, but was it too much to ask that Ellen and her son give some consideration to Nathan's needs while he was there? He was not a monk, for Christ's sake. He was a virile young man. And if his ex-girlfriend no longer wanted to hear his voice or read his letters, well, then, he was going to need to get out of this large, drafty house every once in a while and talk to somebody his own age. He trudged down the stairs to find Ellen watching TV.

Taking a seat across from her in the recliner, he asked, "How's your son?"

"Oh, he's fine. He's doing very well."

"That's great." On television a mile-wide tornado whirled and thrashed across an open prairie toward an old man in a pickup who was speeding down an endless stretch of open road.

Ellen said, "You look handsome."

Nathan turned to find her staring at him. "Oh. Thanks." He glanced down at himself. "I found this sport coat in the closet upstairs."

"In the closet?"

"Yeah, it was the only thing in there, so I'm guessing maybe it was Ralph's? It was kind of dusty but it fits pretty well."

"I suppose it must have been one of Harold's."

"Whoa, I'm sorry. I'll take it off."

"Oh no, no. I like it on you," Ellen said, leaning over to pick up her cane from beside the chair. She took a minute to rest her head against the back of the recliner, eyes closed, as if to gather her energy. Then she leaned forward and asked, "Would you turn off the TV so we can go?"

On the way to the party, Ellen mentioned that her son would be visiting later that summer.

"Oh? When?"

"Pretty soon, I think."

"Did he give any dates?"

"Oh, I'm sure he did." Ellen's brow furrowed thoughtfully until her attention was drawn to the passing scenery. As they turned off Birch Hill

Boulevard, they passed the club, where only two men were playing tennis, then drove on beneath the vaulted boughs of Admirals Way. After turning around in the cul-de-sac, Nathan parked behind a row of cars and escorted Ellen up the long driveway. In the lengthening shadows of old oak trees, warm evening air carried voices and laughter from the expansive coastal home. Made of white brick, with a shale-colored slate roof, the east and west wings extended out like stunted arms welcoming visitors onto the grounds. At the front door, a female caterer in a red bow tie guided them down a softly lit hallway to the large, sunken living room where the partygoers had gathered. A massive gilt-framed mirror above the fireplace reflected the antique furniture and dozens of senior citizens who had separated into clusters in the fading summer light. Nathan inhaled the musty sweetness of old women's perfume.

Later he would wonder why he had been so unprepared for the reception they encountered that evening. Why had he assumed that only Glen would know his mother and Mr. McAlister had "gotten to know each other pretty well" while Mr. McAlister was still married? These partygoers were older, conservative men and women who valued dignity and discretion, and, Nathan was learning, also gossiped like fiends. Heads turned, voices quieted, and standing on the edge of that long, gangplanklike hallway, Nathan felt for an instant that he and Ellen had arrived at their doom. He nervously escorted her down the steps, and helped her to avoid tripping over the living room's large, Persian rug, but it was several moments before the crowd's murmuring returned to full-fledged chatter.

As a few of the partygoers turned with broad smiles and gushing "Hellooooo's," Franny and Carl Buchanan were among a circle of couples who attempted to engage Ellen in conversation. Franny raved about how lovely it had been to watch last year's Fourth of July fireworks from Ellen's porch, and, adopting a more somber tone, expressed how wonderful it was that Ellen had been able to return to "the Cove." Carl's pale cheeks looked flushed with embarrassment or liquor or both, and his lips had the wet gleam of freshly melted wax. He shook hands with Ellen and Nathan, but said almost nothing, gazing over their heads as he absently surveyed the room. When Franny suggested that perhaps Nathan would like to escort Ellen someplace to sit down, Nathan was grateful to move away from them.

At the bar—bottles of wines and liquor arrayed on a white tablecloth—Nathan ordered a sherry and a rum and Coke. He guided Ellen to the upholstered couch at the far corner of the room, where he sipped his drink and tried to make it appear that he and Ellen were actively engaged in conversation. He commented on the baby grand behind them, asking her if she had ever played an instrument (the flute, briefly, as a child), then talked at some length about his own teenage efforts to play the guitar. When this monologue evolved into another—about how well sound traveled across the harbor, and then about the differences in weather between Cleveland and Brightonfield Cove—Nathan sighed heavily and took the final gulp of his rum and Coke. Finding Ellen's drink mostly unsipped, he stood to refill his glass.

The bartender refreshed his drink, and Nathan lifted a stuffed portobello mushroom from a silver tray. Many of the faces surrounding him were familiar from the Alnombak club or St. Michael's. But he saw no sign of Leah. Eldwin was talking with a group of people near the back patio, but Nathan did not try and talk with him. Instead he ate a few more stuffed mushrooms while occasionally glancing at Ellen. An older man with a gray mustache eased himself down on the couch beside her, and Ellen clasped his hand with both of hers. Nathan was about to march back to the couch when Eldwin approached him.

"So, are you bored yet?" he asked. He had tired, hound-dog eyes, and shook Nathan's hand while sidling up to the bar.

"Give me another minute," Nathan said, although he was no longer as bored as he had been. He was wondering about the man with the gray mustache.

"Leah's out in the side yard with the kids, if you want to say hello."

Nathan nodded. "All right."

After asking the bartender to refill his glass of merlot, Eldwin asked, "So what do you do in Cleveland when you're not going to church?"

Ellen and the man were no longer holding hands, so Nathan rubbed his chin and decided he could stay a moment longer. "In the afternoon I've got a job as an assistant at the downtown public library, and at night I usually work on this graphic novel I've been trying to draw."

"Is that like a . . . like a comic book?"

"Well, yeah, but it's not like Superman or Green Lantern or any of those superhero comics. It's more like an illustrated story for adults."

Eldwin sipped his wine and nodded.

"Not a lot of adults know about them," Nathan explained. "A lot of graphic novelists have to publish their own work and then find a company to distribute them."

"Is that what you're planning to do?"

"Well, I've already done it once," Nathan said, affecting modesty about his accomplishment because telling the truth would have embarrassed him. He had published a thousand black-and-white copies of his collection of illustrated short stories, *Let Us Now Praise a Romantic Man,* but he'd never persuaded any company to distribute them. He'd had to do it himself: hauling them around in the backseat of his Civic, hawking them at comic book conventions, cajoling the few comic stores in town to let him place a few issues on their shelves. Roughly six hundred copies remained in the printer's boxes, and so far he'd recouped only half of the $2,000 it had cost to print them.

"Do you have a copy I could buy?"

"I don't have one here, but maybe I could mail you one after the summer," Nathan said. He took another sip of his drink and added, "I'm kind of trying to move on and work on new stuff."

"What are you working on now?"

Nathan shrugged. "Lots of different stuff, actually."

"Well, I'd be interested in seeing your work sometime."

"Yeah, I'll have to show you something," Nathan said, nodding. Deep inside the box of comic books he'd brought with him, there was a copy of *Let Us Now Praise a Romantic Man.* But the autobiographical stories about a young man's romantic tribulations now left him feeling so mortifyingly untalented that he could no longer bear to leaf through the pages, much less show them to anyone else. When he'd tried starting another graphic novel—detailing the last year before his mother's death—he'd found he couldn't work on it without sobbing. So for the last several months he'd done little more than random sketches he hadn't planned for anyone else to see. Nathan picked up another mushroom from the tray and asked, "So what do you do in Boston when you're not at church?"

Eldwin scratched his neck, frowning, as if attempting to remember his life in Cambridge. "I guess I spend a lot of time at home with Rachel and the kids. I used to do more writing, essay writing for journals. And every once in a while we try to do something with friends. But it's been a hard year. Rachel's father was sick for a long time, and he just passed away last February."

Nathan's mouth was full, but he said, "I'm sorry."

Eldwin shrugged. "He wasn't always a nice guy, but he was her father, and her last parent, so she's been having a tough time. That's why she's not here tonight."

"I can understand that," Nathan said, swallowing. "My mom passed away a few years ago, and when I think about it, I still feel like I can't breathe sometimes."

Eldwin nodded.

Nathan glanced at the far corner of the room just in time to see the mustachioed older man put his hand on Ellen's knee as he said something to her.

"Do you know if that guy sitting next to Ellen is Bill McAlister?"

Eldwin followed Nathan's gaze, then said, "Yeah, that's him. I just met him."

Nathan shook his head.

"What?" Eldwin asked.

Nathan informed him of his conversation with Glen, and Eldwin said a woman had already told him earlier that evening about Bill's affair with Ellen. Nathan asked, "Do you think a lot of people know?"

"I think a lot of people in this community know things they're not supposed to know about one another."

"Well, how did the guy seem to you?"

"He seemed polite, in a gruff kind of way," Eldwin said. "I didn't talk to him long. I talked mostly with his wife. I think she said he used to be a hedge-fund manager in New York."

"My God. His wife is here?"

Eldwin attempted to point her out, but he couldn't locate her in the crowd. Giving up, he asked, "Would you like to go chaperone?"

Nathan didn't want to, really—he wanted to grab Ellen and leave—but he followed Eldwin across the room closely enough to be able to smell the cigarette odor wafting from him. As they approached the couch, Nathan kept his eyes on Mr. McAlister. Dressed in crisply pressed khaki pants and a blue blazer, he had the build of a former athlete who had managed to stave off growing fat. His widow's peak of gray hair was thinning to baldness around the crown, and deep laugh lines like parentheses framed his crooked smile. Firmly gripping Nathan's hand, he asked, "So you're helping Ellen out this summer, huh?"

"Trying," Nathan said as he and Eldwin sat down in upholstered chairs across from the couch.

"Don't let her take advantage of you, now. She can be a real taskmaster." The sagging ruddiness of his face was enlivened by the twitch of his mustache and the twinkle in his gray-brown eyes.

Ellen shook her head demurely.

"Well, she can take advantage of me all she likes," Nathan said, and smiled. The words immediately burned in his ears with an unintended sexual connotation, and he sought to disguise his embarrassment by taking a long drink from his glass.

For a while they talked about how—like Nathan—Mr. McAlister had been born in Cleveland. His house had been on Coventry, not far from where Ellen lived, but he had not spent much time there as a child before his parents sent him to boarding school. After graduation, he served on a naval carrier in the war and then moved to New York. "I met Ellen when I started coming up here to the Cove, but I'd actually met her before, many years ago, at her coming-out party, even though I don't think she remembers."

"I remember," Ellen said.

"Well, what was I wearing?"

"You were wearing a *tuxedo*."

"Well, that's right," Mr. McAlister said, shrugging with a she's-got-me-beat expression and then bursting into raucous laughter. Nathan looked away and noticed a few people stealing glances at them. The older man pushed himself farther back on the couch, resting his wineglass between his legs, and said, "Did you know Ellen used to be a great golfer? She was a great athlete in general, good at tennis, but she was a fantastic golfer."

Nathan wondered what it would be like to hear the talents you had enjoyed in life spoken of in the past tense. But Ellen was watching Mr. McAlister with an expression of fond expectation.

"Do you remember the tournament you were in—what year was that, eighty-seven? Ellen played in a mixed golf tournament here when one of the best players got sick and his replacement was Vice-President George Bush."

Eldwin said, "George Bush is a member of the Alnombak club?"

"He's an honorary member."

"Does he have a summer home here?" Nathan asked.

"No, his place is down in Kennebunkport," Mr. McAlister said, waving further questions away with his hand. "Anyway, he was playing in this golf tournament, and then you had Ellen out there—the only woman—but she was playing with the men because that's how good she was. I think you had Rainier out there too, didn't you?"

"I may have." Ellen smiled.

"That would be just like her, taking her dog," Mr. McAlister said, shaking his head. "She was always bending the rules and getting away with it, because no one could say no to her. So anyway, she's in the tournament, and she wins the damn thing and beats the vice-president by how much, Ellen?"

Ellen's smile erupted into a laugh, a delighted, confident laugh that Nathan had never heard from her. "I think by a lot."

"Yeah, I think so too, because do you remember what you said to him when you both were walking into the clubhouse afterward?"

Ellen was still smiling, but she knotted her brow. "No—oh, no, what did I say?"

"You said, 'I hope you'll be a better president than you are a golfer.' "

Ellen laughed again but put her hand over her mouth. "Oh, Bill," she said, letting her hand fall away. "I didn't."

"You did," Mr. McAlister said, chuckling.

Soon, a man with snow white hair sat down and began to talk about a tennis match that he and Ellen had played together. Nathan might have stayed longer, but Eldwin used the base of his wineglass to touch Nathan's knee. "You might want to head out there if you want to talk with Leah," he said.

Nathan wanted to talk with Leah, but because a blade of nervousness twisted inside him at the prospect, he first had to relieve himself. In the bathroom, he did not turn on the overhead light because there was a candle burning beneath the mirror and he much preferred the way he looked in the flickering shadows. Zipping up his pants, he stood in front of the mirror and practiced the close-lipped smile that disguised his too small teeth. Then he unlocked the door. The thought of going back through the living room to exit out of the patio doors did not appeal to him. So he turned in the other direction in search of another way outside. Walking stealthily down the hallway, he found a laundry room with a door leading to the backyard, but he was drawn a few paces farther in the direction of a small library. From the doorway, Nathan could see a matching brown leather couch and chair sitting in front of a marble fireplace, and, on the far side of the room, floor-to-ceiling wooden shelves set into adjacent walls. Looking back to make sure no one was watching, he stepped inside the cozy room. Many of the books were faded, picture-heavy manuals about sailing and shipbuilding, but there was also row upon row of nineteenth-century-edition books by Dickens, Thackeray, and Twain. Pulling the novels from the shelves, Nathan was struck by the high quality of the binding, and even more by how often the books contained illustrations. From beneath the rows of nineteenth-century fiction, Nathan pulled out a massive, old leather-bound copy of *Don Quixote* and paged through intricately detailed illustrations by the artist Gustave Doré. So much of great art is great patience, Nathan thought, optimistically. But staring down at the most famous drawing—of the Don being knocked off his horse by a windmill—Nathan felt a familiar pang of doubt about his talent and abruptly returned the tome to its shelf.

Once back in the hallway, he stepped through the laundry room and out into the backyard. After a moment's hesitation, staring out at the empty back lawn that rolled down for a hundred yards or so to the shore, he heard children's voices floating from somewhere to the east and behind him. Plunging his hands into his pockets, then letting them hang loose at his sides, then plunging them into his pockets again, Nathan walked around the east corner of the house. There Eldwin's children and their nanny were standing on the immaculate lawn amid a course of croquet wickets and stakes. Wearing a tan sleeveless dress, Leah waved at Nathan as Eliot struck a ball that rolled to the far side of a stake. The boy's shoulders sagged, but his face lit up as he said, "Meghan hit her ball twice, so don't I get to go again, too?"

"No, hers went under the hoop, remember? That's why she got to go again," Leah explained.

As he approached, Nathan said, "Looks like a heated match."

"I think they're tired," Leah said. "I had to break up a fight a few minutes ago."

"I'm not tired," Eliot said. He was standing on the head of his mallet, attempting to keep his balance.

"It's *your* turn," Meghan wailed.

"Oh!" Leah said, and stepped forward toward her red ball. "Okay, it's my turn." She smiled at Nathan with feigned embarrassment. She whacked the ball in the direction of the intended wicket, but it wobbled past Nathan and Eliot into the mulched flower bed beside the house.

"Tough break," Nathan said.

"I hate this game," Leah muttered, humor infiltrating her pout.

As they watched Eliot practice his swing, Nathan asked, "So, how was sailing yesterday?"

"It was a gorgeous boat. But I had to keep these two from throwing each other overboard, so it wasn't really that fun. I think I did get a tan, though," she said, peering down at her shoulder. Her skin was an unfreckled ripe golden brown. When she looked up, she said, "Eldwin said you were supposed to come with us, but Kendra wouldn't let you?"

Nathan smiled weakly. As he told her the story, Leah took her turns in the match, sometimes acting as referee between the children, but always glancing back expectantly, waiting for him to continue.

"I can't believe she would do that," Leah said. "It's so *tacky*. I mean, she knew you were working for Ellen?"

Nathan shrugged. "Yeah."

"That's crazy."

"Well, I didn't let it ruin my day," Nathan said. "After I found out you were busy, I went back to the house and popped some popcorn, and Ellen and I watched four hours of television, including an old Jerry Lewis movie."

Leah hesitated, but said, encouragingly, "Oh, well, that's good."

"That was kind of a joke. I mean, we did watch four hours of television. It just wasn't that . . . fun."

Leah smiled at Nathan with puzzled amusement before positioning herself over the ball. Her legs spread as she leaned over, and Nathan averted his eyes to glance out at the bay. She struck the ball hard enough that it rolled halfway up the sloping lawn, then back down, finally resting almost where she was standing. Her shoulders collapsed and she hung her head in a comic expression of defeat.

The croquet match eventually degenerated into a game wherein each child tried to see who could hit the ball the farthest, and as Nathan and Leah watched, she asked, "Why do you think I'm here?"

"I'm not sure. You mean in a cosmic sense?"

Leah smiled and said, "Yes."

"Well, I mean, I don't know you that well, but you seem like a young woman probably gifted with certain abilities, and maybe, you know, maybe your purpose is just to share those—"

"All right, stop." Leah clamped her mouth shut in an apparent effort to stop smiling. "I'm asking why Eldwin would drag me and his kids along with him tonight when it would have been *so* much easier for us just to stay home."

"I don't know," Nathan answered.

Eliot knocked his ball into a row of tall grass and flowers between the trees, and after guiding him in another direction, Leah returned to stand beside Nathan. "Did he know you were coming?"

"Eldwin? I don't think so. I told him Ellen might come, but that if she did, I was probably just going to drop her off."

"Hmmm," Leah said.

Nathan said, "Maybe he wanted to hook you up with one of these old dudes."

"Maybe," Leah said, lengthening the last vowel while her eyebrows rose with mock interest.

"There was a guy in there emptying out his catheter tube who I think might be single."

"You're gross," Leah said, shaking her head. But she grinned and her eyes glinted warmly in a way that gave Nathan hope. Twilight was falling over them when Eldwin approached from the far side of the house. Eliot and Meghan grabbed their father's hands, screeching passionate accounts of how the other sibling had cheated during the match.

"I want to go home," Meghan cried.

"I'm with you," Eldwin said, freeing his hands to light a cigarette.

Nathan helped Eldwin and Leah pull out the stakes and wickets, then carry them, along with the rest of the equipment, to where the station wagon was parked along the curb. Seeing Eldwin's rusted white Ford Fairmont made Nathan feel relieved. He had been so nervous around Leah, and consequently said so many foolish things, that he was looking forward to seeing her humbled by climbing into this dilapidated car.

Nathan turned to Eldwin. "Ellen holding up in there?"

"Yeah, pretty well. What are you doing on Friday night?"

Nathan glanced sidelong at Leah, but she was encouraging Eliot to hurry up and follow them. "I'm not sure, why?"

"We should go kayaking."

"Yeah." Nathan had enjoyed his conversations with Eldwin, but on Friday night, he was hoping to do something with Leah. "That sounds great. The only problem is, I've just got an hour or so free during the day and Ellen doesn't really go to bed until nine o'clock."

"That's not a problem. I was thinking that we'd get started around nine, anyway, after Meghan and Eliot go to bed."

Nathan said, "I've never done it before, though, so I should probably learn how to do it in daylight first, don't you think?"

Eldwin exhaled smoke through his nostrils. "Not necessarily. We'll be on the bay, so there's not much chance we're going to roll. I'll teach you a few things before we head out, but it's a tandem kayak, so we'll be together. And you can swim, right?"

Not very well, Nathan thought. He might have admitted this if he had been walking with Eldwin alone, but with Leah and the children listening, Nathan answered, "Yeah, of course."

"Then we'll be fine," Eldwin said, opening the driver's side of the station wagon. Leah smiled as she waved good-bye, and Nathan felt a moment of longing for a wife, children, and the comfortableness with oneself that driving a rusting station wagon implied. Stepping back from the street, he turned toward the house. Near the front steps, he glanced back to see the station wagon slow to a stop near the first bend in the road, the brake lights burning a brighter crimson until the car shifted into park. After a moment, Eldwin and Leah climbed out from the front seats. Leah's movements seemed quick and purposeful compared to Eldwin's lumbering shuffle. They switched places, closed the doors, then started once more toward home.

Warm coastal wind passed gently through the moonlit bedroom as Nathan lay staring at the ceiling. Reviewing his memories of Leah at the party that evening, he searched for aspects of her personality that might eventually disappoint him. He always felt more comfortable around women who, for one reason or another, he was confident he would never marry.

He had found enough disappointing things about Sophie—including her tremendous need for attention and the way she pressured him to be more appreciative of certain films—that he could feel comfortable even when they were fighting, even when it seemed they were on the verge of breaking up. The fact was, Nathan had broken up with her many times during the roughly two years they'd been dating. But he'd felt such a rush of arousal near her that such breakups lasted only a few days, and usually ended at her apartment with him quickly undressing her. Their relationship had depended on these hot, tear-filled reunions to give it life. But after a while, even the reunions began to seem banal and exhausting. Nathan had started flirting with a Norwegian exchange student he often saw at the library, and began mulling over gentle ways to tell Sophie that perhaps they needed to spend more time apart. He had still been searching for the best way to tell her that this would be a *real* breakup—not like the others—when she invited him to her apartment to announce that she was really breaking up with him for someone else: a burly, mouth-breathing friend of hers named Derek who managed the music store near the floral shop.

Nathan had cried. She'd cried.

A few days later, Nathan had returned to her apartment with a ring made of tinfoil—a pitiable thing with which he hoped to win her sympathy—and lied to her while proposing. His voice broke as he told her he'd never found anything about her to make him second-guess his hope that they would marry. Sophie laughed at this, understandably, and Nathan eventually chuckled, too. They'd waged war after war over everything from her resentment about the lack of time they spent together to her love of Truffaut. So Nathan finally told her the truth: that although there had been moments of second-guessing, he didn't know of anything about their relationship that they couldn't work through, and that he loved her desperately, desperately, more than he had ever loved anyone, and that if she were to agree to marry him, please marry him, he would consider it the greatest stroke of luck in his life.

Sophie's face softened, and raising that fragile piece of tinfoil to her finger, Nathan almost didn't expect the fear and sorrow that suddenly surged and twisted inside him. Did he somehow reveal it to her, too? He must have. She'd clenched her extended fingers into a fist and whispered that it was time for him to go.

Nathan turned over in his groaning bed and stared out at the moonlit sky until leaden memories of heartache were replaced by lighter thoughts of Leah, and a little of his grief lifted when he considered he could be a better person for her.

Late in the night, an ambulance wailed in the distance, rousing Nathan from sleep. For a moment, the siren seemed to fade, but then plunged toward him, again, warbling louder and louder. Dread that the ambulance was somehow for Ellen propelled Nathan from under his blanket and into the hall. He pressed his head to her door and peered through the opening into the milky shadows of her room. When the siren stopped, somewhere still a few streets away, Ellen mumbled in her sleep and Nathan sagged with relief. He wondered for whom the siren had wailed, and in his tired, fretful frame of mind, he hoped it had wailed for Mr. McAlister. Crawling back into bed, Nathan's muscles tightened again when he remembered Glen's request and how flirtatious Mr. McAlister had acted that evening with Ellen. In the soft yellow light of his front porch, the old Lothario had bid good-bye to her with a warmly clasped hand, a lingering kiss planted nearer her lips than her cheek, and a low-spoken promise to stop by soon.

Six

Thayer Woodbridge Shows His Muscles ~ Nathan Kisses Leah ~ Mr. McAlister Regrets to Inform Them of a Death

When the doorbell rang the following morning, Nathan left his breakfast to greet a dark-haired young man whose heavy-lidded eyes seemed to watch him with vague disdain. "Are you Nathan?" he asked.

As Nathan opened the door to shake his hand, the young man said his name was Thayer Woodbridge. "Bill said Mrs. Broderick had a dinghy that I could probably borrow for a couple of hours to row out to our yacht."

"Bill?"

"McAlister. He's my step-grandfather."

"Oh, we were just at his party last night."

"That's what I heard."

Both young men nodded and stared at each other. Then Nathan said, "So, do you want to come in and I'll ask Ellen about the dinghy?"

"I think it's in there," Thayer said, pointing toward the white shed that sat near the end of the driveway on the west side of the house.

A padlock kept the shed doors closed, so Nathan said, "All right, well, come on in and I'll ask Ellen if she knows where to find the key."

Thayer sniffed. "I can wait out here."

When Nathan explained the situation to Ellen, she suggested looking inside the living room desk. Nathan sifted through drawers of loose paper, old party invitations, coupons, and rubber bands, but after a few minutes he gave up. He went outside to break the news to Thayer but found the shed doors already opened.

The near door creaked back and forth in the wind, and Nathan grabbed hold of it as he peered inside. Thayer stood in rays of sunlight that slashed through the wooden sideboards to illuminate a wheelbarrow, assorted gardening tools, fishing poles, three car tires, and a red-and-black dinghy resting on its stern against the rear wall. He tilted the dinghy backward onto his shoulders to carry it out of the shed.

"How'd you get in here?" Nathan asked.

"The key was under that rock," Thayer said, gesturing down at a doorstop-size stone that lay by the grassy corner of the shed. "No one really locks anything around here."

Scabs of paint flaked off the boat as Thayer eased it down on the lawn. In black cursive letters on the rear were the words *Little Red Hen*.

"I don't know, man," Nathan said, remembering the video of Ellen's son in the dinghy when he was just a small boy. "I think this thing is over forty years old. You may not want to take it out."

Squatting in his shorts and T-shirt, Thayer ran his hand along the interior of the boat, saying, "I think she'll be all right."

But Nathan worried about what would happen if Thayer damaged or sank the boat when it was likely it had some sentimental value for Ellen's family. Also, the young man's air of entitlement made Nathan want to deprive him.

"Why don't you just use one of the dinghies down at the yacht club?"

"Bill doesn't belong to the club," Thayer answered. "He just ties his boat up at the bottom of his yard, and all the people I know at the club have taken their boats out to go sailing."

"What happened to the boat you usually use?"

"My friend Crispin took it out with his girlfriend so that they could spend the night on the *Daydreamer*. But they haven't come back."

"You think something happened to them?"

Thayer laughed. "Yeah, I think they got drunk and naked and now they don't want to leave." He grabbed both sides of the *Little Red Hen* and hoisted it up on his broad shoulders. Turning slowly, he asked, "Hey, would you mind bringing the oars from the shed?"

By the time Nathan made it down to the beach, Thayer had already eased the boat down in the shallows of the incoming tide. Nathan stared out across the water, and asked, "Which one's the *Daydreamer*?"

Thayer directed Nathan's eyes toward a roughly forty-foot yacht resting among a flock of other yachts several hundred yards out from shore. A few of the other yachts were larger, or grander, but Nathan admired the handsome sleekness of the *Daydreamer*'s navy blue hull and wood trim. Imagining it out on the open sea with sails billowing made him yearn for the kind of experiences he imagined Thayer and his friends must have enjoyed all the time: shuttling from their exciting, culturally rich lives in New York to their summer homes, unfettered by financial concerns, getting naked on yachts with their sexy girlfriends. He wanted their freedom—to not have to work, to travel, to hang out with the smart, charming women their money would eventually help them to marry.

No one was on the *Daydreamer*'s deck, but a matching blue dinghy drifted behind the yacht's stern. Thayer grabbed the two oars Nathan had been holding and placed them into their fittings. Once inside the boat he promised he would soon return it to the shed. "You're helping Mrs. Broderick out for the summer?"

"More or less," Nathan answered.

"I'm having some people over to Bill's house on Saturday night, if you want to come. Like around nine o'clock. Have you met that girl who's staying a couple houses up from you?"

"Leah?"

"I don't know, she's got dark hair?"

"Yeah, you're probably thinking of Leah."

Thayer pulled off his blue T-shirt to reveal a V-shaped upper body. His sculpted abdomen was like a rock wall beneath the precipice of his bulging pectorals. "Cool," he said, grabbing the oars. "If you see her, tell her she's invited, too."

Nathan had no intention of telling Leah about the party. But after lunch, while Ellen napped, he walked over to see if she was home. Opening the front door, she silently mouthed, "Hey," and waved him into the living room. She was cradling a phone to her ear, and held up a finger, signaling that the conversation was almost over.

The house smelled faintly of damp towels, even though most of the windows were open and sunlight shone in lengthening rectangles across the floors. In the living room, children's books and wood blocks lay on the rug beside a half-completed puzzle of a sailboat plunging through a whitecapped ocean. With Leah still on the phone, Nathan crouched beside the puzzle, searching for missing pieces while glancing through the open doorways into other rooms. The dining room appeared orderly in that "no one really goes in here" sort of way, but the kitchen looked as if it hadn't been cleaned in many days. Plates and crumpled napkins were scattered across the kitchen table, while underneath lay an abandoned village of toy cars, plastic movie figures, and a blond, blue-eyed doll. Near the sink, towers of more plates, bowls, and drinking glasses leaned perilously over torn frozen food boxes and empty grocery bags. When Nathan sensed Leah watching him, he stared down at the sailboat puzzle still in need of a sail.

"I will. You too, though, okay? Okay. Love you," Leah said, pressing a button on the phone to end the call and collapsing onto her back on the couch. She rested her arm over her eyes in a gesture of great weariness.

"How's your mom?" Nathan asked.

"She's fine—but not fine. She's . . . she took a long time to get over her divorce from my dad," Leah sighed, pausing, apparently contemplating whether to say more. "So she's been dating this guy for a while now and she really likes him, but now he's in the hospital and they don't know why he's having these horrible pains in his side."

"She's pretty upset?"

"Yeah, but she's not showing it—or she's trying not to show it."

A moment later, Leah turned onto her side and brought her arm under her head to look at Nathan. "Why am I telling you all this?"

Nathan smiled. He found a piece of the sail and fit it into the puzzle, then cast his eyes up at the ceiling. "Where is everybody?"

"Eldwin took Meghan and Eliot to play putt-putt and Rachel is sleeping . . . or at least lying in her bed." Leah's words tapered into a whisper as she picked at the frayed edge of beach towel that hung over the armrest of the couch. She wore jeans and a blue spaghetti-string tank top whose bottom had bunched up a few inches above her waistline. Glancing at the luminous tan of her stomach, Nathan asked, "So do you think you might have time to take a walk?"

When they were strolling beneath the shady trees of Birch Hill Boulevard, he told her he'd been thinking about the Chekhov quote. He asked her if she had ever had her heart broken and she explained that she and her first real boyfriend, Andy, had started dating when each was sixteen, when he was a half-hearted punk-rock skateboarder and she a half-hearted skater chick. They'd thought they were in real, fated-for-one-another kind of love, the way that maybe you can only believe when you're in high school, and they'd believed it so much that, despite all advice to the contrary—including a threat by her mother to not pay her tuition—they'd both enrolled at Haverford, outside Philadelphia.

Andy had had vague plans to be an actor, then a sculptor, and by the winter of junior year he was spending more and more time in the studio with his art friends, purportedly working on their art. Trailing him one afternoon, Leah watched him leave the studio with a pimply, bird-faced girl Leah recognized from her class on Irish literature. Leah thought the girl was not Andy's type, but after discovering them again the next day, eating bagels together in the bookstore, Leah broke into Andy's e-mail.

After finally guessing his password (Rodin), a roaring filled her ears as she read the flurry of erotic missives that he and the bird-faced girl had been sending almost since the beginning of fall term.

Later, it would be rumored that Leah had chased Andy into his apartment, tearing it apart in a crazy, Shiva-esque tantrum, but it hadn't happened like that at all. She *had* followed him to his apartment and forcefully cleared his desk of some clutter so she could sit down, but all she wanted were answers. She told him what she'd discovered, and he tearfully confessed. He said he'd loved Leah when they arrived freshman year, but, *God,* he was a different person now, and he wasn't so sure anymore. "Well, you better get sure, because I still love *you*!" she had cried, but this did not make him stay.

"But now you're not haunted by him?" Nathan asked.

Leah tilted her chin down and laughed. "No, because I've *processed,*" she said, folding and unfolding her arms as if releasing a captured bird into the air. "I spent almost my entire senior year processing."

"Ah."

"How about you? Have you had your heart broken?"

Nathan saw it as a badge of honor to be able to nod. "Yeah, I have."

He told her a little about his breakup with Sophie, including the story of the last night he had gone over to her apartment. "At the time, I hadn't figured out what her new boyfriend's truck looked like, so I go up to her apartment, and when she opens the door, he's there," Nathan said. "I can see him at the kitchen counter with a bottle of champagne that he's working to open. His back is to me, but he turns around and sees me, so Sophie steps into the hallway and kind of closes the door behind her so we can talk, and somehow it comes out that they're celebrating . . . but when I asked her what they were celebrating, she wouldn't tell me. She said she would call me tomorrow, and started to go back inside the apartment, but I asked her to wait a second and said, 'Just tell me what you're celebrating.' "

"Oh my God, why?" Leah cried.

"Why what?"

"Why did you want to know so badly? You know it was going to be bad news."

"*You* know it's going to be bad news, because we're talking about bad breakups and I'm telling you a story, but do you think that in that moment I should have known?"

"Yes!"

Nathan threw his head back, laughing. "All right, so I shouldn't have asked that question."

"So what did she say?"

"Well, she wouldn't tell me for a long time."

"*Then* what did she say?

"Then she told me bad news."

Leah grabbed Nathan's arm and fixed him with a mock-baleful stare that indicated she was not going to tolerate any further delays in the story.

"Whoa, she gave me that same look, actually," Nathan said. "Right before she told me that they were celebrating the fact that they'd both just tested negative for STDs."

Frowning, Leah said, "Ugh. God. That's horrible."

"Yeah, I don't think it was a knowledge-for-knowledge's-sake kind of thing," Nathan laughed, although he felt idiotically disingenuous for laughing. He wished he had not offered Leah this humiliating snapshot of himself. He'd never told the story to anyone.

"But now you're over it?"

Nathan nodded. "I think I've processed."

Near a sharp bend in the road, where they could see the grayish blue of the Atlantic on the other side of densely rocky shore, Nathan pointed out a gap in the hedgerow on their left. A narrow footpath led up the hill to a grassy plateau overlooking the ocean. On their way up the trail, Leah said that when the summer was over, she was moving into a friend's apartment in New York City. "I think I'm going to try and get into publishing," she said. "Figure out how to sell people the books I like to read."

"That sounds like it would be gratifying," Nathan said. He was a few years older than she was—without a college degree—and he had no idea what he was going to do when he got back home. Even if they gave him his old job back at the library, the idea of shelving books beneath those yellowing neon lights was like a weight on his heart.

At the top of the hill, the trail dipped then leveled out for a quarter of a mile as it circled the rim of a steep peninsula roughly fifty feet above the ocean. When they reached the part of the loop extending farthest out above the exploding waves, Nathan told Leah how, a few days earlier, he and Ellen had taken a shorter route here from a path just off the golf course. It was still a foolish thing for them to have attempted. Once the path grew rocky and uneven, Ellen became increasingly unsteady, and when she sat down to rest on a rock, she had very nearly fallen off the side of the cliff. The vision of her grasping at air as she tumbled over, her wide blue eyes upon him as she fluttered, heavy and wailing, onto the rocks, made Nathan shudder even now.

Leah stood with arms folded across her chest, staring down at the shoreline beneath them. "What would you have done if she'd fallen?"

"Go home, I guess. Maybe there would have been a trial for criminal neglect, but more likely I would have just stayed in my room for a long time, staring up at the ceiling."

"That would be horrible," Leah said, hugging herself as she backed away from the edge. "Then who would I talk to when I'm here?"

"You can always talk to your pastor."

Leah frowned and stepped back to sit beneath the shaded embankment separating the rolling hills of the Alnombak club golf course from the Point. "I can't talk with him."

"Why not?"

"I think he has enough problems with Rachel. All she does is sleep all the time, and she hardly ever goes anywhere, even with her own kids. I think Eldwin was hoping that taking her out of Cambridge to someplace beautiful for the summer would help her kind of get over whatever's going on with her, but it's not happening. She's come down to sit with us at dinner a couple of times, but she doesn't say very much. She's like a ghost."

Lying down beside where Leah was sitting in the shade of a birch tree, Nathan said, "Her father died in February?"

"Hmm, I think so," Leah said, her eyes cast down at the grass.

"Grieving can take a long time."

"How long ago did your mother die?"

"A few years ago."

"What did she die of?"

"Lung cancer."

"She smoked?"

"No, my dad did—or does. He's started up again."

"Oh."

Nathan said, "So what do the kids say about their mom?"

"I guess they've kind of gotten used to it. They lie in bed with her sometimes in the mornings, but they don't say much about her to me. Sometimes Meghan mentions playing soccer or something with her mommy back when she was 'feeling good.' But I think it almost seems normal to them now."

Nathan picked a dandelion and began cutting off pieces of the stem with his fingernail.

"And all Eldwin does is read," Leah continued. "I love reading, you know? I want to go into publishing! But I feel like he uses books to escape from what's going on around him. I think he's depressed too, with Rachel in bed all the time, and I guess it can be a depressing job to have to listen to a lot of people coming to you with all their problems."

"What kinds of problems do people have around here?"

"The same problems people have everywhere," Leah said, frowning at him suspiciously. "I think he's an alcoholic. Did you notice how much he was drinking at the party? I think that's why we left, because he knew he was too drunk to talk to people anymore. I asked him if he wanted me to drive, and at first he was just staring out the window, and I thought for a second he was going to yell at me for embarrassing him in front of his kids or something, but then he just kind of whispered, 'Okay.' He drinks a lot at home, too. He's always got a beer with him when he's reading, and he doesn't really smoke in the house, but he does it all the time when we're in the car. Did you ever see a pastor smoke?"

Nathan gave the question some thought. "I once saw a Catholic bishop at a fancy restaurant smoking a cigar."

"Plus, I think I heard him and Rachel having sex a few nights ago," Leah said. She checked the grass behind her for stones and then stretched out to lie on her side facing him.

"Hmm, and you think that's a sign they're both depressed?"

Leah pushed Nathan's chest. "I'm just saying I think he was probably drunk or something because . . . I don't know. He would have had to work really hard to persuade a woman that depressed to have sex with him."

"Well, what did you hear?"

Leah shook her head and stared down at the grass. Then she stuck out her tongue and panted heavily.

"Whoa," Nathan said.

Leah laughed and covered her mouth. "It really wasn't that impressive."

Nathan smiled down at her and they locked eyes for a moment, but he glanced away. Her face seemed too far away from him. In front of them, the wind was bending the long grass and wildflowers, and sunlight danced across the windblown surface of the ocean. For a while they didn't speak. Then Nathan looked over to where Leah lay with her head cradled in her arm, eyes closed, like a sleeping angel.

"What are you thinking about?" he asked quietly.

"I'm trying not to think about Eldwin and Rachel having sex. What are you thinking about?"

Nathan's hand pulled awkwardly at her hip, and he had to scoot closer to her, but they kissed. He ran his fingers through her dark, tangled hair and felt the fluttering warmth of her against him. Nothing this romantic had happened to Nathan in months, maybe years, and it was enough to persuade him, for at least a moment, that his life was not a series of random incidents but the fulfillment of a destiny.

Long after he'd kissed Leah good-bye, Nathan could still smell the faintly musky scent of her hair and taste her cherry-lip-balmed lips. Luxuriating in the sense memories of the afternoon, he watched television with Ellen, but the images rarely penetrated his reverie. During dinner he sat with his chin in his hand, nodding as Ellen spoke, until he noticed she was waiting for a response.

"I'm sorry, could you say that again?" Nathan asked, leaning forward, as if the problem was with his hearing.

"I just said that I don't think I'm going to be able to finish all of this steak, so perhaps we should give some of it to Rainier?"

Nathan thought there was still something he had missed. "Rainier? You mean your dog in Cleveland?"

Ellen looked at him long enough for Nathan to see the shock of recognition appear in her eyes. "Yes, that's right," she mumbled, staring out the window at the harbor. Then she smiled apologetically. "I guess that wouldn't be terribly practical, would it?"

"No, but he seemed like a special dog," Nathan said, shrugging, as if the idea of air-mailing leftovers was not so insane. To admit that something was seriously wrong with Ellen—that it was probably imprudent for her to be left alone for any part of the day—was to admit that he should call Glen, pack their bags, and put her on a flight home.

When they finished dinner, Nathan grabbed his sketchbook and followed Ellen onto the porch. She rocked gently in the swing, reading her book, while Nathan arranged himself in the chair beside her. He wanted to draw a picture of himself and Leah lying beside each other on the Point. He knew he would have to pay special attention to his pronounced nose and slight build for it not to seem mawkish, and knowing it would be difficult made him exhausted almost as soon as he began. He took a couple of breaks, to go to the bathroom and to pour himself a drink, and he was staring absently at the harbor when he noticed Mr. McAlister slowly marching between the rocks of Parson's Beach, wearing khaki pants and a gray polo shirt, his head hanging as if searching for shells. When he came closer, he squinted up at them and raised his palm.

"Here comes Mr. McAlister," Nathan said, but Ellen was already waving in her regal way as the older man climbed the embankment into the yard. Halfway to the house he raised his hand to them again, but the gesture seemed strangely solemn.

"Mind if I come up?" he called from near the base of the stairs. He carried with him the sweet, dying-leaves smell of a smoked cigar, and the swollen pouches beneath his eyes made his banker's face look even longer. On the porch, he shook hands with Nathan and sat down on one of the wooden chairs beside the swing. He declined Nathan's offer of something to drink, and when Ellen commented on the beautiful evening, he smiled weakly at the boats anchored out in the harbor.

Nathan said, "I met your step-grandson, Thayer, when he came over to borrow Ellen's dinghy this morning."

"I'm glad," Mr. McAlister said, nodding, as he pressed his tongue along the inside bottom of his cheek. He stared down at nothing in particular in the yard before turning to Ellen. "Did you talk with Franny today?" he asked quietly.

Ellen shook her head. "No."

"I thought someone might have called here." He glanced up at Nathan, but Nathan shook his head also.

Mr. McAlister leaned forward and clasped his hands between his knees. "I wasn't expecting to be the one to have to tell you . . . but Carl passed away last night."

Ellen's face drained of expression and she brought a hand to her mouth. "Oh . . . How?"

"They think maybe he had a heart attack. Franny didn't give me a lot of details. I think she's just trying to let people know what happened."

Ellen looked down at her lap, her eyes beginning to water.

"So," Mr. McAlister sighed. He stood and took a seat beside her on the swing, steadying them with his feet. He put his arm around Ellen's shoulders and held her left hand, saying, "I know. He cared an awful lot about you."

They sat for what seemed a long time as the sun fell behind the White

Mountains. Pale, golden light reflected off the white porch columns and clapboards. Nathan asked Ellen if she would like her shawl, and Mr. McAlister suggested they all go inside. In the dimly lit living room, he and Ellen sat down on the couch—Mr. McAlister still with his arm around her—as Nathan went into the kitchen to fetch them glasses of water. Unsure of what to do when he returned, he sat down by the fireplace, stuffing newspapers between the logs. He said, "You don't know when the funeral's going to be, do you?" And Mr. McAlister said that no, he didn't know. He didn't even know if there would be one in Brightonfield Cove, given that Carl would presumably be buried in Boston. The logs were just beginning to burn when the phone rang. Instead of answering it there in the living room, Nathan hustled through the dining room and into the kitchen. Along the way it occurred to him, with sudden dread, that the call might be from Glen.

Nathan picked up on the third ring and was grateful to hear the raspy, brusque voice of the local nurse who bathed Ellen. She was calling to confirm an appointment for the following morning. Normally, Nathan would have gone in and asked Ellen. But he was afraid of embarrassing her in front of Mr. McAlister, so he told the nurse tomorrow would be fine. He stared out the kitchen window at the first stars in the lavender darkness above the water, then walked back into the living room, where Mr. McAlister held Ellen's hand in her lap. The fire cast tall, flickering shadows along the walls, and despite Mr. McAlister's dignified demeanor, he and Ellen looked smaller, somehow more vulnerable than Nathan remembered them. Standing with a hand on the banister, Nathan announced that he was headed upstairs.

In his room, he stripped down to his boxers and flopped on the bed. He paged through his art books and comics for more than an hour. But mostly he was thinking about Carl. Nathan hadn't known him well enough to grieve. Yet it was difficult to comprehend that if he wanted to visit the man who only nights ago had been drunk on the porch, hurling his wineglass at the ocean, that man was no longer available. The particular amalgamation of atoms that allowed for the sound of his voice and that look in his eyes would never occur again, ever. Nathan still had a hard time internalizing this fundamental truth with regard to his mother. Even now, some part of his body expected to see her open his parents' front door before he knocked, hug him, then lead him to newspaper clippings about comic books or a local teen's triumph over adversity, and into the warm air of the kitchen, where, if he liked, she could heat up the soup she and Nathan's father had made earlier that afternoon. Nathan remembered the days after she drew her long-expected last breath—how he lay in his bed, barely eating, hiccupping with sobs, and occasionally hurling books and other mostly unbreakable objects around his room. As a boy, he had embraced the idea of the Rapture, which would allow him to escape death, and even though his faith had evaporated before he was even out of his early teens, Nathan could never completely let go of the feeling that the end could not be the end. He wondered about Leah's experiences with loss, and if similar sorrow might bring them closer together, until these thoughts led to others—more arousing—about her warm, slender body and the cherry taste of her mouth.

Seven

The Nurse Discovers Ellen ~ Leah Talks of Leaving ~ Kendra Explains Her Actions ~ Nathan and Eldwin Kayak to the Mouth of Albans Bay

Pounding on the front door awoke Nathan again the next morning. He pulled on shorts and a T-shirt and hustled down the stairs to see the nurse's face squinting through the curtained window. As he opened the door to let her in, he noticed it hadn't been locked.

"Morning. I'll go wake her," Nathan said. But about halfway up the stairs it occurred to him—with sudden, muscle-tightening force—that he had fallen asleep the previous evening without hearing Ellen return to her room. There had been no familiar creak of her footsteps on the stairs, or scuffing of her shoes against the carpet, and now, when he reached the open door to her room, he found that the bed was still made. He ran down the hallway, peering through open doorways at empty rooms, until the nurse yelled, "She's down here!"

Nathan hurried back toward her voice. Stumbling down a few stairs, he crouched and stared into the living room, where Ellen was sitting on the couch. "Fuck," he said quietly. Ellen's hair had shed its hairpins and hung in tangles as she brushed them back from her face. She wore a badly wrinkled, seashell-patterned dress, and the hem, bunched up above her right knee, revealed a little more of her pale and veiny leg than Nathan wanted to see. Even if he hadn't recognized the dress as the same one she'd worn yesterday, her disheveled appearance strongly indicated that she'd spent the night on the couch.

Nathan stood and walked casually down the remaining stairs. "Taking a little nap, Ellen?"

Ellen finished wiping the wisps of hair from her face and then drew her thumb and forefinger down the sides of her mouth.

"A long nap," she said, finally.

Nathan smiled down at her and placed his hand affectionately on her shoulder. "Yeah, you napped for a while." He shook his head as if to say, "What a funny, sleepy-headed woman!" but the nurse's arms were folded across her chest and her mouth was a slit.

"Are you ready for your bath, Mrs. Broderick?" she asked quietly, sympathetically, as if this were the one kind gesture that Ellen was likely to receive all day. The two of them shuffled toward the stairs, and Nathan thought of rushing ahead of them to fling back the covers on Ellen's bed, but the nurse frowned at him as he hesitated, forcing him to retreat into the kitchen.

Sunlight broke across the kitchen table and landed in trapeziums of light on the floor. Nathan fixed himself a glass of orange juice and a piece of toast, then walked out to the porch swing. Seagulls glided above the water. He breathed deeply to try and calm himself, but thoughts about how the nurse must be disgusted by him were tangled up with thoughts about Ellen, Mr. McAlister, and Carl Buchanan, and how an urgency to live propels some lives, but not others.

Nathan remembered how a few weeks after Sophie had dumped him, he'd taken a bag of groceries to his father's house because the older man was laid up in bed with the flu. Nathan often tried to avoid his parents' bedroom because it still contained so many things that reminded him of his mother. Her musical jewelry box, a collection of her shoes stuffed in boxes at the top of the closet, and a badly painted portrait of her as a young girl that she had always seemed to love anyway. Nathan's father had the bedcovers pushed down past his knees and lay in his briefs and white T-shirt watching *Wall $treet Week with Louis Rukeyser.* He turned down the volume and asked Nathan what he'd been up to.

Since Sophie had left him, Nathan had been wondering with total seriousness whether he had reached the limits of human suffering. He had called in sick to work a few times, hadn't been eating or sleeping, and had even stopped drawing. In general he didn't feel comfortable talking with his father about romantic issues, but he had no close friends besides Sophie, and the few housemates he talked with had failed so miserably to console him after the breakup ("Look at it this way, dude, you got to date a super-hot girl for two years!") that he couldn't help telling his father what had happened. His father made a few inquiries about the details, but not many, and Nathan soon changed the subject. He listened to his father talk about the ongoing landscaping he was always doing in the backyard, and the performance of the stock market, then Nathan said he had to go. He was already halfway down the hall when his father called him. Nathan returned and stood in the doorway.

"Listen" his father said, pulling on his unshaven face. "Life, you know, it seems short to you now, because you're so young, and part of why you're anxious and upset is because life seems so short. But it isn't, and you'll understand that eventually. Your life lasts a long time."

Now this memory drifted in and out of Nathan's thoughts about his mishandled past and indeterminate future until the weight of such considerations began to make him feel he hadn't gotten enough sleep. He sat with his arm across the back of the swing and rested his head, blinking out at the ocean, then closing his eyes. He had almost fallen asleep when a dog barked in a neighbor's yard, and minutes later, children's voices cried from somewhere behind the house, on Harbor Avenue. Nathan sighed and grabbed his empty glass off the little table beside him. Opening the French doors, he glanced back through the spaces in the railing in time to notice that the children moving through the side yard were Eldwin's.

They wore matching blue-and-yellow bathing suits and Leah followed behind them, carrying a large canvas bag. Nathan stepped quietly into the house to watch them walk down to Parson's Beach.

They spread their towels on the sand and the children skipped toward the water. Leah unfastened her shorts, letting them drop to her ankles, then pulled off her white T-shirt, so she was wearing only her black bikini. She ran her hand through her hair, then sat down on the towel and took a bottle of suntan lotion from her bag.

Nathan hurried into the bathroom, did a quick check in the mirror, then ambled down the yard toward her.

The spaghetti straps of Leah's bathing suit were tied in a loose bow around her neck, and propping herself up with one arm, she glanced over her shoulder to smile at Nathan through windswept hair. "Hey there," she said as Nathan sat on one of the empty cartoon-themed towels beside her.

"So what did you do yesterday after I left you?" Nathan asked.

Leah stretched out on her side and held her head in her hand. "I thought about you."

"Yeah?"

"And I also talked to my sister, Lindsey. She's getting married in February and freaking out, so I was trying to calm her down."

"What is she freaking out about?"

"Did I mention she's getting married?"

Nathan said, "Fair enough."

"I have to leave on Sunday to go down to New York and help her plan," Leah continued. "She's got this friend who's a big designer and she's going to do Lindsey's wedding dress and the bridesmaid dresses, and we're meeting with her on Monday."

"How long will you be gone?"

"Not too long. I'm supposed to come back on Wednesday."

"Who will I talk to while you're away?"

"You can always talk to your pastor."

Nathan lay alongside her, peering into the contents of the canvas bag near her feet. In addition to her hair clip, suntan lotion, and lip balm, the bag contained issues of *Cosmopolitan* and *Vanity Fair,* and the same book of Chekhov short stories she had disparaged just a few days ago.

"Do you feel ready to get married?" Nathan asked.

"We've only just met."

Nathan smiled. "No, I mean do you feel like you're emotionally ready to get married—to someone—if you met the right person?"

"Probably not for a while. My sister's five years older than me but that still seems really young. I don't even feel like an adult yet, you know?"

"You are."

Leah shrugged. "Maybe." She sat up and dug her hand into her bag to withdraw her sunglasses and a can of Coke. "How about you? What did you do with the rest of your day?"

Nathan groaned and told her the whole story about Carl and Franny's visit to the house a few evenings before, and then about Bill McAlister's visit last night to tell Ellen about Carl's death.

"Yikes," Leah said, putting on sunglasses so dark Nathan could no longer see her eyes. "Do you think he was in love with Ellen?"

"I think so, calling her the most beautiful woman he'd ever met in his life, but the guy was also married to his wife for forty years."

"So?"

"I'm just saying it was probably emotionally complicated for him."

Leah said, "Maybe he would have left her in a minute if Ellen had wanted him."

"Maybe," Nathan answered. But this uncharitable perspective on Carl depressed him, and it seemed like bad luck to talk with Leah about people's capacity for betrayal.

In front of them, the children worked in focused silence, dripping wet sand from a bucket to form the lopsided turrets of a castle. When Nathan heard a distant screen door slap closed behind them, he glanced back to see the nurse glaring down at him from the porch. He stood and shouted, "Okay!" and waved his hand to indicate that he'd seen her. But the nurse just shook her head and turned back into the house.

Nathan explained to Leah that he had to go. "Do you feel like taking a walk this evening?"

"I think you're supposed to go kayaking with Eldwin."

"I am?"

"He said if I saw you, to tell you he would plan on coming over around nine o'clock."

"No. I didn't tell him I'd *definitely* do it, did I?"

Leah sipped her drink and watched him.

Nathan ran his hands up both sides of his head and clutched his hair. "All right. Well. What are you doing tomorrow evening?"

"I was invited to a party."

"Whose party?"

"Thayer Something. It's at the same house we were at a few days ago, if you want to come."

Nathan told her about his meeting with Thayer when the young man had borrowed the *Little Red Hen.* "It doesn't sound like the party's going to be very big, though," Nathan said. "He made it sound like it's just going to be a few of his friends."

"Hmm."

The synapses of Nathan's brain were crackling with far better ideas of how he and Leah could spend the last night before she left for New York. He wanted to kneel down and kiss her, but with the children watching, he just waved and backed away, saying he'd call or stop by soon but that the party sounded like fun.

At the club that afternoon, older men ran back and forth across the courts, wiping sweat from their brows. Ellen smiled occasionally at things they said or the way one man kept lunging after the ball, grunting like he'd been punched in the stomach, but Nathan was too preoccupied with Kendra Garfield to pay much attention. She was sitting just three rows ahead of him beneath the same green-and-white-striped canopy. She wore a white skirt and polo shirt, and the hairs on the back of her slender neck were dark with perspiration. The blond woman beside her said something, and Kendra threw her head back, laughing, as her ponytail slid down between the damp crescents of her shoulder blades, visible through her shirt. "That's right. That's exactly right," she said, nodding gaily. But soon, Nathan thought, she would get up from that chair and notice that he and Ellen were there, too. He felt pleasurably nervous waiting for Kendra's confident laughter to wilt and die as she anticipated the awkwardness of having to say hello.

In the meantime, Nathan made idle conversation with Ellen about the tennis matches and about how the windy weather must be wonderful for sailing. She had spent much of the early afternoon on her porch watching a man stand broad legged on a catamaran in the harbor as he instructed a group of children in pint-size sailboats on how to harness the wind. She had shaken her head, laughing, as the children tacked haphazardly through the shallows, and sitting beside her, Nathan wondered if perhaps she had forgotten her grief. He did not mention Carl's death or inquire as to how she'd ended up sleeping on the couch, and was now heartened to see her taking pleasure in the tennis matches in front of them. They'd been sitting there for half an hour when—having exhausted his capacity for mostly one-sided small talk—Nathan fell silent.

"Would you like something to drink?" Ellen asked him.

In the clubhouse, the mousy lady took a long time to fill his order of two half-and-halves, asking Nathan about himself and telling him about her daughter who had recently married a man from Cleveland. But Nathan was too distracted by the view through the window. Kendra and her friend were getting up from their seats. "On the tab—Broderick," Nathan said, hurriedly gathering the two drinks from the counter. On his way down the porch steps, he saw Kendra, her friend, and two men who had been playing tennis gathered around Ellen.

"Here you go," Nathan said, handing Ellen her drink. But the ice-filled glass was so cold in her bony hands that she whimpered and looked around for someone to take it from her.

Nathan stepped forward to help, but Kendra was already taking the glass. "Here, Aunt Ellen. I'll put it right down here by your seat, and you just let me know when you want a drink. I'm sorry, Nathan, you were probably sitting here, weren't you?"

Kendra stepped away from where she'd been standing in front of Nathan's chair.

"I'm fine," Nathan said, pulling up another chair to sit on Ellen's far side.

"Are you sure?"

"Sure I'm sure."

Kendra glanced at her companions—perhaps wondering whether to introduce them—but they were already talking among themselves, waiting for her to finish.

Kendra crouched in front of Ellen and Nathan like an adult squatting down to have a private moment with her children. "You know, Nathan, Lucien and I were talking about the confusion down at the yacht club and how embarrassed I feel about what happened. With your different clothes on, and in all that glare from the sun, I think I just didn't recognize you."

Her clasped hands suddenly opened with spread fingers to indicate that she was at a loss for any other explanation. She shrugged and smiled apologetically as Nathan watched in stunned silence. Did she actually expect him to believe her? Or was she expecting him to see through this explanation, but hoping he would demonstrate enough forgiveness or cowardice to permit her to save face?

"I thought it was the other way around."

Kendra stared back at him blankly. "How do you mean?"

"I thought you wouldn't take me sailing because you figured out who I was."

"Oh, of course not, Nathan. I was just so preoccupied with trying to get everyone on the boat that I didn't know who anybody was!"

Her rounded cheekbones were flushed and her eyes were filled with pleading and resentment. Nathan glanced past her. Fluffy white clouds drifted over the fairway toward the horizon, where an older woman in a blue tracksuit was powerwalking near the Point.

Kendra looked down and stroked a few blades of grass. "Anyway, I'm sorry about the confusion. Maybe you can go out with us another time."

"All right," Nathan said, nodding. He did not want to carry on this uncomfortable conversation any longer, particularly in Ellen's presence. He sensed her watching the tennis match in front of them with somewhat feigned concentration. Kendra stood and moved to Ellen's side to face the golf course. With arms folded across her chest, she appeared to be contemplating her exit, but then she raised a hand to her mouth. "Oh, there's Franny Buchanan, the poor thing."

Nathan followed Kendra's gaze to the woman he'd noticed earlier, in the blue tracksuit, still tramping around the coastal edge of the fairway.

One of the two men in Kendra's party stepped away from where he'd been talking behind Ellen's chair. Kendra introduced him as her husband, and the tall man said to Nathan, "I'd shake your hand but I don't think you want my sweat all over you!" His blond arm hairs were still slick with perspiration, but when he touched his wife's shoulder, she reached up and patted his hand affectionately.

"We're going inside to get drinks, hon," he said, swinging his racquet casually beside him.

"Oh, I'll go with you. I'm dying of thirst myself." Kendra picked up her racquet and bent down to kiss Ellen's cheek. "Bye-bye, you two," Kendra said, walking backward and smiling, as if everything had been resolved and she was once more carefree. She turned and skipped to catch up with her party, laughing once again as she followed them up the front steps of the clubhouse.

Tennis matches were still being played on three courts, so Nathan and Ellen stayed awhile longer. Then Ellen widened her eyes hopefully, asking, "Are you ready to go?"

Walking back across the lawn, they saw a man with a closely cut beard standing on the far side of a black Toyota pickup parked behind Ellen's car. In the bed of his truck stood a tripod and camera with a telescopic zoom lens. The man vanished momentarily in the shadows of a large maple tree, but then pulled his face back from his camera to glance at Ellen and Nathan.

He was wearing a tan photographer's vest, with lots of little pockets, and said he was taking photographs for *Down East.* Nathan had never heard of the magazine, but months later, during a drizzly gray November, while at a newsstand, he would look longingly at the sunny places featured on the covers of travel magazines, and pick a copy of *Down East* from the rack. The cover story was "The Ten Best Places in New England You've Never Heard Of" and the cover photograph was of the Alnombak Golf and Tennis Club. Beneath the perfectly puffy white clouds and surrounded by impeccable landscaping, handsome men and women played golf or tennis and looked very good doing it. It was the kind of photograph that can make your own life seem hopelessly joyless and plain, and Nathan felt something like relief when he noticed in the far right-hand corner, where the golf course met the sky, the profile of Franny Buchanan moving determinedly over the earth.

When Eldwin arrived at Ellen's house that evening, he smiled the close-lipped smile of a man amusedly aware of his appearance. Dressed in a black wet suit, which covered his body from wrist to ankle, he looked like an overweight superhero.

Nathan followed him up Harbor Avenue toward the aluminum shed abutting the east wall of Eldwin's house. The blue tandem kayak lay on its side against the doors. The two men grabbed hold of the carrying rope on either end, portaged it across the gravel, then set it down in Ellen's yard.

Crouching over the storage compartment at the front of the kayak, Eldwin pulled out something black and rubbery. "You might want to wear this old wet suit of mine. I can't fit into it anymore, but it might fit you."

Nathan held the wet suit in both hands. "Yeah?"

"It's not full size—with arms and legs—but you'll be a lot warmer with it on if we tip over."

"Are you thinking we might tip over?" Nathan said, baring his teeth in a pained expression.

"No, but sometimes the water gets a little choppy. Have you been in the water?"

"I put my foot in far enough to know it's damn cold."

"Yeah, it's about fifty degrees during the day, so it'll just be safer to have it on."

Reluctantly Nathan crept back upstairs to his bedroom, careful not to awaken Ellen, and pulled off his sweatshirt and shorts. He was uncertain whether to remove his boxer shorts, but the idea of resting his testicles where another man's had once lain disturbed him. Pushing his legs through the wet suit, the rubber felt cold and damp and he began to suspect that he was not supposed to be wearing his boxers. The rubber was like a second skin, except that it only extended as far as his thighs and elbows. Zipping up the front of the wet suit, encasing himself like a link of sausage, Nathan stared into the mirror with shame. He looked skinnier than he'd thought possible. Folding his arms across his chest, he persuaded himself for a moment that he was in fact more robust, but the utter blackness of the wet suit made him look vampire pale. Sighing, he let his arms dangle, as if drained of their blood. He pulled on his sweatshirt and turned in front of the mirror a few times. Then he stepped into his shorts and hurried back out to the lawn.

Standing up where he'd been squatting beside the kayak, Eldwin said, "You're not going to put it on?"

"No, I've got it on."

Eldwin stared at him.

"Underneath."

Once on Parson's Beach, they donned their life jackets. Eldwin explained how to paddle, what to do if the kayak flipped, and so on, and asked Nathan if he preferred the front or back seat. Nathan opted for the back and walked behind Eldwin as they eased the kayak into the harbor and helped each other to climb aboard. The water was dark and frigid, and in his seat Nathan rubbed his soaked tennis shoes together to try to warm up his toes.

When they had settled into a steady rhythm of paddling, Eldwin said, "There's going to be a funeral service for Carl Buchanan on Sunday at St. Michael's, so you should probably plan to bring Ellen."

"All right," Nathan said, nodding. "I actually met him a couple of times. He and his wife came over once to visit."

"What was he like?"

"You never met him?"

"I may have shaken hands with him at church or at some party, but I don't remember meeting him. I've been talking with Pastor Russell and other people to try and learn a few things about him so I can say something meaningful during the service."

Nathan gave an account of Franny and Carl's visit to the house and of Carl hurling his wineglass at the ocean. Toward the end of the story, Nathan wondered why Eldwin's shoulders seemed to be shaking, but then Eldwin's big head tilted back and he let out a deep, full-throated laugh.

Nathan grinned. "What's so funny?"

"I was just imagining the expression on your face."

Lights from the coastline reflected off the water as they paddled toward a narrow quarter-mile stretch of land, named Stone Island, located near the mouth of Albans Bay. Rocks and seaweed hugged its shoreline, and Nathan used his oar to help navigate while staring at the island's lighthouse. It was the kind of white, conical lighthouse seen in children's drawings or Maine postcards. Towering above clusters of shrubbery on the island's edge, the lighthouse's luminous eye slurred across the Atlantic and then away, as if both fascinated and horrified by the empty vastness of the ocean.

"You want a beer?" Eldwin asked. He rested his paddle on the kayak and rooted around in the compartment in front of him.

"Uh, sure," Nathan said.

The popping open of the cans echoed loudly across the water as they let the kayak drift along next to shore. A warm, pine-smelling breeze blew over them from the island, and Nathan leaned back in his seat to gaze up at the silvery clouds gliding across the moonlit sky. Eventually, he asked, "So what have you learned from other people about Mr. Buchanan?"

"Let's see . . . he served in the Second World War . . . worked at Boston College for thirty years, even though with his wife's money—she's heir to the Goodyear fortune—he didn't need the job to pay the bills. They had one daughter who died of leukemia in her thirties. He did not like to travel on planes . . . loved reading about art history and apparently did like to drink . . . and he was very fond of Ellen."

"Who told you that?"

"Russ—Pastor Russell—the guy I'm replacing."

"What did he say exactly?"

"Well," Eldwin said, sighing. He sipped his beer, perhaps contemplating how much to say, but then continued, "We had finished talking about Carl, and I was just telling him how glad I was that Leah had found a friend here, and I mentioned who you were—that you were up here taking care of Mrs. Broderick, and that's when he told me about her driving her car into that boulder." Eldwin tilted his head back to finish his beer. "You finished with yours?"

"Uh, no, not yet."

"All right, well try and drain it so we can circle around the island. The tide's going out, so we're going to be fighting the current."

"All right, but what does Carl have to do with why Ellen drove her car into the boulder?"

Eldwin paddled a few strokes in silence and then told him that by the time Ellen's husband died, she had already been having summer affairs with Bill McAlister. When she came back to the Cove the summer after her husband's death, Carl had asked her to marry him.

"Did Franny know?"

"I don't know, but Ellen had been having the affair with Bill and was apparently more interested in marrying *him.* Bill had only been separated from his wife a short while, though, and apparently wasn't ready to get married again right away."

"How does this guy know all this stuff?" Nathan said, frowning.

Eldwin said, "When you're pastor of a church, it doesn't take long to learn about the lives of your congregation, particularly in a gossipy community like this one. Russ was also a good friend of Carl. He wants to be here for the funeral, but I don't think he's going to be able to come."

"So, what, Ellen drove her car into the rock because Mr. McAlister wouldn't marry her?"

"I don't think that's it entirely. When Russ saw her at the hospital after the accident, he said she seemed disoriented, as if she was having a nervous breakdown, probably due to the combination of everything that had happened: her husband dying, the pressure of Carl wanting to marry her, and Bill not wanting to . . . it just seemed like maybe she felt isolated and abandoned and was just trying to find some way of escape."

Nathan sat staring back at the yellow porch light of Ellen's house and listening to the quiet rippling of the water around him.

"You still nursing that beer?"

"That's crazy," Nathan mumbled. He finished his beer in a few gulps and felt a slight buzz in his head as he stuffed the can beneath his seat and began to paddle. The current was stronger than he'd expected, and his shoulder muscles were soon burning. On the far side of the island, the world existed in a wedge of darkness, cut off from the reflected house lights of Brightonfield Cove, smelling of pine trees and brine. They paddled wordlessly for several minutes, and when they rounded the east corner of the island, they were once again on the glimmering surface of the harbor. The dotted house lights along the coastline were a comfort, allowing Nathan to feel away from town, but still within shouting distance. Eldwin said they could let the tide carry them for a while and asked Nathan if he wanted another beer. As they drank, Nathan asked, "Did you always know you wanted to become a pastor?"

"No," Eldwin said, shaking his head. "I don't think anybody who knew me growing up would have thought I was going to be a pastor. I didn't."

"What did you think you were going to be?"

"I don't know. A musician, maybe. I didn't come from a very religious family and I got pretty involved in the punk scene growing up. I had the liberty spikes," he said, gesturing with one hand to demonstrate the foot-long horns of gelled hair that had once run down the middle of his head. "I was a bass player in a punk band and I got pretty involved in everything that went along with that, including drugs."

"Whoa, so how did you become a pastor?"

"It took a long time. I've only been a pastor for three years. I was in graduate school in philosophy at the University of Michigan, but I just didn't feel that what I was studying was addressing life as I was experiencing it. I didn't feel like there was any accounting for the possibility of the miraculous. So I started attending an Episcopal church and talking more and more with the pastor there until she said the church would sponsor me so I could go to seminary if I wanted to."

Nathan said, "Are you glad you made the switch?"

"Hell, yeah. The job market for professors is terrible."

Nathan laughed as he sipped his beer, debating whether to ask Eldwin what he meant about the possibility of the miraculous. Nathan prided himself on seeing, or at least *trying* to see, the world rationally, and he was concerned that if he and Eldwin confessed to profoundly different worldviews, they might end up thinking less of each other and spoil what up until then had been a pleasant evening.

Eldwin said, "So what's going on with you and Leah?"

"What's going on? I don't know. We're going to a party tomorrow night." Nathan stroked the dark water with his fingertips. It had been a long time since dinner and he was beginning to feel the mind-muddling effects of the alcohol. He added, "I guess it's one of those things where we both know that at the end of the summer, she's going to New York to do her thing and I guess I'll be headed back to Cleveland."

"You got a lot keeping you there?" Eldwin asked.

Nathan tried to explain, but he knew his life back home didn't sound very alluring. Maybe—if he begged—his manager would rehire him to work part-time at the library. Then life would resume as before. Living in his small, one-window room in the shared house, he would return to work on his art, endure the company of three emotionally retarded housemates, and occasionally visit his father.

"My father's been pretty depressed since my mother's death," he said, gloomily. This was the truth, but not the whole truth. His father had wrestled with depression long before Nathan's mother grew ill, but she had always been an optimist capable of tempering his pessimism, a light illuminating his darkness. And it was obvious to anyone who cared to look that his father was suffering tremendously from her loss. Nathan certainly did not have such illumination in him, and he sensed within himself and within his father a muted frustration at not being able to provide it for each other. Nathan loathed feeling this way, like he was failing his father because he couldn't help him, and he was keenly aware of how much he and his father depended on the women in their lives to sustain them.

"What were you saying earlier about your belief in the miraculous?" Nathan asked. His head lolled back and he stared openmouthed at the sky.

Eldwin said, "Just that I've had some things happen to me that I don't know how to talk about or explain in other terms."

"Like what?"

"Well, just strange occurrences that seem to suggest something more than just strangeness or coincidence . . . that seem to suggest something like a plan. When I was younger, in junior high, my parents got divorced and I moved around a lot with my father. We moved into one house where my bedroom had this wall-size photographic mural of an incredibly tall and beautiful waterfall out in Yosemite National Park in California. And I used to lie in my bed and stare at that picture and have this powerful sense that that was where I needed to go, that I would have some kind of life-changing and liberating experience there. When I was fourteen or fifteen, I even tried to go there. I left the house and walked a couple of miles to this marina. I broke into a houseboat and stole a bottle of vodka and then walked to the train tracks and climbed into this coal car and lay down with my bottle, waiting for the guards to pass by, and when the train started moving . . . I felt this incredible sense of freedom, like I was on my way to great adventure, to this new life and maybe this new way of living. Then the car slowed to a stop. I waited, and then the car crawled another thirty yards and stopped again. To kill time while the car crept along, I ended up drinking enough of that vodka that I passed out . . . and when I woke up in the morning, we were only about a fucking mile out of the train yard, so I just got disgusted and jumped off."

Nathan laughed. "So where's the plan?"

"Well, then not that long afterward, I was at this girl's house where she was living with some other people, and I had sex with her—more or less in exchange for heroin. And afterward, while she was sleeping, I stepped out into the living room where other people were sleeping, and this porno was on television and it was of a priest fucking a woman. I sat down in a chair and suddenly saw a blinding flash of white light and experienced this overwhelming calm, where I felt like I was going to be okay—like I was aware that I had bottomed out but that something was telling me I was going to be all right."

"Had you shot up the heroin before you went into the living room?"

"No. I wasn't high at the time. So fast-forward several years and I'm in graduate school and at a party in an old gym on the outskirts of Ann Arbor, and I'm talking with a beautiful woman—more beautiful than anyone I ever dated growing up—in the middle of this old boxing ring, and something happens in this conversation. Some kind of connection takes place so that the next week she and I are traveling across the country together and we end up camping at Yosemite National Park. We hike to the falls—to the same falls I used to stare at on that mural when I was growing up, and there was a moment when I kissed her—or she kissed me—and I've tried to describe this before and always fail. But it was like there was a real electrical charge, not a metaphoric one but a real one passing between us, and when we pulled away tears were streaming down both of our cheeks. There's a passage in the Zohar—this classic text of Jewish mysticism—about a kiss of true love, which sounds kind of like what I experienced, and I don't know how else to explain it other than in these mystical terms because I think they are experiences outside of what we can give a rational explanation."

"Was the woman your wife?"

"Yeah, Rachel."

Rational explanations for what happened had been flickering in Nathan's mind throughout the conversation. Eldwin's overpowering sense of Yosemite Falls as a place of liberation had grown out of a young man's endless nights of longing to get away from a troubled home. The blinding flash of white light had been a biochemical explosion in his brain from having injected so many drugs. And the kiss was about trying to make the simply wonderful seem unique by taking a hackneyed metaphor and making it literal.

But even as Nathan doubted Eldwin's outlook on life—doubted that the white gull soaring above them, so strange to see so late at night, could be more than a random, meaningless occurrence—he could not help searching his past for moments of significance in a plan he might not yet recognize or understand. As he and Eldwin rowed toward shore, the possibility that perhaps he was meant to come to Brightonfield Cove and meet Leah instilled within him an uncertain hope. Thoughts of his father made Nathan feel netted down by grief and responsibility, but he did not want to end up one of those people who spend their whole lives tangled up in a parent's miserable and life-sucking neediness. His life back home was already almost as lonely as his father's. Maybe it would be better for both of them if Nathan did go someplace else, maybe even New York. He knew a guy from college who now lived there. Maybe Nathan could stay with him for a month or so, just until he could find his own apartment. Of course he didn't mention any of this as he and Eldwin paddled ashore and carried the kayak back to the shed. Nathan thanked Eldwin for inviting him and wanted to tell him how heartened he felt by their conversation and how long it had been since he had experienced an evening of male camaraderie that left him feeling less alone. But the alcohol was wearing off, so he just shook his hand and turned to go. He was concerned that Eldwin already viewed him with some pity and Nathan did not want to make it worse.

Eight

More Friends Are Dying ~ Thayer's Party ~ Visiting the George and Barbara Bush Estate ~ A Volkswagen Commercial ~ The Morning of the Funeral

For much of the next day, Nathan ruminated about the upcoming party. He wouldn't know anyone except Leah, and he was certain the place would be congested with young men like Thayer—with polished Ivy League confidence and rowers' builds—who would make Nathan's own boyishness and skinny frame seem much less appealing by comparison. He brooded about this all afternoon at the club and was still thinking about it in the early evening when he smelled the lushly sweet scent of a cigar wafting into the living room. Through the open window above the couch, he saw Mr. McAlister flicking embers into the flower bed beside the front steps. When Nathan opened the door, he noticed the old rogue looked better than he had when he'd visited to break the news about Carl. His rugged face was freshly shaved around his mustache, and his gray-brown eyes indicated a melancholic generosity. Ellen had been nodding off in front of the television but looked up when she heard Nathan greeting him at the front door. Mr. McAlister took a seat beside her on the couch and asked her in a low, still-in-mourning kind of voice, "You been doing okay?"

Nathan wandered into the kitchen to wash the dishes and then went up the back stairs to his room. At the wooden desk in the corner, he worked on a drawing of himself and Eldwin in the kayak as they'd drifted idly through the bay. In the drawing, Eldwin held a can of beer in one hand and his big forehead in the other while Nathan slouched in the back seat, staring up at the sky. An hour passed, and as Nathan grew more and more pleased with his work, he began to hope Mr. McAlister would stay another couple of hours. That way—without Ellen safely in bed—Nathan would have a good excuse not to go to the party. Maybe Leah would say she didn't want to go without him and ask if she could just hang out with him on the porch, or at least these were the thoughts he was entertaining when Mr. McAlister called from below. Nathan opened the door into the hallway and saw him standing with his hand on the banister at the base of the stairs.

"Hey, I was just telling Ellen that Carl's funeral is tomorrow afternoon at one o'clock at St. Michael's."

Nathan nodded. "All right, we can be there." He glanced down into the fading light of the living room where Ellen remained on the couch.

Mr. McAlister ran his hand over his widow's peak. "Okay, then, I'll see you both there at one. Good night, Ellen ," he said, leaving.

Nathan came downstairs and sat across from Ellen in the burgundy recliner. After the wooden chair upstairs, the cushiony seat felt so comfortable that Nathan stifled a yawn. Ellen smiled and glanced down at her hands.

"You doing all right?" Nathan asked.

"I'm okay," Ellen said feebly. She nodded as if to persuade herself, but then added, "I guess I'm just a little . . . concerned."

"Yeah? What are you concerned about?"

"Well, a lot of my friends are dying," she said, her lower lip trembling as she picked at the upholstered arm of the couch.

Earlier that afternoon at the club, an old woman with wispy hair had told Ellen about a friend of theirs who'd died of heart failure, and another who was now battling pancreatic cancer, but Nathan could not remember their names. He got up and sat beside her, telling her that he understood her sadness, but, look, she had also been making new friends, younger friends, all her life, hadn't she? Nathan had seen them at church and at the club. Those friends were still around, and they would eventually have to suffer losing her the way she was suffering the loss of other friends now. That was the way it worked, Nathan thought, and he didn't know what else to say. Her concerns about growing older and dying were the same concerns already twisting within him. He knew no way to assuage them except through religion or weariness, so he eventually stopped talking and just held her hand.

Nathan had told Leah he would pick her up around nine, but because of his conversation with Ellen, he arrived half an hour late. "I was just about to call you," Leah said, opening the front door before he'd knocked. She was wearing jeans and an army green T-shirt with the Red Cross symbol on the front. "Did you bring your bathing suit?"

"No."

"Oh, you should get it," Leah said, evidently not joking. "Thayer told me there was a hot tub we could use."

Nathan glanced down at the canvas satchel that he supposed contained her bikini. "Well, he didn't mention it to me and I'm not sure I feel like hot-tubbing it tonight. Plus, I'm kind of afraid if I went back inside, I might wake up Ellen and then I'd have to wait for her to go back asleep."

Leah shrugged as she closed the door and then followed Nathan away from the house. With their shoes scuffing through the gravel of Harbor Avenue, she asked, "So how was it kayaking with Eldwin?"

"It was good. It was more fun than I expected."

"Did you guys drink when you were out there?"

"I think we each had a couple of beers."

Leah frowned doubtfully, and said, "I was going to call and tell you that Eldwin had already drunk a six-pack by the time he left. I was afraid for you going out with him. I know he can drink a lot without getting drunk, but I thought for sure you would notice it. You didn't smell it on him?"

"No, I mean, we were outside—and he wasn't stumbling around or slurring his words. How long did he take to drink the six-pack?"

"Like half an hour—I'm serious!—while he was reading the paper."

"Well, I guess the guy can hold his booze, because I didn't notice anything different about him and I never felt like we were in any danger." Nathan looked up from his shoes at Leah. "I'm touched you were concerned about me, though."

"For an artist, you're not very perceptive," Leah said.

"Well." Nathan smiled. Her admission of being worried was acting on him like the best kind of liquor, invigorating him and giving him confidence, so he was no longer as anxious about the party. When he told her a little of what he and Eldwin had talked about while kayaking—including why Ellen supposedly drove her car into that rock—Leah said, "Oh, that's so sad. How does Ellen react when she's around Mr. McAlister's wife?"

"She seemed more than okay at the party. Given how everyone seems to know about her affair with McAlister, it seems incredibly bold for us to have been there. Why the hell would that guy have invited her if he knew his wife was going to be there?"

"I don't think he knew she was going to be there. I think they were angry at each other for a while, but now Thayer says they're talking and that they might get back together."

"She doesn't live with him?"

"Not since they separated. She's been staying in their completely gorgeous house near the Point."

Nathan nodded distractedly. He often thought of his late teens and early twenties as a period of romantic tumult that he must pass through until he found refuge in the warm embrace of a marriage like his parents'. He disliked remembering that sometimes the romantic tumult never ended, that alliances were always vulnerable, and life-changing heartache was always a glance away.

Leah continued, "Thayer says that his grandmother was really upset after her first divorce and that she had a hard time adjusting to living with Bill, but now she really, really wants him back. By the way, do you know who Thayer's real grandfather is?"

Nathan shook his head.

"Brent Delphy. He's the publishing director at Epoch—and Thayer says he's going to let him know about me so maybe I can talk with him when I go to New York this fall."

"That's great," Nathan said. He wanted to ask how often she was talking with Thayer to have learned all of this about his family, but he wasn't sure it would help his confidence to know the answer. Searching for ways in which he was better than Thayer, passing by the Alnombak club and the stately homes of Admirals Way, Nathan was heartened to remember that being wealthy often weakened a person's character—not to mention his abilities as an artist. Look at what money had done to Hemingway! And weren't R. Crumb's comics a lot worse now that he was cozily ensconced in the south of France? Wasn't Nathan more likely to be not just a superior artist, but a superior man, because he was connected by the gnarled cord of suffering to what was *real*?

Moon shadows were stretching across the gray lawn as Nathan and Leah walked toward the warmly lit portico of Mr. McAlister's home. The young woman who opened the oak door was petite, with sandy brown hair and a dense constellation of freckles across the width of her face. "Hey, cool, more people," she said, smiling. After introducing herself with a name Nathan immediately forgot, she led them through the sunken living room—the epicenter of Mr. McAlister's party—to the screened-in back porch. A corner floor lamp illuminated roughly a dozen college-age men and women lounging on the two adjacent couches or on the floor. The multicolored digital display of a portable stereo flickered festively as jam-band music played at a low volume and a few of the young men occasionally nodded their heads to the rhythm. Thayer was sitting on the floor with his legs extended—playing a card game—but when Nathan and Leah entered, he glanced up with an inebriated grin. "Hey, hey, you made it!" he called, getting up and stepping over a few people to approach them. His T-shirt was tucked in only above his belt buckle, and his eyelids hung so heavily that he seemed to tilt his head back to see. He hugged Leah and shook Nathan's hand, then guided them over to the mini-refrigerator against the wall to pull a few Coronas off the shelf.

In the awkward pause that followed, Thayer said, "So, you want a tour?"

He didn't know much about the house, really, except for the purposes of the rooms and which ones had the best views of Albans Bay. So as they walked down the hallway, peeking into the bathroom and laundry, Nathan broke the silences by asking Thayer questions about himself. He was a senior at Columbia, he said, majoring in history and theater. But it was the theater he really loved. And not just acting, but directing, too. He'd already directed *The House of Yes* last year, and next year was planning to direct Tony Kushner's *Angels in America.*

When they followed Thayer into the library, Nathan tried to demonstrate that he was a learned person, too. He inquired about the old, leather-bound copy of *Don Quixote* he'd noticed during Mr. McAlister's cocktail party, and drew attention to the quality of Doré's illustrations.

Thayer took the tome from him and paged through a few illustrations, not spending much more time on one than any other, then slid the book back onto the shelf, saying he didn't know where it had come from. "Bill bought this place about ten years ago, but he only started living here again in the summers after he and my grandmother separated . . . so . . . I think he uses this room to smoke his cigars."

"Just you and Mr. McAlister live here?" Nathan asked.

"No, it's just him. I mostly stay with my grandmother. I just thought this would be a better place to have people over, and Bill said it was cool."

"These books are really beautiful," Leah said, paging through an illustrated 1906 edition of *Huckleberry Finn.* Nathan stepped closer to look over her shoulder at the illustrations and smell her vaguely apple-scented hair.

Thayer stared at the wall of books, then said, "Do you want to check out the other side of the house?"

Nathan and Leah followed him back through the sunken living

room toward another long hallway offering separate rooms for playing billiards, watching a large-screen TV, or stewing in a hot tub or sauna. This last room was wood paneled, with a large bay window through which Nathan could see the distant porch light of Ellen's house.

"Did you bring your suits?" Thayer asked.

Nathan said, "She did. I didn't."

"Well, if you want, when we go upstairs I can try and scrounge you up one."

With Leah watching him, Nathan shrugged. "Yeah . . . if you do, that's fine." As they exited the room, a young couple wearing bathing suits and carrying towels approached them from down the hall. The young man had a broad, sculpted chest and a handsome lantern-jawed face, and he was laughing alongside a petite, buxom blonde with a perfectly proportioned smile. As Thayer introduced everyone, Nathan shook hands and laughed with them, but he was rankled by the conventionality of the couple's attractiveness and the fact that—unwittingly or not—they were pressuring him. If Thayer found Nathan a swimsuit, and everyone, including Leah, climbed into the hot tub, what excuse would Nathan have not to join them? He wasn't opposed to revealing his body to Leah. He had just envisioned doing it in a darkened room where she wouldn't be able to see him very well.

Upstairs he and Leah followed Thayer down the hall and into a room with an imposing, four-post, oak bed—the kind for men named Odysseus or Achilles—and a pile of clothes on a corner chair. From a mirrored bureau on the far side of the room, Thayer pulled out a green bathing suit with a white flower print. Lobbing it at Nathan's chest, he said, "See if those work." The bathing suit was long legged, more like a pair of capri pants than shorts, but Nathan nodded, and said, "Cool," as they walked back out of the room.

They peered into a few other guest rooms, then into an office with an old rolltop desk and a view overlooking the harbor. While Leah and Thayer stared out the window, Nathan entertained a vision of his future wife seeing him at such a desk, his head cradled in his hands, nobly suffering for his art. It was a vision he had in different variations all the time, with variously beautiful wives, and it usually ended with her moving to wrap her arms around him, admire his work, then ask if he wanted to have sex. Nathan was half-adrift in this pleasant dream of his future when he heard the click of a door opening a few yards to their left.

The sound of the television—lively voices and laughter—emanated from the room, making it seem pitiable when only Mr. McAlister trudged into the hall. Wearing black dress socks and a gray bathrobe, he had the swollen, saggy eyes of the recently awakened. "Hold on, Peewee, I'm getting it for you," he mumbled, rubbing his whiskered face as his dachshund trotted behind him. When his eyes narrowed at the three people staring back at him, he pulled the folds of his bathrobe closer to cover the wispy hairs of his chest. "What? Is the party spreading up here?"

Thayer said, "No. Sorry, Bill. I was just showing them around the house."

"Well, don't let my privacy stand in the way of your tours," Mr. McAlister grumbled with semi-ironic indignation as he proceeded into a room across the hall. When he came back into the hallway, he carried a rolled-up magazine and a jangling blue ball that he immediately dropped for the dog. "Things going okay downstairs?" he asked, folding his arms across his chest as he watched Peewee bite the ball and carry it back into the bedroom.

"Yeah, it's okay," Thayer said.

"Well, make sure you wipe the blood off the walls."

"We will."

"Ellen already in bed?"

Nathan's eyebrows arched with surprise at the question, but he stammered, "Yeah. Yeah, she was sleeping soundly when I left."

Mr. McAlister nodded and sighed. "Okay, I guess I'll see you tomorrow."

On the way back down the stairs, Thayer told them how a friend of Mr. McAlister had given the ridiculous-looking wiener dog to him after his first wife died of cancer—to provide him with a companion, but also to remind him of the comedy in life's absurdity. Nathan smiled an appropriately jaded smile, but the notion of life as absurd always made him uneasy, and this uneasiness was compounded by his wondering whether he should return to Ellen's house. He'd told Mr. McAlister that she was sleeping soundly when he left, but perhaps he'd been irresponsible to leave her on the night before Carl's funeral. She'd been upset earlier that evening. What if she was awake, searching for him, or just wandering aimlessly around the house? And wouldn't his concern be a good excuse to avoid donning the stupid bathing suit he was carrying?

When they returned to the back patio, Nathan was about to ask Leah if she felt like meeting up with him later at Ellen's house, but she excused herself to use the restroom, and Thayer returned to where he'd been sitting on the floor. Nathan lingered in the patio doorway, trying to look occupied with the view of the harbor and then with the selection of beers inside the mini-refrigerator. Casually leaving the bathing suit behind the leafy plant on top of the fridge, Nathan pulled out another Corona and took a seat on the nearest couch. The freckled girl who had answered the front door was sitting beside him, her bare feet tucked beneath her, but she was talking with a bearded young man to her right. Another young man, with round eyeglasses, changed CDs on the portable stereo while Nathan continued sipping his beer, saying nothing, sometimes smiling at people who glanced at him.

"Did you know that?" the freckled girl asked, abruptly turning to face him.

Nathan stopped drinking and wiped his lips. "Know what?"

"That I was the mascot for the New York Mets last summer?"

"No, I didn't know that. What is a Met, anyway?"

The girl had her mouth open to say something, but nothing came out. "I don't know," she said, frowning. She turned and interrupted her friends to ask them, but no one else knew.

"It doesn't matter, anyway," she said. "I wasn't a Met. I was a baseball."

"Was it hot wearing that outfit?"

"Oh, my God, yes," she said, falling back on the couch as if the mere memory was exhausting. "I had to wear a bathing suit inside it and even then I nearly passed out."

She leaned forward to pick her beer can from the floor and cupped it between her crossed legs. She said her uncle knew one of the publicity directors and that they had needed someone small to fill in for the last few weeks of the season. "I wouldn't have been small enough if my mother hadn't smoked when she was pregnant with me."

She continued telling Nathan what it was like to be *the* New York Mets mascot, and Nathan was interested for a while, and then less so, until he was just grateful to have her near him so that Leah—who had reappeared in the doorway, talking with others—could witness how easily he was able to converse with other attractive young women. After the freckled girl had talked at some length about her mostly dysfunctional family, the bespectacled boy near the stereo popped in a much more frenetic song and a few people stood up to dance.

The freckled girl began rocking her head, singing along with the music, and occasionally smiling at Nathan. "Do you want to dance?" she asked. The volume had been turned up so loud that she almost had to shout into Nathan's ear.

Nathan smiled and shook his head. "I'll embarrass you."

The young woman pushed out her lower lip in a pout. When Nathan continued to shake his head, she took his beer, set it down, then led him by the hand to where the others were dancing. Nathan was hesitant at first, but soon most of the people who had been sitting stood up to dance, and he felt less and less self-conscious as he glanced at the young men and women around him. He assumed they came from wealthy families, but they were dressed in the faded jeans and thrift-shop shirts that perhaps demonstrated a longing for the authenticity they associated with the poorer classes. Nathan too longed for an authentic-feeling life and also wore a faded T-shirt. As other, similarly spirited songs played, Nathan smiled at the bobbing faces surrounding him. Maybe some of it was the beer, but he felt somewhere deep within him the warmth of those faces smiling back at him. They were sunny, life-filled faces, and for a little while Nathan felt not only that he could dance, but also that, despite everything, people were basically good at heart. Turning in place, flapping his hands periodically against his chest, he saw Leah step across the patio toward him.

"You're a dancing machine," she shouted, moving in a little circle around him.

"Machines don't have this much soul."

"What?"

"Machines don't—"

But Leah had already glanced away, grinning, attempting to ignore his lame joke. Nathan took the beer from her hands and drank.

"Do you want to go in the hot tub in a little bit?" Leah asked.

"I do, but Ellen was acting so anxious earlier, I was kind of thinking maybe I ought to go home and make sure she's all right."

Leah nodded and touched his shoulder to pull him closer. "Let me know if you want me to go with you," she said, her warm, boozy breath in his ear.

Nathan hoped that dancing at the party had let Leah see the side of him capable of expressing spontaneous joie de vivre. The suddenly roisterous atmosphere of the evening encouraged Nathan to feel as if they were the desirable young people in movies who are always doing zany things like dancing on top of beds, or just laughing and driving down long country roads, a hopeful pop song playing in the background, and he didn't want to lose this momentum. On the way up from Cleveland, he had overheard a gas station attendant giving directions to the coastal edge of Kennebunkport, where you could see George and Barbara Bush's estate. Nathan suggested to Leah that, after checking on Ellen, they take a late-night drive. They stopped at the house so Nathan could creep inside and get the car keys and make sure Ellen was still asleep. Then Nathan grabbed a bottle of cabernet from the dining room and hoisted it victoriously as he trotted outside to the car.

As he drove, they talked about how good the music had been, how the right song at the right moment can totally transform the nature of a party, then Nathan made the mistake of telling her what he thought of Thayer. "I think the guy comes off a little presumptuous—he was that way when he came over to borrow Ellen's boat, and I thought he was kind of that way tonight—like I felt he assumed that we would want a tour of the house."

"You didn't want the tour?"

"No, I did," Nathan said. "But I didn't like him assuming that I would, you know? I just feel like there's an arrogance about him."

"Yeah, but I think it's funny," Leah said. "I was talking with that girl Danielle, who is sort of seeing him? And she kind of thinks the same way."

"What way?"

"Just that . . ." Leah paused, grinning as she stared out the passenger window. "It's like what he was saying about *Angels in America.* Have you read that play?"

"No."

"Well, it's a really hard play—a *really* hard play to do—and the fact that he thinks he can pull it off is kind of funny but also pretty cool too, you know?"

Nathan grunted noncommittally.

Leah said, "I think he was trying really hard to be nice to you."

"What reason does he have *not* to be nice to me?"

Leah frowned at Nathan as if he was not being very sympathetic. "He wants his grandmother and Bill to get back together again, Nathan, and you took Ellen over to Bill's party while Thayer's grandmother was *there.* The woman was so upset she had to leave. He doesn't know if you knew about Ellen and Bill's affair, so he's trying to give you the benefit of the doubt."

"I didn't know!" Nathan laughed and glanced out at the gray-blue of stone wall that separated the road from the woods. "Who told you he was trying to be nice to me?"

"Danielle."

Nathan disliked being cast as a beneficiary of Thayer's benevolence, so he tried to attack the statement's veracity. "Did you tell Danielle that Thayer was apparently so furious with Ellen that he came over to her house wanting to borrow her dinghy?"

"I think he had to do that . . . to get out to the *Daydreamer*."

"Well, how about inviting me to his party?" Nathan added, even though he knew Thayer had only invited *him* when he thought he might not be able to personally invite Leah.

If Leah knew the answer to Nathan's question, she was merciful enough not to reply. He pulled back the sunroof so that moonlight filled the front seat and they could smell the surrounding birch and pine. After a while, Leah asked, "Were your parents still happily married when your mother passed away?"

Nathan tried to let go of his earlier irritation and exhaled loudly before answering. "Yeah. I mean, it wasn't a happy time while she was sick, and they had fights every once in a while, but I think they loved each other very much." He took a moment to remember his father in the hospital, holding his wife's hand when she was no longer coherent, her eyes sunk into her sallow head—but he tried not to let the memory overwhelm him. Rubbing his face, he asked, "How old were you when your parents divorced?"

The question rang so familiarly in his ears, and seemed so *routine,* that it felt almost trite. But as they drove, Leah told him how, when she was eleven years old, she had unwittingly participated in a stakeout with her mother to catch her father leaving his mistress's apartment. "There's Daddy," Leah remembered saying. Her mother stalked across the street, cursing, until she was close enough to try and scratch out her husband's eyes. But he grabbed her wrists and pushed her down so that she collapsed to her knees on the pavement. He picked up his briefcase, which had fallen, and stumbled backward up the street. Glancing at the car where Leah sat, geography homework still in her lap, he climbed into his own car and drove away.

The dramatic details of her story swirled through Nathan's consciousness along with other details of other girlfriends' parents' breakups as it occurred to him that he had never been in a serious relationship with someone whose parents were still together. Outside, the pine trees were gradually replaced by sidewalks, wooden signs, and the clapboard storefronts of downtown Kennebunkport. They stopped at a gas station for directions, turned around, and were soon cruising along a winding coastal road with the windows open, the sea breeze fluttering the map Leah held down against her legs.

"I think this is it," she said, directing Nathan to pull over where the road's shoulder broadened for sightseers to park. Climbing from the car to the embankment of moonlit, rocky shoreline, they both stared at the Bush estate. Despite the half dozen pine trees in the yard intended to shield the grounds from public view, Nathan could see a sprawling ranch house, a tennis court, and what appeared to be guest quarters, all spread out on a little peninsula like a finger bent into the sea. House lights illuminated a driveway with a golf cart and two black SUVs, and several hundred yards away from these vehicles, a tall, chain-link fence separated their property from public coast. Nathan and Leah walked slowly over the rocks toward the compound—holding hands occasionally, for balance—until they sat down on a flat boulder.

Once they had made themselves comfortable, and Nathan was opening the bottle of cabernet, he told Leah the story about Ellen telling Vice-President Bush that she hoped he was a better president than he was a golfer.

"Yikes," Leah said, holding up her cup for him to fill. "That's harsh."

"I'm sure she was just teasing him."

"So you like her?"

"She's okay. It's kind of hard to say because I feel like I'm getting to know a kind of handicapped version of the person she was, but she seems all right."

"She doesn't seem suicidal?"

"No. I don't know. I don't think so."

"Danielle says Thayer thinks Ellen was pressuring Bill to marry her and they must have had some kind of blowout the night she drove her car into the rock. Did you know that they had gone out to dinner that evening?"

"Yeah, I think I heard they were together."

"Well, Thayer thinks Mr. McAlister must have told her no, and then she tried to kill herself in a way where she probably knew she wasn't going to die."

There was a coldness in these words that cooled Nathan's libido.

Leah asked, "What do you think?"

"I think that sounds kind of soap operaish."

Taking his hand, Leah said, "Yeah, but lots of soap operaish stuff happens in life, don't you think?"

"That's true. Maybe the evil identical twin sister you don't know about is planning to kill you right now."

Leah gave him one of her frowning-through-a-grin looks and leaned back so that she and Nathan faced one another, propping their heads on their hands. They talked for a while about people they'd known who had killed themselves, and Nathan asked, "Have you ever thought about doing it?"

Leah pushed out her lower lip and frowned. "No. If I did, my mom would probably dig me up and kill me again." She pushed her finger over the rock through a few granules of sand. "Have you?"

"No, not really," Nathan sighed, although after his mother died, and Sophie dumped him, and his father continued to collapse even further into himself, Nathan *had* thought about it. He'd thought about it on dark mornings when he felt beyond crying, beyond grief. It was impossible to calculate the distance between thought and action, but Nathan remembered that the act—which had seemed baffling to him when he'd first learned of it, as a child—had begun to make a certain cold sense.

"Well, what keeps you from thinking about it?" Leah asked, reaching over to take his hand again.

Nathan shrugged. "Lots of reasons. I guess I always thought about the stuff I'd be missing if I did. Like I'd never have had the opportunity to take care of a deranged old woman for an entire summer, or watch lots of geriatric tennis, or lie on this cold, uncomfortable rock . . ."

"Or kiss me."

"Or kiss you."

On the way home, Nathan felt invigorated by the experience of kissing Leah, her hair draped over his face, his hand on the small of her back. At a red light, he leaned over to kiss her again, and she laughed and told him the light was green. He drove out of Kennebunkport and onto the winding country roads, the moon turning the surrounding forest shades of silvery gray. The wind through his opened window smelled of the earth, and glancing at the young woman beside him, her feet pulled up beneath her, it was easy for him to wonder if he might be falling in love.

"It feels like we're in a Volkswagen commercial," Leah said.

Nathan smiled wanly. He'd experienced a similar *this feels like we're in a movie* moment too, but he'd been careful not to say so. He knew the commercial she was referring to: several friends in a convertible Volkswagen, driving along a lushly moonlit country road. Nathan didn't mind the commercial. But Leah's comment made him wonder how much of his enjoyment of the drive was because it reminded him of an experience he'd seen advertised on television. It made the romantic, almost nostalgic feeling he'd been having seem tainted and inauthentic.

"It's better than a Volkswagen commercial," he said, although the words sounded silly to him and he wasn't even sure what he meant. Leah smiled—admiringly or indulgently, Nathan couldn't determine—but she ran her hand through the back of his hair, and by the time he kissed her again, outside her house, he had almost forgotten his disappointment.

Back at Ellen's, Nathan walked up the stairs with his feet far apart to reduce the moaning of the wood. The hallway lamplight shone through the slender opening of her door, and Nathan could see her head on her pillow, her mouth partially open. He paused long enough to observe that she would probably look much the same when she died.

In his bedroom, he glanced at the lacy white drapes billowing like sails from the window. Knowing they would do very little to keep out the approaching sun, he pulled off his clothes, then draped his shirt over the curtain rod. Usually the sounds of Ellen's grating bedroom door and her coughs were enough to wake him in the morning, but because he felt so bleary, he set the alarm for 8:30 A.M. Pulling the sheets over himself, he worried that he would not be able to stop imagining what it would be like to make love to Leah, but not long afterward, he fell asleep.

When he awoke to the creaking of Ellen's door, Nathan rolled over and squinted at the blazing numbers of the alarm clock: 6:27 A.M. He did not move. He listened to his own breathing, and the gulls already squawking outside his window. He suggested to himself that perhaps he'd mistaken a gull's squawk for the grinding of an unoiled door hinge. He closed his eyes and had almost drifted back to sleep when he heard the sound of Ellen's pink slippers shuffling down the carpeted hallway.

Nathan stared at the wall with angry hope—that she was merely en route to the bathroom, and that in a few minutes they'd both be back asleep—but then he heard her on the stairs. He struggled out of the bed, wrapped a towel around his boxers, then flung open the door.

"Ellen!" he said, loudly enough that her head snapped in his direction, eyes wide. She was in her blue bathrobe. One hand clutched the railing, while the other was braced against the far wall, as if the staircase were a highwire she was attempting to cross.

"Where are you going?"

"I'm going to eat breakfast," she said. But Ellen had not prepared her own breakfast since they'd arrived. Nathan knew she did not have the strength to twist the cap off the applesauce, or the technical know-how to operate the Mr. Coffee. His muscles were tense with lust for sleep, and after taking a deep breath, he felt a lot like a father talking to his wandering child.

"It's very early, Ellen," he said.

"What time is it?"

"It's six thirty in the morning."

Ellen turned to look down the stairs at the sunlight pouring in the front window. "That is early," she said, although her voice revealed no surprise.

"So why don't we go back to bed for a while? That way we'll be rested for the day."

Ellen glanced down at her feet, perhaps calculating the maneuvers required to reverse direction on a staircase, then looked back at Nathan with an embarrassed smile. "All right."

Nathan waited to see her make the first tiny, turning steps. "I'll see you in a couple hours, then?"

"Fine."

Back in his room, Nathan slid a macramé-covered brick against the warped door and eased back into the little nest he'd made for himself with the bedsheets and extra pillows. Eyes closed, he lay listening to the distant groaning of the stairs. Then he flung the covers back, cursing. The groaning was not growing louder but more faint.

"Ellen!" Nathan called, this time not bothering with the towel as he strode into the hall. She stood at the base of the stairs and seemed to hesitate, as if uncertain whether to stay or make a run for it. But she stared up at Nathan with a befuddled innocence in her eyes.

"Where are you going?" he asked.

"The kitchen."

"I thought you were going back to sleep."

Ellen nodded and surveyed the drab living room furniture. "Well, I'm hungry."

Nathan glared at her, suppressing the ugly violence he felt, then nodded, defeated. He went back to his room. After dressing again—thrusting each leg into his pants as if to punish them—Nathan fixed Ellen her cereal, toast, applesauce, juice, and coffee, then sat across from her at the kitchen table. Outside, seagulls seemed to laugh at him over the gleaming surface of the water. Nathan rested his head in his right hand, facing the window, ostensibly fascinated by the languorous swooping of the gulls, and closed his eyes. He hadn't slept in a sitting position since high school, but he slept, awakened only occasionally by the clinking of Ellen's mug upon its saucer or her shallow, early morning coughs.

When she pushed her chair back from the table, Nathan stood and cleared the dishes, then followed her back through the living room, toward the stairs.

"Do you feel like getting some more sleep?" Nathan asked, hopefully.

Ellen wrinkled her nose and said, "I'm going to change clothes."

"Okay, well, maybe we'll hang around here this morning and then go to the funeral this afternoon?"

Ellen nodded as she climbed the stairs, and Nathan congratulated himself for not mentioning that it was Sunday. He liked Eldwin's sermons well enough, but he didn't want to spend the whole day at St. Michael's. By the time she came downstairs—dressed in a funereal blue dress and pearls—Nathan was drifting in and out of consciousness on the couch. With half-open eyes, he watched her ease down in her recliner and pick up her book. Nathan closed his eyes and contemplated going upstairs to his bed where he could set the alarm, but he was already too comfortable amid the old pillows of the sagging couch, and this way he could keep tabs on Ellen. He would just enjoy a brief rest, then get up with enough time to take a shower before the funeral.

When the clanging phone woke him, Nathan scrambled over to the other side of the couch and picked it up. "Hello?"

"Hello, Nathan. This is Bill McAlister. I was just calling to remind you about the funeral this afternoon."

"Yep, one o'clock," Nathan said, struggling to sound relaxed and in control. Ellen was no longer in her recliner. He glanced at the clock on the mantel: 11:53 A.M. "We were just about to have lunch and head over."

Nathan stood with the heavy black rotary phone in his hand, yanking it around the living room, head swiveling in search of Ellen. He finally found her sitting with her back to him, on the porch swing. When he hung up the phone, he sat back down on the couch to wait for his heart to resume its normal rhythm. He felt an angry desire to explain that he wouldn't have overslept if Ellen hadn't acted like such a freak this morning. On his way up the stairs, he glanced through the French doors to where she sat with her book at her side, staring out at the glassy ocean, serene.

Nine

Carl Buchanan's Funeral ~ Nathan Kisses Leah Good-bye ~ Ellen's Remembrance of Things Past ~ A Symbol of the Comedy in Life's Absurdity Dies a Horrible Death ~ The Battle Royal

It surprised Nathan to see Carl again, but there he was—dressed in a navy blue suit with a blue-and-white-striped tie, surrounded by a semicircle of mourners lingering around the open casket in which he lay. Nathan led Ellen through the crowd and overheard an old woman murmuring what someone always murmurs at funerals: how the dead person looked so peaceful. And Carl did look peaceful, of course, in the same way that a mannequin can look peaceful. But he bore little resemblance to the person Nathan had encountered a few nights ago on Ellen's porch. His broad, blotchy face had been uniformly dusted with makeup, and his lips were now fixed in a position of dull imperturbability.

Ellen stared at the corpse but soon moved over to peer at the photographs on a nearby table. There was one of an almost unrecognizably young Carl, dressed in a crisp army uniform, and another where he was middle-aged, standing with his arm around a pigtailed girl in horn-rimmed glasses—his daughter?—in front of an old, two-story clapboard home. Nathan stared longest at the photograph of Carl and Franny on Big Beach, hugging, a Labrador celebrating their happiness by bounding through the ocean behind them. A few people spoke with Ellen to affirm how much Carl would be missed, and she agreed, smiling feebly, then let Nathan escort her into a pew.

Dust particles drifted in and out of shafts of light from stained-glass windows, and the church smelled of damp stone and perfume. Eldwin read a few verses of scripture and made general comments about the qualities that apparently made Carl such a great friend and neighbor. But it was mostly others who assumed the pulpit, honoring Carl's memory in a way that turned out to be much more generous and heartfelt than Carl perhaps would have expected. One man talked of how impressed he had been by Carl's appreciation of art and art history when walking with him through a museum, and another spoke of how Carl had driven to Massachusetts General Hospital to stay with the man's son, who had just been in a car accident, until he and his wife could get home from where they'd been on vacation. Whether or not Carl had ever come to see himself as one of them, many of these summer people seemed to have loved him. He was, by all accounts, somewhat excitable and reckless, but also deeply kindhearted, and he and his wife had often traveled (by car, rail, or sail) with many sitting tearfully in the pews.

Nathan hadn't felt especially fond of Carl's wife in his brief encounter with her at Ellen's house, but it was hard to maintain such feelings at the funeral. She did not speak, and her makeup and glasses did little to hide her sagging grief. When the pews emptied and people passed once more by the casket to say their final good-byes, she put a hand on her husband's stomach, inadvertently emptying his chest of air. His fat head tilted back on his silken pillow, sighing through the dark stitching intended to have sewn his mouth shut. Franny pulled her hand to her own mouth, sobbing, as a lanky gentleman put his arm around her shoulder and led her a few steps away.

Before they exited, Nathan glanced back into the nave of the church to see Mr. McAlister, arms folded across his gray suit, talking with a group of people near the altar. Nathan had not noticed him earlier, so he doubted Ellen had either. But outside on the stone walkway, she stepped off into the grass to join Eldwin and the others lingering out front, and said, "Maybe we can wait a moment for Bill."

A thin-faced man with jug ears approached and shook his head at Carl's death, then told them a story about Carl getting roaringly drunk on the plane that he took to attend his father's funeral. It was a funny story (Carl had apparently attempted to disembark in midair), but it lasted a long time. Mr. McAlister still had not left the church when it was over. The jug-eared gentleman and two others excused themselves, leaving Eldwin, Nathan, and Ellen to simply stare at the dispersing crowd. When there seemed nothing else they could say about Carl, Nathan and Eldwin made vague plans to kayak again sometime soon. Then Eldwin thanked them for coming and walked back through the front door of the church.

Nathan said to Ellen, "I guess Mr. McAlister's still talking with some people. Do you want me to let him know you're waiting for him?"

"No," Ellen said, quietly, shaking her head.

"Do you want to head home and maybe try and meet up with him later?"

Ellen smiled weakly, then shrugged in an effort to demonstrate that it made no difference to her. She took Nathan's arm and walked with him out of the lengthening shadow of the church.

Nathan sat in the living room watching *Shadowlands,* a movie about the late-blooming romance between the English novelist C. S. Lewis and an American woman who died of cancer soon after they were married. In a lecture Lewis gives in the movie before his wife dies, he wonders why a loving God would allow for human suffering, and he comes up with this answer: Suffering is God's instrument. As a sculptor wields his chisel, so too does God wield the instrument of suffering to forge us into better selves.

This was only modest consolation to Nathan as he suffered Ellen's nervous pacing around the house, which she'd been doing for the past half an hour, including in front of the TV. Craning his neck to see around her, Nathan asked, "What are you thinking about, Ellen?"

Ellen stopped and frowned at the harbor before looking over at Nathan. "Well, I was thinking that perhaps we should go and see Bill."

Nathan nodded and pursed his lips as if genuinely considering the idea. "Well, he may still be at the church right now. Do you want to give him a call a little later in the afternoon?"

It had been more than an hour since the funeral, so Nathan doubted Mr. McAlister was still at St. Michael's. But the man had made no effort to find Ellen while she was there, and Nathan did not want to help her chase him down if he was not interested in talking with her.

When she finally went upstairs to take her nap, Nathan glanced at the clock on the mantel and picked up the phone. He had tried to reach Leah immediately after the funeral, but no one answered. He was afraid she had already left for New York. The phone rang a few times, but then she finally answered, sounding rushed, and asked if he could come over to say good-bye.

Eldwin's son, Eliot, answered the doorbell, carrying a wooden block like a weapon, and screaming for Leah with a ferocity disproportionate to his frame. When she stepped out the screen door, she led Nathan off the porch, into the yard, where they could talk away from the opened windows of the house.

"You look handsome," she said. She was wearing jeans and an old gray T-shirt, while Nathan was wearing the same pants and sport coat he'd worn to Mr. McAlister's cocktail party.

Nathan said, "I wear this for parties and funerals."

"How was it?"

"Sad."

"Did Eldwin talk about Aristotle?"

"Not this time. When are you leaving?"

"Soon, like in a couple of minutes. But hey, listen to this! You know how I was saying that Thayer's grandfather is the publisher at Epoch?

Well, Thayer asked him if he would meet with me when I'm there, and he said he could probably meet me on Wednesday!"

"That's great," Nathan said, smiling briefly. "But aren't you supposed to come back here on Wednesday?"

"Well, I can come back a day later. Isn't that exciting, though?" She pushed herself up on her toes and stared at Nathan with eyes that encouraged him to share her enthusiasm.

"Yeah, absolutely," Nathan said, furrowing his brow with renewed conviction. "Hell, yeah. Is it going to be an interview kind of thing?"

"I think it's going to be more informational, like I'm just asking him for advice on how to get into the business. But he's the freaking head of Epoch, so who knows? If he likes me, maybe he'll hire me, or maybe he knows somebody who would hire me."

"That's great that you're going to meet him."

Leah grinned as she absently pointed her toe at the gravel that was mixed up in the grass at the edge of the yard. "So, wish me luck. What are you going to do while I'm gone?"

Nathan shrugged and glanced back at the house. "I don't know. Work on some sketches, try and figure out what the hell I'm doing when I leave here this summer."

"I thought you have this job at the library and this graphic novel that you're finishing."

For a moment, Nathan considered telling her the truth—that there was no job waiting for him and that he hadn't worked on the graphic novel in months. But he said, "Yeah, I do. I am. I've just been thinking that maybe I need a change."

Leah stared at him with expectant, sympathetic eyes, and Nathan shook his head as if he'd been caught talking nonsense. "I didn't get a hell of a lot of sleep last night." He told her how Ellen had awakened him at 6:27 that morning, and Leah laughed in the easy, lighthearted way of people with reasonably optimistic plans for their future.

With only semi-ironic desperation, Nathan asked, "What the hell am I going to do without you here?"

"Well, you have Ellen and Eldwin to keep you company."

"But they can't kiss like you do."

Leah said, "Maybe they just need practice." She laughed a little at her own joke, then pouted, "Hey, that was a pretty good one."

Nathan grunted his approval.

Moving forward to kiss him, Leah briefly balanced on his shoes, then stepped back. "Okay—I should probably finish getting ready. Eldwin's driving me to the train station and I think he wants to go soon."

"I'll miss you."

Leah leaped toward him again, embracing him longer this time, but it was still a painfully short, *someone might see us* kind of kiss. Watching her skip excitedly toward the house, and toward New York, he resisted the urge to hurry after her so he could hold her again.

The rain fell in gray torrents that evening and continued into the next morning. Nathan turned on the lamps in the living room to fight off the weight of the leaden clouds, but the old house with its old furniture seemed to deepen his listlessness. Ellen sat in her recliner, watching golf on television, while Nathan lay on the couch, drifting in and out of sleep. When the downpour finally stopped, he yawned and asked Ellen if she felt like taking a drive.

They drove inland for half an hour, down winding, country roads, through forests and one-church towns, stopping at a little gas station with a general store. Nathan bought them both ice cream and they sat in the car, eating, staring across the street at a few horses in a pasture on the other side of a wooden fence. On the mantel at Ellen's house there was a photograph of her on horseback, and when he mentioned it to her, she said, "Oh, yes, I used to love to ride. My father put me on a cow when I was a year old so I could learn."

Nathan noticed an uncommon lucidity in Ellen's eyes, and he asked the kind of specific question he had for the most part stopped asking. "Was that your horse in the photo?"

"Harold bought me that horse not long after we were married."

"Your husband looked like a handsome guy in that home movie."

Ellen licked the chocolate ice cream off her upper lip, nodding. "Yes, he was. I don't think I'm the only one who thought so, either."

Nathan continued to stare out at the pasture in front of them as he asked, "Other women thought he was handsome, too?"

He felt Ellen glance at him, frowning, as if perhaps he did not understand, but then she made a low sound of acknowledgment and looked back at the horses. "Yes, that's right," she whispered, before taking another bite from her cone.

On the way home they didn't talk much, and Nathan turned on the radio with the volume low. They cruised along the coastline until they were on Oceanside Avenue, the narrow strip of road between the Atlantic and the cove, and very near the town proper. Because Nathan had no plans, and because driving around a little longer seemed preferable to watching TV, he turned right onto Birch Hill Boulevard, in the opposite direction from home. He turned right again on Haley, driving until the street became Shore Road and he could gaze out Ellen's window at the whitecapped waves of the ocean. When Shore Road circled back onto Birch Hill Boulevard—near the main entrance to the Point—Ellen asked him to slow down.

Nathan eased his foot off the gas, but remembering Ellen's near-death experience last week, when she had nearly fallen from the cliff, he said, "You don't feel like hiking again, do you?"

"No, turn in here."

Nathan turned right and drove between two stone pillars, up a sloping cement driveway. As the incline leveled off, he could see over the tops of pine trees the turreted stone house he'd seen before from the Point. Towering over a deep green half-acre lawn that dropped precipitously toward the ocean, the house looked as if it should have been obliterated by tall waves long ago. Yet there it was—looking steadfast and permanent. Judging from the absence of a garage and the apparent age of the stones, Nathan wouldn't have been surprised if it had been there for more than a century.

"Who lives here?" Nathan asked, parking the car in the narrow driveway.

Ellen tilted her head to stare up at the house. "Oh, just an old friend."

Nathan helped Ellen out of the car and up a stone path leading to a wooden wraparound porch. It was the only porch Nathan had seen in Brightonfield Cove with a view that rivaled the one from Ellen's house. Ellen seemed uninterested in the heavy-looking front door, and instead led Nathan to the railing overlooking the glinting waves of the ocean.

"Do you want me to knock?" Nathan asked. Through the drapery-bordered windows behind them, the interior of the house, with its hardwood floors and antique furniture, looked shadowy and vacant, but Nathan still thought it odd to be standing there without attempting to notify the owners.

Ellen shrugged as she stared out at the ocean, suggesting—as Nathan understood the gesture—that notifying the owners was something they could do in a moment. From this height, they could see on the left the jutting nub of peninsula that rose to the Point, and on the right, the rocky shore that curved deeply inland then straightened out to become the sandy stretch of Big Beach. This was where Leah took the children and—Nathan had learned—where she often talked with Thayer and his friends. Nathan squinted to see distant figures in colorful bathing suits scattered along the tide's edge.

"Who came up with the name Big Beach?" he asked.

Ellen shook her head without looking at him, and Nathan had the sense that he was interrupting a moment of contemplation. A lock turned behind them with a clunk, and a woman with short, spiky gray hair stepped into the doorway, her eyes adjusting to the light. Nathan recognized her as one of the women who had been standing near Mr. McAlister at the funeral.

"Can I help you?" the woman asked.

Ellen looked expectantly at Nathan, and after a moment's hesitation, he let out a nervous laugh. "Ellen and I were just driving around and she thought maybe we'd stop by and say hello. I'm Nathan Empson, a friend of hers from back in Cleveland."

The woman let Nathan shake her hand. Then she took off her reading glasses to stare at Ellen.

"Is that why you're here, Ellen?" the woman asked, sliding the glasses into her pants pocket and folding her arms across her pink blouse. A slender woman with a narrow, high-cheekboned face, she had traces of a softer beauty now more wizened and severe.

"I suppose so," Ellen said, smiling abashedly, already shuffling in the direction of the car.

"All right, well, nice to meet you," Nathan said. He raised his palm to say good-bye. He offered Ellen his arm and they walked, listening to the sound of the woman's bare feet padding across the wooden floorboards as she followed behind them. "It's a beautiful view," Nathan said. He glanced back with an expression of confused helplessness, to help explain the intrusion, but the woman only glared and shook her head.

At the car, after helping Ellen into her seat, Nathan felt the need to say something to make the situation seem normal. "Thanks!" he said, smiling as he waved good-bye.

"I didn't invite you here," the woman said.

"I know. Sorry," Nathan said.

"Bill doesn't live here anymore."

"Oh. All right."

"So why did you bring her?"

"I don't know." Nathan shook his head. "Fuck it," he murmured, climbing back into the car. He wanted to get out of there as soon as possible, but the driveway was so narrow that it was difficult to turn around. He worked the car's gearshift into drive, then reverse, then drive, then reverse, glimpsing out of the corner of his eye the whitish blur of Ellen's head lunging back and forth beside him. He finally backed the car up enough to wrench the wheel to the right one last time, then pushed hard on the gas. He passed closer to the walkway than he'd intended, and the woman took a few hurried steps back, but the car was finally pointing down the long driveway. Glancing in the rearview mirror to make sure the woman was all right, Nathan saw not one figure but two. The woman was hugging a young man whose face was obscured, but whose dark hair and muscled arms Nathan thought he recognized well enough.

"Two months of doing nothing" was how his father had described this summer job, and Nathan was looking forward to disabusing him of this notion. Nathan was simply not emotionally, intellectually, or even physically capable of handling the responsibility of watching over a mentally unstable woman twenty-four hours a day for eight weeks. To pretend otherwise was to invite more painfully awkward episodes like the one that morning and perhaps even to court disaster. With Ellen upstairs taking her nap, Nathan fixed himself two drinks and then dialed his father's office number on the rotary phone. When the receptionist answered, saying that Nathan's father had been out sick since last Thursday, Nathan tried him at home. The older man sounded tired when he answered but grew slightly more animated at the sound of Nathan's voice. They talked about what was wrong with him—the flu, maybe? He felt exhausted and had slept the previous evening for fourteen hours.

"Have you been working late at the office?" When Nathan was a child his father had often left the house before Nathan awoke for school, and didn't return home until after he and his mother had eaten supper.

"Nah, not so much. I think they're learning how to get along better without me," his father answered.

"Yeah?"

"They're bringing in a lot of new people, young people."

Nathan did not know how to answer, but he was afraid that if his father ever had to retire from his job, he would most likely retreat even further into his already cloistered existence.

"How are things going up there?" his father asked.

Nathan sighed as he told him that things were not going at all as he'd hoped. He'd already told his father about Ellen sitting in the car that first morning, for how long?—minutes? hours?—waiting for an escort to church. Since then she had encouraged him to accompany her on a hike to the Point, even though the shortest path there was still clearly more than she could handle (Nathan omitted the part about her nearly falling off the cliff), and conscripted him into the afternoon's absurd adventure at the home of Mr. McAlister's wife.

Nathan said, "It's hard for me to see how—I don't know, maybe you haven't seen much of her lately—but it's hard for me to see how you and Glen could have sent me up here with her alone."

In the heavy silence that followed, he could hear his father sinking back into whatever dark bog of the mind he had been slogging through before Nathan had pulled him out with his call.

His father said, "I thought she was okay. But I'm sorry that things are turning out this way. If you want, I can call Glen this evening and we can make arrangements for bringing her home."

Even before his father finished speaking, Nathan's face prickled with the flushed recognition that he did not want to return to Cleveland. He had simply wanted to establish himself as a kind of martyr—but dammit! Ending his arrangement with Ellen would mean no more thousand dollars a week, no Leah, and a return to the drudgery of his life back home. His heart fluttering in his chest, he said, "I don't know if that's necessary . . . yet."

"I know you'll watch over her when you're together, Nathan, but are you thinking she might hurt herself again when you're not around?"

"I'm not sure. I mean, how can you ever be sure of something like that, you know? Everybody knew that she hurt herself with the car and they still sent me up here!" His father did not respond immediately, and Nathan took a moment to figure out what he was trying to say. "I don't think she's acting purposefully self-destructive, not totally," he said, cradling his forehead with his palm. "It's just . . . frustrating . . . she's just not all there all the time."

"I'm not all here all the time."

Nathan laughed despite himself. "That's true."

"Well, just let me know if anything changes, if it seems too much to handle, and we'll make arrangements," his father said. When the conversation moved on, they talked for a while about his father's plans to plant a tall hedgerow in the yard for privacy from a neighbor's aboveground pool. The call didn't end badly—Nathan wished his father a swift recovery and promised to check up on him soon—but he still hung up feeling aggrieved. If something had happened to Ellen in the past, Nathan could have shared the blame with his father and Glen. But now he had just told his father, quite explicitly, that he thought it was fine for him to take care of Ellen all by himself.

An hour passed, during which Nathan fixed himself three more drinks and watched TV, often cursing as he changed the channels, wondering what kind of summer home did not have a fucking remote. Feeling sufficiently inebriated, he checked to see if Ellen was still asleep, then crept out of the house. He ambled down Oceanside Avenue to Big Beach and made a mental note to himself that he needed to purchase a portable container to carry a drink with him next time he walked. From the glimmering, moon-gray sand of the beach, Nathan stared at the ocean with arms folded across his chest—hoping that some attractive woman somewhere was watching him stare contemplatively at the ocean—then moved back up the landing and into town, all the way along Shore Road to the Point. He pushed his way through the hedgerow surrounding the entrance and stumbled up the moonlit trail. From the rock where Ellen had nearly fallen, he was squinting down at the lamplit windows of Mr. McAlister's wife's house when it occurred to him why Ellen may have wanted to hike here. Nathan had not paid much attention to the house on the day of their hike and he wondered what, if anything, she had been able to see of Mr. McAlister or his wife. Maybe Ellen had just wanted to see the home that no doubt held pleasant memories for her. For a misguided instant, Nathan wanted to share with her what he thought he might be learning this summer—a lesson in love about the virtues of letting go and starting over. But almost immediately, he understood that starting over was a luxury of the young. Ellen's powers were failing, and when she'd hobbled and scraped her way up here that afternoon, nearly killing herself in the process, she had probably done so to see the house, but also because it was a view she'd seen all her life, with different companions, and she understood—if not at the beginning, then halfway up, certainly—that this would probably be the last time.

Nathan felt ashamed for not being more attentive to such things when they'd been hiking together, and he tried to distract himself with activity. He turned and rambled over the golf course, past St. Michael's, then under the heavy boughs of Admirals Way. He gazed at the imperious homes set back from the street and was surprised to see the silhouette of Mr. McAlister, standing in the middle of his front lawn. His cigar ember burned in the darkness while his wiener dog wandered in front of him between the thick trunks of old oak trees. When he suspected that Mr. McAlister was peering at him, Nathan raised his palm and said, "Evening."

"Who is that?"

"Nathan. Ellen's . . . friend."

"Oh," Mr. McAlister said, sounding vaguely disappointed. "I was going to call you."

"Yeah?"

"Yeah. You got a minute to come inside?"

Nathan hesitated, but said, "Sure."

As he walked onto the yard, he could see that in the cool evening air the older man was not wearing a sweater, only a short-sleeved, navy shirt, his bare arms pale in the dark. Mr. McAlister called for Peewee a few times, saying, "Hurry up now, piss," but the dog continued to sniff around different tree trunks.

"Ah, he'll come in through the flap in the laundry room," Mr. McAlister mumbled. In the house, he flipped on a few lights and led Nathan through the sunken living room into the dimly lit library Nathan had so much admired. A lamp burned softly between the two couches and a fire in the marble fireplace cast shadows over the bookshelves surrounding them.

"Have a seat. I'm going to get something to drink. You want anything?"

"Do you have Coke?"

"I can get you one."

Nathan looked over the bookshelves, glancing at *Don Quixote,* but he felt too uncertain about himself this evening to want to look at the illustrations again. When Mr. McAlister returned, they both sat in front of the fire with their drinks. Mr. McAlister's drink looked like a gin and tonic and Nathan wondered if it was too late to ask for a shot of rum in his Coke.

"Let me know if the cigar smoke gets too much for you and I'll open another window," Mr. McAlister said. "Do you make many fires at the house?"

"Not a lot. Sometimes, when it's really cold. I've been surprised by how cold it can get up here at night, even though it's the summer."

"When you get older, your bones get colder a lot quicker. With Ellen as slender as she is."

Nathan nodded at the implicit suggestion. "Yeah, maybe I should ask her if she wants me to make more fires."

As Mr. McAlister puffed on his cigar, tendrils of smoke billowed out of his mouth and dissipated into the flickering shadows around them. "In Boston I lived for a long time in an old brownstone without a working fireplace, so I like to make fires here in the evening sometimes even when it's not so cold."

"Huh," Nathan said. "You know, I don't remember where the kitchen is, but is there any way I could put some rum in this?"

An instant later—still pointing sideways at his glass—it occurred to Nathan that to have asked the question meant he probably still had a good deal of rum in him. Mr. McAlister's smile faltered and he slid his cigar into the ashtray, his long face slackening into an expression of gloomy fatigue. Reaching for his own glass, he said, "Why don't you tell me what happened today first?"

"What, you mean at your wife's place?" Nathan asked, his heart quickening at the question even as he pushed himself back on the couch to make himself more comfortable. "There's not a whole lot to tell. Ellen and I were driving around and she said she wanted me to pull into this friend's driveway, so I pulled in, and about the same time we got on the porch, your wife came out. I didn't know she was your wife, but she wasn't particularly happy to see Ellen, so we left."

"What did Jean say?"

Nathan recounted the conversation as best as he could remember, and the older man ran a hand over his thinning widow's peak in what seemed a gesture of impatience. Mr. McAlister said, "Then what?"

"Then—like I said—I helped Ellen to the car, and we left."

Mr. McAlister sipped his drink and worked his tongue around the inside of his mouth as if searching for something. "Jean says that you told her to fuck off. Or to go fuck herself."

Nathan's mouth opened to let fly a nervous laugh, but he managed only something like a dry cough. "No. That's very definitely not what I said. I didn't say anything remotely like that."

"What did you say?"

"I think I said good-bye! I think I might have cursed to myself, or cursed myself for bringing Ellen up there, but I would never have said anything like that to your wife."

"She seems to remember the incident differently. She also claims you tried to hit her with the car as you were leaving."

"That's insane!" Nathan cried. "I didn't try to hit her either." While he spoke, he heard Peewee's paws scratching across the hardwood floor as the dachshund trotted into the room on its stubby legs and crossed onto the throw rug in front of him. The dog had gotten into something—thin streaks of what looked like black tar ran down the short, caramel-colored hair of its back. But apparently not noticing, Mr. McAlister patted the seat beside him on the couch. "I think your dog—," Nathan muttered, but Peewee had leaped onto the cushions and was already nuzzling the older man's hand.

In an instant, Mr. McAlister peered at his palm, then at the dog, then swept Peewee off the couch at the same time that he himself stood. "Goddammit!" Mr. McAlister bellowed. He held his drink in front of him like a lantern as he inspected the seat cushions and his pants. "This is the second time he's come in here with that shit on him and I can't figure out where he's getting it."

The dog had landed miraculously on all fours. It stared at Mr. McAlister and Nathan with a plaintive expression, then circled around the throw rug as a preliminary ritual to lying down.

Mr. McAlister said, "No, Peewee! No, now come here." He set his drink and cigar on the end table then led the dog down the hall. Nathan stared into the fire, wondering if it was possible Mr. McAlister's wife really thought he had been trying to mow her down. He thought about the way she looked when he passed near her with the car—all the righteous indignation drained from her face—and for a moment he wished he'd driven closer. As the minutes passed, however, and Mr. McAlister still hadn't returned, Nathan's resentment began to fade in and out of a defeated and somewhat drunken melancholy. A dog walked in circles before lying down because of hundreds of thousands of years of dogs flattening grass to create a space to fall asleep. Two men in front of a fire arguing over the mistreatment of a woman. The same stories again and again.

"All right," Mr. McAlister said, sighing as he reentered the library. He glanced back down the hall as Peewee trotted after him to circle and finally lie down on the rug. When Mr. McAlister eased himself once more onto the couch, his long face and narrowed eyes indicated that most of his patience had left him. "So, why would Jean think you tried to hit her if you didn't?"

"I have no idea. I was trying to pull out of that narrow driveway, and there's no way to turn around without coming close to the walkway. But I wasn't going very fast, and I certainly wasn't trying to hurt her or even scare her. I don't even *know* her, for God's sake."

"You know she was rude to Ellen."

Nathan hesitated, then said, "Yeah. I do know that. But that wouldn't have been enough for me to try and hit her with the car."

For a moment, the only sound in the room was the faint keening of wind through the windows and the crackling of the logs in the fire. Mr. McAlister said, "Jean is thinking about pressing charges against you."

Nathan stared openmouthed. "You have got to be . . . that's absurd."

"Both she and Thayer thought you could have hit her with the car."

"Well, both she and Thayer have greatly misinterpreted what happened."

"I just wanted to let you know."

"Well, is she going to?"

"I don't know. I think that's something she's debating at the moment."

Nathan said bitterly, "You know what I think this is about? I think this is your wife knowing that if I have to leave, that means Ellen probably has to leave, too."

"I don't think that's what this is about, Nathan."

"Yeah, well from what I hear, it would probably be less complicated for everybody if Ellen wasn't here. I know you guys were involved and that Ellen still wants to spend time with you, but at the funeral the other day, you wouldn't even walk over and say hello to her because you were so busy chitchatting with your wife."

Mr. McAlister held his glass with both hands in his lap and glowered at Nathan, pausing to choose his words. "I wanted to say hello to Ellen, and I would be very saddened if she had to leave."

Nathan said, "Well, so would Ellen."

Mr. McAlister nodded and cast his eyes down. He said, "I can tell Jean that—" But he didn't finish the sentence. A knot in one of the logs in the fireplace exploded, and a flurry of red embers arced through the air. Most landed safely on the dark tile in front of the hearth, but one settled on Peewee where he lay stretched out on the edge of the rug. The ember ignited a few hairs on his hindquarters and remained contained for a moment, allowing Nathan to chuckle when the dog yipped and lifted his head. Then that small patch of burning hair rocketed up the full length of Peewee's body and enveloped the dog in crackling flame. Because Nathan had been drinking earlier, he questioned what he was seeing, but when he glanced at Mr. McAlister and saw his stricken expression and outstretched hands, he understood it was true. What had initially seemed a minor accident was becoming something ghastly to behold. Peewee scrambled up on his paws, yelping wildly, until he scurried, howling, out of the room before either man had time to stand.

By the time they found Peewee on his side a few feet away from the living room's patio doors, scorched and whimpering, he had already tried to extinguish himself by rubbing against the heavy white curtains. Flames leapt and snarled up the thick folds with a voracious hunger. For an instant, Nathan stood, stunned, as Mr. McAlister took a throw pillow off the couch and alternately tried to beat out the smoking cinders on his dog and the flames already licking the ceiling. Then Nathan grabbed another throw pillow and tried to smother what had become a wall of fire. Mr. McAlister waved him back. His flushed face squinting into the shimmery heat, the older man grabbed at a section of the curtain not yet burning, and yanked. The muscles in his face and neck strained with the effort, but the wooden curtain rings defied him. He stepped back and stared into the roiling fire then called for Nathan to follow.

Mr. McAlister hustled into the kitchen and fumbled inside a closet a long time to finally pull out a fire extinguisher. As they rushed back down the hallway, the older man was walking quickly, not running, and flakes of spittle clung to the corners of his mouth. "Do you want me to use that?" Nathan asked, but Mr. McAlister shook his head.

In the living room, the fire rushed like upside-down rapids across more than a quarter of the ceiling. Nathan darted over to grab a shawl from the couch and use it to scoop Peewee into his arms. He carried him back into the hallway just as Mr. McAlister took a few steps into the room to spray the walls and ceiling. Acrid-smelling smoke billowed toward them in dense clouds, forcing them deeper into the hallway. Nathan inspected the still smoldering dog for signs of life, but he knew the poor thing was no longer breathing. He cradled the dead dog in his arms as both men stared in mute astonishment at how quickly the fire was raging across the ceiling and along the side walls.

Mr. McAlister let the fire extinguisher fall, then hurried over to the near corner of the room to pull a few photographs off the piano. His face wincing from the heat, he carried the frames into the hall and gestured again for Nathan to follow him. In the kitchen, Mr. McAlister's armful of frames clattered across the marble counter as he picked up the phone to dial 911. He barked the address and a few directions, then sputtered, "When you've gotten that far, you can just follow the goddamned smoke." His skin was a sweating, reddish-gray, and when he hung up, he beckoned Nathan. "I need your help to take some things out."

First they deposited Peewee, the pictures, and a seascape painting Mr. McAlister had pulled off the foyer wall onto an illuminated semicircle of driveway near the front lamppost. Then Mr. McAlister said, "Don't go near the fire or upstairs. Just grab anything that looks important and try to get it outside."

For the next few minutes, Nathan did what he could, shuttling china, silverware, chairs, and paintings out onto the driveway. When he had finished carrying out a framed aerial photograph of Brightonfield Cove and a drawer full of letters, he paused, panting, to survey how much of the house the fire had already consumed. No longer able to see the lamplight through the library window—the room was thick with black swirls of smoke—he thought he might rush around to enter through the laundry room and perhaps at least rescue *Don Quixote.* But when he took a few hesitant steps in that direction, he heard Mr. McAlister.

"Nathan! Can you get these for me?" The older man was standing in the doorway, his chest heaving, waving Nathan into the house. He led him through the faintly smoky hallway to a stack of drawers at the bottom of the stairs. Peering down into the jumbled mess of old stock statements, socks, and bills, Nathan coughed and shouted, "I think the fire's reached the library." Mr. McAlister crouched beside him, hoisting a stack of drawers, and nodded grimly.

Outside they could hear the rising wail of approaching fire trucks. They returned for more salvage, but Nathan was increasingly aware of the progression of the smoke and how foolish it would be to die trying to save this rich man's possessions. When Nathan stumbled back outside with a rolled-up Persian rug, he was relieved to see a fireman approach to lead him out onto the street. Red lights flashed against the white facade of the house. Firefighters bustled around their trucks, then dispersed, weaving the long hose through the trees and alongside what looked like a high-end, late-night yard sale. A fireman led Mr. McAlister out of the house as the older man tried explaining what other belongings might be saved.

The dog dead, the library lost, and Mr. McAlister safely removed from the house, Nathan took a deep breath. He was disturbed by the memory of the dog's gruesome death, and grieved by the loss of so many beautiful books, but he was safe. The sympathy he had for Mr. McAlister was overwhelmed by the thrumming postadrenaline excitement of having experienced something bizarre and life-threatening and now being able to tell the tale.

The fireman by Nathan's side asked if there was still anyone in the house, and if he felt okay, then told him to wait near the fire truck for the paramedics to check him out when they returned. "Are you cold?" The fireman pulled a blanket out of the back and draped it over Nathan's shoulders. Listening to the sounds of breaking windows and watching the smoke billow out of the house, Nathan felt like a character in one of those videos he'd watched in grade school about the importance of fire safety. A few feet away, a heavy, ruddy-faced fireman was asking Mr. McAlister questions and jotting down the answers on a clipboard.

"So no one else lives in the house besides you?"

"No."

"And you said your dog died in the fire?"

"Yeah."

"Do you know how the fire might have started?"

"Yeah, the dog. Peewee. He caught fire."

The fireman nodded, but his lips grew smaller within his goatee. "How did the dog catch fire?"

Mr. McAlister shook his head and said, "I don't know." He was staring off to where neighbors were already gathering on the left side of the yard.

"Any guesses?"

Nathan pulled his blanket more closely around him and stepped nearer to where the two men were talking. How *had* the dog caught fire? he wondered, with increasing indignation. He had hated seeing the terror in those eyes, and smelling its charred wiener-shaped body, and he wanted to know why God would have allowed such a deviation from the normal laws of combustion. A stray ember could have burned Peewee mildly, igniting a small portion of his hair, but what the hell had turned that dachshund into a miniature rocket of howling flame?

Mr. McAlister straightened up and chewed on his lower lip as if he might bite it off. "The goddamned dog had tar on him again, so I rubbed some paint thinner on him to get it off, but then he came back into the"—Mr. McAlister shook his head before his voice trailed off into a whisper—"into my study there, and sat down by the fire."

Nathan stared, slack-jawed, at Mr. McAlister, then the fireman. The stocky young man had been listening sympathetically to Mr. McAlister, but when the older man said "paint thinner," the fireman's mouth twitched to one side and he looked down at his clipboard with suddenly rapt concentration.

The fireman eventually asked what happened next, but Nathan wasn't around to hear the answer. A paramedic had walked over and began asking Nathan questions to see if he was all right. When it was over, and he had fielded many of the same questions from a policeman, Nathan watched as the firemen launched thick cords of water into the house until the fire no longer seemed to be spreading. Mr. McAlister stood nearby, already surrounded by several neighbors with shaking heads. Nathan listened to the neighbors' stilted conversation about the things Mr. McAlister had been able to save, and how lucky it was that they had a volunteer fire department to respond with such dispatch. The fire was now mostly smoke, and other neighbors were mingling with the firemen, policemen, and paramedics to talk about what had happened. Nathan walked past the couple talking with Mr. McAlister and shook his hand, telling him that he was going to head home.

"You sure you're all right?" Mr. McAlister's eyes looked much more compassionate than they had when he was barking orders at Nathan, trying to lug everything out of the house.

"Yeah, I'm fine. Are you okay? Do you need any help taking this stuff somewhere?" He gestured at the furnishings clustered in the front driveway.

"No, I'm all right for now," Mr. McAlister said, turning to face the sight of his smoldering home.

Nathan dropped off the blanket at the back of the fire truck, then headed down between the expansive lawns of Admirals Way. On the street, an older couple in tracksuits asked him what had happened.

Nathan said, "Mr. McAlister's house caught on fire," and hurried onward. At Ellen's house, he checked to make sure she was still sleeping, then mixed a drink. He walked down Parson's Beach and far enough up Mr. McAlister's backyard to see that the firemen were still arcing a thick stream of water into the house, but that they were also packing up their gear. It wasn't until he was walking back along the beach, mulling over the best way to recount the story to Leah, that he wondered where Mr. McAlister would spend the rest of the summer.

In the morning, Nathan told Ellen what had happened, and a fissure deepened between her eyebrows as she stared at him.

"You weren't here?" she asked.

"No, I went out for a walk," Nathan said, taking a sip of his juice. He felt frustrated by what he took to be an implicit expectation from her and from her son—perhaps even from his father—that Nathan's every waking hour should be spent at her beck and call, and he was increasingly worried about the ramifications of last evening. The dozens of neighbors who had seen him outside Mr. McAlister's would want to know why he had been in the house, and wouldn't the older man reclaim some respect (after such an embarrassing episode) by explaining that he had called Nathan over to dress him down for driving so recklessly—putting Ellen's safety in jeopardy as well as nearly killing his wife? Even if Nathan wasn't prosecuted, how long would it be before the gossipmongers told Glen and he yanked him out of Brightonfield Cove?

Nathan wanted to talk this over with Ellen, but he was uncertain about her capacity to understand the full implications of everything that was happening. He said, "I thought the more newsworthy part of what I said is that Mr. McAlister's wife is very angry with us, thinking of pressing charges against *me,* and that Mr. McAlister's house burned down."

Ellen smiled and shook her head incredulously but continued eating her toast, glancing out at the yachts sailing toward the sunny horizon of the Atlantic. In the living room, she demonstrated little interest in watching the tennis match on television, and after a while, walked over to riffle through the drawers of her desk. From a bottom drawer, she pulled out a red address book and carried it with her to her recliner, where she eased down and reached for the phone.

This would be the first call Nathan had ever seen Ellen initiate, and he wondered if the laws of etiquette required him to leave the room. Ellen sat facing the French doors and blue sky while Nathan remained in his recliner, hoping it would be enough for him to just feign interest in an old *Sierra* magazine.

Of course Ellen would try to call Mr. McAlister, Nathan thought, so he was not surprised to see her hold the phone to her ear for a while and then set it back on the receiver. But then she flipped through the yellowed pages of her address book and appeared to dial a different number.

Cradling the phone to her ear, Ellen said, "Yes, may I speak with Bill, please?" There was a pause, then a heavy sigh. "This is Eleanor Broderick."

Ellen listened, then pursed her lips in irritation. "Well I don't—," she began, then stopped. "Hello?" she said, and finally set the phone back on the receiver. Settling herself deeper in her chair, she looked at Nathan, but he was careful to act as if he was too engrossed in the article about snow leopards to notice whether she was still talking on the phone. When she stood up to shuffle around the house, and then onto the porch, Nathan waited a few minutes before he stepped out to join her. She was sitting on her swing, pushing herself back and forth gently as she stared out at the harbor.

Sitting down in one of the nearby wooden chairs, Nathan asked her if she wanted something to drink, but she declined. Even though he knew he'd already told her this earlier, Nathan said, "I don't know if I told you this earlier, but Mr. McAlister is completely fine. The paramedics checked him out while I was there and gave him a clean bill of health."

Ellen nodded and said, "I'm relieved to hear he's okay."

But her uncomfortable smile left Nathan wanting to do more. Frustrated, he said, "If you want, we could drive by his place so you can see what happened."

Long before they pulled out of the driveway, Nathan knew this was a stupid, *stupid* idea. Mr. McAlister's home no doubt carried many fond memories for Ellen, and the fact that he would most likely not be there would only exacerbate her nervousness. Still, Nathan had told her he would take her, and so he drove beneath the arching trees of Admirals Way until, on the horizon, the smoldering mansion inched into view.

Yellow police tape stretched around the trunks of old oak trees to surround the perimeter of the yard, and all the furnishings they'd rescued last night had been removed. The west side of the house appeared untouched, but the east side was more devastated than Nathan remembered. Most of the tile roof had collapsed into a blackened maw from which wispy ribbons of smoke twisted out into the air. The outer brickwork was still standing, with upturned tongues of ash above the windows, but the interior appeared to have been mostly hollowed out by the flames.

"Can you see it?" Nathan asked, pushing back against his seat to allow her to see past him.

"Yes, I can."

Nathan turned the car around in the cul-de-sac to give her a better view. He let the car idle as they both stared out at the house. Ellen began to fumble with her door handle.

"Whoa, where are you going, Ellen?"

"I want to talk with Bill."

"I don't think he's here. I think the yellow tape means they've closed it up so that nobody disturbs anything before the insurance company gets here."

Ellen paused. "I think he might still be here."

"What makes you say that?" Nathan asked, looking out at the house for something he hadn't seen. The windows on the west side had their draperies closed, and he tried to remember if they had been that way before the fire.

"I just think he might."

"All right, well, I tell you what," Nathan negotiated. "Why don't I go out and check. That way you won't have to make a long walk for nothing."

On his way toward the house, he stepped between puddles of soaked grass and pulled the yellow tape over his head to pass underneath. He rang the doorbell and no one answered. Turning to look back at Ellen, he gave her a *no one's answering* shrug, then walked around the east side of the house. He stared through broken windows into the blackened jutting of charred floor and furniture still smoking below. When voices began to call to one another from the opened windows of the neighbor's house, Nathan retraced his steps across the lawn.

"Well, nobody answered," he explained, once back in the car. "I'm sure he probably just spent the night at a neighbor's. Or who knows? Maybe he spent the night here and just went out to get lunch or something."

Ellen nodded and pulled her white cardigan more closely around her neck. As Nathan drove away from the house, he asked if she'd like to watch tennis at the club, but she just sniffed and shook her head. "Turn here," she said, pointing left down Birch Hill Boulevard, in the opposite direction of her house. Nathan turned as she directed, driving in silence. Long before they reached the end of the road, he tried to lead them away from the destination he suspected Ellen had in mind. He took an abrupt right on First Street, but she guided him onto Shore Road, where they curved along the Atlantic and ended up approaching the Point.

"Turn here," Ellen said, gesturing at the next driveway, ahead of them.

Nathan's hands tightened on the wheel as he let his foot up on the gas. "Why do you want to go there, Ellen?"

"To visit a friend."

"Which friend?"

"Well, my friend Bill McAlister," she said, her gaze fixed on the curving slope of the driveway.

"But we were just at his house."

"I want to check his other house."

"Ellen, I don't think that's such a good idea."

"Why?"

"Well, because she was so rude to us the last time we were here."

Ellen turned to stare at him blankly, then looked up at where the slate roof of the house could be seen above the pine trees scattered along the hillside. "She may not be here."

"Well, we don't know that. So why don't we just head back home and try calling him again later on. We'll give him a call in a little while to find out where he is, okay?"

Ellen didn't answer, but as the car rolled past the driveway, Nathan pushed his foot on the gas and propelled them quickly toward home.

Without Leah around, Nathan's life seemed to creep at a glacial pace—making breakfast for Ellen, eyes glazing over at morning television, watching tennis at the club, sitting out on the porch—with nothing to break up the routine. As expected, Leah did not return on Wednesday. But on Thursday, while Ellen napped, Nathan checked the post office box and discovered two cocktail party invitations, a flyer for the Brightonfield Cove Lobsterfest and Firehouse Fund-raiser, and a distinctive pink envelope. His blood surged through his veins and he felt a shortness of breath. Instead of walking back to the house, he decided to walk down to Big Beach, where he could sit undisturbed and devote his whole heart-wrenched attention to the letter. He thought he would wait to sit down before he opened it, but after a minute or so of speed walking, Nathan discovered he couldn't wait. He tore open the envelope and read while staggering like a drunk between the blacktop road and sandy berm.

Hello there, Nathan—

If you received my last letter, you're probably surprised to be hearing from me, but it's late on a Saturday night and I don't feel like talking to anyone except you. The new apartment wasn't working out, so I've moved back into my parents' basement for a little while.

I can remember how once I felt beautiful and successful and confident here, but I'm not so comfortable now, and part of it is that I've been thinking of you. Sometimes it feels like our relationship has been plagued by so much trauma, apprehension, and fear that I can't remember what it was like for us before. I just want things to be normal. Normal, where I am feeling things that could lead to gleeful outcomes. (I think a person should say the word "gleeful" once a day and then meditate on it.) And because I like you so much and we haven't done anything really evil to each other yet. Let's not.

I have pleasant wishes for your summer and for when you return. May you breathe lots of warm summer air, redirect the faith of a certain Sophie Hurst, have your car fixed, stay healthy, think in terms of poetry, learn to love Truffaut, hear a wealth of love songs to create new memories to, eat apple dumplings (my mother just heated some my grandmother made and they are very good), have lots of stars to look at and blond hair (mine) to touch. I miss you.

P.S. And the trauma, apprehension, and fear, well, you figure out what to do with that.

Love,
Sophie

On the beach, Nathan reread the letter several times, sitting with his elbows on his knees, his hands clamped over his ears. He sighed and lifted his head to squint at the families on beach towels and beneath oversize umbrellas, scattered along the ocean's edge. So they hadn't done anything really evil to each other yet.

No, not evil, he supposed. But then what was it to fuck someone else while knowing how much Nathan still loved her? Taking off his shirt, he arranged it behind him so that his back wouldn't touch the hot sand. He draped an arm over his eyes to shield them from the sun and visualized Sophie fucking her dull-eyed, Cro-Magnon boyfriend. The Cro-Magnon kissed her, then bent her over and fucked her with a thick-dicked ferocity that left her panting for more. Nathan had never had these kinds of dark fantasies before Sophie dumped him, fantasies about other, often hugely endowed men having sex with his old girlfriends, but lately he imagined such scenes all the time. At first he worried he might be gay. But remembering that "my cheating wife" stories appeared often in *Penthouse* letters, Nathan felt more at ease. He suspected the fantasies had something to do with self-loathing, and he wondered if dating Leah and eventually feeling better about himself might mean such thoughts would no longer plague him.

Turning to lay his head on his arm, he raised a hand over his eyes to stare at the parents in low, canvas beach chairs, their children in Day-Glo bathing suits frolicking in the shallows of the ocean. How enviably simple and wholesome their lives seemed! After squinting at them for a while, he was surprised he hadn't noticed Eldwin earlier. Even from fifty or so yards away, his heavy-looking head was recognizable. He was sitting in a beach chair, and after a few minutes, Nathan pulled on his shirt and approached him.

"How's it going?" Eldwin said. Despite his wraparound sunglasses, peering up from his book, his face was still pinched by the sun.

"All right. How's it going with you?"

Eldwin stopped craning his neck to look at Nathan and faced the ocean. "Okay," he said, nodding, as if testing the word to find out if it agreed with him. In the shallows of the incoming tide, Eliot and Meghan were searching for shells to take to older children who were constructing a castle.

"What are you reading?"

Eldwin held up the hardback and said, "*Homo Ludens,* by Johan Huizinga. It's about play, about the importance of play."

"I'm for play," Nathan said.

"Me too, but it was the wrong book to bring to the beach."

Nathan crouched down beside Eldwin's chair.

"So what have you and Mrs. Broderick been doing?" Eldwin asked.

"Not a lot. Mr. Buchanan's funeral, and then we've been taking a few drives, but that's about it." Nathan considered telling him about the fire, but he couldn't figure out how to tell him without also mentioning his encounter with Mr. McAlister's wife. Nathan figured the less he talked about it, the less other people would talk about it, and the less likely it would be that he would end up in jail. Instead, he said, "What have you been doing lately?"

"You're looking at it."

"Looks like a good life."

Eldwin said, "Yep." He pulled a pack of cigarettes from his pocket and stuck one in his mouth.

"Have you heard anything from Leah?"

"She's supposed to get back tonight."

"That's good."

"How are things going with her?"

"Okay, I think. Pretty casual. Has she said anything to you?"

"About dating you? I haven't asked her. I think it's probably good that you're keeping it casual, though."

Nathan nodded as he watched the children lift shells out of the water and throw them back behind them into the sea. "Why do you say that?"

Eldwin answered quickly, as if anticipating the question. "I just mean that talking with her mother about her relationships in the past—I'm sure I'm not telling you more than you already know—she had this really serious boyfriend in high school and into college and then she started soon after with this musician guy who wanted her to move with him to New York after they graduated, until they just recently broke up."

Nathan nodded, and grunted affirmatively, trying to remember if Leah had ever mentioned the latter boyfriend.

"So I think Renee—Leah's mother—has just been hoping that Leah would have some time to not be in any serious relationship for a while."

Nathan looked above the children's heads out at the ocean and wanted to be on the distant sailboat billowing across the horizon. "Yeah. It's not that serious. I was actually dating a girl for two years before we broke up a few months ago, so I'm not really looking for anything too hot and heavy, either."

"That's good," Eldwin said. But through his sunglasses it was difficult to tell if he'd been persuaded. To change the subject, Nathan asked about the differences between sea kayaks and river kayaks and this segued into a much more lighthearted conversation about where each of them would like to go kayaking if he had the resources and the time. Nathan thought of maybe paddling around the Pacific coastline of the U.S., but Eldwin talked about navigating through the middle of the country, following the route of Lewis and Clark.

"That'll have to wait for a while, though."

"Because of the kids?"

"Yeah," he said, sounding as if that wasn't the only reason. "That."

"You could always store them in the hatch."

Eldwin flashed a smile in acknowledgment of the joke, but Nathan sensed that jokes about storing children like supplies were probably not as funny to the children's parents. He glanced at Eldwin's watch and said he should probably be heading back to check on Ellen.

"Do you want to go kayaking later this evening?" Eldwin asked.

"What time is Leah supposed to get home?"

"I think not until late."

"What time were you thinking of going?"

"Well, why don't you just come get me after Ellen goes to bed?"

"That sounds good," Nathan said, feeling strangely resigned. For some reason, he had been trying to come up with an excuse for why he couldn't commit to this plan. But what the hell was he afraid of? That Leah would come home early? That he'd be kayaking for an hour—something he had *enjoyed* doing the last time—instead of rushing immediately out to find her? He knew guys back home who were this way: so afraid of missing out on the possibility of something better that they could never say for certain if they would be at a party, or would be interested in hanging out on a given evening, and Nathan disliked this quality in them. He did not want to be like that himself, and for a few moments, while walking home, he was dimly conscious of the way in which a love of freedom can leave you standing still.

On the couch that evening, Nathan reread the letter Sophie had sent him. Then he just stared at the words. There were sentences he did not understand completely, but the general anxiousness of her tone left him feeling like a great weight had lifted from him. He did not want her to fall apart, but, by God, if she was experiencing a little of what he'd experienced—sleepless nights, vomiting due to anxiety, the perpetual hand-wringing over whether the person you love still loves you—well, fine! Wonderful! It was a balm to his heart to think that, when the summer was over, she would be waiting expectantly for him. He would let her sweat it out for a few more days then write a letter or call.

"What do you think about this?" Ellen asked. She was sitting in her lounge chair, sifting through the other mail Nathan had tossed on the end table.

"What do I think about what?" Nathan scooted over to take one of the invitations from her. It was for a cocktail party at one of the houses on their street, scheduled for seven o'clock that very evening.

"Huh," Nathan said, inspecting the card like an artifact while remembering his plans with Eldwin.

"Shall we go?" Ellen asked.

"We could. Do you want to wait a little while and see how we feel?"

Ellen pursed her lips and nodded, as if Nathan had just demonstrated excellent judgment. She returned to her book and he picked up a collection of Jack London short stories he'd found while idly inspecting the living room shelves a few days earlier. They read for more than an hour, until Ellen's eyes closed. Nathan pulled himself quietly from the couch and in the kitchen he mixed a drink. Through the window, the first stars were appearing in the deep indigo sky. When he returned to the living room, he crouched down beside Ellen, and her milky eyes opened.

"Hey, Ellen," he said, touching her arm.

Ellen eyed him blearily.

"You pretty tired?"

"I guess so."

"Do you feel like going to bed?"

Ellen looked around as if searching for something that had changed, but then said, "Why not?" She smiled and patted his hand with such affection that Nathan almost convinced himself he was a quality caregiver after all.

With Ellen tucked safely beneath her comforter, Nathan refilled his drink, then trotted upstairs to change his clothes. In the bottom of his closet lay the wet suit, but the rubber felt so cold and damp he decided to wear just his shorts and hooded sweatshirt.

Outside, the air smelled of cut grass and the sea, and despite the glow of nearby houselights, the sky looked heavy with stars. For a few moments on Harbor Avenue, the only sounds were a distant car starting, and the scuffing of his feet against the gravel, but he soon heard the murmuring of young men behind him. Nathan turned to see Thayer and two others on their way up Ellen's lawn from Parson's Beach. One of Thayer's companions was the handsome, lantern-jawed young man who had been wearing a bathing suit at Thayer's party; the other was a squat, dark-eyed juggernaut with thick lips and curly black hair.

None of the young men returned Nathan's smile when he raised his hand in greeting. "Hey, how's it going?"

Thayer said, "Don't fuck with me, cocksucker."

Nathan watched the three men continue up Harbor Avenue toward him. "What?"

"I said don't fuck with me." Thayer stepped in front of his two companions to put his clenching jaw in Nathan's face. "Just tell me why you were acting so fucking stupid."

"So stupid about what?"

"I said don't fuck with me!" Thayer barked. He slammed his palms into Nathan's chest, propelling him backward a few steps so that Nathan had to wave his hands in front of him to keep from toppling over.

"What the fuck, man?" Nathan said when he had regained his balance. "You mean over at your grandmother's? I was just trying to get out of the fucking driveway. I wasn't trying to hit her."

"Who said anything about trying to hit her?" Thayer asked, turning to both of his friends in mock inquiry. "I didn't say anything about trying to hit her. Why would you say something like that unless you were trying to fucking hit her?" Thayer's voice rose in anger as his hands flew up to push Nathan backward again.

"I wasn't trying to hit her! Mr. McAlister told me that's what you guys thought. But that's not what happened."

Advancing toward him, Thayer said, "Yeah, he told me your bullshit story, but I want to hear the truth, okay? Just tell me the fucking truth and maybe I won't shit down your throat."

"I was just trying to get out of there," Nathan said, "but that driveway is so narrow, I came closer to her than I thought I was going to."

"So why didn't you fucking stop and apologize?"

"I don't know. Your grandmother seemed so pissed off, man, and—I don't know—I should have. I'm sorry."

"Did you ever think that maybe she was angry because you told her to fuck off?"

Nathan smiled at the misunderstanding. "I didn't tell her to fuck off."

Thayer's hands hammered Nathan's chest, sending him backward again. "Don't fucking laugh at me, cocksucker. You think this shit is funny?"

"No, I don't think it's funny. We were just—I just mumbled 'Fuck this' or 'Fuck that' or something, because the whole situation was so fucked up. Ellen didn't know what the hell she was doing, and I was just—"

"Bullshit she didn't know what she was doing! She was up there trying to play some fucking head game, and you were helping her!"

"Man, I'm just her driver."

"You're her fucking bitch is what you are. But you didn't expect to see me there did you, motherfucker?"

Thayer deflected Nathan's outstretched hands to shove him so hard it was like two simultaneous punches that forced Nathan off his feet and into the white cedar hedgerow lining the road. The branches clawed under his sweatshirt and raked his back, but after he sat on the ground a moment, stunned, he pushed himself back up.

"C'mon, you bitch," Thayer taunted. He stood with his feet spread apart, fists raised in anticipation of Nathan's counterattack.

The juggernaut shouted, "Hit him!"

Nathan shook his head and muttered, "Fuck this, I'm not fighting you." He took a few steps toward Ellen's house, but heard crunching gravel and heavy breathing as Thayer sprinted toward him. Nathan swiveled and held his hands close to his head—a defensive posture he'd seen boxers use on television—but it didn't work. Thayer's fist connected just beneath Nathan's right temple and he staggered backward once more into the row of trees. He heard a roar, as if a wave had knocked him over and was still swirling around him. The moist earth soaked through his shorts, and gauging the stiffness of his jaw, he opened his mouth as if to sing his own requiem.

Thayer stood a few yards in front of him while the juggernaut yelled at Nathan to get the fuck off the ground. The lantern-jawed young man stood about thirty yards up Harbor Avenue, nervously glancing at well-lit neighbors' houses. In a loud whisper, he pleaded, "C'mon, dudes, let's just *go!*"

Thayer nodded at his friend's suggestion and took a few steps backward, but then, as a parting gesture, he chuckled, "Stupid fuck," and spat. The wax-colored strand of mucus landed on Nathan's cheekbone just as he was pushing himself out from the hedgerow.

Nathan wiped his cheek with the sleeve of his sweatshirt, then clenched his fists and screamed, "Motherfucker!" as he hurled himself up the hill.

He punched the muscled thickness of Thayer's neck while Thayer swung and missed and hooked his arm around Nathan's head to drag both of them onto the gravel. Wrestling with each other on the small, jagged stones, Nathan struggled free and was halfway into a standing position when Thayer yanked the hood of Nathan's sweatshirt over his eyes and punched him squarely in the forehead.

Nathan managed to stay upright, but his feet worked back and forth beneath him as if trying to balance something very heavy. He pushed the hood off his head and struggled not to go down. He focused on a small willow tree in a neighbor's yard and tried to stop the roaring world from lurching. His jaw ached and his lungs burned and he wondered with contempt why no one had stepped out of a house to rescue him.

The juggernaut snarled, "Now finish the fucker!"

Thayer stood and advanced with a bobbing, fist-raised posture that made Nathan wonder whether they might have taught boxing at Thayer's boarding school. His approach was impressive and fear inspiring, so Nathan crouched, grabbed a handful of pebbles, then whipped them at his opponent's head. Most of the stones missed him entirely, landing softly in the grass or sounding off the clapboards of a nearby house, but a few struck their target. Thayer crumpled, his hands on his face, like a man wracked with grief, and Nathan ran at him, low, wrapping his arms around his midsection and driving them onto the neighbor's lawn.

They landed in a jumble of flailing arms and legs. But seconds later, the juggernaut's hamlike forearms dragged Nathan from the melee to where he could be more easily kicked. The young man's tennis shoe buried itself once in Nathan's stomach, robbing him of his breath, but then Nathan got an arm down to deflect the blows as he inched backward on his side. Unable to see Thayer, Nathan waited for the kick from behind that would rupture his kidneys, or irreparably damage his spine, but in the midst of this panic, he heard an old man's voice.

"Hey, that's enough, you hear me! I said that's enough!" a white-haired man croaked as he pushed open the door of his screened-in porch. He hobbled down the front walk as Nathan coughed and pulled himself up on his knees.

The lantern-jawed young man was already near the top of the road, backing farther and farther away. The juggernaut backed away also, while Thayer, his hand clutched over his right eye, shouted that if Nathan ever came over to his grandmother's house again he'd fucking sew Nathan's dick in his mouth. Later, Nathan would wonder what gangster movies or prison dramas Thayer must have seen to be able to make such vivid threats.

The old man's face recoiled at what he heard. "Hey, hey, I said that's enough. What the hell do you think you're doing out here?"

"Kicking that motherfucker's ass!" Thayer said as he and the juggernaut walked backward up the road.

"I should kick *your* asses!" the old man sputtered.

The man was so *old,* so profoundly incapable of kicking anyone's ass, that except for a snort of laughter from the juggernaut, the comment ended the confrontation entirely. Thayer and the juggernaut turned to walk up the gravel road, occasionally looking behind them, and once erupting in laughter. The old man asked Nathan, "Are you okay?"

Nathan picked himself up and wiped the dust from his clothes. "Yeah, I think so. Thanks for coming out."

"What did they want with you?"

"I'm guessing they wanted to hurt me."

"But why?"

"I don't know."

"Do you want me to call the police?"

Nathan hesitated. He *could* call the police, he realized. The last time he'd been in a fight was in junior high school, but now he was a legal adult. They were *all* legal adults, which meant that with a witness like the old man, Nathan potentially could have Thayer and the juggernaut arrested. Nathan said, "I might call them in a minute, but I want to think."

"Well, all right. How do you feel?"

After assuring the old man he was fine, and thanking him again, Nathan lumbered back to Ellen's house. Inside, it was quiet. Ellen had slept through the war, so Nathan made a beeline for the bathroom. He stared into the mirror a long time, moving backward and forward to assess how noticeable his facial wounds would be to others, and, in particular, to Leah. His right ear looked flushed with embarrassment, and his right cheekbone was scraped and swollen, but he was optimistic that by applying ice to these injuries they would be much less noticeable by morning. What concerned him most was the little knot of exploded blood vessels smack-dab in the middle of his forehead, where Thayer had punched him. Nathan pushed and pressed around the bruise with his thumb and forefinger, attempting to mollify the angry veins and minimize what would otherwise be a mortifyingly conspicuous reminder of his defeat.

He was sitting on the living room couch with a stiff drink and two bags of ice when he heard footsteps on the front porch. Lunging up in hopes of preventing whoever it was from awakening Ellen, Nathan's world tilted. He rested his forearm against the door frame, to keep his balance, and quietly opened the door.

Dressed in his wet suit and black cross trainers, Eldwin looked abruptly confused. "Jesus. What happened?"

Nathan said, "I was getting ready to call you. I was on my way up about a half hour ago when a couple guys kind of attacked me." He barely managed to smile as he stepped further into the porch light and pointed at the dark star on his forehead.

Eldwin grimaced. "Who were they?"

"Mr. McAlister's step-grandson and a couple of his friends. I'd made it to about there when they jumped me." He pointed to where, in the moonlight, he thought he could see bare patches of gravel and broken branches in the hedgerow.

"Why did they want to beat you up?"

Nathan tilted his head and shrugged. "It's kind of a long story." He let go of the door frame. The world seemed momentarily to have righted itself, so he stepped out onto the porch. Bringing the ice bag to his cheekbone, he said, "Have you heard about the fire at Mr. McAlister's house?"

"Yeah, I heard about that," Eldwin said, his voice low with grave concern about how this might pertain to the fight.

Nathan chuckled, but smiling caused a searing pain beneath his right ear. "Fuck. My jaw," Nathan groaned, putting his palm to his cheek. His awareness of how pathetic he must have looked made him laugh again, which made him groan again. Eldwin laughed tentatively with him despite a lingering expression of concern.

"I didn't start the fire," Nathan explained, smiling awkwardly. He sighed and told him the story of the ill-fated visit to Mr. McAlister's wife's house, the conversation with Mr. McAlister, the fire, and then concluded with a blow-by-hurled-gravel account of being pummeled by Thayer and his friend. It was a long story, during which they sat down on the porch chairs, overlooking the harbor, and Eldwin pulled a pack of cigarettes from inside his wet suit. He was well into his second smoke by the time Nathan paused for a reaction.

Eldwin said, "Fuck."

"Yeah," Nathan agreed.

"Do you want me to take you to the hospital?"

"Nah, I think I'm fine. Thanks, though." Nathan removed the ice pack from his cheek and added, "I'm trying to decide whether or not to call the cops."

Eldwin nodded as he took a long drag on his cigarette.

Nathan continued, "I want to call the cops right now and prosecute their asses, put Thayer in fucking jail instead of back at Columbia. But then I think: A) that's a lot of work. That means *I've* got to meet with a lawyer and come back here for the trial, however long that takes, and B) maybe if I don't prosecute them, Thayer and his grandmother won't prosecute me for supposedly trying to hit her with the car."

"How long ago did the incident happen with you supposedly trying to run her over?"

"It's been a few days."

"And you haven't heard anything from the police?"

"Not yet."

Eldwin shook his head. "I don't think you're going to hear anything."

"Yeah?"

"I think if they were going to do it, they would have done it by now. The police would wonder why she waited so long to call them."

Nathan nodded. "It would still be a lot of trouble to come up here after the summer for a trial, though."

"Yeah."

In the silence that followed, Nathan thought about the drink he'd left inside by the couch. "You want anything to drink? I've got wine, or rum and Coke if you want one."

"I haven't had a rum and Coke in a while."

Nathan stood and slowly, carefully, walked inside for the drinks. When he returned, he asked, "Have you ever been in a fight?"

Eldwin exhaled a stream of smoke, squinting as if to see into his past. "I had something like this happen to me when I was in junior high. This guy and his friends chasing me around for a while, and then I got really into ninjutsu—like training to be a ninja." Eldwin tilted his head back and let out a deep laugh, which, noticing Nathan's anxious glance at the upstairs windows, he soon stifled. "I bought some weapons, like throwing stars and nunchucks. But I never used any of it, at least not on *anyone.* I did pretty much destroy my bedroom. The only real altercation I had after junior high was with a police officer when I was in college. I was coming home from a punk show and the officer stopped me because he thought I was drunk. I think I called him a fascist, and he maced me and pushed me down on the ground."

"Whoa—then what happened?"

"He threw me in the back of the car and they put me in the drunk tank overnight, and I had to go to trial and take some classes. I didn't get my license back for a year."

"So you had been drinking?"

"Yeah."

Nathan looked into his glass. "Yeah, you got to be careful with this stuff."

"They say that," Eldwin said.

Sipping their drinks, they watched anchored sailboats bob and tilt almost imperceptibly above the dark water.

"I wish I'd had some throwing stars and nunchucks when Thayer and that fucker attacked me," Nathan announced.

Eldwin reacted to Nathan's half-feigned sincerity with the requisite deadpan nod.

"I would like to take boxing lessons or something," Nathan continued. "When he started coming at me, and even when he was pushing me, I was just kind of paralyzed. I should have been able to react sooner."

Eldwin said, "Aristotle says in the *Ethics* that nobody is born brave, but you become brave by doing brave acts, by making a habit of acting bravely."

Nathan drank and contemplated this wisdom, but something about the notion of bravery turned his thoughts to Leah. When enough time had passed that he thought it would be all right to change the subject, he said, "You know how you were saying this afternoon that you think it's probably wise for Leah and me to keep it casual? Does either of us seem in danger of not taking it casually?"

Eldwin pushed out his lower lip and said, "No, not that I can see. Why?"

"Just wondering," Nathan said, keeping his eyes fixed on the harbor. He took a long drink, finishing off what was left in the glass. "I think I'm in danger."

Eldwin had his elbows on his knees and looked over at Nathan before looking back out at the water. "Yeah?"

"Yeah."

"Well, you can't control those things anyway, so I don't know why I said anything. You think she feels the same way?"

"I don't know. That's what I was trying to get from you."

Eldwin leaned back in his chair. "Everything I know about her I know from her mother, and that's the reason I guess I said what I did a couple days ago. Those first few weeks I think Leah was getting a little stir-crazy up here. That's why I took her to McAlister's party, so that you two could talk. But then the more she went out with you, I began to feel bad because the main reason her mother wanted her to come up here was to help her avoid getting into another serious relationship." Eldwin smiled regretfully. "That woman. My God."

"Her mom?"

"Yeah. She's done an amazing job of making my summer much more complicated. I was debating whether or not to have a nanny come with us, and I made the mistake of mentioning that to Renee before I decided whether it would be a good idea—with Rachel the way she is—or if we could really even afford it. Once I mentioned it to her, though, she just pushed and pushed. She thought that otherwise Leah would end up going straight to New York to be with that musician." Eldwin shook his head. "I'm going to tell you something, but you *cannot* tell her—because if you do, she'll probably leave and go home."

Nathan said, "All right."

"We're able to have her because her mother is supplementing what we pay with her own money, but we're not allowed to tell Leah."

"Whoa."

"So that's why I feel a little guilty about taking her money and then setting Leah up with you."

Nathan laughed, but the sudden sharp pain in his jaw made him whimper.

Eldwin nearly choked on his drink, chuckling. "Are you sure you don't want me to take you to the hospital?"

"No, no. I think I'm good."

"Well, I'm glad you survived. I would have been angry if those guys had killed my kayaking partner."

Nathan smiled, then winced. "Thanks."

"All right. I'm supposed to pick Leah up at the train station at eleven thirty, if you want to come."

Nathan hesitated but shook his head. "Nah." He did not want to look so badly beaten when he saw her again. "I think I should just stay here and keep some ice on my injuries. Try and keep Mount Vesuvius from erupting on my forehead."

Eldwin glanced at his watch. "I should probably walk the dog before I go."

Nathan apologized for not being able to kayak. They made vague plans to do it some other evening, then shook hands good-bye. Inside, Nathan went straight to the bathroom mirror. If all he had suffered had been the scratched and swollen cheekbone, he would have been okay. The abrasion added a tough-guy quality to his face that might have given him a rugged kind of sex appeal. But the blotch on his forehead looked like a sprouting fungus.

He refreshed his drink, then collapsed into Ellen's chair. A police drama was on television, and Nathan watched with a bag of ice cradled against his head. He considered calling his father or even Sophie and telling them an edited version of the fight, a version in which he did not seem so timid and had perhaps landed more blows, but his jaw still felt tight when he yawned, and he couldn't muster the energy.

When the news came on, Nathan turned off the television and trudged upstairs to his room. Stripped down to his boxers, he punched at his reflection to see what he might have looked like during the fight. Then he crawled into bed. With the doors and windows locked, the only sound the quiet lapping of the tide against the shore, Nathan nestled beneath the covers and sighed. He hoped Eldwin would not tell Leah too much about the fight. Nathan was looking forward to telling her his own version of the story, which he hoped would elicit her respect and compassion.

Staring at the wallpaper, he rolled over on his other side and felt immediately dizzy. He closed his eyes, but this only made his nausea worse. So he kept his eyes fixed on the nicked corner of a nearby dresser. The world eventually stood still, but Nathan's face remained hot and his heart pounded againt his chest. Maybe he did have a concussion after all. He tried to remember what he knew about concussions, but all he knew was that sometimes people suffered a severe blow to the head, went to sleep, then never woke up. After a while his face no longer felt flushed and his heart began to beat in normal time. He rolled slowly onto his back, gauging how the nausea increased depending on how quickly he turned. The smart thing would be to drive himself to the hospital and get himself checked out, but how could he drive in this condition? Also, he couldn't just leave Ellen by herself. It was too late to ask Eldwin for help, and besides, Nathan ached with soreness and exhaustion. He wondered if he would die, and what others' reactions would be to his death, until at last his breathing slowed into sleep.

Ten

The Stigma of the Beaten ~ An Unexptected Encounter at the Club ~ Eldwin Speaks of Demons ~ Leah Explains ~ Almost Another Conflagration ~ Ellen Visits Nathan's Bed ~ A Portrait of Desire ~ Consummation on Stone Island

Waking felt like a little victory until he attempted to yawn. Sharp pain radiated through the right side of his face, and as he threw back the sheets, a dull ache swelled in his ribs. He approached the mirror and found that the purplish blotch on his forehead had developed a sickly yellow ring.

"Fuckin' A," he murmured, leaning forward over the bureau for a closer inspection. After he'd dressed, he noticed Ellen was not in her bedroom, and he hurried downstairs into the kitchen.

She was sitting in her bathrobe at the table, chewing an unbuttered piece of toast.

"Morning," Nathan said. Reluctant to explain his injury, he'd already pushed as much hair as he could over his forehead and kept his back to her as he prepared their breakfast.

"Good morning" Ellen said.

Nathan glanced sidelong and was glad to see her staring out the window at the sailboats. He prepared for each of them orange juice, buttered toast, and cereal, and then assumed a weary pose at the table, his forehead resting in his hand. As the minutes passed and the posture became more uncomfortable, however, Nathan accustomed himself to the fact that Ellen would inevitably notice his injury. He couldn't hide it from her forever, and the more uncomfortable his posture became, the more he wanted her to recognize the suffering her madness had caused. Sitting back, he was in the middle of prattling on about the forecast for the next couple of days when he noticed Ellen no longer looking at his eyes but about an inch above and between them.

"What happened to your—?" she asked, pointing to where her own age-spotted forehead was now furrowed with concern.

Nathan gave a pained smile. "Do you remember how I told you that Mr. McAlister's wife was very angry with us for visiting her house, and how she thinks I tried to hit her with the car? Well, her grandson saw me outside last night, and he and a few of his friends attacked me."

"My word," Ellen said, shaking her head. She was still staring at the bruise and Nathan fought the urge to cover it.

"Did they take your money?" she asked.

"Uh, no."

Ellen shook her head sympathetically and picked up her spoon to eat her cereal. They ate in silence for a while, then Nathan cleared his throat and resumed his monologue about the weather.

Later that morning, after the nurse had given her a bath, Ellen asked the question Nathan had hoped not to hear.

"Would you like to go to the club?"

Nathan had spent much of the morning striding in and out of the downstairs bathroom to assess and reassess the garishness of his bruise. In front of the mirror, he would tilt his head in different directions, hoping to discover that the bruise didn't really look as ridiculous as it initially had seemed. But then the unrelenting reality of the purple-yellowish blotch would overwhelm him. Cursing, he would retreat into the living room to flip through a magazine or watch TV, until it occurred to him that perhaps the bruise was not really as bad as he thought, whereupon he would return to the bathroom.

Nathan answered, "We could do that. Or, it's so nice out, we could drive over to Kennebunkport and maybe stop along the way by that place that sells ice cream."

Ellen fingered her chin, looking away, as if to better imagine this possibility, then she wrinkled her nose and asked, "Why don't we go watch some tennis?"

After fetching his keys and wallet, Nathan searched a few of the closets for a baseball cap, but found only Ellen's pastel yellow visor, which, given the situation, he might have worn, if it had not advertised a women's golf tournament. In the upstairs bathroom, after scrounging for makeup that might diminish the obviousness of his injury, he discovered an old tin containing a peach-colored cream. Ellen probably hadn't used this makeup in years—its surface was as cracked as a dried-up riverbed—but Nathan mixed it with some water then spread some onto his bruise. A moment passed during which he stared into the mirror, wondering whether it was better to appear like he'd been beaten, or like he'd been beaten and tried to conceal it by smearing clumpy makeup across his forehead. He washed it off, muttering, then trudged back down the stairs.

At the club, Nathan arranged himself in what was now a familiar pose: head propped in one hand in order to cover his forehead. But as the minutes wore on, he wondered why he felt embarrassed, anyway. This unsightly blotch should shame everyone else at the club, not him! Two of their own had attacked him like animals. Nathan was trying out this new, emboldening way of viewing his bruise—as a kind of third eye whose knowing stare should make *others* uncomfortable—when Kendra Garfield bounded off a near tennis court toward them.

"Ouch," she said, squinting as she wiped the perspiration from her brow. "What happened to you?"

"I was in a fight."

"With who? Oh my God, I think I heard about this. You were fighting Jean's grandson, weren't you?" She gestured out to where Thayer was playing with his back toward them on the far-left-corner court. It shocked Nathan to see him, and he wondered how he could have been so preoccupied with his bruise so as not to have noticed. Thayer and the young woman beside him wore the requisite tennis whites, both listening to the instructions the tennis pro was calling to them across the net. It was impossible to determine the damage the gravel might have done to Thayer's face, even if that had been what Nathan had cared most about at that moment. He leaned forward in his chair to get a better look at Thayer's partner. When the tennis pro served, both Thayer and the young woman waited for the other to hit the ball, letting it bounce out of bounds. The young woman pushed Thayer playfully on the arm, then skipped behind him to pick up a few of the balls scattered along the base of the fence. Crouching, her dark hair fell over her face, and as she pushed it away, tucking a lock behind her ear, Nathan knew it was Leah. For one paralyzing moment, he thought she glanced over and saw him sitting there slack-jawed on the other side of the courts. But if she did, she didn't wave, and he saw no change in her frisky behavior on the court.

"Thayer and one of his friends attacked me," Nathan corrected, although he felt detached from Kendra's inquiry.

"Are you okay?"

"I'm fine."

"Did they do it because of your accident with the cigarette?" Kendra asked, her voice lowered in a tone of genuine sympathy.

Nathan frowned at her. "I don't smoke."

After glancing at Ellen to judge the truthfulness of Nathan's statement, Kendra threw her head back in laughter. "Well, then, I am *all* mixed up about you. Were you even there for Bill's fire?"

It took a while for Nathan to realize she was serious, and that she had heard from someone who had heard from someone that Peewee had been ignited by a stray ember not from the fireplace but from Nathan's carelessly handled cigarette. In grade school Nathan's teacher had played a game wherein she would whisper a sentence to one student and that student would whisper it to another, until it finally arrived at the last student in the class, who then would stand and report what was almost always a hilariously distorted version of what the teacher had initially said. Nathan had loved the game as a child, but now he found its lesson grim. Even as he was explaining to Kendra in detail what had actually happened and, inevitably, why he had been at Mr. McAlister's that evening, he knew that other, competing versions of the story were now circulating and that it was only a matter of time before one of them would be related to Glen.

"So Thayer attacked you because he thinks you tried to hit Jean?"

"That's the reason he's angry with me. He attacked me because he's an ape."

Kendra shook her head.

It seemed almost incomprehensible to Nathan that the conversation could segue to other, less dramatic subjects, but for minutes that seemed like eons, Kendra proved how easily it could be done. She told Ellen that Lucien had to go back to Boston to finish up a real estate deal involving an abandoned theater space that she would help him renovate and convert into condominiums. Ellen nodded politely while Nathan tried not to be obvious about his anxious staring at the far-left-corner court. If Kendra already knew of the fight, then for God's sake, how could Leah not know of it, too? The tennis pro continued serving balls while Leah laughed and talked with Thayer as if he hadn't tried to maim Nathan last evening. Or as if Nathan no longer mattered. When Kendra's daughter came over, hanging on her mother's leg and begging for something to drink, Kendra said gaily, "Good-bye, you two. I hope you feel better, Nathan." She took her daughter's hand and accompanied her into the clubhouse.

Nathan waited a minute, then said, "Ellen, do you mind if we go back to the house for a little while? I'm not feeling very well."

"Oh?"

"Yeah, I just feel kind of achy, and a little bit nauseated."

Ellen tilted her head at him conspiratorially. "Are you bored?"

Nathan hesitated, taken aback by Ellen's sudden watchfulness for deception. "No, I'm not bored at all. It's kind of the opposite. I just feel like going home and lying down for a while." He lifted his forehead from his hand in the hope that revealing his wound might make her feel more sympathetic toward him.

She glanced at the tennis match in front of her and sighed. "Okay, let's go."

On the way back to the car, Nathan had an uncomfortable sensation that Leah and Thayer had stopped their lesson in order to watch him and Ellen leave. His muscles felt coiled with the need to turn and ask Leah what the fuck she thought she was doing, or to sprint to the car and drive away. But he neither turned nor moved faster. He remained beside Ellen, holding her hand against his arm, walking in slow, deliberate steps beneath a sweltering sun.

While Ellen napped, Nathan took great pains not to do something dumb and/or destructive. The view of Albans Bay would be calming, so he sat out on the porch with his sketch pad and Sophie's letter. After sketching for a while, he picked up the pink sheet of paper and initially felt reconnected to her not only because of her alluring words, but because he was touching something that she had touched. He sketched for a while longer, then picked up the letter again. He had hoped having it with him would remind him that she was waiting for him back home, and would make him feel less anxious about what he had witnessed that morning. But the longer he meditated on the letter, the more he remembered all the things that had made his relationship with Sophie so fraught with tension and high drama.

Wearing Jim Beam belt buckles and Harley-Davidson T-shirts with an indeterminate amount of irony, Sophie often made clever, disparaging remarks about brooding artistic types while at the same time voicing genuine enthusiasm for Nathan's art. She made him feel—well, big. Bigger and different from other brooding artistic types, and it was harder to feel that way without her. But she had also been a black hole of neediness, with shockingly little patience when she felt Nathan was taking her for granted. And he had taken her for granted. Many Fridays had passed with Nathan working on his comic instead of accompanying her to some art show or party, and by the time he had realized that he'd lost her, it was already too late.

"If you fuck this guy, it's done," he'd told her the night she announced she was dating someone new.

"It is done, Nathan! It's *over.*"

Nathan hesitated, unsure if she had just admitted to having slept with the Cro-Magnon already, and whether he even wanted to know. "I mean I could never forgive you."

Sophie had had a blemish on her cheek, and Nathan kept hoping that her self-consciousness about it (her pale skin was almost always perfect) would make her softer, more forgiving, but she only whispered, "Well, maybe that will make things easier."

Now, after rereading certain portions of the letter again—*because I like you so much . . . redirect the faith of a certain Sophie Hurst . . . have lots of stars to look at and blond hair (mine) to touch*—Nathan took it with him into the bathroom. He tried imagining having sex with her again, but these thoughts morphed into fantasies of sex with Leah, and then of sex between Leah and Thayer, until Nathan's desire passed from him and he rested his head against the cool, blue tile wall.

Drained of the energy to sketch, he poured himself a drink and fell into Ellen's living room chair. Clouds passed in front of the sun so that rhomboids of light at his feet became the same drab mauve as the rest of the carpet. Nathan turned on the television and watched an old G.I. Joe cartoon he used to watch as a child after school, while his mother cooked supper upstairs. All of this contributed to Nathan's sense of being slowly suffocated by the stale atmosphere of the afternoon. He reconsidered going out onto the porch to sketch again, but sketching required concentration and he now could think of little else besides Leah. Hearing her explain the situation—if only to confirm Nathan's suspicion that she was more attracted to Thayer—would be preferable to his own darkly churning thoughts. After mixing another drink, and watching the rest of

G.I. Joe, he conducted another fruitless search for a man's hat, then walked outside to find her.

Eldwin answered the door of his house, massaging the imprint of a wrinkled bedsheet on his left cheek. "Come on in," he said, yawningly, pushing open the screen door for Nathan to follow him. The interior of the house looked much as Nathan remembered. In the living room, blocks and puzzle pieces were strewn over the throw rug, while clothes and beach towels were draped haphazardly across the furniture. But most of the disorder was in the kitchen. Eldwin leaned over a sink stacked high with dirty dishes to peer out the window at the empty play set in the yard. "I guess they're not here. Maybe they went down to the beach."

"Did I wake you up?"

"Yeah, but I was just dozing on and off. I should probably get up, anyway. If I get on Rachel's sleep schedule, I'll never leave the house. You want anything to drink?" He opened the refrigerator. "We've got soda, orange juice, beer?"

"I'll have a beer."

They sat at the kitchen table with their beers among a scattering of bowls of half-eaten cereal. Nathan counted nine of them and wondered how long they had been there.

"How's your head feeling?"

"Better than it looks." Nathan leaned back in his chair, resisting the temptation to put his hand over his forehead. "I think I'm going to buy a hat."

"Could you maybe pop the darker parts—let some of the blood out?"

Nathan glanced around for a mirror, but couldn't find one. "I don't know. Jesus. Can you pop a bruise?"

"I don't know," Eldwin said, slowly peeling the label from his beer. "It just looks like you've got some blood trapped in there."

"I think I'm just going to buy a hat."

"It doesn't look that bad," Eldwin said. "People won't shriek when they see you. Children, maybe. But not adults."

"How did it go picking up Leah last night?" Nathan asked.

"Her train got delayed so she didn't get in till one thirty in the morning."

"What did she say about her trip?"

"She said it went okay. We didn't talk that much, it was so late."

"Did you tell her about Thayer attacking me?"

Eldwin shook his head. "No. I didn't know if you wanted to tell anyone."

"I saw her today at the club, playing tennis with him."

"Thayer?" Eldwin asked. "Are you serious?"

"Yeah. I don't know if she knows about the fight, though. I guess she does. I mean, other people at the club knew about it, and I'm guessing he would have some scratches and bruises he'd have to explain."

The family Labrador had begun barking in the side yard, and Eldwin stood to open the side door. "Harmon!" Eldwin called. Then, turning to Nathan: "Do you feel like walking down to the beach?"

Outside, the sun burned through the clouds to make for a hazy, humid afternoon. As they walked over a small rise in Ellen's yard to allow them to survey Parson's Beach, he saw no sign of Leah. Two older women were lying out beneath an umbrella near the dunes. After he and Eldwin had walked past them, both women glancing twice at Nathan's head as they said hello, Eldwin took the leash off of Harmon and let him bound through the water. Eldwin asked if Nathan had been doing much drawing lately, and Nathan admitted he'd been doing some.

"What kind of stuff?"

"Just occasional landscapes and portraits, some scenes that have taken place while I've been here."

"Are these scenes you think you'll use later in a graphic novel?"

Nathan said, "I don't know. I don't know if I'm going to do graphic novels anymore. It's solitary as hell, and I'm never really happy with what I've done."

"Sounds like being a pastor."

Nathan smiled. "But it's not *that* lonely, is it? Your job seems pretty social—going around, talking with people, spreading the good news."

Eldwin tucked his chin down into his neck. "Yeah, but most people don't want to hear their pastor tell them about his own demons or his own crises of faith."

"You're talking about metaphorical demons, right?"

"Right."

"Hmm. I would be more interested if you had literal demons."

Eldwin chuckled in a constricted way that seemed to push down something within him.

Nathan said, "So why do you do it?"

"Why do I continue being a pastor? Fuck. Well, there are moments when it makes me happy, definitely, but I don't think life is just about achieving your own happiness. Happiness is important, although it's interesting that no one really talked about happiness before Socrates. But I think that living a virtuous life is more important."

"Yeah?"

"I'm married to a woman who right now is . . . I don't know what's going on, Nathan. But she's seriously, seriously depressed. So depressed that I can barely get her interested in what our kids are doing, and our last attempt at sex was like necrophilia." Eldwin was fumbling to pull a cigarette out of its pack. "But what am I supposed to do? I have to believe that making some sacrifices, enduring some hardships, is part of living a virtuous life. And that in the end, the reward of such a life might be a deeper, more substantive happiness than I could otherwise have known."

Eldwin lit the cigarette and inhaled deeply.

Nathan asked, "Is she on any medication?"

"Yeah, she's on Zoloft now, but it gives her gas," Eldwin said. He called Harmon out of the water.

On their way up the yard, Nathan glanced at the house and was startled to see Ellen standing on the porch, hands perched on the railing, overlooking the harbor. In her tatty blue bathrobe, her long, white hair billowing back off her shoulders, she looked like an aged Penelope still waiting for Odysseus to return.

They did not have enough food, Ellen said, and after a quick look in the refrigerator, Nathan agreed to take her to Gilman's. The cashiers and clerks there had asked about her so often in the past that Nathan escorted her through the screen door, ready to bask in the glow of her celebrity. Meg, the cashier, waddled out from behind the counter with arms outstretched; then, perhaps deciding a hug might be too presumptuous, simply clasped Ellen's free hand.

"Hey, Frank? Cindy?" Meg called out above the aisles in her low, cigarette-scarred voice. Only Frank was available. He emerged from the back of the store, donning his glasses and smiling broadly, as if he'd sensed all day that something good was going to happen, and here it was. They talked about the new aisle of organic food they'd added to the store and the fresh seafood they'd just received, and after enough time had passed for them to understand that Ellen would smile and say things like, "Oh, that's wonderful," but would no longer talk with them in the way, perhaps, they remembered, Nathan escorted Ellen to the dining booths along the back wall. There was a newspaper on a nearby counter, and Nathan brought it over to where she sat beside a window overlooking the bay. He had been shopping for just a few minutes, crouching down to survey the cans of clam chowder, when the front screen door creaked open and he heard sandaled feet slapping across the linoleum floor.

"Don't run," came a woman's voice, and Nathan recognized it as Leah's.

He stayed crouched as the children opened and shut the sliding glass refrigerator doors, but then he stood to peek over the aisles. Eliot and Meghan stood with their backs to him, dressed in bathing suits and T-shirts, picking through the lower shelves of ice-cream sandwiches and freezer pops, chirping to each other about which would be the better option. Leah stood behind them in a T-shirt that stretched down to the back of her thighs.

"You don't have to keep the door open," she admonished, but apparently noticing Ellen at the back of the store, Leah abruptly turned to look behind her.

Nathan stared down at the can of clam chowder he was holding, and then, although he knew his face was flushed, looked up and feigned surprise. "Hey," he said, lifting the can of soup in salutation.

Leah reminded the children to keep the door closed until they made their choice, then she walked over to talk with Nathan. Her flawless, radiant face compelled him to raise a palm to his forehead and force a smile.

"So, how was New York?" he asked.

"It was really good. Is that from the fight?"

Nathan let his hand drop. "Hmm. Yeah."

"Are you okay?"

"I'm fine. Did you hear about it before or after your tennis lesson?"

Leah looked pained. "He told me after the lesson. He'd left a message for me earlier asking if I wanted to join him, because Danielle couldn't make it. I didn't know at the time you'd been in a fight with him."

Nathan shrugged but said nothing.

"So you were there at the club today?" Leah asked.

"Yeah, I was."

"Why didn't you say something to me?"

"You were having your lesson and Ellen wasn't feeling well, so we had to go."

Leah glanced back at where Ellen was staring out the window at the water.

"Is she okay?"

"Yeah, she seems better now."

Eldwin's children wandered uncertainly behind Leah, Meghan carrying her freezer pop and Eliot already chomping into his ice-cream sandwich. Dark crumbs clung to his lips, as if he'd been eating dirt.

"Are you guys ready?" Leah asked.

Eliot said, "What happened to your head?"

"I got hit."

"By what?"

"Well, I'm not sure. I couldn't see."

"But what do you *think* it was?"

"I think it was an ape."

"An ape?" Eliot screwed up his face at Leah, wondering if he was supposed to believe such an answer. But Leah only cocked an eyebrow at him in feigned confusion, then asked him and Meghan to follow her to the checkout. Her assistance in keeping information from the children made Nathan feel close to her again, and he sensed that such collusion must be one of the pleasures of parenting.

"Do you want to take a walk later?" Leah asked, prying Meghan from her leg to hold the child's hand.

"Yeah, I could probably do that."

Walking backward toward the cashier, she said, "I'll try and stop by after they've gone to bed."

Nathan peered down at the autumn-colored soup cans arrayed in front of him, but he could not stop glancing at Leah. After she paid, she held the front door open, letting the children pass beneath her outstretched arm. Eliot bounded outside to shout at someone, and Leah glanced back at Nathan, smiling and shaking her head. Nathan smiled down at the can of clam chowder in his hand and read and reread the label several times before the words began to make any sense to him.

For dinner Nathan decided to grill salmon. He'd found some old coal downstairs in a corner of the cellar when he arrived. But when he tried to throw it out, Ellen had entered the kitchen just as he was stuffing the crumpled bag into the trash.

"Are there still coals in there?" she asked.

"Yeah, but they're really old. I tried using them last night and they don't light very well."

"They don't light at all?"

"Well, they *light.* It just takes forever to get them going."

Ellen pulled one of the coals out of the bag and held it up like a giant diamond. "Well, why don't you try and use them up?"

Nathan used the old coals, but he doubted it saved Ellen money. He had to empty nearly a quarter of the container of lighter fluid just to get the briquettes to light. It was even more difficult when the briquettes were damp. This had occurred a few times because the grill lid was missing a piece to close its ventilation, and because it had not occurred to Nathan until recently to pull the grill into a corner of the porch where it could be shielded from the rain by a nearby tree.

Due to a sticky wheel that made the grill frustrating to maneuver, on this sunny evening Nathan pulled the grill away from overhanging tree branches, but not very far from the house. When he tossed the match onto the coals, the flames jumped two to three feet into the air, which he expected, but then licked at the house's clapboards, which he had not expected at all.

Almost unconsciously it occurred to Nathan that if he burned down this house, the story about igniting Peewee with his cigarette would now be considered more sinister by those who didn't know any better. Had it really been an accident? Might it be more than coincidental that he was involved in two devastating house fires? Nathan crouched to grab the handle and drag the grill a few feet more toward the railing, but the clapboards were already aflame. Swiveling his head, scanning the empty beach, he breathlessly murmured, "Oh help," before realizing that the only time to prevent disaster was now. He tried pouring his rum and Coke on the fire, but the stream splattered too far to the right, and it was only after he pulled off his favorite gray T-shirt to beat the flames that he was finally able to subdue them. An ashen streak roughly a foot wide and three feet high remained on the white siding. Nathan cursed as he inspected his shirt for singe marks, then, half-blinded by the alabaster sheen of his chest, he pulled the shirt back over his head.

When Ellen hobbled out of the kitchen, Nathan tried to situate himself between her and the burnt clapboards. But Ellen gestured behind him with her cane.

"What happened there?"

Turning behind him to face the damage, Nathan found it just as bad as he remembered. "You know how I was telling you those coals I've been using were really old?" he began. He omitted the part about the initial proximity of the grill to the house, but concluded by saying, "I'll get it fixed in the next couple of days."

When Ellen ambled back inside, Nathan licked his thumb, pleased to find he was able to rub some of the smoke stain off the otherwise pristine siding. Perhaps he could perform the repair himself. He flipped the salmon over and leaned back on the railing, inhaling deep lungfuls of air that smelled—depending on which way the wind blew—of charcoal and salmon or of flowering trees and the ocean. The twilight had turned the white porch such a luminous seashell pink that if Ellen had been a better conversationalist, he might have asked her to dine outside. Most of their meals now took place in the living room, in front of the television, which was why, when the salmon was ready, Nathan found Ellen in her recliner, waiting for him to pull her TV tray out from alongside the couch. In those rare, delightful moments when the television made no sound, it was possible to hear live voices and laughter wafting up to them from Parson's Beach. That was where real life was being lived. The fading light of the room and *Wheel of Fortune*'s strained conviviality and Ellen's still clinking silverware all felt like a heavy shroud on Nathan's soul. He had started clearing the dishes and dismantling Ellen's TV tray when Mr. McAlister appeared at the door.

"Anybody home?" His blue oxford shirt looked freshly ironed, and he was smiling inscrutably. As Nathan allowed him inside, Mr. McAlister said, "I hope I'm not barging in on you; I was just down on the beach, and thought I'd come up and see if you two were still alive."

Ellen had leaned forward in her recliner to see him better, and remained perched on its edge. "Oh, Bill, you're not barging in at all."

Nathan turned off the television. "Would you like anything to drink?"

When he finished clearing the dishes and poured Mr. McAlister a glass of wine, Nathan returned to find him on the couch, his right hand resting on Ellen's. The older man let go of her hand to take the glass, his face uncharacteristically open and inquisitive. "I was just telling Ellen about what happened the other night. I . . . that didn't happen to you during the fire, did it?"

Nathan shook his head and stopped himself from touching his bruise. "Thayer and his friends attacked me last night."

Mr. McAlister licked his lower lip, saying, "I heard about that. I'm sorry that happened. I had a long talk with him about it, and I think he feels sorry too. I think he and his friends had been drinking, unfortunately. He said you threw some gravel at him?"

Nathan stared at Mr. McAlister with eyes that dared him to continue this line of questioning. "Yeah, I did."

Mr. McAlister looked away and sipped his merlot. "Well. You didn't get a lot of smoke in you during the fire, did you?"

"I think I'm fine."

As Mr. McAlister talked more about the plans for his home, Nathan quietly refilled Ellen's sherry glass and returned to the kitchen. He washed their lunch and dinner dishes, then retreated up the back stairs to his room.

Stretched out on his bed, he watched the dying twilight leach the blues and yellows from the unmanned sailboats on his wallpaper. The evening's darkness weighed heavily, and to slide out from beneath it Nathan stood, turned on his desk lamp, and flipped to an empty page in his sketchbook. He drew several rough sketches of the scene that afternoon at Gilman's. But the more he thought about his conversation with Leah, the more he stared out the window. In the hours after their encounter, why had he felt so relieved? Sure, she may not have known about the fight until after her tennis lesson, but hadn't he seen her flirting with Thayer?

In his sketchbook, Nathan had not yet drawn the moment when Leah came into the store, and now the idea of depicting his conversation with her exhausted him. With a sigh he returned to his bed and thumbed through some of the comics he had brought from home.

From downstairs he could occasionally hear the low rise and fall of Mr.

McAlister's voice. There was eventually an exchange of good-byes, and then the front door rattled closed. The stairs moaned as Ellen climbed them, and Nathan was struck with sudden dread that seeing his light on in the bedroom, she might visit, when what he wanted was for her to sleep. It was too late for him to scramble under the covers, but with only a minor whimpering from the bedsprings, he leaned over to turn off the lamp.

The stairs stopped their moaning. He waited, listening for the sound of her bedroom door creaking open, but heard the macramé brick door-stop of his own room slowly sliding across the hardwood floor. As the beam of hallway light widened across his room, Nathan closed his eyes. He waited for Ellen to draw the door shut, but the light remained, and a moment later he could hear her shuffling, and the gentle thud of her cane on the floor. Nathan kept his eyes closed, lying fetally on top of his white comforter. When she halted, her labored, whistling breath close enough that he knew she could reach out and caress him, she turned and eased herself onto the bed, sinking Nathan a few inches in her direction so he was almost spooning against her. He wondered if she could hear his throbbing heart. He twitched and made a grunting *I'm deep in REM sleep* kind of noise and turned away from her. For what seemed a long time, he felt his backside against hers and waited for the tremulous sound of her voice or the gentle stroke of her hand. But when she finally pulled herself up to leave, and Nathan no longer worried about her touching him, the shuffling of her white sneakers seemed like the loneliest sound in the world.

In the shadowy living room light—where he hoped his bruise would not be so noticeable—Nathan read on the couch, wishing he knew what time Leah planned to come over. It was too late to call her now. He read for another half hour and felt relief as much as surprise when she tapped on the window behind him. She apologized for being late and explained that Eliot had drunk two glasses of soda during dinner and could not keep his hypercaffeinated self in bed. Glancing up at the ceiling, she whispered, "Is Ellen asleep?"

On the outer edge of the soft lamplight, Leah's face reminded Nathan of an old master's painting, and he might have leaned over to kiss her if she hadn't been looking at his bruise.

"Yeah, I think she's probably asleep by now." He told her about Ellen's visit to his bedroom, and Leah's dark eyes grew wide. "Whoa, that's cuckoo. What do you think she was thinking?"

"I have no idea."

"Maybe she thought you were her husband, or Mr. McAlister."

"I think she probably just wanted to talk or something."

"What if she does it again and tries to kiss you?"

"With tongue or without?"

Leah cinched her mouth to the right and shook her head. Nathan maintained his innocently inquisitive expression, but she ignored him. "So what were you drawing when she interrupted you?"

Something about the way she elongated the word "draw-ing" made Nathan sense that she half-expected him to say, You. So he shrugged and told her that he'd just been doing some sketches of Albans Bay.

"Can I see them?"

Taking a seat on the couch, Nathan left enough room for her to sit comfortably between him and the armrest. "Ah, I'm just starting on them, plus they're upstairs."

"I want to see them."

"Well, I'm flattered."

"They're in your bedroom?" Leah looked at him with a child's hopeful expression. She was wearing a long-sleeved black T-shirt pulled up to her forearms and a black and tan headband to keep her hair out of her eyes.

"Yeah, they are, which is right next door to Ellen's bedroom, so it's probably not a good idea to go in there now."

"I'll be quiet," she whispered, raising her fingers to her lips as she ascended the first few steps of the staircase. Once she saw he was following, she laughed, covering her mouth with her hand. She was stepping in the dead center of the stairs—making them groan more than necessary—but they made it into the bedroom. Nathan shut the warped door as far as it would go, then pushed the macramé doorstop against it to keep it closed. Leah sat down on the bed with so little restraint that the springs virtually screamed. Nathan gave her a stern look, raised his hand, then put his ear to the crack in the door.

On his way to the bed, he whispered, "We have to be super quiet."

"What about moaning?"

"No, no moaning."

"You moan."

"I do not."

"Yes, you do. You moan every time we kiss," Leah said, kicking off her sandals and pulling one foot up to rest against the inside of her thigh. "Now come here and let me see your forehead."

Nathan did not want her to see his bruise in the harsh light of the bedside lamp, so he sat a few feet away from her. She edged closer and put a hand on his forehead to inspect his injury. "You poor baby. Okay, so tell me how this happened. You were on your way to visit Eldwin?"

"We were going to go kayaking," Nathan said. He was grateful for the manly sound of that statement before he gave an account of the attack, which inevitably became a blend of what actually had happened and what Nathan wished and sometimes came to believe had happened: an account in which his hesitancy was not a coward's paralysis, but a mature man's desire for peace, and where, once peace was no longer an option, he struck back with shocking force and ability.

Still, the part about whipping gravel at Thayer's face had to be handled delicately. Nathan might have omitted it altogether, but he was sure she would hear about it sometime. So he said he only threw the gravel when it appeared that he was going to have to fight the juggernaut, too.

"Was his name Brett?" Leah asked. She provided a physical description that matched the juggernaut, but failed to give his densely muscled features their due.

"I don't know." Nathan lay down on his side with his head propped on his hand. "You didn't see any marks on Thayer, like on his face, where the gravel hit him?"

"No, but I wasn't looking for it, either. Would it make you feel better if he had marks on him?"

"Fuck, yes."

"Well, I'll look closer next time I see him."

"Has he asked you to do something else with him?"

"No, but I think Danielle goes back to New York a lot and that's who he signed up for lessons with, so I don't know. Do you care if I take lessons with him?"

It took a moment for Nathan to see she was being serious. Then he said, "No. I mean, that's up to you."

"I just think he was upset with you because he thought you were trying to hurt his grandmother. Plus, he was drunk. And I kind of have to stay friends with him so that his grandfather might help me get a job."

"Hmm."

"I'm sorry you got hurt."

"I'm not hurt. The motherfucker just sucker-punched me where it looks bad."

Silence filled the room. Leah reached for Nathan's hand. "Will you show me what you've been drawing?" She looked at him with such innocent eyes that Nathan couldn't determine if she was being ironic or sincere.

He retrieved his sketch pad from the desk and laid it in front of them on the bed. He sat close enough to her that their bodies often brushed against each other. For the most part, his sketches were done in more of a cross-hatching style than he often employed in his graphic novel. He tried to flip through some of the earlier ones he'd done of his parents, and the library where he'd worked, and the other renters in the house where he'd lived, but she slowed him down. "Is that your mom?" she asked.

The sketch was of his mother in the middle of his parents' backyard garden. She was dressed in jeans and an old sweatshirt and had her arm propped on top of a freestanding birdhouse. Her face was already thin and jaundiced due to her monthly chemotherapy treatments but she was still smiling in the broad, life-filled way that often made Nathan wonder if such happiness could be had without religion. "Yeah, that was her."

"That's a good drawing."

Nathan continued flipping the pages—identifying different people from his past and attempting to skip over occasionally vulgar illustrations, which Leah inevitably fought to see. She looked for a long time at a woman with a gigantic vagina that contained a small, scruffy man. He was leaning against a vaginal wall, crying, *I just want to go home.*

"I think I was drunk when I did that," Nathan lied.

He turned the pages to find more illustrations of himself and Ellen on her front porch, overlooking Albans Bay, and of Mr. McAlister racing out of his burning house, beads of perspiration jumping from his forehead, teeth clamped on a lit cigar. Then Nathan turned to a more intricately detailed, cross-hatched illustration of Leah sitting in her bathing suit on Parson's Beach, smiling at the viewer through windswept hair.

"Is that me?" Leah whispered.

"Well, it's going to be. I'm kind of still working on it."

"It's beautiful."

"Lord, you're vain."

"I think your *drawing* is beautiful, stupid."

Nathan was about to lean over and kiss her without moaning, but she asked if he would do a sketch of her so she could watch.

"Draw one right now?"

"Yeah, I want to see how you do it. I want to see the artist at work."

"But I don't have my beret with me."

"Your beret?"

"Yeah, I usually wear it at a rakish angle while I'm creating beautiful works of art."

Leah leveled her gaze at him. "Just tell me where I'm supposed to sit."

"This isn't going to be very good. It takes time to do a good drawing."

"I have time," Leah said, affecting a regal air as she sat down in the desk chair. "How's this?"

"Quit posing like the queen of England, and sit in a way that's going to be comfortable for a while," Nathan instructed. While he turned the pages of his sketchbook, he asked about her trip to New York. She said she had fun, hanging out with her sister Lindsey and their mom, looking over Lindsey's dress and helping decide what the bridesmaids were going to wear. But it was also kind of crazy, because one night when their mother had gone to bed and they'd stayed up late talking, Lindsey confessed to Leah about having cheated on her fiancé. It was not the first time she had cheated on him, but it was the first time she had cheated on him since they'd been engaged. Her fiancé, Justin, worked as a—well, Leah didn't know what you called him, but he worked on TV show sets arranging outdoor scenes and mostly moving equipment around. Last month while she was visiting the set of *NYPD Blue* (which normally filmed in L.A. but was being shot in New York for a few weeks), Lindsey had been talking to an actor named Ryan Parker, and when he'd invited her inside an empty trailer, they'd made out like teenagers for half an hour.

Nathan looked up from the first rough lines he'd drawn to try and center the portrait around her warm eyes. "So what is she thinking now?"

"Oh, she's still getting married. I think she just thinks of it as a bump in the road."

"You sure it wasn't a hump?"

"Noooo, all they did was kiss."

"For half an hour."

"Yes."

Nathan nodded and refocused his concentration, wanting to make sure that he had drawn the amused curve of her lips before compelling her to speak again. When a few minutes had passed, he said, "Did you visit your ex-boyfriend when you were there?"

Leah hesitated but then shrugged. "Yeah, he fixed me dinner at his skanky co-op one night. Eldwin told you about him?"

"He assumed I already knew." Nathan let her acknowledgment of this most recent boyfriend—a boyfriend she'd never mentioned to him—linger like a ghost in the room. "So what was skanky about his co-op?"

"It was just dirty. The kitchen was dirty, the bathroom was dirty, *they* were dirty. It's like the whole house was all artists and musicians, and none of them could take the time to wash a glass."

"Hmm." Nathan nodded sympathetically, although more conscious now of the pile of dirty clothes beside his closet.

"And I think they wanted me to have group sex with them."

Nathan smiled uncertainly but kept his eyes on his drawing. "Yeah? What makes you say that?"

"After dinner, I was in Marcus's room and we were just talking, but you could hear other people in the room next to us having sex, and it sounded like it was more than one woman."

"Maybe it was a lesbian couple."

"No, I heard a guy's voice, too."

"What was he saying?"

"He was just mumbling and grunting. I did hear him say, 'Now back that up.'" Leah tried to imitate the man's guttural voice, but then she broke down laughing, leaning over with hands clasped.

Nathan told her to hush and waited for her to right herself again. "Well, what makes you think they wanted to have sex with you?"

"First of all, who wouldn't want to have sex with me?" Leah smiled with an only slightly ironic glint in her eyes. "Second, we'd just had dinner with these people. I mean, we were all sitting around, and when they got up to leave there was just a weird, kinky vibe in the room. I don't know. I don't think I would have thought anything of it, but Marcus said we should go over and knock on the door."

"Whoa, he said that?"

"Mmm-hmm."

"What did you say?"

"I said, 'Hell, no.' I wasn't going to interrupt a group of people having sex."

"So you think Marcus wanted you to participate in group sex with him?" Nathan asked, wonderingly.

"Yes, Midwestern boy. That's what I'm telling you."

Nathan shook his head but did not look up from the drawing.

"Would you ever have sex with more than one person?" Leah asked.

Nathan's eyes widened. "You mean at the same time? I don't know. It sounds kind of complicated. I'm not sure where everything would go."

"I thought that was every boy's dream. Two girls at one time. I don't think you can know until you've been asked."

"That's probably true."

"Lindsey went down to this resort in Jamaica with this friend of hers and they said there was tons of group sex going on—that people would just meet in the pool or in the hot tub, and then you'd see a group of them leaving together."

"Did Lindsey do it?"

"Well, she said this one guy who looked just like Richard Gere invited her to go with him and his wife upstairs to their room to have drinks, but she didn't go. She said it was happening *so* much that it began to seem normal. For one week she could resist it, but she said if she was down there for two weeks, she wasn't sure."

A moment passed and Nathan sighed. "All right, we've got to talk about something else. How was your interview with what's his face?"

Leah laughed. "Why do we have to talk about something else?"

"I can't concentrate."

"Oh."

"So how was your interview with what's his face?"

"I think it went okay, but who knows?"

"What'd you talk about with him?"

"Books—about the kind of fiction I like and want to help publish. I think I kind of ended on a good note with him. When we were getting up to leave, he asked me if there was anything else he should know about me, and I told him I was addicted to lip balm, and he said he was, too."

They talked for a while about her job search until it was clear that she wasn't searching for a particular job in publishing—as an assistant editor, say, or publicist—but for almost any job in the industry. Her fondness for books was intertwined with an idea of life in New York City as she'd witnessed it in early Woody Allen movies. Such people—hadn't she just met some at Epoch?—spent their days performing thoughtful, gratifying work, then retired to friends' spacious, book-lined apartments to laugh and drink wine with other smart and stylish New Yorkers. Leah wanted to find a way to be included.

Nathan occasionally looked up to view the lovely, shadowed hollow at the base of her neck, or the loose, lustrous curls of her hair. He was aware of the sound of his pencil scratching against the paper and how long it was taking to draw her.

"What are you thinking about?" Leah asked.

"I'm thinking about you."

"What about me?"

"I was thinking about how much you've slouched from your original posture."

Leah sat up and resumed a ridiculously regal demeanor, then sighed into a pose that was not quite as she'd originally been sitting.

Nathan said, "I was also thinking that for the next portrait, you should be stretched out nude on top of my bed with a pencil tucked behind your ear . . . like you're copyediting or writing a press release or something."

"Weren't you just talking about having problems concentrating?"

"The nudity wouldn't be about your . . . nudity . . . but about creating a representation of the purity of your devotion to the craft."

"What craft?"

"Nude copyediting, or nude press release writing."

Leah sighed as if disappointed with his tactless methods of trying to see her naked. But a moment later she asked, "Would it be any easier for you if I sat closer—to make sure you're getting it right?"

Nathan feigned indifference, but she sat on the edge of the bed, close enough that he could smell the apple scent of her shampoo. She tucked a lock of hair behind her ear and stared up at him through long lashes. Nathan pretended to concentrate on the drawing as Leah leaned far enough forward that he could feel her breath on his neck. She looked down at the sketch. "I look blurry," she whispered.

"Well, it's a rough sketch—like an outline."

"Am I blurry to you?" she asked, leaning closer.

"You make me feel blurry," Nathan said, which was true, generally, but right then he felt like he'd been holding his breath a long time and that kissing her was like breathing. The sketchbook dropped to the floor as he and Leah scooted back on the bed with one of Nathan's hands clasped behind her slender neck. In time, as they kissed, he brought the same hand over her right breast and then underneath her shirt to feel the warm smoothness of her skin.

Leah flinched and whispered, "Your hands are cold."

"I'm trying to warm them."

Her forehead pressed against his, and he moved his head away to kiss her, but also to take the excruciating pressure off his bruise. They pulled the covers back and scrambled beneath them, kicking off shoes, pulling off shirts, until the creaking springs sounded so much like the cliché sex sounds of movies that they stopped. Leah laughed into Nathan's shoulder. He reached over to turn off the lamp. When they were both undressed to their underwear, Leah whispered, "I don't think we should have sex."

"All right." Nathan had an old condom in his wallet, and he had been hoping that the evening would end in lovemaking, not wholly for the sensual pleasure—although that was no small part—but also because it would be a way of pulling her closer, of establishing, implicitly, that he had nothing (besides bodily harm) to fear from Thayer or any other young man.

"Is that okay?" she asked.

"Yeah, no, of course," he said, wrapping his arm around her and pulling her toward him. As his eyes adjusted to the darkness, and he glanced down at her lovely, moonlit shoulders, Nathan's discontent evolved into something like gratitude. Sex was apparently a gift she bestowed only on the most worthy, and Nathan's heart lightened at the possibility that he might be worthy, if he tried.

By the time Leah arrived Saturday evening, Nathan had already filled a picnic basket with a bottle of pinot noir, a wedge of Brie, a baguette, and a blanket from one of the spare bedrooms. As they left the house, he pulled a flashlight out of his back pocket and she followed him toward the shed. Opening the white wooden doors, Nathan shone the broad beam of light over old fishing poles, garden tools, and finally the *Little Red Hen*.

"You might have to go alone," Leah said, frowning beside the small rowboat.

"Why?"

"Because I think we're both going to drown if we go out in that thing."

"We're not going to drown. It just looks old. It *is* old, but it works." Nathan pulled the boat down off its stern to conduct a more thorough inspection.

Crouching down to pull a piece of flaking paint off the interior, Leah asked, "How do you *know* that it works?"

"Because Thayer borrowed it a little while ago and unfortunately survived the experience." Nathan pressed his hand against the floor of the boat to check for dampness even though he knew any water that had seeped in while Thayer was using it would have already dried. In the flashlight's sickly beam, the boat looked older than Nathan remembered, and now that he was planning to use the boat himself, the amount of peeling paint disturbed him. He had been looking forward to the trip, but now he hoped Leah would try again to dissuade him.

"All right," Leah sighed with arms crossed, shifting her weight. "But if you kill me, I'm going to be pissed."

Leah picked up the oars, picnic basket, and blanket while Nathan pulled the boat upright and carried it out onto the lawn. He positioned himself under the boat, knees bent, then hefted it above him. He staggered forward a few steps to find his balance.

"Do you want me to help you?" Leah whispered.

"No, I'm good," Nathan said, frustrated by the heaviness of the boat, remembering how easily Thayer had borne the weight. As Thayer had done, Nathan held on to both sides, with the boat a foot or so above his head, but a few steps down the lawn he let the boat rest upon his stooped shoulders.

"Are you sure? That looks painful."

"It is painful," Nathan said.

He tramped a few yards farther, then bent his knees to let the stern rest on the ground. Stepping out from underneath, he held the boat up with one hand while massaging the back of his neck.

Leah said, "Why don't we put the oars and food in the boat and then we can both carry it?"

"You mean besides the fact that I'll feel less masculine?"

"Oh, don't feel less masculine. I saw you pick it up." With lips pursed in mock admiration, she wrapped her hand around his slender bicep. When they had deposited the oars and picnic items on the floor of the boat, Leah lifted the stern, her flip-flops flopping behind Nathan as he guided them through the tall grass to the bay. Setting the boat down in the shallow incoming tide, he pressed his hand along the rough bottom and used his flashlight to check for leaks.

Leah put a hand on his back for support as she absently brushed at a pebble beneath her foot. "Do you think it'll hold both of us?"

In the reflected glow of the boat's bottom, Nathan smiled with grim satisfaction at his own thoughtlessness. During all of his planning, and the shoulder-searing experience of lugging the *Little Red Hen* to the shore, how had he not considered that question? Thayer was muscular, but he was not the size of *two* people. And although Ellen's husband and son had used the boat in the father-son derby, that was more than forty years ago, while Glen was still a small boy. Nathan doubted his ability to swim the breaststroke for very long, particularly in such frigid water. But if the boat had a leak or could not hold them, he figured they would find this out long before he'd rowed too far from shore. "I'm sure it's fine," he told her.

There was only one seat for a rower, and Leah eased herself down in front, knees pulled to her chest, watching Nathan arrange the two oars. He rowed the boat thirty yards, then withdrew the oars and turned on the flashlight to see if they were sinking.

"You feel anything?"

"Lust," Leah said. She had already uncorked the bottle of wine and was drinking out of the plastic cup. "You look very masculine when you're rowing."

So Nathan continued to row. Initially he'd been undecided about which of the harbor's islands they should visit. But the farther he rowed from the well-lit shore, the more he steered toward the closest: Stone Island. The sweeping glow of its lighthouse also offered refuge from the uncertainties of the dark.

"Would you like a sip?" Leah asked, apparently undisturbed by the fact that they were now hundreds of yards from the coast or the island.

"I try not to drink and row."

"Hmmph—since when?"

On the island's narrow shore, Leah helped him pull the boat past the nearly continuous strand of seaweed that marked the farthest reach of high tide. Nathan carried the basket and blanket as they stepped carefully among the rocks and crunching seashells toward the far side of the island. Clusters of dense shrubbery on their left thinned into a grassy, dandelion-speckled clearing beneath the towering lighthouse.

When they had spread out their blanket and drunk half the bottle of wine, Nathan lay back, looking up at the stars. He pulled her toward him to kiss her. When he let her go, he asked, "What do you think about those relationships where the woman wears the pants?"

"I think that's the only way to have a healthy relationship."

Nathan said, "No, no. This is going to be hard. This is going to be really, really hard, but try not to be ironic and funny about this. Don't you have contempt for the guy?"

Leah opened and shut her mouth before speaking. "Okay. This is the thing. I wish you could've met my parents. When they were married, I mean."

"Fuck. Your mom wore the pants?"

"It's not about wearing the pants. I mean, my mother is a drama queen. She'll burst into tears, on command, and when my parents were having arguments, you would only hear my mother's voice. Earlier on in life she had been very quiet about her . . . about the things that displeased her. So she learned to be vocal, and she learned to be dramatic, to bring attention to herself. It's just a personality trait, you know? You have to find the right person who can handle it, and my father was that man. He was quiet, but adamant, and just as stubborn in a subtle, silent way that could be almost as unnerving as my mother's drama queen theatrics. And he never came across as being less of a man . . . until they divorced. He came across as being more of a man because he could handle it."

"In other words, the more of your bullshit I endure, the more manly I become."

"In my eyes."

"I think I need more wine to persuade me."

"We're almost through."

"Refill my cup."

"We have to pace ourselves."

"Refill my cup!"

"Why are you shouting? Did I not just finish telling you that if I'm going to be a drama queen, then you have to be quiet?"

She had started the sentence with feigned indignation, but ended it in a cooing, pleading voice that Nathan heard as an invitation. Pushing his empty wineglass and the picnic basket away from them, he pulled her toward him again. This time she unfolded her legs to lie on top of him. During their deep, wine-soaked kisses, Nathan fumbled to unbutton her shorts and slide them off, in as fluid a motion as possible, down over her knees and feet. When he rolled on top of her she helped him pull his shirt over his head, but seemed content to paw at his chest and gently rake her nails down his back. After a while, Nathan eased himself onto his side and she helped him unbutton his jeans and tug them down, along with his boxers. Then she climbed on top. She pressed her warm stomach against his and Nathan slid his hands down her back, underneath the elastic of her black cotton panties until she slid farther down from him and stood. Nathan did not ask what she was doing. And, for a long time afterward, whenever he thought about what it meant to be overwhelmed by pleasure, and maybe even by love, he thought of Leah standing in her faded blue T-shirt—head tilted to one side, grinning as she rolled her black panties down her hips and let them fall into the grass. When she stepped out of them, kneeling with her legs on either side of Nathan, he could feel the wet warmth of her brushing the base of his stomach and then surrounding him, tentatively at first, until they were both rising and falling and she had taken him in whole.

Eleven

Nathan Confesses His Plans ~ A Chilling Cry ~
Paramedics Provide Succor and Shame ~ Night at the
Hospital ~ Eldwin Draws a Circle

Leah, it turned out, was on the pill, and the combination of this news and the wine allowed Nathan to sleep like the dead. At church the next morning, Eldwin preached about the value of the soul, and of the importance of play, but Nathan was too awash in lovely memories of last evening to really listen. It was not until he was at the club that afternoon, watching men and women swat a neon green ball with apparently endless enthusiasm, that his thoughts began to circle around the things Leah had told him about her trip to New York. Her ex-boyfriend, a musician, lived there in a house full of other artists and musicians who, when not making art or music (which Nathan assumed was quite often), undoubtedly took lots of drugs, and apparently had lots of sex.

Group sex.

Nathan had not wanted to ask Leah if she'd slept with Marcus, but maybe she had. And because she was on the pill, maybe she'd had sex with him without a condom.

Ellen asked, "Are you thirsty?"

"You want a half-and-half?" Nathan said, grateful for the distraction. In the clubhouse he chatted amiably with the old lady at the counter about her daughter who would soon be moving to Cleveland, and persuaded himself that because he was chatting and laughing, everything would be fine. He hadn't contracted some venereal disease. How many people out there lived lives much more reckless than his and had not had anything terrible happen to them?

On his way out of the clubhouse, however, he saw the old photos of the dead club members, and then, passing Ellen's glass into her bony hands, he remembered that the Dark Diceman doesn't always care how carefully you're living. More health-conscious and careful people than Nathan had died of cancer, or heart failure, or even AIDS.

As lunchtime approached, tennis matches ended and not as many began. They watched an old married couple play in a way that seemed more about volleying than winning.

Nathan did not want to go back to the dull emptiness of the house, so he suggested they go out to eat at the clam shack halfway down Oceanside Avenue. There they sat outside on park benches overlooking the cove. Ellen ate all of her BLT, but Nathan couldn't finish his clam chowder. He barely spoke. And afterward, when he asked whether she wanted to take a drive, he almost immediately wished he hadn't. Ellen often fell asleep during such trips, and Nathan had little to distract him from his thoughts. His mind was a stormcloud of imaginings about the possible repercussions of what he'd done. What if he had to explain to the woman he someday wanted to marry, *Oh, by the way, I just wanted to let you know that I have this highly contagious wart (or lesion) that will periodically appear, and if we have unprotected sex will probably transmit said wart (or lesion) to you, raising your risk of cervical cancer* . . . or . . . *Oh, hey, listen, I don't want this to upset what we've got going on here—because I think it's something really special—but I'd just feel, I don't know, remiss if I didn't mention that I have this disease that's working to dismantle my immune system until I'm emaciated, muttering nonsense, and shitting myself to death.*

Nathan could handle a genital wart, or herpes. He would just resign himself to a mostly celibate lifestyle and take solitary comfort in his art; he'd become the Henry James of comics. But HIV, AIDS! Nathan could not bear the disgrace of explaining how, after suffering the loss of a wife, his father must now suffer the loss of his only son because—because of what? *Well, Dad, we're talking about a girl I was falling in love with—who is smart! With this beautiful body, standing in front of me with her pants off. I mean, I know—safe sex safe sex—but . . . I mean, c'mon . . . she didn't seem . . . HOW WAS I TO KNOW SHE WAS A SEETHING CAULDRON OF DISEASE WAITING TO POISON ME!*

Back at the house, Nathan waited for darkness to fall. Dinner and the game shows on television seemed interminable while he waited for Ellen to finally trudge upstairs to go to sleep. The moment he heard her door close, he called Leah. When she came over, they walked quietly upstairs and lay together on Nathan's bed. He endured a brief conversation about her day with the children, then reached for her hand. They lay facing each other on top of the covers, and he worked his thumb across her soft palm. He whispered, "Hey, I was thinking about last night, and I was wondering, do you normally use the pill as your only birth control method, or do you usually use condoms, too?"

"Normally just the pill."

Nathan nodded.

"Why?"

"I was just wondering."

She looked at him amusedly and then told him that earlier that evening, Rachel had come downstairs for dinner and had gone through the whole meal without saying much of anything. "Normally she doesn't eat dinner with us; and God, I hope she doesn't anymore because this was so creepy I wanted to scream. The kids would ask a question and she would just say, 'I don't know,' or nod and then just take another bite of her spaghetti." Later, when Rachel had gone back to her room and Leah was putting the kids to bed, she heard through the floorboards the sound of Eldwin smashing dishes. "At first I thought it was an accident, but it was just one after the other, and I think the kids were so freaked that they acted like they believed me when I told them their daddy must have dropped some things with his soapy hands. When I went down into the kitchen before I came here, there were wet sponge marks all over the wall—I guess he'd cleaned up where he'd been throwing everything—and in the trash can, there were tons of pieces of bowls and plates. He was just sitting in his living room chair, drinking a beer, reading, and when I said good-bye to him, he nodded at me like nothing had happened. Isn't that cuckoo?"

"That is cuckoo," Nathan said, nodding, but in his smile it was evident that he was only half-listening to her story.

"What's wrong?"

"Nothing. I don't know."

"Tell me."

Silence enveloped them like a heavy cloak until Nathan whispered, "I don't know. I've just been thinking about how you were in New York last week visiting your ex-boyfriend who—I don't know the guy, but he might have slept with some of the people who were having group sex the other night. And then we had unprotected sex last night. So I just didn't know if there's anything I should be worried about."

Leah looked down at the comforter.

"Do I?"

"No," she whispered, shaking her head.

"Okay."

Nathan wanted to leave it at that—and did for a long moment. But he could not help asking, "Are you sure?"

"Yes."

Nathan continued to rub his thumb gently against her palm. His whole body began to relax, free from the tremendous weight of the anxieties he had been shouldering. But when he looked up, he found Leah's dark eyes glaring at him. "What?"

"Nothing . . . it's just that how do I know you haven't given something to me?"

Nathan exhaled and smiled indulgently at her hand. "I haven't. I was tested two years ago and since then I've only slept with one person."

"Your ex-girlfriend?"

"Yeah."

"You always used a condom with her?"

"Well, she was on the pill for a little while. But she'd only slept with one guy before me and they were both virgins at the time. So it kind of doesn't matter."

Leah frowned at him. "They never had oral sex with other people?"

"I'm not sure," Nathan said, slowly, realizing his error in logic.

"Also, how do you *know* she was a virgin, or that she didn't cheat on you?"

Nathan withdrew his hand from hers. "Don't get nasty."

"I'm not being nasty. I'm just asking how you know for sure."

"Well, I know. Plus, the last time we slept with each other was over six months ago. So I don't think you have anything to worry about."

The fact that he hadn't had sexual relations with anyone in over six months was more than Nathan cared to divulge, but he felt it was necessary to assuage her anger. A moment passed and Leah said, "Well, I don't think you have anything to worry about either." They lay in silence for a long time until she rubbed her nose with the outside of her hand, eyes closed, like a sleepy child. "I can go and get tested if you want."

"That's okay," Nathan answered. Even if either of them had contracted something, he knew it wouldn't always show up right away.

"Please don't worry."

"I'm not."

After a time, Nathan went downstairs and brought back a bottle of wine. He showed Leah a few of his favorite comics, but he was relieved when she whispered that it was probably time for her to go. In bed that night, mulling over the conversation, Nathan willed himself to believe that although she never actually stated she'd refrained from having sex with her ex-boyfriend, in so many words, this was in fact what she'd told him. That was why she seemed so defensive and indignant. She didn't want to have to come out and say directly, "I didn't have sex with my ex-boyfriend just a day or so after I kissed you." That would have been demeaning, perhaps for both of them, and her unwillingness to say such a thing revealed a decorousness Nathan couldn't help but find admirable. He told himself to take a deep breath, relax, and maybe the next time they were together, the bitter aftertaste of the conversation would be gone and they could simply put it behind them.

Leah declined to take a walk with Nathan the following evening, explaining that the children had awakened her very early and she could barely keep her head up. But when he called the next afternoon, wondering if she'd like to share a sunset picnic on Big Beach, she said okay. He spread the blanket near the dunes and poured their wine, listening to her talk about funny things Meghan and Eliot had said or done recently. When he asked if she wanted to have children of her own, Leah said, "Why do you think I wanted to have sex with you without a condom?"

Nathan closed his eyes. "Not funny."

Leah laughed and then swore that she was truly and honestly on the pill. She promised. She wasn't sure she wanted children. "Sometimes when I'm with Meghan and Eliot I feel like I might like to, but it also reminds me of how hard it would be. Like yesterday, I was in the car with them, and in the backseat Eliot had this old educational toy where you push a button and it plays a little song about each letter of the alphabet." Leah sang, " *'So N is the sound that goes nuh, nuh, nuh,'* which is fine, but Eliot kept hitting the button so it would go, *'So N is the sound that goes, So N is the sound, So N, So N, So, So, So,'* so I was about to tear the thing out of his hands and throw it out the window."

Nathan refilled their glasses of wine.

"I'm sure it's different when they're your own children," Leah continued. "I know it is. I think when my parents got married, my father was a lot like I am now, but I think he kind of grew into parenting, you know? He used to come into my room at night to tuck me in, and he'd do this thing where he worked his hands down my arms, starting at the shoulders and ending with my fingertips, and he would say that he was massaging the energy out of me so that I would sleep better."

"Did it work?"

"It worked great," Leah said, her lowered voice sounding a note of wistfulness.

Nathan gave a sympathetic smile as he sat up. He had been trying to lie on his side—facing her—but he found it difficult to drink this way and so sat with his legs stretched out in front of him. "Do you think the fact that your father cheated on your mother has affected your relationships with men?"

Leah frowned with such incredulity that Nathan laughed and said, "All right. Well, in what *way* do you feel it's affected your relationship with men?"

Leah shrugged. "I don't know. I'm sure it's probably made me less trustful of people in general—more cynical—to know that even your own father can act one way and be another."

"How trustful do you feel toward me?"

"I had unprotected sex with you."

"Mmm. Right. We did do that, didn't we?"

"How trustful do you feel toward me?" Leah asked.

"I had unprotected sex with you."

"Yeah, and then you freaked."

"I did not freak. I was just concerned."

"Well, the time to ask those questions is *before* you have sex with someone. Not afterward, when you make the other person feel like a whore."

"Tell me you didn't feel like a whore."

"I did! Because you were acting like I might be diseased!"

Nathan said, "There are lots of people out there with venereal diseases who aren't whores, and I'm sure there are lots of people who have STDs and don't even know it. I was just trying to put both of our minds at ease."

Leah snorted.

"What?" Nathan asked.

"I think you were trying to put *your* mind at ease, to make sure I hadn't infected *you.* When I said I was willing to get myself tested, you could've said you were willing to get yourself tested too, you know?"

Nathan looked down into his mostly empty glass, wondering if the families in the houses behind them had heard their raised voices. Quietly he asked, "Would you like for us to go get tested?"

"No, but that's because I trust you."

To Nathan this wasn't about the trust between them. This was about whether her ex-boyfriend's ex-girlfriend's ex-boyfriend might have unwittingly infected everyone his sexual partners had had as sexual partners. He opened his mouth to say this—but he was already exhausted by the conversation, and his thoughts were further muddled by how beautiful she looked—even angry—and how much he wanted to kiss her. "I trust you," Nathan answered. "Sometimes I think I might be falling in love with you."

Leah whispered, "Don't say that." She shifted onto her side to face him, but stared down at the patterned blanket now colored shades of moonlit gray.

"Why?"

"Because we're going to be leaving here soon."

"But that doesn't mean we can't see each other again."

Leah picked at stray threads in the blanket without responding. So Nathan continued, "I've actually been thinking lately about maybe leaving Cleveland and checking out someplace else for a while . . . like maybe New York."

"You mean live there?"

"Yeah, maybe."

"What would you do there?"

"I don't know. I mean, anything, really. But I was thinking maybe I would get a job where I could do illustrations, like making storyboards for TV shows or movies or something."

Leah frowned. "Do they still use storyboards?"

"I don't know. Maybe it's with computers. But if it is, then maybe I'd try to work for DC or Marvel Comics."

"I thought you hated those comics."

"I don't *hate* them. I'm not that into superheroes, you're right, but maybe I could do that during the day for money and then work on my own stuff at home."

"Hmm," Leah said, her lips pressed together in an expression that seemed noncommittal.

Smiling, Nathan said, "You don't sound very excited."

"No, if that's what you want to do, you should do it," Leah said. "I just don't want you to move there for my sake, because I don't really know what I'm doing right now."

"Yeah—no—I wouldn't be moving there just for you."

Eying him with impatient sorrow, Leah explained, "I just had a really hard time with my first breakup. And the reason Marcus and I aren't dating anymore is because I didn't want to get into anything too serious again. He wanted us to move in together in New York and I didn't want to. I mean, I did but I didn't. I just wanted time to figure out how to be happy on my own for a while." She let her gaze fall back to the blanket. "You know?"

Nathan managed to nod and say, "Yeah, no, that makes total sense. I wasn't saying we should move to New York *together*. I was just saying that there may be a time when I move to New York, down the road sometime, and then we could see each other."

"Well, I think you should if you think you'd like it there."

"Yeah, well, it probably wouldn't be for a while, anyway." Nathan drank the last of his wine and then stared out at the surf. In the more primal and inarticulate depths of his brain, the dark, unrelentingly churning, chaotic ocean seemed to him like the force of life, always threatening to drown him. Eventually he would be too tired to resist, but, inspired by a flickering memory of resistance, Nathan flung his glass toward the Atlantic, where it landed in a barely noticeable puff of sand.

Leah flinched and tilted her chin down as if attempting to swallow something. "Whoa, are you okay?"

"I'm fine," Nathan said, seriously at first, until he chuckled at the pathos of his gesture. To leave the wineglass where it fell seemed like an unnecessary theft from Ellen, and if broken, the shards of glass would be a danger to the children who would be frolicking on the beach the next morning. Nathan stood and ambled over to pluck the glass from the sand.

"What?" Nathan asked on his way back to the blanket.

Leah smiled, and said, "I'm the one who's supposed to be the drama queen."

"What am I supposed to be again?"

"Subdued, restrained."

"All right." Nathan was tired of the high irony that characterized so much of their conversation and also of the different conceptions of manhood the world thrust confusingly at him. He wished he knew what Aristotle had to say about manhood because what he said about bravery sounded true. You become brave by doing brave acts. Pushing a stray tendril of hair from her face, Nathan caressed Leah's cheek, and she let him. He kissed her uncertainly at first, then more deeply, warring against the possibility that from now on he would be kissing her good-bye.

For most of the next day, Nathan thought about Leah. He thought about her while watching tennis balls steadily volleyed across the Alnombak courts, he thought about her while having lunch, and he thought about her later that afternoon while taking a long drive with Ellen. He told Ellen he was looking for a particular kind of candy—what the name was, he couldn't remember, but he thought she would love it—while he stopped at two gas stations and a grocery to find the brand of extra-thin condoms he feared were the only kind thin enough to allow him to maintain an erection.

Once home, however, Nathan found he couldn't wait for Leah. He hustled into the upstairs bathroom and performed the minor exorcism necessary to allow him to think about other things.

When Ellen trudged up to her bedroom after the game shows were over, Nathan turned the channel on the television and eased himself into her recliner. He was finishing his third rum and Coke as large, handsome TV faces filled the darkened room with flickering light. Having ridden the wave of lust that crested upon him that afternoon, Nathan was now in the trough, contemplating the possibility that he had made his affection for Leah too obvious for her to think it worth having. Of course, she'd said she wasn't interested in getting involved in a serious relationship because she'd been wounded in the past, but for the love of God, who hadn't been wounded? And isn't that what people always said until they met someone who really interested them? Convinced that she was taking him for granted, Nathan picked up the phone.

When Leah answered, sounding buoyant, his conviction faltered. She said she had to bathe but she would be over in half an hour.

Nathan stammered, "Actually, I don't think I can tonight, or at least not till later on."

"What happened?"

"It's nothing with Ellen. A friend just called when I was making dinner, and I was so tied up that I didn't have time to talk with her for very long. But she's making this documentary film about graphic novelists and she wants to profile me. So I have to give her a call back in a minute."

"Wow," Leah said, sounding excited for him.

"Yeah, well, we'll see. I don't know how much of my part will end up being included in the final film."

"That's great, though. How long do you think it'll take?"

"I don't know. I think she's got some personal stuff going on right now, too. So I'm not sure. You're not mad, are you?"

"No, I'm sure I'll see you soon."

"I just thought that since our relationship is a summer fling it wouldn't be that big a deal."

Leah didn't reply.

"I'm joking, *joking,*" Nathan said, his nervous laughter sickening him even as it erupted from his mouth. "That was a joke. I'm sad about not being able to do anything with you, but she's just someone I'm kind of close with, and I'd feel bad if I didn't call her back. Do you want me to give you a call if I get off with her early enough?"

"That's fine. Some people were getting together at Danielle's, so I may just go over there, though."

"Okay," Nathan said. He asked her questions about what she'd done with the kids that day—hoping he could cause her to forget his foolish comment—and Leah answered briefly before reminding him to hurry up and call his friend. Nathan hung up and stared down at the black rotary phone as he sipped his drink. Then he picked up the phone with both hands and tried to break it in two. He grunted and slammed the unbroken phone back onto the receiver. The house was quiet except for the almost inaudible murmuring of TV voices and tree branches occasionally scraping the house. He decided he would wait another twenty minutes for Leah to take her bath and then go over and catch her before she left for Danielle's. If she asked about the conversation with his friend, Nathan would say: Oh, well, they had talked about her dissatisfaction with her boyfriend, and she'd asked some interesting questions about Nathan's art, but she mostly wanted to make sure he'd swing by New York on his way home so they could hang out and she could film him. Nathan glanced at his watch. He was on his way into the bathroom to check the diminution of his bruise when an unearthly sound echoed from upstairs.

"Dora!"

Nathan froze, his heart attempting to burst from his chest. The raspy voice had called out in a long, plaintive tone—but then stopped so abruptly that he almost wondered if he'd imagined it. He listened to the low whistling of the wind.

"Doraaaaa!"

Openmouthed, Nathan stared up the shadowy stairwell until his frightened, booze-addled brain finally comprehended that Dora was Ellen's cook. He cursed and hurried back to the phone. He wanted someone to tell him what was happening. When he dialed Ellen's home in Cleveland, the answering machine picked up, and Nathan sputtered, "Hey, Dora, Ralph, this is Nathan up in Maine, and I'm calling because Ellen's talking really loud in her sleep, and I was just wondering if you guys had ever had something like this—"

"Doraaaaa!" Ellen howled. Nathan hung up the phone and ran up the stairway to her room.

The door was slightly ajar, but Nathan hesitated to push it open out of respect for her privacy and because he didn't want to see her half-naked. His first evening in Maine, Nathan had carried Ellen's three leaden suitcases up the staircase to her room, then said good night and gone downstairs where, a few minutes later, he'd heard her calling his name. Five feet and a few inches tall, Ellen had stood on the top steps, wearing an essentially translucent gown. Beneath it Nathan had seen the outlines of her panties, the waistline lost beneath the sag of her belly, and the white no-frills bra containing her freckled, potato-skin-colored breasts. She had only wanted help unfastening one of her suitcases, but Nathan had never seen a woman so old so scantily clad, and he didn't want to see her that way again.

"Ellen?" he said softly, tilting his head toward the narrow space between the door and its frame. "Ellen? Are you all right?"

"I think I'm . . . ," Ellen said, but her voice trailed off into murmuring.

Nathan took a step backward, breathing easier. "Ellen, you're all right. You're just talking in your sleep."

For what seemed a long time, Nathan listened to the sound of tree branches clicking against her bedroom window and the distant, high-pitched whine of the television downstairs. Then Ellen laughed a rumbling, bitter laugh Nathan had never heard before: a gurgling noise that developed into a wet, congested cough. "I—I don't think I'm sleeping."

Nathan pushed open the door, turned on the light, then stared in disbelief at Ellen's bed. It was still made. The lacy white draperies billowed away from two opened windows, and Ellen was nowhere to be seen. He took a few steps farther into the room and found her sprawled on the carpet on her side, legs splayed like opened scissors, her pale hair fanning out across a dark stain of blood.

"Jesus!" Nathan cried, kneeling beside her. She was wearing the same white cardigan and navy blue dress she'd worn all day. He placed his hand on her hip to comfort her as she abruptly vomited—a thick, gray-pinkish liquid. Nathan clenched his teeth and turned away. When she'd finished, he asked, "What happened?"

Ellen only shook her head and glanced down at the grayish goo as it seeped into the carpet and congealed with blood and more vomit. "It's disgusting, isn't it?" she croaked.

"No, it's not that bad," Nathan said, even though he was leaning back so he would not have to see. "You're going to be fine. I'm going to call an ambulance, and we'll take care of you, okay?" Nathan let go of Ellen's shoulder and leapt over the bed to the phone.

In retrospect it would seem to him that all of his mealtime monologues that summer were in preparation for this moment. After calling the ambulance, Nathan knelt beside Ellen with his hand on her shoulder, and spoke in the warmest, most soothing voice he could muster about whatever passed through his mind. He reasoned that she must have fallen skull-forward into her dresser, then slumped onto the carpet, where she had lain drifting in and out of consciousness until he'd heard her. He told her that she was tough, that she had to be tough to suffer a blow like that and still have the strength to call for help, and each time she vomited or coughed, Nathan squeezed her shoulder and reminded her that the ambulance was on its way.

When he finally heard the siren—faintly, at first—then growing louder as the ambulance navigated the hairpin turns of the neighborhood, Ellen's eyes widened with apprehension as he attempted to reassure her. The siren stopped some distance from the house, but soon Nathan heard tires crunching the gravel, ambulance doors opening and closing, and men's voices. Nathan told Ellen he would be right back, he was just going to let the paramedics inside. But as he approached the stairs, three men in blue jumpsuits were already opening the front door. They marched up the stairs and past him. Two of them squatted beside Ellen while the short, crew-cut man hung back beside Nathan.

"Do you know how she fell?" the man asked.

Nathan said, "No. I think she probably tripped and hit her head on the dresser, but I didn't know about it until I heard her calling me . . . or, actually, she was calling for her cook in Cleveland, so I think she's a little disoriented. She's definitely a little disoriented."

"How long ago did you hear her calling?"

"Like half an hour ago."

"Is she currently taking any medication?"

"Yes."

"What kind?"

Nathan wasn't sure. Luckily, on the day after they'd arrived, Nathan had been in Ellen's bedroom, helping her to move her suitcases, when he'd noticed a box of see-through pill containers on top of her bureau. Each container was divided into seven rows, one for each day of the week, and each row was filled with colored pills. When he'd called the house to ask about them, Dora had said some were vitamins, others were prescribed by Dr. Peters, and that it was important that Nathan give them to her every morning at breakfast. Nathan told the paramedic that Ellen took the pills every day, but that he had no idea what they were. "I can bring them with us, though, if that helps."

"Yeah, bring them. But can you call someone to find out what medication she's taking?"

"Yeah, I have phone numbers for her doctor and some relatives."

"Okay, bring those, too. And do you know if Mrs. Broderick has a living will?"

Nathan was watching the other two paramedics as they hunched over Ellen, moving her onto a flat wooden board with handles cut into both sides. Ellen moaned as they strapped her down, one of them using his gloved hand to pull a vomit-soaked lock of hair from her cheek, then securing her neck with a brace. Ellen's frightened blue eyes stared at the ceiling as Nathan felt the gravity of the paramedic's question weighing heavily upon him.

"I don't know. I'm not sure if she has one," he said as they carried Ellen into the hall. The crew-cut man picked up the large canvas bag the men had used and carried it with him as he ushered Nathan along with his clipboard.

Nathan said, "I can try to get hold of her son to find out."

"What relation are you?"

"I'm not any blood relation. I'm her helper," Nathan said, although the irony of the words frightened him. He was half-drunk, trying not to get too close to anyone for fear they might smell his breath, and when asked several potentially life-or-death questions about Ellen, he had been virtually no help at all.

In the kitchen, Nathan grabbed two containers of Ellen's pills from the counter. But in the living room, on the desk, he could not find the piece of paper containing the phone numbers of Ellen's doctor and Glen. The desktop was a mess of old bills, invitations, letters, and flyers that Nathan sifted and resifted like a frantic magician who had misplaced the object everyone was waiting to see. Cursing, he grabbed his phone book and bounded out the front door.

Outside, the white-haired man who had broken up Nathan's fight with Thayer was standing with his wife within their screened-in front porch. Nathan nodded at them and glanced at Eldwin's house, but he saw no sign of Leah. The crew-cut paramedic helped Nathan into the back of the ambulance, where he sat on what looked like a large metal toolbox. The paramedic in back with him had sliced through the sleeve of Ellen's white cardigan and her dress to insert an IV. He attached to her chest a few probes that looked like the suction-cupped tentacles of a beeping monitor that was attached to the wall. Ellen stared wincingly at the harsh ceiling light and moved her lips as if attempting to speak.

"Ellen?" Nathan said, leaning in from his seat so she could see him. The ambulance made a hairpin turn and he lurched forward, almost falling on top of her, until the paramedic extended a forearm that pushed Nathan back into his seat.

"You've got a seatbelt behind you," the man said, checking to see if Ellen's IV had been disturbed.

As Nathan strapped on his seatbelt, he said, "I thought she was trying to say something."

"Mrs. Broderick?" the man asked, leaning forward so that she could see his mustached face.

"Bill?"

"No, I'm not Bill," he said, glancing at Nathan.

Nathan said, "Bill's not here right now, but he knows what happened, and he said to let you know he's thinking about you and is going to come see you." He thought such a lie might help her find the will to survive. He squeezed her hand, and her eyelids fluttered, but otherwise her ashen face betrayed no response.

The thirty-minute ride to Brightonfield seemed to last an eternity, and even though Nathan felt relieved to have more qualified people now looking after Ellen's health, his relief didn't last very long. At the hospital, two of the paramedics wheeled Ellen's gurney through the emergency-room doors while Nathan and the crew-cut paramedic followed behind them. The man asked, "Do you have her son's number to call about the living will?"

"I don't have the number with me," Nathan explained. "But if there's a phone I can use, I think I can call someone to get it."

At the nurses' station, he dialed his father, but because his father did not keep a telephone in his bedroom, Nathan was not surprised when he didn't answer. He dialed the number at Ellen's house in Cleveland—optimistic about reaching Dora—and when she didn't answer, Nathan cursed, then dialed Ralph's private line.

"Hello?"

"Hey, it's Nathan. I'm glad you're there. Ellen's had—"

"Hello?"

"Ralph? It's Nathan. Can you hear me?"

"I can't hear you."

"Ralph! It's Nathan. I'm at the—"

Ralph's voice said, "All right, all riiiiight. I can't get to the phone right now, but leave your message at the beep and I'll try and get back to you when I've finished testing out my Ruger Blackhawk revolver." Gunfire—or at least what sounded like real gunfire—exploded from the receiver, followed by the opening chords of Guns n' Roses's "Welcome to the Jungle." The answering machine finally beeped, and Nathan shook his head bitterly.

"Ralph, this is Nathan. I'm calling because Ellen has had a serious accident and I'm at the hospital trying to—"

There was a click, the clatter of a phone dropped and retrieved, then Ralph actually answered. "Hello? Nathan?"

"Ralph, for God's sake, man," Nathan said, quickly telling him what had happened.

"Fuck, all right, hold on," Ralph said. He rooted around in his room for what seemed like ages, then returned to the phone with Glen's number. Afterward he babbled something about maybe swinging by on his way up to Portland rather than on his way home, but Nathan was too distracted to listen closely. He mumbled, "Yeah, okay, keep me posted," and hung up.

A broad-faced, bespectacled doctor took the number, and after watching him walk to the other side of the counter, toward a glassed-in office and a more private phone, Nathan glanced back at the waiting area. An old man sat sleeping with his mouth open in one of the blue plastic chairs, and a skinny, stringy-haired woman rocked a crying baby in her arms. Above them a TV had been bolted to the wall, broadcasting eruptions of laughter from an old episode of *Cheers.* Nathan wondered how much of the recycled laugh track was the laughter of people long since dead.

With the doctor still on the phone, Nathan walked to the far side of the room, where nurses had pulled a tan curtain around Ellen's bed. He had expected the partitioned space to be a hive of activity, but found only a chubby female nurse checking the clear bag of liquid that dripped into

Ellen's arm. Ellen looked much cleaner. Her hair—cleansed of most traces of blood and vomit—was pulled back from her closed eyes, revealing a dark crescent of broken blood vessels on her cheek.

"Is she going to be all right?" Nathan asked.

The nurse flashed a perfunctory smile, but as she began to explain how Nathan would need to talk to the doctor, the doctor appeared behind him and guided him a few steps outside the curtain. He was a short, compact man, with the kind of efficient, doctorly compassion Nathan sensed would disintegrate if he took more than a few minutes of his time.

The doctor said that Glen had been informed of the situation and would be faxing a copy of the living will. "Meanwhile we're going to send her to the ICU for some tests to find out what happened and what kind of injuries she might have sustained during her fall. We don't expect any dramatic changes overnight, and it's probably been a long night for you already. I'd go home and get some rest."

Back inside the curtain, Ellen was sleeping, but Nathan felt the need to talk to her anyway. He told her things he wanted to be true: that the doctors would take great care of her, that Glen would be there soon, and that it wouldn't be long before they were back on the porch, watching sailboats tack lazily across the harbor while the sun set over the White Mountains. He was staring at her slackened, swollen face when two orderlies yanked back the curtain, like stagehands interrupting a scene.

He followed them as they wheeled Ellen past the waiting area, down the hall, toward a pair of swinging doors marked "Treatment Area—Patients Only." As they approached the doors, one of the orderlies pointed to the sign and reminded Nathan that he would not be permitted to go with them any farther. Nathan held on to one of the swinging doors and watched through scratched Plexiglas as they continued wheeling Ellen down the hall.

The cab company said they could be there in half an hour, but Nathan told them he'd have to call them back. Dressed in a black polo shirt, Eldwin was walking through the hospital's pneumatic doors, carrying his

Bible. Nathan told him what had happened, and afterward Eldwin left his phone number with the receptionist in case the doctors thought it time for Ellen to receive her last rites.

Nathan stared at the heavy woman, waiting for her to smile and say that the need for last rites seemed unlikely, but she merely nodded and took his number, then answered a ringing phone.

On the way home, Eldwin explained that he must have been in the shower at the time of the accident, but that a next-door neighbor had told him what had happened while Eldwin was outside emptying his trash.

"Was Leah still there when you left?" Nathan asked.

"I'm not sure. I think she may have already left. I thought she'd gone over to visit you."

"We were going to try and meet up later."

In the dim glow of the dashboard lights, Nathan reflected on the questions that had haunted him since he'd found Ellen bleeding on the floor: What would have happened if he had gone out as usual that evening with Leah? What if he had not found Ellen until morning? To escape such contemplation, he asked, "Do you do a lot of this back in Boston? Visiting people in hospitals?"

"Not too much. Russ—Pastor Russell—he still does a lot of it. I usually do it once every couple of months."

"Seems like it would be pretty emotionally exhausting work."

"It is and it isn't. You get used to it, I think, and it's not as if I'm bringing them bad news. People are usually pretty relieved that I'm there."

"What exactly is it that you do when you're giving someone the last rites?" Nathan asked. The evangelical minister of his mother's church—a rosy-cheeked man with thinning hair—had performed them for her the day she died. But Nathan had been outside the room, struggling with a soda machine and simply wandering the halls, so that when he returned, the pastor had already left. His mother, lips cracked and flaking, tried to smile at him as he apologized and broke down, bringing her hand to his cheek. Even if he wasn't sure he believed in it, he'd wanted to ease her passage into the new life she thought she was about to begin.

Eldwin sighed, "Well, there's anointing the person with oil, and offering communion if the person's able to receive it, but it's mostly a series of prayers. The ritual is supposed to remind the person that they're part of something much larger than themselves, which can be a comfort to them before they die."

Outside, strip malls and corner gas stations gave way to fenced yards and then the dark blur of passing forest. As they turned down Oceanside Avenue, traveling the narrow stretch of land between the Atlantic and the cove, Nathan asked, "Where does your faith come from?"

"Where does my faith come from?" Eldwin repeated. He was searching one of the car's cup holders for his cigarettes.

"Yeah. I mean, how do you explain why you believe what you believe?"

Eldwin said, "Well. I can't explain human suffering, why it happens, but the way I usually answer this question is to say imagine a circle. And say that circle represents *all* there is to know about the universe. And keep in mind that the Hubble telescope has detected something like fifty million galaxies and is still finding more, so we don't even have any evidence that the universe ends. It may be infinite. But let's say that the circle represents all that there is to know about the universe and how it works. Everything humanity has learned about cosmology, history, physics, biology, and everything else that remains to be learned." Eldwin lit his cigarette, then used his finger to draw a large circle in the thin layer of dust on the windshield. "Now put your finger up there and make a dot to represent how much you know."

Nathan put his finger inside the circle and left a fingerprint.

"Whoa, bold."

"Ah well," Nathan said, smiling, raising his finger to diminish the fingerprint but only making it larger. "Shit."

From the corner of his mouth, Eldwin exhaled a stream of smoke that curled out of the window. "Yeah . . . realistically I probably wouldn't even make a mark on there that you could see. I know so little about the universe, I can't make any reasonable assertion about the order of things, or about whether that order negates or affirms the existence of God. I can only have faith, either in the absence or presence of God, and I choose to believe in God's presence."

"Why not in God's absence?"

"Well, partially because of those strange things or patterns I told you about that have happened to me in my life. But also because I think belief comes naturally if your perspective on the universe is both deep and broad enough."

"Are you saying *belief* comes naturally to you, or the longing? Because I'm with you if you're saying the longing."

"I think I'm saying both."

Eldwin had stopped the car in Ellen's driveway. It was late and he did not cut the engine. Nathan thanked him, and Eldwin said to let him know if there was anything else he could do. Then Nathan climbed out of the car. A few of the house lights were still on, and he opened the front door quietly, out of habit. But glancing up at the staircase, it occurred to him that for the first time all summer, he was in the large house all alone.

Twelve

The Son's Arrival ~ Ellen Awakes ~ Mr. McAlister Accuses Nathan of Intemperance ~ Nathan Rattles His Father ~ An Unforeseen Houseguest

Nathan went to bed that evening with his door ajar. The following morning, a strangled metallic crash caused his eyes to flutter open. Stumbling into Ellen's bedroom in his boxers, he flopped over the bed and picked the heavy rotary phone up from where it had fallen onto the floor.

"Nathan?"

"Yeah?"

"Are you all right?" It was Glen.

"Yeah, I'm okay," Nathan said, trying to untangle the cord and lift the rest of the phone from beneath the nightstand.

"Have you heard anything from my mother's doctor?"

"No, I haven't." Nathan rolled over to sit upright on the bed. "I mean not since the doctor said they were going to run tests on her last night. Have you?"

"No, nothing yet. The doctor told me what I guess you told him, but could you just tell me again what happened?"

"Yeah, absolutely," Nathan said. He took care to omit the parts about his having been semidrunk and almost leaving Ellen to die in her own blood and vomit, and not having been able to find the emergency numbers Glen had given him. But otherwise he told the story as it had happened.

Glen sighed. "Well, she's very fortunate to have had you there."

"Well, I'm very glad to have been here." Nathan glanced at the hands of Ellen's old alarm clock. Nine forty-five. "I was just finishing up breakfast here and was about to head over to see her."

"All right, well, I'm on the plane now, but I'll be landing in Portland about eleven, and then I'll take a taxi over."

Nathan said, "Oh. Well. Why don't I come pick you up?"

This allowed no time for breakfast or bathing, but what else could he do? He dressed, hurriedly scrubbed the dark, vaguely Texas-shaped stain of blood and crusted vomit on Ellen's carpet, then drove at a steady seventy-five with his window down, wondering how to recognize Glen. A photo of him had sat on the grand piano at Ellen's home in Cleveland, but Nathan remembered only that in the photo he'd had a beard. From conversations with his father, Nathan knew that Glen had used some of the family money to buy an enormous ranch in Wyoming, where he now lived with his wife. He did not need to work but taught occasionally at the state college and every few years published a book about the paleontological history of Wyoming.

Having a vague sense of Glen's fondness for western country, Nathan had been expecting someone cowboy lean, but the burly, bearded man near the baggage claim seemed naggingly familiar. He was wearing old blue Teva sandals, faded jeans, and an untucked T-shirt with printed, multicolored frogs hopping across his barrel chest. While other men sat on an unfilled row of plastic chairs, holding paperback thrillers or balancing laptops, the bearded man sat cross-legged on the carpet. He was reading

Non-Dinosaurian Lower Vertebrates Across the Cretaceous-Tertiary Boundary in Northeastern Montana.

"Glen?"

"Hey, Nathan?" Glen pulled off his old, tinted glasses and let them dangle against his chest. His eyes were milky blue, like his mother's, and his shaggy, peppery black beard helped disguise his narrow lips. They shook hands and Glen slipped his book into a beat-up army duffel bag with G. BRODERICK stenciled on the cloth, then led them toward the exit with the bouncing stride of a younger man.

"Have you heard anything more?" Glen asked.

"No, nothing yet."

The drive to Brightonfield took half an hour, and although the conversation revolved mostly around Ellen, Nathan learned that Glen had gone to boarding school, then the army, then to college in Wyoming, where not long afterward, he'd purchased the ranch. There was an understated pride in the way he spoke of the choices that had brought him so far from the world of clubs and yachts and cocktail parties—the world of Brightonfield Cove—but he evidently had a tremendous fondness for his mother.

"How have you and the old girl been getting along this summer?"

"Pretty good, I think."

Glen stared out the window. "I'm sure she's very fond of you."

"She was in the hospital last summer, too?"

"Yeah, I was telling this to the doctor last night. Mother has had a few mini-strokes over the last couple of years, and I was wondering whether that might be what caused her to fall."

"Is that what they think might have caused the accident with the car?"

Glen's face clouded as he shook his head. "No—they weren't able to say for sure what happened then." Later, fingering his mountain man–style beard, he asked, "What happened to your head?"

Nathan touched his bruise and glanced at Glen, wondering how much the man knew. He hesitated, but then said, "Your mom and I were driving around one day and she asked me to drive up to what I thought was a friend's house, but the woman who met us on the porch was actually

Mr. McAlister's wife. She told us to leave, and we did, but her grandson was angry that we came, so he and his friends jumped me a few nights ago when I was outside by myself."

"Are you all right?"

"Yeah, I'm fine."

"Why were they angry with *you*?"

Nathan shrugged.

"Have you had any trouble with them since then?"

"I haven't seen them," Nathan said. He smiled wanly because he already regretted telling such an edited version of what had happened. He was driving Glen to Brightonfield Cove, after all, where the man surely knew people who would be happy to update him on all that he had missed by being away. Glen turned, shaking his head, and gazed out at the passing restaurants and gas stations of Brightonfield. "I'm very sorry that happened."

Nathan couldn't figure out a good way to fill in the details of the story, so he tried convincing himself that perhaps Glen, who did not seem to be in love with Brightonfield Cove, would stay at a hotel in Brightonfield—to be closer to his mother—and not visit the Cove at all. While nurturing this hope, Nathan realized that Glen had not breathed a word about his mother's desire to visit the home of Mr. McAlister's wife. But Nathan did not ask him for his thoughts. He understood the compulsion to believe—despite mounting evidence to the contrary—that one's mother was going to be all right.

At the hospital they took the elevator to the third floor, then walked in silence to Ellen's room. She was on the near side of the room's curtain, propped up in bed, white sheets pulled up to her waist. The crown of her head had been shaved and a white bandage had been applied like a strapped-on yarmulke. Tubes ran into her nose and right arm, and her left cheekbone had turned so densely purple it was almost black.

"Oh, Momma," Glen whispered, standing beside her and grasping her hand. Ellen's watery eyes half-opened to stare at him, then at Nathan; but her swollen face revealed no emotion. Nathan patted her foot where it poked up beneath the tight bedsheet. He told her how relieved he was to see that she was doing better than last night. But she didn't really seem better. She looked miserable. She didn't speak. And when she closed her eyes again, Nathan didn't know what else to say. The silence overwhelmed him. He whispered to Glen that he was going to step outside and use the restroom. Glen nodded distractedly as he smiled down at his mother.

"It's Glen, Momma. Do you want to squeeze my hand if you recognize me?" he asked, only he couldn't get all the words out. His voice rose a little before it caught, and he clenched his quavering jaw shut.

Nathan didn't need to use the toilet, but the restroom was empty, so he locked himself in a stall, put the seat down, and sat with his chin in his hands. He spent several minutes wondering about Ellen, and what he would do with the rest of the summer, until a heavy-breathing guy entered the stall beside him, grunting out sounds like someone squeezing a bottle of clogged shampoo. Nathan fled and didn't breathe until he was back in the hospital hallway.

A lean Indian doctor was standing outside Ellen's room, his smock so perfectly white that his skin looked like tanned leather. He stared down through bifocals at the clipboard in his hand, his index finger crooked beneath his lip, then he entered the room.

Nathan lingered near a leafy plant and sat down in one of three blue plastic chairs wedged into a corner of the hallway. He picked up a copy of *Us Weekly* that lay on the end table. The magazine opened to show photos of stars performing the same boring chores he often performed. Taking out the trash, loading groceries, paying the pizza delivery person. In this way the stars were just like Nathan. In case this fact had been lost on him, the photographs had been lumped together beneath the banner "Stars—They're Just Like Us!" He flipped a few pages and was reading about how Meg Ryan was starting over with a new life *and* a new love, when, glancing up, he was startled to see Glen approaching. Nathan rolled the magazine into a tube.

"Did you find the restroom?" Glen asked, rubbing his nose, his lilting tone belied by the watery pinkness of his eyes.

"Yeah, I was just waiting out here while you talked with the doctor. Do they have the results back from last night?"

"Well, he knows my mother has had her mini-strokes over the last couple of years, but right now it doesn't look like it was another stroke that caused her to fall into the bureau last night. So that's good news. It looks like she just fell, but the trauma to her head caused a hematoma, which he says is clotting in the space between her brain and her skull, so that bandage on her head is where they had to drill to relieve the pressure." Glen clamped his lips and sniffed as if he'd just smelled something malodorous. "The doctor thinks that with some rehabilitation, she should be able to recover."

Nathan nodded and said, "That's great. She's tough. I'm sure she's going to be all right."

When they reentered the room, Nathan was surprised to see Ellen smile lopsidedly at them.

"Hello, Momma," Glen said. He smiled warmly as he sat down in the chair he'd pulled beside her. "I was just talking to your doctor and he says you must be a tough old girl to have hit your head so hard and still be able to call for help."

"Oh?" Ellen croaked, but then she glanced at Nathan as if wanting him to make sense of what Glen had just said. Nathan blathered on about how relieved he was to hear she was going to be all right, but her eyes shifted from his face to his chest, and his words trailed off into silence. Ellen lifted her arm from the tight bedsheet and pointed a bony finger at Nathan's heart. He moved closer toward the bed as she extended her arm and pressed her fingers against him. She pulled a golden hair from his shirt and held it a few inches from her face. It was a hair from Ellen's golden retriever Rainier. The dog's hairs were everywhere in Ellen's car and Nathan was constantly picking them from his clothes. "Rainier's hair," Nathan said. He smiled, but Ellen's cloudy blue eyes were still uncertain. She slowly set the hair down on the white bedsheet and shook her head. She could not remember, Nathan thought. But Glen's eyes flickered with expectation. "Ol' Rainier sheds a lot doesn't she, Momma," he said quietly, more as a statement than a question, so it wouldn't seem so bad when she didn't answer.

When Glen asked him later if he might like to go home and rest, Nathan was eager to get back to try and disguise how he had nearly torched the family's home. Much of the damage was cosmetic, just a layer of soot, and a vigorous scrubbing with soap and bleach (as well as an arsenal of different brushes) wiped away more than Nathan had allowed himself to hope for. He scrubbed for almost an hour, the sun scorching the back of his neck, but after spending so much of the day at the hospital watching baseball on Ellen's television, the labor felt good, as if he was sloughing off the sickness he'd felt creeping up on him while he was there. When he finished, the broad column of ash that once stood a yard high had been reduced to the burned edge of a clapboard and a narrow, foot-high streak of faded gray. Nathan pushed the grill closer to the wall, hoping to cover up the charred clapboard until he had time to paint. To reward himself for his hard work, he mixed a drink and lay down on the shaded floorboards of the porch. Amid thoughts of Leah and his immediate future, he was also dully aware of how exhausting the last sixteen hours had been. His arm made a surprisingly comfortable pillow. Drifting in and out of sleep, Nathan tried to listen for the sound of a car in the gravel driveway. He wasn't expecting the heavy footsteps that suddenly made the floor tremble.

"Are you drunk?" Mr. McAlister asked.

Nathan sprang into a sitting position, squinting at the bright white of the porch. "No, I'm not drunk." He wiped the beginnings of drool from his mouth and glimpsed down at his nearly empty glass of rum and Coke. "I was just taking a nap."

Mr. McAlister watched him with gimlet eyes. "How's Ellen?"

"She's at the hospital." Nathan began to tell him the story about what had happened, but Mr. McAlister cut him off.

"I saw her at the hospital this morning."

"Oh."

"Have you been to see her yet?"

"Yeah. I was there this morning, too. I picked Glen up at the airport and then we headed over. We must have just missed you."

In a tone less scolding, Mr. McAlister offered, "She looked like she must have hit that bureau pretty hard."

"Yeah. But the doctor says he thinks she's probably going to be all right. He says he doesn't think it was another stroke."

"Well, that's good news, huh?"

"Yeah. It's great news," Nathan said, now awake enough to be irritated by Mr. McAlister's initial, presumptive anger. "Do you think it was a mini-stroke that might have caused her to drive her car into those rocks last summer?"

The older man's leaden eyes searched Nathan's face. Licking his lower lip, he murmured, "I don't know."

"I was just wondering."

Mr. McAlister ran his hand over his widow's peak and said, "It could have been. Anyway, I was just stopping by to make sure Ellen had somebody who was watching over her." As he turned to walk off the porch, he added, "Do you know how soon Glen is planning to take her back home?"

"I don't know."

"I imagine this is probably the end of her summer."

"Maybe." Nathan shrugged. "Have you been able to find someplace else to stay?"

Mr. McAlister glanced out at the sunlight glinting between the yachts in the harbor. "No. No, I'm looking, but every place is booked up at this time of the season, so I'm staying with a friend for the time being." Raising his hand in farewell, he forced a smile. "Anyhow, tell Ellen that I'm thinking about her and that I'll try and get back up there to see her soon."

In the early evening, Nathan decided to call his father and fill him in on what had happened. They talked in low, somber tones at first, but when his father started asking about Nathan's future—about what he intended to do when he returned home, and, more specifically, about whether or not he would try to return to his job at the library—their voices grew strained and Nathan fought the urge to hang up on him. Implicit in the conversation was the idea that Nathan needed to quit fucking around. He'd had his fun working only part-time for a few years, indulging his love of drawing, but now he needed to start thinking about what he was really going to do with his life. In junior high, playing goalkeeper for the school soccer team, Nathan's ability to bark commands at his fullbacks had instilled within his parents the absurd belief that he could be a great manager. Had Nathan ever considered managing a hotel? If he wanted to go back to school, his father would pay his tuition. The generosity of this offer, however wrongheaded, quieted Nathan for a moment. But when his father suggested a career in advertising, Nathan asked, "How about your plans?"

"What about my plans?"

"I mean, what is *your* plan?"

"I have a job, Nathan."

"Yeah, but how about a life?"

His father chuckled. "I have a life."

"Yeah?"

"I may not be jet-setting around the world, but I have my garden out back, and . . . Paul and I go do something every once in a while."

The Stuebners, Paul and Linda, had been longtime friends of his parents, but since Nathan's mother's death, he knew his father's contact with them had grown less and less frequent. "When's the last time you saw him?"

"It's been a little while, but I don't need you setting my social schedule for me."

Nathan said, "That's great to hear, because I may not be around for much longer. I'm thinking I might move to New York."

The announcement had its intended effect. Hesitating, his father cleared his throat. "New York? What do you plan on doing there?"

"I plan on living there, and I know a guy who's involved in cartoon animation. I showed him some of my drawings and he wants me to work for him."

"What's the name of the company?"

"Uh, Animatronix or something . . . I think it's new."

"Well," his father said. "Well, I sure would miss having you around here, but you've got to live your own life, I guess."

Nathan offered his father nothing.

"New York's expensive, though, Nathan. Is he going to pay you enough to live in a decent place?"

"Yeah, we're talking about that. But listen, I've got to get going here."

They hung up and Nathan stared out the French doors at the glittering water a long time. In the kitchen, he picked up an old *New York Times,* then opened the door to the back porch. The sky was releasing its first stars, and the air smelled of the ocean. Nathan read a few articles, then closed his eyes, listening to the sounds of the rattling rigging and snapping sails in the harbor. It was still early in the evening, but it was late enough that Nathan could stop brooding about his father and start wondering why he had not heard from Leah. He had tried to call Eldwin's from the hospital, but there was no answer, so he'd left a message on their machine saying he would try to reach her later that evening. But why hadn't she tried to reach him? There was no answering machine in Ellen's house, so maybe she'd called that morning. But, still: Why hadn't she called again that afternoon, or left a note expressing concern about Ellen's accident?

He opened his eyes and read more of the paper. Not long afterward, a car pulled into the gravel driveway, and assuming Glen had arrived, Nathan decided to wait in his chair. When he heard knuckles rapping on the screen door, however, he walked around the corner of the house. He found an unshaven young man in cutoff army shorts and a black T-shirt, peering with cupped hands through the window.

"Ralph?"

"There you are," Ralph said. He grinned as he shook Nathan's hand.

"How did you get here?"

"I drove the beast."

"But Jesus, we were just talking last night, and you were in Cleveland."

As they walked out to Ralph's pickup, Ralph repeated what he claimed to have already told Nathan on the phone: He'd been getting ready to leave for Portland, anyway, and when he heard of Ellen's accident, he'd decided to swing by on his way up.

"But you must have left right after I called."

"Nah, I got a few hours sleep. Dude, what happened to your head?"

Nathan touched above his eyes until he felt the familiar soreness. "Ah, I got in a fight with some guys. I'll tell you about it later."

"You got in a fight *here*? You didn't punch anyone in their pacemaker did you?"

"No, they were younger guys."

Ralph shook his head. "How's the monkey holding up?"

Nathan had heard him use this nickname before, on the phone, but he paused and repeated the word before remembering that Ralph was speaking of Ellen. He told him of her prognosis as Ralph pulled a large gym bag from the front seat of the rusting Ford Ranger. The back window of the truck cab was plastered with bumper stickers and Nathan read them as they talked. A few advertised bands including the Misfits and the Pogues, others demonstrated support for the FOP and NRA, and one in the center declared, "This Truck Protected by Angels."

"So Glen doesn't know I was coming?"

"No, man. I wasn't expecting you so soon, but I can't imagine it'll be a problem. I'm sure he'll be glad to see you."

In the living room, Ralph set his bag down and spent a moment gazing out the French doors. "Fourteen hours," he sighed as he walked over to flop down on the couch.

"You drove it straight?"

"Except for hitting a few drive-throughs and taking a major-league shit."

Nathan stepped out onto the porch to grab his glass and newspaper, then returned to the room. "Well, you wouldn't know it by looking at you—that you drove that long, I mean."

In truth, Ralph looked as if he had just been thrown from a bull. One leg was draped over the arm of the couch, and he removed his old Yankees cap to wipe the sweat-matted hair from his forehead. "I thought I'd stop by here before heading on up to the hospital, but it sounds like she's doing okay, huh?"

"Well, I mean she's stabilized, but we don't know how much she'll recover yet." Nathan glanced down at his watch. "It's seven thirty, though. I think visiting hours are over around eight o'clock, so it probably wouldn't make much sense to go up there now."

"The monkey is tough."

"She is tough."

"Tough monkey," Ralph sighed, shaking his head.

Nathan held his nearly empty glass aloft and asked Ralph if he wanted a drink. When he returned from the kitchen, Ralph was stretched out on the couch, a pillow tucked beneath his sweaty head. Nathan made a mental note never to use that pillow again.

"Aaaaaah," Ralph said, wrapping both hands around the glass. He sipped and nodded his head appreciatively. "So how's it been going up here, all in all?"

Nathan felt too fatigued by his conversation with his father to express his frustration at not being told the whole story about Ellen. So he just shrugged. "It's been all right."

"Yeah? What have you guys been doing up here?"

"Watching fuckloads of tennis."

"Yeah. I warned you about that."

"We spice it up every once in a while by raising hell in town."

"You have to be careful when you let the monkey out of her cage."

"Yeah, you do."

"Crazy monkey."

Nathan gingerly touched his forehead. "Speaking of crazy monkeys," he said, taking a deep breath. He told him about the fight, and Ralph laughed with disbelief.

"Fuck, man. How do they look?"

"I don't know," Nathan admitted. "I haven't really seen them."

"I should have brought some heat for you."

"Heat?"

"A burner, man, a gun."

Nathan smiled. "Has Ellen ever done any crazy stuff around you?"

"Does the pope shit in a funny hat?" Ralph fingered the bristles on his chin and explained how his living arrangement, receiving free room and board from Ellen, also required him to take her out to dinner once or twice a week on her dime. A few months ago, he had taken her to a Tex-Mex restaurant where Ellen had repeatedly asked Ralph if the bearded bartender—a man wearing a gaudy sombrero—was in fact her son, Glen. Although the details of the story were not by themselves hilarious, Ralph's impersonation of Ellen was so exact—with his shoulders slightly hunched and a tight-lipped, quizzical expression on his face—that Nathan nearly exhaled rum and Coke through his nose.

Nathan asked, "Do you think Glen knows—you know, how fucked-up she acts sometimes?"

"I don't know," Ralph answered. He said it could be difficult to speak with Glen about his mother—that, once, after Ralph had taken Ellen to an Indian restaurant, she had ordered something spicy and shit herself on the way home. "I tried to tell Glen about maybe getting her some of those diapers for adults? But he just exploded at me and said that maybe I should stop taking her to such stupid fucking restaurants."

"Were those his actual words?"

Ralph nodded, saying, "Don't let the scholarly, gentle outdoorsman shtick fool you. The dude has a fucked-up temper. He talks with Dora about Ellen, but I think Dora probably doesn't tell him everything because she doesn't want Glen to get upset and take Ellen to Wyoming."

They were talking about what it meant to have a mini-stroke when the nurse phoned to set up an appointment for Ellen's bath. Nathan knew the nurse did not think well of him, so he took some pleasure in telling her how he had been there to hear Ellen's cries and escort her as quickly as possible to the hospital. The call took no more than ten minutes, but when it was over, Ralph was already asleep. He had turned on his side, mouth open, loudly snoring into another pillow Nathan would not use again.

In case Glen arrived at the house, instead of staying at a hotel near the hospital, Nathan wrote a note explaining that Ralph was upstairs sleeping and that he himself was taking a walk. His hopes had been lifted by recent thoughts as to why Leah still had not come over to see him. Perhaps, not seeing Ellen's car in the driveway, she assumed he was not home; or perhaps, seeing Ralph's truck, she thought that since family had arrived, it would be an inappropriate time to visit. He looked forward to sorting out the misunderstandings when he found her.

Outside, the air was warm and carried the faintly sweet scent of a neighbor's flowering bushes as Nathan walked up Harbor Avenue. The lights in the living room of Eldwin's house were on, so Nathan knocked lightly on the door and was surprised when Rachel answered. Her straight blond hair hung wispy and uncombed, and her pale, angular face squinted beneath the orange porch light.

"Hey," Nathan said. "I'm sorry if I woke you. I was just wondering if Leah was around."

Rachel turned to glance up the house stairs. Rubbing the side of her mouth, she said, "No, I don't think she's here."

"Oh. Okay. Do you know where she might be?"

"I don't have any idea."

"Do you know how long ago she might have left?"

"About an hour ago?" she said, as if asking for affirmation.

A nearly full moon hung in the starry sky as Nathan continued up the road. On Big Beach, the ocean shimmered like molten lead. Older men and women walked along the shore with him as he strolled west toward Mariner's Rocks. The only young people he saw were joggers and, on his way back, a group of young men surrounding a few burning logs near the dunes. Their laughter reminded Nathan of Thayer and his friends, so he walked far away from them—near the tide's edge—and trailed an old couple up the boardwalk onto a neighborhood street.

He had been gone over an hour, and worrying that Glen might have returned, wanting to talk about his mother's condition, Nathan decided to head home.

He followed Shore Road along the rocky edge of the Atlantic, glancing through warmly lit windows into maritime-theme living rooms. But the old couple he'd been following began to seem oddly familiar.

The slender woman was wearing rolled-up tan chinos and a white, round-brimmed hat. When a robust wind blew from the ocean, she clamped her hat down with one hand to keep it from blowing away. Nathan would not have paid her much attention if it hadn't been for her companion. The older man had changed clothes since Nathan had last seen him, but his broad shoulders and bald spot were the same, as was the generous, barking laughter Nathan remembered from listening to him at his party. Squinting at Mr. McAlister and his wife, Nathan slowed to follow them. They were not holding hands, but strolled together down the street, then up the winding driveway toward her home. Nathan lost sight of them behind the tall hedgerow separating the house from the road. But hustling a few yards up the driveway, he watched them walk inside the front door.

Lights flicked on throughout the first floor, and eventually in a corner room upstairs. Suspecting he might be able to see them better from higher ground, Nathan scrambled up the footpath toward the Point. Moonlight gave the gray earth a silvery luster and touched the tops of large cumulus clouds rolling slowly above the ocean. Near the top of the hill, however, Nathan realized he would not be able to see into the house any better than he had on the street. Because curtains hung in most of the second-story windows, he couldn't see more than moving shadows, and after the first-floor lights were turned off, he ambled back down the hill.

Of course, Nathan had suspected for some time that this was where Mr. McAlister was now living. But having his suspicions confirmed was depressing. He thought of Mr. McAlister's ability to laugh even though

Ellen now lay in the hospital, and it reminded him of the last time he'd seen Sophie with her new boyfriend. She had been on the way out of Dugan Florist, the Cro-Magnon's heavy arm draped casually around her neck, and the sound of her laughter, so lighthearted, had made Nathan tremble in the heat of the summer.

On Harbor Avenue, he walked off the gravel and onto the grass, where his steps made less noise. He paused in Eldwin's front yard. The house was dark, but lamplight shone faintly from Leah's bedroom window. He walked closer to the house and whispered her name, waited, then glanced behind him at the gravel road. Gathering up a few pebbles, he lofted them as gently as possible toward her window. The first rattled off the clapboard siding, but the next two pinged so loudly off the pane that Nathan was torn between wanting to run and wanting to wait for her to respond. He could hear his heart beating. He whispered her name again and tossed another pebble just as a nearby window blazed like a searchlight, illuminating almost half the front yard. A shadow moved across the ceiling, but Nathan ducked along the side of the porch, then sprinted across the back lawn.

Thirteen

An Early Departure ~ Ralph's Girlfriend ~ Leah's Party Plans ~ Nathan's Fury ~ Beer, Badminton, and Dancing

In a dream he had that night, Nathan was on Ellen's porch when he noticed Leah. She was in her black bikini on the beach, waving for him to join her.

"I'll be there soon!" Nathan called.

Leah yelled something back to him—something reassuring, Nathan could tell—but he couldn't hear her over the creaking coming from somewhere inside the house. He wandered back through the French doors, climbed the stairs, and opened the door to Ellen's room. He found her leaping on the bed, her khaki dress billowing up to midthigh.

Nathan raised his hands and shouted, "Ellen, my God! Be careful! Stop bouncing!"

But through the loose wisps of hair, she only stared at him, her brow knitted in a familiar expression of embarrassed confusion, as if she didn't know how she'd started, or how to stop. Nathan begged her to come down. Then her lips parted into a toothy, knowing smile. She pushed off hard from the bed, leaping high, like an airborne dervish, twirling head-first toward the bureau, so that Nathan awoke with a start.

A seagull had perched on the gutter above the room's nearest window, its talons scraping against the aluminum rim. Nathan clapped his hands and yelled so that it flew away, and then—aware that he might have awakened someone—he listened for sounds of movement in the house. The red numbers on his alarm clock read 9:26 A.M., later than he and Ellen usually awoke. But he heard no talking or footsteps. He dressed and peered through his door at the empty hallway, then walked quietly downstairs. Returning from his walk last evening, he had discovered Ellen's Volkswagen in the driveway and an additional bedroom door closed, so his hope that Glen would stay in a hotel had already crumbled when he saw the note on the kitchen table.

Nathan,

Sorry I missed you last night. Ralph and I didn't want to wake you, but we wanted to get to the hospital early. See you there? We're taking Mother's car, but the keys to Ralph's truck are beneath the driver's side mat.

Glen

By his own admission, Nathan was not a tidy person. The one time his father had visited Nathan's room in the shared house, a year or so ago, when they were still trying to meet every Wednesday for lunch, his father couldn't help curling his lip at what surrounded him: empty glasses and half-eaten dinners, opened art books and comics, clean and unclean clothes, all of which looked as if it had been tied up into a bag—along with his bedding—and then struck like a piñata until its contents had exploded across the room. Still, even Nathan's tolerance for this kind of disorder did not allow him to feel at ease in the driver's seat of Ralph's truck. Two gnarled and blackened banana peels lay directly in front of him on the dash, and when Nathan reached with two fingers to throw them out, he found they were fixed to the dashboard, along with a few coins and a half-empty pack of cigarettes, by a paste of sun-hardened cola. Crammed-in cigarette butts overflowed from the ashtray, spilling out onto a pile of empty cans, newspapers, mail, and fast-food bags that covered the passenger-side floor. A deodorizing cardboard Christmas tree hung from the rearview mirror, but the truck still reeked so badly of cigarettes and decaying food that Nathan rode with all the windows open, his face pinched and frowning until he pulled into the hospital.

Ralph and Glen sat on either side of Ellen's bed, although only Glen was awake. Ralph sat on the far side with a *National Geographic* on his chest, his arms folded across it like a beloved manuscript. A bouquet of red and white tulips stood on Ellen's nightstand, and Glen sat with his elbows on his knees, his glasses halfway down his nose as he read aloud from *The Collected Jack London.*

"Hey, Nathan," Glen said, removing his glasses and shaking Nathan's hand. He reached over and laid a hand on his mother's forearm. "Momma's doing much better today. Aren't you, Momma?"

Ellen smiled faintly. Tributaries of broken blood vessels still fed into the dark lake of bruised skin around her left eye and along her cheekbone. Opening her mouth, she pulled a white piece of pulp from inside her lip and held it up for them to see.

"I'll take that from you, Momma," Glen whispered, as he took a tissue from a nearby box. He took the pulp from between her fingers and dropped it into the trash. Patting her hand he said, "You're doing much better today than you were yesterday. You even ate some applesauce this morning."

Ellen raised her hand from the bed and circled her index finger once in the air, a feeble gesture of celebration. Glen and Nathan both laughed so loudly that Ralph opened his eyes to squint at them, shifted position in the chair, and went back to sleep.

"Oh, Momma, you're going to be fine," Glen said and smiled.

Ellen nodded blankly and stared up at the muted baseball game on the television bolted into the wall above them. As they watched the game, Nathan apologized for not getting there sooner. But Glen shook his head, saying he had just wanted to get there early to talk with Dr. Sahni and a couple of private medical plane companies about when they might be able to take his mother home. "Dr. Sahni says she's stabilized now. They'd like to run some more tests and keep her under supervision for another week, but a lot of that can be done in Cleveland. I've been trying to find out when a private plane would be available with one of these companies. Right now I've got one that says they can do it a little over a week from now and another that says they can do it tomorrow."

"Whoa," Nathan said.

Glen frowned as he glanced back at his mother. "Well, we don't want to do anything reckless. But I'm going to talk with Dr. Sahni again this afternoon, and we'll discuss whether or not it's possible. So we'll see. I know my mother would like to be home." He glanced down at Ellen and said, "You're a tough old girl, aren't you?"

Ellen nodded and then rested her head back on the pillow and closed her eyes.

For lunch they purchased hamburgers from the cafeteria and took them back to the room. They found a tennis match on television—for Ellen's benefit—and for a little while, Ralph regaled them with stories about his quest for the photograph that would capture the quintessence of the inner city. "I wandered into this crack house one time, and this big dude—I mean, a *big* dude, way too fat to be a hard-core junkie, so he must have just been a dealer—shouted that he'd give me thirty seconds to get out or he was going to burn me. Slang for a gun is a 'burner,' so I'm not sure if he was talking about shooting me or actually burning me. But, anyway, I hit the road."

After suggesting that Ralph be more careful, Glen said, "Allison has taken some absolutely breathtaking photographs when we've been on our trips." For decades, Glen's willingness to occasionally guide tourists through important archaeological sites in Wyoming allowed he and his wife admission to other, eco-educational trips offered by the same company, and the trips were part of the reason Glen did not travel to Brightonfield Cove very often. Glancing sideways to make sure that his mother was still asleep, he said, "Summers are short in Wyoming, so I've got a limited time for doing field research, and the free time I have—if it's a choice between watching tennis at the Alnombak or going with Allison on a kayaking expedition in Alaska, I'll almost always go to Alaska."

By late afternoon, Ellen was occasionally replying to questions. Her answers were limited to shaking or nodding her head, or slurring a monosyllable, but the fact that she was responding at all buoyed everyone's spirits considerably. Nathan and Ralph stayed until dinnertime, when Glen thanked them for coming and let them know he could "hold the fort" by himself. Nathan protested half-heartedly, but by the time he was finished, Ralph was already waiting for him in the hall.

Out at the truck, Ralph opened the passenger-side door to try and clear out a space for Nathan. He threw armfuls of clothes, cans, newspapers, paper bags, and audio cassettes from the seat and floor into the already garbage-filled truck cab. Then he stood back and wiped his brow. Most of the trash was off the seat, except for a Ziploc bag and some pennies, and on the floor all that remained were a few empty cans and scraps of paper.

"That work for you?" Ralph asked.

"That's gorgeous," Nathan said, already cranking down the window.

During the drive home, Ralph lit a cigarette from the pack on the dash and sighed, "Fuck. Hit me if I fall asleep."

"You still pretty wiped from the drive?"

"Yeah, I would've been rested up. But I heard Glen banging around in his room this morning and woke up about ready to eat my sack off, I was so hungry. I went down to the kitchen to try and find something to snack on, and he found me down there. Guess what time we got to the hospital?"

"I don't know—eight o'clock."

Ralph frowned at Nathan. "You're pissing on my parade, man—we got there around nine o'clock."

"That's still early."

"Hell yeah it is, man, and the doctor didn't even show up for like another hour. So I was trying to stay awake, but I'm dragging ass." Ralph blew a stream of smoke out his window.

"You really think Glen might put her on a plane tomorrow?"

"I don't think so. I think she's going to be fine, but it seems kind of quick to be jetting her home."

"I think so, too," Nathan said, staring out at the blur of passing trees.

Ralph asked, "So does this suck for you or are you glad to be going home?"

"Well, it sucks to see Ellen injured. It scared the living shit out of me when it happened. But it also sucks because there was this girl I was seeing, and I don't know what's going to happen now."

"You were seeing a girl up here?"

Nathan told him a little about Leah, and Ralph nodded with a knowing, Cheshire grin. "So that's what you were doing last night? A little boinky-boinky on the beach?"

Nathan shook his head. "I actually didn't meet up with her last night. I think she thought I was still at the hospital, so I ended up just taking a walk."

"You gonna see her tonight?"

"Yeah, probably. Maybe."

Ralph leaned over and pulled his wallet from his back pocket, opening it to show a photograph of himself and a young woman. "That's my girlfriend, Shannon."

"She's cute," Nathan said, holding the wallet. The girl in the photograph was not cute, not really, although the pale fleshiness of her face made her appear very young. In the photo, she stood beside him on a beachside balcony, wearing cutoff jean shorts and an oversize gray Case Western sweatshirt. Her dirty blond hair was pulled back tightly, and the toothy overbite of her smile reminded Nathan of the braying of a reined-in horse. Ralph said they had been dating for almost two years. She was majoring in art history, but she also knew a lot about photography, and it was great to be with someone who didn't have all kinds of emotional baggage, who could offer him intelligent criticism and suggestions about his work. Ralph winked, and said, "Plus, if she's drunk, she sometimes lets me give it to her up the pooper."

At the house, a glass-dish casserole sat on one of the chairs beside the front door. Nathan picked it up to read the note attached to its aluminum-foil cover.

Dear Glen,

I thought you might like something other than hospital food this evening, and this spinach casserole is one of the few things I can make! I thought it might spare you and the boys from having to worry about fixing dinner. Our thoughts and prayers are with you and your mother.

Love,
Kendra

"Thank you, Jesus," Ralph said.

"Do you know Kendra?"

"She's my cousin."

Ralph went upstairs and Nathan carried the casserole to the refrigerator. After pouring himself a drink, he sat down at the kitchen table, then picked up the phone.

Ralph's voice trumpeted from the receiver, so Nathan set the phone down and pulled an old *Sierra* magazine across the table. An article about wildlife preservation quoted a letter the writer Sherwood Anderson had once written to a friend. In it he asked, "Is it not likely that when the country was new and men were often alone in the fields and the forest they got a sense of the bigness outside themselves that has now in some way been lost . . . Mystery whispered in the grass, played in the branches of trees overhead, was caught up and blown across the American line in clouds of dust at evening on the prairies. . . . I can remember old fellows in my home town speaking feelingly of an evening spent on the big empty plains. It had taken the shrillness out of them. They had learned the trick of quiet. . . ."

Nathan looked up from the page to stare out at the sea. He wasn't anywhere near big empty plains, but he was near a big empty ocean, away from Sophie, away from his father, away from all the shackles of home. In the days before he'd left for Brightonfield Cove, Nathan had begun to hope that being away from everything would give him time to clear his head. He had allowed himself to envision a quiet summer of drawing and watching ships pass and just recuperating from the last few years of his life. But this was not how things had turned out. He still wanted the shrillness taken out of him, but his dreams of quiet were now tangled in a vision of a future with Leah. He thought about how romantic it would be for them to take a road trip to a place where they could stand on the big empty plains, letting the mystery whisper in the grass around them. He was biting his thumbnail and holding a fistful of hair in one hand when Ralph traipsed into the kitchen.

"Are you through with the phone?" Nathan asked.

Ralph opened the refrigerator to pull out the casserole. "Yeah, but I'm supposed to be getting a call back in about fifteen minutes."

"I'll be off before then," Nathan assured him. Using the phone in the living room, he cleared his throat and dialed Leah's number. His blood jumped when she answered.

"Nathan! Oh my God, how are you?"

He inhaled deeply and almost laughed. "I'm all right." He told her about Ellen's accident the way he'd practiced telling the story to his father, and he had her attention for a while. But maybe he made the story too long, or too unnecessarily detailed, because near the end he heard her whisper something to one of the kids.

"So," Nathan concluded.

After a moment, Leah said, "That's so sad! And scary! Were you scared?"

"Yeah, I was a little bit."

"I would have been terrified. I probably would have run out of the house screaming."

"No, you wouldn't."

"How is she doing now?"

"She's doing okay. It looks like there's a decent chance she's going to recover enough to walk and talk again. But she's not going to do it here. They don't know how long it's going to take for her to get back to normal or even how much she's going to recover, so Glen wants to fly her back to Cleveland. He was talking about doing it tomorrow, but I think he's probably going to wait until next week."

"Oh."

"Yeah, so I may not be here much longer."

"You have to go home when she does?"

"Yeah, I guess. I would have to get the car back to them, anyway."

"Wow."

"Yeah."

There followed a heavy silence. Then Leah said, "Well, swallow it and go to bed."

Nathan's mouth hung open. But it turned out she was not talking to him. Leah said, "I'm sorry. Meghan has an ear infection, so I have to give her her medicine."

"What have you been doing since I last saw you?"

"Mostly taking the kids to the beach. Meghan can't go in the water, so I've been making loads of sand castles with her. I usually ask them, 'Don't you want to lie on this nice towel, work on your tan, maybe read some of my *Cosmo*?' But they always want to make castles. I'm getting pretty good at making them."

Nathan said, "I came over last night, but Rachel said you weren't there."

"Yeah, I didn't see your car, so some people were getting together over at Ethan's and I went over there."

"Who's Ethan?"

"I think you met him at Thayer's party that night? Brown hair. He was getting into the hot tub?"

Nathan remembered a young man with a sculpted chest and lantern jaw. "So what did you do over there?"

"Just ordered pizza and hung out. He's having a party tonight if you want to come."

"This is the same guy who's friends with Thayer, right? The same guy who was with him when he was trying to kick my ass?"

"Yes, but he's really nice, though," Leah said, laughing embarrassedly. "I think you'd like him. He was the one who was trying to get them to stop, remember?"

Nathan looked through the French doors at the sailboats tacking across the slate-blue water. Deciding he was too tired to argue, he said, "I don't know. I'm pretty beat. Do you feel like just taking a walk or something?"

"I would, but I think this is going to be one of the biggest parties of the summer."

"I'm pretty exhausted," Nathan said.

"I'll bet. You've had a super-stressful couple of days."

"Hello?" Ralph's voice came on the line.

Nathan said, "I'm getting off in two minutes."

The line clicked.

To demonstrate that he was not afraid of Thayer or his friends, Nathan took down directions to the party. "So should I expect to see you?" she asked, and Nathan wondered if she felt anything like his own heartsickness when he told her he didn't know.

An hour later Ralph stood in the living room wearing a white T-shirt, cutoff army pants, and a pair of blue-and-orange running shoes. He said he'd been jogging for almost a year, and although he still carried a stubborn paunch, he'd already lost twenty pounds. Nathan sat in Ellen's chair, eating spinach casserole, while Ralph ran in place in front of the television, slapping his knees.

Not long after Ralph left, a car pulled into the driveway, so Nathan turned off *Entertainment Tonight* and picked up *Audubon* magazine. Glen entered carrying a Gilman's grocery bag and two bottles of wine. They greeted each other and Nathan asked about Ellen's condition, but Glen did not seem in a good mood.

"I think she was just getting tired toward the end of the day," he muttered, glumly. "Having young men around seems to liven up my mother, so I think you and Ralph probably saw her at her best this afternoon."

In the kitchen, Glen uncorked a bottle and unpacked groceries.

"Ralph went out jogging, and he and I ate some of this casserole that Kendra Garfield cooked for us," Nathan said, opening the door of the refrigerator.

After Glen microwaved the casserole, they both walked out onto the porch. Thin streaks of clouds lay on top of the horizon, reflecting the salmon glow of the setting sun. Glen glanced at the grill, but if he noticed the ashen streak on the clapboards, he said nothing about it as he sat down. Placing the plate on the small wooden table Nathan had pulled over for him, he raised his glass and stared at Nathan. "To my mother's recovery."

Nathan raised his glass and drank.

Glen took the first bite of his casserole and said, "Mother had a surprise visit this afternoon from Bill McAlister."

Nathan's heart skipped, and he worried that this was the beginning of a conversation he had been dreading almost since Glen's arrival. "Yeah?"

"Have you and Mother seen much of him?"

"Well, we haven't seen a *whole* lot of him, but he came over every once in a while, and I never really knew how to handle the situation. Because your mother would know he was there, and clearly be interested in seeing him, and it would have been really awkward to ask him to leave."

Glen nodded as he chewed. "I don't think there's much you could have done in those situations."

Nathan felt both relieved and aggravated by this reply. If he had known Glen felt this way, Nathan could have saved himself a great deal of hand-wringing. But he wiped his mouth and smiled good-naturedly. "How did you handle him today?"

"I let him try and talk with Mother, but she was already very tired, so we ended up talking a fair amount about you."

"Yeah?"

"Yeah."

"I don't think he's my biggest fan."

"No, I don't think he is either."

Nathan's face fell. He had half-expected Glen to protest, and consequently, he felt short of breath. "What did he say?"

"Well, he had a very different account of what happened at his wife's house that day with Ellen, for one thing—he said you told his wife to fuck off."

"That's a lie."

"He also said that both his wife and his step-grandson thought you tried to hit her with the car."

"That's a lie, too."

"Why didn't you tell me that's why those boys attacked you?"

"I did tell you."

"You told me that they were angry—that Bill's grandson was angry—because you had brought Ellen over to his grandmother's house, not because they thought you cursed at her or tried to hit her with my mother's car."

Nathan nodded. "I should have told you . . . but I was just . . . Mr. McAlister talked about them maybe pressing charges for this thing that never happened, and I was just in this mode of not telling anybody anything more than was necessary."

Glen stared at Nathan with blue eyes that revealed more intensity and gravitas than Nathan would have thought possible from someone born into a life of ease and privilege. Glen said, "I don't know what to believe at this point. I'm more troubled by his suggestion that you weren't very attentive to my mother this summer."

"That's definitely not true."

"Then why was that asshole able to rattle off about half a dozen parties where my mother was invited but somehow didn't show up? You took her to *his* party—the one party I told you I would rather my mother not have attended—but somehow managed not to bring her to anyone else's party this summer?"

"I didn't know how to stop her from going to Mr. McAlister's party, short of standing in front of the door and preventing her from going!" Nathan exclaimed. "And the other parties . . . I don't know what happened. Sometimes when I got to the post office, the parties had already happened, but Ellen was also tired a lot, and said she didn't feel like going."

"Bill says it was probably because you wanted to go out with this girlfriend you have here."

Nathan shook his head. "That's not why."

"He also said you were planning to go out with her the night my mother fell?"

Nathan was stunned. He took a moment to figure out how Mr. McAlister could have known. Then in a quieter voice he admitted, "That's true."

"Well, then, how lucky are we? How lucky is my mother?"

"I was planning to go out after your mother was asleep," Nathan explained, his indignation suddenly rising to match Glen's. "I was with her practically every conscious moment of her day, and when she was asleep, yeah, I sometimes took a walk with this girl Leah. But you obviously thought that your mother was okay enough to be able to send her up here with just—"

"She isn't okay!" Glen shouted.

"Well, then why the fuck did you send me up here with her alone? You think *I* would have been responsible if I hadn't been around to hear your mother that evening? *You* would have been responsible! Did you expect me to camp outside her bedroom every time she went to sleep?" Nathan leaned forward and felt like standing up from his chair.

"I expected you to take care of her."

"I expected when I came up here that I would be helping out someone who was mentally stable. That wasn't the case, and I sure as fuck should have been told."

"If you didn't think that was the case, then why the fuck didn't you tell me?"

Nathan opened his mouth, but no words came to him immediately. This was the question that had haunted him almost since his very first morning in Ellen's home. He answered, "I don't know. I wanted to believe she was okay."

Glen observed Nathan a moment, then drank the last of his wine. The crimson flush of his face began to fade, and he pushed himself back in his chair.

Silence opened between them, and Nathan stared out at the sunlight reflecting across the surface of the harbor. "I'm very fond of your mother and I did the best job I could."

"All right, it's over now, anyway," Glen said, waving his hand dismissively as he looked out toward the ocean. "I was just hoping this could have been a more enjoyable time for her."

"We did have some fun together."

"I'm sure you did," Glen admitted. He went back into the house to microwave his cooled casserole. When he returned, with a refilled wineglass, his face was no longer clouded with resentment. He told Nathan about a long, reassuring conversation he had finally had with Dr. Sahni about his mother's condition. The doctor said that although ideally he would like for her to stay a few days longer, he understood the situation with the medically equipped planes, and he didn't expect she would have any complications on the trip back to Cleveland. Glen had been on the phone with the airline for the rest of the day.

"We're leaving the hospital tomorrow at noon, and we'll leave the Portland airport at two o'clock," Glen said.

Nathan managed to utter, "All right."

"I wish we could wait longer, but I've got to get back into the field and Dr. Sahni doesn't think we should have any problems. Another thing is that if we do it tomorrow, the airline can provide us with a doctor on the plane."

"That's good."

Glen lifted his glass and pushed back the little table in front of him in order to climb out of his chair and sit with legs outstretched on the wooden floor. It was a boyish gesture, and Nathan waited for him to explain why he preferred sitting this way. A bad back, perhaps, or the need for better circulation in his legs. But apparently he was just making himself more comfortable. Propping himself up with one arm, he sipped his wine and said, "Regardless of Bill's complaints, I am grateful you were able to come up here with my mother this summer. She wouldn't have been able to come up at all if it weren't for you, and you probably saved her life."

Nathan was recovering from the fact that they had been shouting at each other just moments earlier, and he marveled at how relaxed Glen appeared, when his own heart still felt constricted with apprehension. "I just did what anybody would have done," Nathan said, repeating the words of soldiers and local news heroes, and immediately wishing he had said something else.

Glen was frowning as if deep in thought. "How long were you supposed to be here with her, again?"

"Until Labor Day."

"Well, remind me before I go, and I'll write you a check for the rest of the summer."

Nathan's lips puckered with surprise, and he said, "That . . . that's not necessary."

"No, that's what you were planning on, and you probably made all sorts of arrangements, so that's what you should get."

"Well . . . that's very generous," Nathan said. He felt as if a tremendous burden was lifting from him, and he might have laughed if he hadn't worried that Glen would take it the wrong way. Even if Glen still thought he was a fuck-up and was only offering the payment because he wanted to do right by Nathan's father, at least it would be a while before Nathan had to worry about money again.

They were taking their glasses into the kitchen when Ralph returned from his jog. His flushed face and stubble gave his chin a faintly strawberry appearance, and the darkened hourglass of perspiration on his shirt revealed dense swirls of hair. He greeted them and opened the door of the refrigerator, stared inside, then walked over to the sink and filled a glass with water. Glen had started to tell Nathan more about the details of the plan for the next day, but he stopped and repeated the information so that Ralph was aware of it, too.

"You're taking her home tomorrow?" Ralph asked. He stole a glance at Nathan, but Nathan kept his eyes fixed on Glen.

They remained in the kitchen, sorting out the details, then Ralph trudged up the front stairs and Glen followed behind him. The older man carried a bottle of wine and his empty glass as he told both of them good night.

Nathan wandered over to stare out the French doors. His spirits had been momentarily lifted by the knowledge that he would be paid for the entire summer. But the fact remained that in a few days he would be back in essentially the same drab situation he'd been in before the summer began. He didn't have to stay in Cleveland, he knew, but the more he thought about his old college friend in New York, the more he realized how much time had passed since they'd spoken and how presumptuous it would be to ask to stay at his apartment for more than a couple of days. Nathan wasn't ruling it out—maybe a couple of days was all the time he would need to find an apartment—but would it make sense to go there without knowing what he would do to make money, and whether Leah would want to continue to date him? When he called Eldwin's house, Nathan was not surprised to learn she wasn't there. He sat back in his chair and sighed, wondering if it would be brave or senseless for him to go to the party. Leah knew he didn't have much time left in Brightonfield Cove, yet she was asking him to meet her at a party that would most likely be attended by the same apes who had attacked him. He was settling into the idea of not going—of just hanging out around the house with Ralph, drinking—when Ralph bounded downstairs, freshly shaved, wearing a blue button-down shirt.

"Looking snazzy," Nathan said, toasting him with his glass.

"Yeah, I passed a party when I was jogging, and I think I'm going to head over."

"Whose party?"

"I don't know," Ralph said, distracted by a nearby mirror. "There were a lot of people going in, though, so I don't think it really matters. Are you doing something with what's her name?"

Nathan felt a nervous tightening in his stomach, but he rubbed his jaw and nodded. "I am. I think so. I think I'm actually supposed to meet her there."

The story of Glen's paroxysm of anger did not impress Ralph. As they walked beneath the trees of Birch Hill Boulevard, he said, "That's just the way Dr. Jekyll deals with things. He goes all Hyde on you for a little while and then he's Mr. Milquetoast Professor again. Who gives a hootenanny what the guy says, anyway? You know you were doing the best that you could and you're getting paid for the rest of the summer."

"Is it hard for you to deal with him when he's staying with you at the house?"

"Nah," Ralph said. "I'm not even going to be there much longer. I'm moving into a house with these friends of mine who have their own darkroom, which should be cool."

They talked a little about his new living arrangement, then Nathan asked, "How did you end up at Ellen's, anyway?"

Ralph explained that when Ellen's husband died, Glen had wanted someone to live in the house with her. "At the time, I wanted out of the fraternity house I was living in because they didn't like Carter—my boa constrictor—and they wouldn't let me have my guns."

Nathan smiled, but Ralph appeared genuinely resentful, recalling the injustices he'd endured.

"Plus, my mom wouldn't pay for me to live in an apartment when Aunt Ellen lives so close to campus. That's why I got a job at this frame shop—to pay the rent on the room in this house. I don't hate living with

Aunt Ellen, but it's like going through college living with your grandma, you know?"

"Doesn't she have any friends her own age who want to live with her?"

Ralph said, "I could probably count on one hand the people who have stopped by the house since I've been there. How many people have come to visit her here?"

This was something that had been on Nathan's mind. Despite the demonstrations of affection from people at the club and at church, very few had actually stopped by the house to visit. Nathan counted. "Three."

"How many of them were men?"

"Two."

"I'm surprised it wasn't three."

"Why?"

"Because, dude, you haven't noticed? For the most part, Aunt Ellen only wants to be around men. I'm sure if it was five years ago, she'd have no problem finding somebody to go play golf with or whatever. But now that she's older, I think you can tell she didn't have any real friendships with women. None of them comes around to hang out. I think she was just one of those people always looking for romance to save them."

The site of the party was a rehabilitated red-and-white firehouse, with a rectangular tower that rose to a windowed room overlooking Brightonfield Cove. As they walked up the front porch steps, music wafted through open windows, and Nathan glanced inside at the shadowy mingling of people. The door was opened by Ethan, the same lantern-jawed young man who had been on his way to the hot tub at Thayer's party, and who had continued moseying up the road while Nathan battled Thayer and the juggernaut. Ethan had the air of a broad-chested, Ivy League swimmer who did not want to be seen as just a jock. His dark, carefully mussed hair seemed an affectation of restless creativity, and his faded Merge Records T-shirt advertised his deep awareness of what was cool. Waving them in distractedly, he said, "Hey, come on in," although his smile slipped when he glanced at Nathan.

College-age men and women were scattered throughout the high-ceilinged living room, lounging on couches and leaning against the walls. Nathan didn't see Thayer or his thickly built friend, but, pushing forward, he glimpsed Leah in the far corner of the kitchen, talking with Danielle. Leah was wearing the same faded blue T-shirt she wore the night Nathan had rowed her out to Stone Island.

He and Ralph stood in front of the keg beside the refrigerator, filling plastic cups with beer. "Some of the guys I was in that fight with will probably be here," Nathan said. "The guy who opened the door was with them, but he didn't fight."

"How big are the rest of them?"

"Medium build. They look like they probably work out every once in a while."

"Well, I've got your back," Ralph said.

"Thanks."

"And if it looks like we're losing, I'll feign a seizure."

Nathan gestured forward with his beer. "C'mon over and I'll introduce you to Leah."

They wove through the knots of people until Nathan could distinguish Leah's voice from the others. "That's my situation, too," she was saying as he stepped behind her and rested his palm on her back. When she turned, Nathan wondered if he glimpsed in her expression disappointed surprise that he had come. Leah and Danielle introduced themselves to Ralph, and there followed an awkward moment during which no one seemed to know what to say.

"So who the hell are all these people?" Nathan blurted.

"Some of them are from here, but I think a lot of them are probably Ethan's friends from Harvard," Leah said, glancing at Danielle for confirmation. Danielle stared out at the mass of people in the living room and nodded.

"Did you find out from Glen when he's taking Ellen home?" Leah asked.

"Yeah, it looks like they're going to fly her home tomorrow."

"Tomorrow?"

Ralph said, "It's too fucking soon if you ask me. I think Glen just wants to go home."

Nathan explained to the young women that Glen studied dinosaurs and needed to get back before the early winter in Wyoming in order to gather samples from the field.

"So when do you have to leave?" Leah asked.

Nathan hoped he and Leah could have at least one evening alone in Ellen's house before he had to drive the car back to Cleveland, and he was afraid of saying anything in Ralph's presence that would encourage him to remain. "I'm not sure," Nathan said. "I imagine I'll have to leave pretty soon after they do because they need to have the car back in Cleveland."

Leah looked up at him sympathetically and Nathan gave the same wan, tragic smile he might have given if he'd just announced he was going to war. Then he gulped the rest of his beer. He had envisioned having this conversation with her somewhere else—on the beach, or in his room—where they wouldn't have to act so casual and could talk with greater candor about their feelings. But now the news was out and the conversation moved on. Danielle was answering Ralph's questions by telling them about her life in Boston and her aspirations of working as a TV news producer. Nathan tried to listen, but he could barely hear her over the din of conversations behind him. Turning to Leah, he said, "Glen got kind of angry with me on the porch this evening."

Leah looked at him, surprised. "Why?"

"Lots of things. He heard that I was spending too much time with you, and not paying enough attention to Ellen, but he was also pissed off because Mr. McAlister told him I almost wasn't there the night Ellen fell."

Leah shook her head in commiseration as she glanced out at the people in the living room.

Nathan said, "I'm trying to figure out how Mr. McAlister would have known."

When it occurred to her what Nathan was asking, Leah looked back at him, disgruntled. "I didn't tell him."

"Did you tell Thayer?"

Leah hesitated, the decision to tell the truth or not wavering within her dark eyes, but she kept her gaze level. "I told some people last night."

"Why?"

"We were just talking. I don't know. I was just saying how lucky it was that you were able to be there for her. I didn't think Glen would hear about it or be mad at you." Her last words were clipped with resentment, and Nathan wondered if she was drunk.

"Anyway," Nathan said. "He's going to pay me for the rest of the summer."

"That's great," Leah said, her face brightening.

Nathan wondered if her response was due to relief at changing the subject, or whether she was genuinely delighted for him, but he wanted to believe in what would make him happier.

"Yeah, so that'll give me a little launching pad if I decide to leave Cleveland." Gesturing down at her mostly empty cup, he asked, "Do you need a refill?"

"Okay."

Nathan left to refill their cups, but when he returned, Leah and Danielle were no longer where he had left them. Ralph was still in the corner, engrossed in conversation with a guy wearing a train engineer's cap. Nathan half-listened to them talk about the fact that many of these people were from the same housing unit at Harvard, and leaned closer when the young man asked if they had been out back. "I've got to go find my girlfriend, but you guys should check it out."

"They've got badminton," Ralph said, looking to see if Nathan shared his enthusiasm.

Nathan didn't, but he was ready to leave the congested corner and finally breathe some fresh air. They lingered long enough for Nathan to finish one of the beers he was holding, then they opened the sliding glass doors onto the deck. The backyard was separated from the neighbor's by a small forest of trees alive with the blinking of lightning bugs and the steady chatter of crickets. Lamp lights affixed to the house shone down onto the grass where two couples—one on either side of the net—volleyed the shuttlecock back and forth in what may or may not have been an actual competition. Nathan and Ralph leaned against the railing with their beers and watched them play.

Ralph asked about Danielle, but Nathan wasn't able to tell him much, and he wasn't interested in talking about her, anyway.

"I'm trying to figure out what I'm doing when I leave here," Nathan said. He explained how as a low-income, aspiring graphic novelist, his low-rent, low-responsibilities life in Cleveland still dimly appealed to him. When he spoke of maybe moving to New York to be near Leah, Ralph discouraged a life of wage slavery.

"You should take over my room at Ellen's, man, not have to pay rent at all."

Nathan laughed. "I don't think Glen would be crazy about me living there."

"He would probably like you living there more than he's liked me living there."

"I just had a shouting match with the guy."

"I've had a dozen shouting matches with him and I'm still sucking on the sugar tit. I'll talk with him. You'd have it even easier than I did. Aunt Ellen's not going to be going out to dinner anytime soon, she'll probably have a full-time nurse at home, and you could just sit upstairs and work on your stuff."

Ralph explained that he would be doing this favor for Nathan because he could not help but see him as a kindred spirit. Both of them were artists and both needed time to work and did not want to have to worry about money. Although Nathan suspected that Ralph's motivations for wanting Nathan to replace him were more complicated, he nevertheless felt grateful to him. They both drank and watched a slim gazelle of a girl swing at the shuttlecock and miss entirely.

"How's your badminton game?" Ralph asked.

"About as good as my polo game."

"Have you ever played?"

"Every once in a while. When I was in third grade, I was playing barefoot in our backyard and impaled my foot on one of the metal spikes they used to hold up the net."

"Is your foot okay now?"

"It only hurts when I play badminton."

Ralph said, "We should play. You think you're going to be any worse than them?" Ralph gestured at the couples fecklessly volleying the shuttlecock to one another. One of the male players glanced up at Ralph then returned his attention to the match.

"Don't you feel like we just got here?" Nathan asked.

"I feel like I was born here."

"Anyway, who knows how long they're going to want to play."

Minutes later the couples took a break to stroll over near the lawn chairs where they had left their beers. Ralph slapped Nathan on the arm and promptly skipped down the steps. Near one of the poles he crouched down beside an open box and picked out two racquets.

The young man who had been eyeing Ralph called out, "Oh, we were going to play another game in a minute."

"That's cool, we'll play with you," Ralph answered, waving a racquet at Nathan to come down.

Perhaps noticing Nathan's reluctance, the slim gazelle and her boyfriend acted friendlier toward him than the opposing team did to Ralph. Ralph's team played the first match in muttering communication. But as the matches wore on, his teammates—a goateed young man and his small-eyed, elfin girlfriend—began to interact differently with him. They still laughed at his ungraceful intensity, but he laughed with them, and they eventually applauded his effort. When they had played several matches, they all retired to the lawn chairs near the deck to drink their beers. The elfin girl and her boyfriend were soon to leave for San Francisco. The girl wasn't sure what she wanted to do there, but the boyfriend had a degree in computer science and planned to sign with a company in Silicon Valley.

When the young man asked what Ralph and Nathan did in Cleveland, Ralph told them about his photography, and because Nathan occasionally shelved fiction, he told them he managed the library's literature department.

The elfin girl said, "Oh, that sounds so cool. I know everybody says this, but after I've worked for a few years and made some money, I want to try and start my own bookstore."

"That sounds great," Nathan said. They discussed her vision of a cozy little store where people would feel free to sit and read books and magazines, but Nathan's encouraging words rang hollow to him. He knew independent bookstores rarely survived the competition from chain stores, so he suspected the project would consume years of her life and then fail. Nathan wondered if he was traveling a similar path: chasing dreams of artistic greatness and romantic success that he should know were doomed to failure. The elfin girl did not seem unintelligent, and because listening to her quixotic dreams somehow made his own seem more quixotic, Nathan abruptly excused himself to look for Leah.

Inside, the air hung heavy with heat and perspiration, and the stereo speakers worked like magnets, pulling partygoers toward them. Nathan stopped at the keg, then moved forward. Living room couches had been pushed against walls, and the weight of the dancing crowd caused the hardwood floor to tremble.

Standing on the periphery of the crowd, the musty smell of spilled beer, sweat, and cologne wafted over him. UB40's "Red Red Wine" played on the stereo, and although the resurgent popularity of eighties music struck Nathan as evidence of a stagnant culture, the effect on nearly everyone else was narcotic. Heads bobbed smilingly at one another, conveying ironic detachment from the song, as well as real pleasure at being reminded of a shared history and younger, perhaps less self-conscious selves. For the most part, the men seemed restricted to casually thrusting their fists, as if warming up for a fight, but the women's bodies moved like waves. Some backed themselves up into men who nodded their heads affirmatively, as if something they'd earned was being awarded them. Nathan spotted Thayer near the far wall, grooving with closed eyes, while Danielle undulated beside him, one hand stuck in her hair. Nathan's gaze slid away but then returned when he caught sight of Leah. He lost her behind Danielle, but then she reemerged, looking flushed. Her blue thrift store T-shirt had been pulled farther above her waistline and the sleeves rolled up above her shoulders.

Nathan set his empty cup down on the mantel and began to maneuver across the dance floor. He was feeling audacious with booze as he bobbed his head and tried with one hand to pat his chest in time with the music, but his courage waned. As he inched forward, the thought that perhaps he should wait for a better time to approach—when she wasn't so close to Thayer—began to seem increasingly reasonable. Then Leah met his gaze. She smiled a broad, languorous smile, and seemed to tilt her head in a gesture encouraging him to approach. Closing her eyes, she turned, holding her arms above her head and letting him see the whole lithe and glistening body he'd be missing if he did not continue his march forward. Danielle smiled as Nathan came closer, but Thayer's charcoal eyes remained heavy-lidded with contempt.

"Hey there," Leah said, smiling, revolving closer to him and then away again. Nathan shifted his weight from side to side as he stared over the heads of other dancers and occasionally smiled down at Leah. When the song was over he asked—prematurely, he knew, but he couldn't help himself—if she wanted to take a break.

"Oh, I will in a while, but why don't we dance a little longer?"

The first percussive beats of the Violent Femmes's "Blister in the Sun" blasted out of the room's corner speakers, and although Nathan had never figured out how to dance to that song, no one else seemed to have any problem. Leah and Danielle turned in place, preoccupied with the movement of their hips and feet, and when the song crescendoed, Thayer began to bounce up and down as if trying to strike something above him with his forehead. Young men all over the dance floor began to dance in this semicontrolled, moshing way, knocking and flailing into one another.

But Thayer danced like a man possessed. Each leap into the air seemed like a painful attempt to slough off his affected ennui. Each time he fell to earth, he fell against someone, and once he even collided with Nathan.

Nathan endured this performance by trying very hard to seem as if he wasn't noticing and also by staying a few feet away from where he thought Thayer's next leap would propel him. When the song ended, Nathan remained long enough for Thayer to leave and a few more girls to join the circle. Then he shouted to Leah that he was going to get himself another beer. Leah nodded. At the opening chords of the Cure's "Just Like Heaven," she flashed a thousand-watt smile. She said, "I'll take a break in a few minutes."

Nathan turned and angled back to draw himself another beer. He stood just outside the doorway to the kitchen, waiting through several songs as Leah danced in a congested circle with Danielle, Ethan, and other people Nathan did not know. Then he retreated to the back deck. The elfin young woman and her boyfriend stood on either side of the net, lazily swatting the shuttlecock back and forth as they talked between long silences about their friends. Nathan drank his beer and noticed Ralph and two girls sitting where the light from the house faded into the verdant shadows of the woods. As Nathan stepped down to join them, he found one of the trio, a cherubic-faced girl, talking about her guilty fondness for *Forrest Gump.* He sat in a wooden chair a long time, listening to their excited chatter about movies, but he wasn't listening attentively. He was drunk. He stared up at the stars to remind himself of how little Leah's inattention to him meant within the context of the Grand Scheme. But as was often the case, contemplating his insignificance and the possibility that there might not even *be* a Grand Scheme, made the events in his life seem not less anxiety-inducing, but even more so. If there was no God, and none of Nathan's suffering meant anything—*anything!*—then wresting a few felicities out of existence seemed like the only possible hope.

With these thoughts surging inside him, Nathan left and reentered the party. The climate inside was like a hothouse. Setting his cup down on the mantel again, he pushed through the mass of dancers—sliding past warm, sweat-slicked skin—and into the heart of the crowd, where he could barely move. He turned in place, nodding and patting his chest distractedly, but in the throng of bodies surrounding him, he saw neither Leah nor the people with whom she'd been dancing. He pushed himself back out of the jostling mob and stood against the wall, both to wait to see if she'd emerge and because he didn't know where else to go. Nathan turned to ask the guy next to him the whereabouts of a bathroom.

"There's one there near the kitchen, and then there's another one upstairs at the end of the hallway, but I don't know if it's cool to use it."

There was a line for the bathroom near the kitchen, so Nathan trotted upstairs with his head down, as if performing an errand. The staircase emptied out into a hallway of closed doors and framed photographs of Maine lighthouses. He used the bathroom and exited back into the hall just as Ethan was bounding up the stairs in front of him. The solidly built young man's cheeks were flushed from dancing, and after acknowledging Nathan with a surprised, "Hey," he stepped inside a hallway door. Music pounded up through the floorboards as Nathan reluctantly trudged back toward its source. With his head turned toward the dancing crowd, he failed to notice Leah until he was almost at the base of the stairs.

"Hey," he said, smiling. "I'm glad I found you."

"Me, too," she said, her face momentarily blank with surprise. "Is there a bathroom up there?"

They made idle chatter about how great the music was for dancing while Nathan guided her up the staircase, toward the bathroom. While waiting for her, he stared at a photo of a lighthouse—a phallus rising out of what the photographer must have noticed were distinctly labial-looking crashing waves—until Ethan emerged from his room.

He glanced down the hallway at Nathan. "Is there someone in there?"

"Yeah, my girlfriend," Nathan said, folding his arms across his chest, and repositioning his feet for greater balance. Ethan stared at him, shook his head, then turned to walk back down the stairs.

When Leah opened the door, Nathan asked her if she would step back inside where they could talk for a moment in private. In the yellow bathroom, with the door closed, he asked, "Did you really come up here to use the toilet?"

"Why else would I have come up here?" Leah said, tilting her head in apparent confusion. When he continued to look at her searchingly, she asked, "Nathan, are you okay?"

He sat down on the closed lid of the toilet and briefly buried his face in his hands. "I'm fine. I don't want to leave."

"I wish you didn't have to go."

"Yeah? I feel like you've been acting kind of strange toward me lately."

Leah sighed. "And you seem like you're wanting to pick a fight."

"I'm not," Nathan said. "I don't know. Maybe I am because that would make things easier. But I'm going to be leaving here in a day or two and I just didn't want you to . . . I didn't want to leave here without . . . did you come up here to be with Ethan?"

"What?" Leah crossed her arms, then shook her head in exasperation. "No, I did not come up here to be with Ethan."

Nathan stared at her a long time, and at the moment he thought she might be getting ready to say something more, to clarify how her no might not really have been a no, he said, "Okay." He nodded and stared down at the white and yellow tiles between his feet.

"Why are you freaking out tonight?" Leah asked.

"I'm not freaking out . . . I'm just . . . I know you're moving to New York after this summer and a lot of these people live there, so . . ." Nathan hesitated a moment, wondering whether to remind her how a few of them had tried very hard to rupture his spleen, but he continued, "So I know it's a good idea for you to have fun and make friends with them so that you'll have friends to be with in New York. Maybe they can even get you a job. I'm not . . . I'm not angry with you for doing that."

"Good," Leah said. She still had her arms folded across her chest, and Nathan was groping for the words to unfold them.

He smiled at her quizzically, as if her brusqueness indicated she must not be understanding him. "I just . . . Because I'm not going to be here much longer and because I've kind of felt you drifting away from me the past couple of days—"

"Nathan, the woman you take care of nearly died, and you've been at the hospital a lot of the time. So I think it's been you as much as me."

"All right. I just want you to know that if I haven't seemed so . . . so confident lately . . . I just want you to know that that's not me. I know these guys all have a lot of money and are—"

"Nathan."

"No, I know it's not the money, I know they're smart, and probably funny, and charming, and they're probably more accomplished than me in a lot of ways, but I'm just letting you know that I have a lot going for me, too." Nathan wasn't sure what, exactly, he was going to point to as evidence, so he was relieved when she finally unfolded her arms and sighed, "I know you do."

"This all must sound pretty pathetic," Nathan said, smiling and shaking his head. "It's just that a lot of bad stuff kind of happened to me all at once . . . with my mom . . . and I didn't handle it as well as I probably should have." He was surprised to hear his voice tremble, but Leah stepped forward and crouched to put her hand on his knee.

"I probably shouldn't have left college," he continued, roughly wiping the dampness from his eyes. "I know I shouldn't, and I'm not sure right now about what I'm going to do, but I'm going to get sure. That's what I want you to know . . . I'm going to get sure because I want to be that kind of person for you."

Leah's dark eyes softened with understanding, and Nathan gently brushed a lock of hair from her upturned face. "Does that make sense?"

"Yes," she whispered, smiling compassionately. "But, Nathan, I haven't known you that long and you're leaving in a few days."

Nathan said, "I know I'm leaving in a few days, but so long as I have money, I can go anywhere I want. And I have money now. Maybe I can come back here or maybe I'll go to New York, but it'll be fine. Let's not worry about that now . . . I'm drunk . . . are you drunk?"

Leah laughed and rubbed her nose. "A little . . . maybe more."

"Me, too. I know exactly what I'm saying, but I'm drunk and I just want to kiss you again."

She kissed him long enough that Nathan began to feel that the conversation had been a success. He had told her how he felt about her and now, through her kiss, she was telling him how she felt about him. Resting her forehead against his, she asked, "Do you mind if I go dance again?"

"I want you to dance," Nathan said. "But I can't dance, so I'm going to watch you for a little while and then maybe wait for you in the backyard."

Even in Nathan's boozily optimistic frame of mind, wherein almost anything seemed possible, the dance floor still seemed too crowded to do much more than bump into other people while making your hands flutter in front of you. But Leah was enjoying herself, occasionally smiling over at Nathan where he stood beside the mantel. He watched her until his legs began to grow weary. Then he retired to the back lawn. Ralph and others were still gathered at the edge of the woods and Nathan sat down in the grass beside them, not so much to join the conversation as just to be in their company. He felt a deep love for humanity, and all those people he'd seen throughout his life carrying signs that said things like "Peace" and "Love Not Hate," well, maybe he shouldn't be so cynical about them. He lay back and closed his eyes, chuckling at the things he overheard Ralph and the others saying about the way they were in high school. He wanted to share with them how wonderful it felt to lie on this grass beneath a moonlit sky and to be in love with a beautiful person you thought probably loved you. He was thinking of letting them know, whenever they stopped talking about their worst haircuts, but when he cradled his head in his arm that was all sleep needed to overwhelm him.

Fourteen

The Morning After ~ From Ellen's Chamber to Her Carriage ~ An Unfortunate Sighting at Mariner's Rocks

The next morning Nathan felt woozily hungover as he squinted out his windows and got dressed. He smelled coffee. He didn't drink coffee himself, but he had brewed a cup in the mornings for Ellen, and smelling it reminded him that this was the last day he would see her in Maine.

In the kitchen, Ralph grunted in greeting. He sat at the table, unshaven, in the same blue shirt he'd worn last night.

Pouring himself a glass of juice, Nathan mumbled, "Glen still upstairs?"

"No, he just left for the hospital." Ralph lifted his eyes from the newspaper to peer at the digital clock on the coffeemaker. "We're supposed to meet him there in a couple hours."

Nathan blew his nose, nodding.

"I asked him about you maybe filling in for me after I leave."

"Yeah?" Nathan asked. He glanced over to see Ralph still reading the newspaper. "What did he say?"

"He seemed cool with it. He said he would think it over."

Nathan toasted a piece of bread and sat down at the table, sipping his juice. He stared out at the sunlit harbor. "Did you see Leah after I left?"

Ralph glanced up as if surprised to see Nathan sitting there. "Yeah," he said, finally, as he pushed himself back from the table. He raised his arms above his head and stretched as if being tortured on a medieval rack. "I saw her in the kitchen. I told her you went home and then I didn't see her after that."

Nathan rubbed the back of his neck as he considered this troubling information. Last night, when Ralph shook his shoulder to tell him he and his new friends were going to dance, Nathan stumbled drunkenly through the house a few times before deciding that Leah had very likely gone home. In his dark jeans and black T-shirt, he thought he must have been difficult to find, sleeping so close to the woods. Now he wondered if he should feel guilty for having left the party without telling her.

On the way to the airport, Ralph confessed—with some pleasure—that he had spent most of the night on Big Beach, feeling up the girl who loved *Forrest Gump.* But now he wondered what it would mean for his relationship with his girlfriend back home.

"Have you ever cheated on her before?" Nathan asked.

"No. Well, once. In the very beginning, when we had just started dating."

"How do you feel about what happened last night?"

Ralph continued staring out the front windshield and massaged the right side of his face. "I actually feel all right."

"Yeah?"

"Yeah."

"I have a theory about this if you want to hear it."

"All right. Hit me," Ralph said.

"Well, I think that if you've cheated on your girlfriend and you're sick to death about it and you know it's not going to happen again, you shouldn't tell her. It's making your own burden easier by giving it to her to share, and she shouldn't have to. *But* if you've cheated on her and you feel okay with it—if you're not wracked with guilt about it—then that suggests you may not feel as strongly about her as you might have imagined, and the odds are you're going to do it again. So you have a moral responsibility to tell her."

"Hmmm," Ralph said. "What if I feel okay with it and then guilty about it and then okay with it again?"

Nathan laughed. "Yeah, I don't know what to tell you then."

As Ralph reached to turn on the radio, Nathan said, "I think that's the problem with most of my theories—they all sound pretty good until I try to apply them to life."

Ellen understood something significant was about to happen. The swelling of her face kept her left eye from opening fully, but she followed with mute suspicion the white-clad figures moving in and out of her room. Glen stood at the foot of the bed, raising his glasses to peer down at the paperwork brought for him to sign, while talking with Nathan about the plan for the next couple of days. Glen asked, "Will it give you enough time to spend today and tomorrow here to wrap things up and then start home on Monday?"

Both men knew that the few things Nathan had to do at the house—packing Ellen's clothes, calling the handyman to tell him they were leaving—would not take two days; and although Nathan would have preferred to stay longer, he was grateful for Glen's thoughtfulness and said he'd leave Monday morning at the latest.

For a few minutes, the bustle of nurses to and fro suggested an on-time departure. But after the flow of paperwork stalled, Nathan and Ralph sat down on either side of Ellen, watching the tennis match on television above them. It seemed inappropriate to talk about things as trivial as tennis while Ellen was about to embark on a journey that might conceivably kill her. But when Glen commented on the match, asking who was supposed to be the better player—Pete Sampras or Andre Agassi—Ralph said he thought Sampras was supposed to be better, although Agassi was more fun to watch, and for a little while it felt like each word about tennis was another buffer against tragedy. The more they spoke as if nothing could happen to Ellen on that plane, the more likely it was that nothing would. When Sampras and Agassi took a break, the program flashed back to a match featuring Jana Novotná and Martina Hingis. Remembering his initial interview at Ellen's home, Nathan asked, "What do you think of Martina Hingis, Ralph?"

Ralph opened his mouth to answer, but the corner of his lip lifted in a smile. "I think she's good," he said at last.

Not long afterward, Dr. Sahni entered and supervised two nurses as they prepared Ellen for her ambulance ride to the airport. They hoisted her from the bed to the gurney, one of them rolling the portable pouch that fed the tube leading into Ellen's bruise-blackened arm.

"It's going to be all right, Momma," Glen assured her. Dr. Sahni continued speaking quietly to him as the nurses guided her out of the room. Two stocky orderlies grabbed either side of the gurney and rolled Ellen down the hallway in silence. Trailing them down the empty corridor, Nathan felt as if they were acting out some ancient procession, liveried footmen escorting a frail, aged queen from her bedchamber to her carriage. Then the exit doors swung open into the glare of sun-blasted pavement and the whooshing roar of the nearby highway.

Nathan put a reassuring hand on Ellen's shoulder as the orderlies collapsed the legs of the gurney and slid her through the opened ambulance doors. Staring out from the shaded interior, Ellen clenched and unclenched the white bedsheet tucked beneath her, and shook her head, as if baffled by all the commotion.

Glen put his glasses back on and signed a few forms that one of the nurses from the private plane service handed him. Finally, he shook Nathan's hand, saying, "Ralph said you might be interested in moving into the house with my mother?"

Nathan stammered but said, "Yeah . . . Ralph was just mentioning it to me as a possibility."

"Well, think it over." Glen handed him the keys to the Volkswagen and, glancing at Ralph, who was bumming a cigarette from one of the orderlies, added, "You don't have any pets, do you?"

"No."

Glen nodded somberly. "Good." He walked over and shook hands with Ralph, then threw his old army bag into the front of the ambulance and climbed into the back. He held one of his mother's hands and smiled crookedly as a nurse shut the doors. Nathan and Ralph watched without speaking as the ambulance circled and pulled out of the parking lot into the slow-moving flow of traffic. Ralph took a long drag of his cigarette and exhaled with squinting eyes. "So long, monkey," he said.

Nathan was looking forward to driving back in the Volkswagen, away from the stench of Ralph's truck, and where, alone, he could consider all the unanswered questions about Leah that now besieged him. Alcohol had allowed him to speak more freely than he perhaps would have otherwise last evening, but it was also blurring his memory of what they'd said. He remembered that it went well—she had kissed him so soulfully!—but had she still seemed reserved when Nathan spoke of leaving Cleveland? Back at the house, while Ralph slept on the living room couch, Nathan went into the kitchen to phone her.

Eldwin answered and said that Rachel's sister was visiting and had taken the kids to Freeport to do some school shopping, so he'd given Leah the afternoon off. He didn't know where she'd gone. Perhaps noticing the disappointment in Nathan's voice, he added, "I was getting ready to take a walk if you feel like getting out of the house."

Nathan wanted to walk and look for Leah, but he was afraid Eldwin would slow him down and make any encounter with her awkward. So he said he was too exhausted and planned to nap. For a while after he hung up, he stared out the kitchen window and bit his thumbnail. Then he quietly exited out the back door and squinted up Harbor Avenue.

He saw no sign of Eldwin.

Hurrying up the gravel road, Nathan thought about strategy. He decided he would no longer be looking for Leah to say, "Yes, absolutely, come and be with me in New York." That was a stupid thing for him to have wanted from her anyway. It would put too much pressure on her, and on them. He would simply look for affirmation that she loved him, and then say cautiously, "Well, let's take it slow. I'll go back to Cleveland, wrap things up there, and then, if it seems like a good idea, I'll see if I can find my own place in New York." If he got there soon enough, he could still probably take the train here a few weekends before the summer was over.

On Big Beach, parents lounged in deck chairs beneath umbrellas as their children scuttled crablike along the farthest reaches of the tide. When he spotted Eldwin, fifty yards or so in front of him—head bent down toward the sand—Nathan slowed and trailed behind him. Every now and then Eldwin would crouch down to pick up a shell, and Nathan would have to stop and pretend to tie his shoes or just stare contemplatively at the ocean. They walked several hundred yards in this way until Eldwin had crouched more than a dozen times and Nathan—too tired of the charade to continue—just kept walking toward him.

Eldwin was wearing dark wraparound shades that made it impossible to see his eyes. Nathan told him he had changed his mind about the nap, and Eldwin nodded as he picked a broken seashell out of the sand. "Meghan's been collecting seashells, so I've been trying to find some good ones for her," he explained, brushing it off and slipping it into his pocket.

Strolling down the beach, Nathan asked Eldwin's advice about whether to accept Glen's invitation to live with Ellen in Cleveland.

"It sounds like it would be a great place to devote some time to drawing your next graphic novel, or just to read," Eldwin answered. He said he had a writer friend who was working on the second volume of a memoir while at the same time having to teach at a junior college, and who would relish the gift of time being offered to Nathan. In this comment lay much of why Nathan felt grateful for Eldwin and had begun to see him as a friend. Whereas most people he knew would ask the obvious question—*Why would a twentysomething man want to live with an old woman, even if it is for free?*—Eldwin was like-minded enough to understand why this might be a great opportunity. He was also generous enough to suggest that Nathan and this writer were men of the same kind. Which was why Nathan struggled to say what he was thinking without diminishing Eldwin's respect for him.

"Yeah, I mean, it could be good, but I also feel like I want to go out and *do* something. It's hard not to feel like being at Ellen's would be part of the holding pattern I feel like I've been in for a while now."

"What else do you think you might want to do?"

"I don't know," Nathan said, although what he meant was that he wanted a life with more apparent success. There had to be lots of easier ways to be successful than as a graphic novelist.

"You would be *doing* something at Ellen's, right?"

"Yeah, I would," Nathan said. He knew Eldwin envisioned him hunkered over his desk, drawing, or poring over the great works of the Western world. But Nathan saw himself sitting in that dimly lit living room, making idle conversation about the tennis on television, or at restaurants, explaining to Ellen that each bearded man who passed by was not Glen. Nathan understood the romance of the notion of living at Ellen's—the artist in his garret, forging out of his private anguish something beautiful—but he felt the part about the private anguish wasn't being given nearly enough consideration. He wanted to tell Eldwin that he had spent almost three years working on a meticulously illustrated book of stories that now embarrassed him and lay yellowing in the backseat of his car.

Near Mariner's Rocks—where the dunes gave way to sandstone boulders that curved east, forming a narrow peninsula—Nathan noticed Thayer on a beach towel roughly fifty yards away. He was wearing a gray-and-blue bathing suit and lay propped up on his elbows, watching a young woman alone in the ocean. Nathan squinted. Dressed in a red bikini, Danielle pushed rippling waves in front of her as she high-stepped toward the shore.

"There's your sparring partner," Eldwin said. He nodded toward where Thayer lay as Danielle walked over to kneel down beside him. She searched inside a canvas bag then toweled off her wet hair.

"Is it wrong to pray he gets skin cancer?" Nathan asked.

"Yeah, it is," Eldwin sighed, as if saddened to have to say so. He glanced over at the boardwalk that led back onto Oceanside Avenue. "You want to go up or go back the way we came?"

"Why don't we go up?" Nathan said. It might have been more scenic walking along the beach, but it would have been the same scenery, and also, Nathan was tired of the constant mild anxiety of wondering whether each distant figure might be Leah. At the top of the boardwalk steps, he stopped because Eldwin had turned to look over the coastline. It was a breathtaking view, charming clapboard homes presiding over the leaden blue of the Atlantic. Nathan inhaled the ocean air, then noticed on his right a young woman suddenly sit up on the beach. He hadn't noticed her earlier because she was lying close to the dunes, obscured by the boardwalk. But now he could see her plainly. Even from fifty yards away, he knew it was Leah. On her far side, a young man—Ethan, the host of the previous evening's party—lay in knee-length blue swimming trunks, propped up on one elbow to face her. When the wind blew, Leah turned her head in a familiar gesture, pushing a lock of hair from her brow and holding it above her forehead as she talked.

"You ready?" Eldwin said.

"Hold on," Nathan said. His face had flushed so suddenly that he felt momentarily faint.

Leah drank from a soda can and then lay on her side facing Ethan. She pulled her bikini bottom higher on her hip.

"Fuuuuck," Eldwin said, following Nathan's gaze to where Leah was lying on the beach.

Nathan could see only the back of her—naked except for the dark triangle of her bikini bottom and the string over her shoulder blades. As they talked, Ethan occasionally reached out to touch the side of her face. She pulled back as if in protest, but remained steady as he leaned forward to kiss her.

"Nathan," Eldwin whispered. But Nathan did not answer. Leah and Ethan had stopped kissing, and Nathan thought that perhaps she was explaining to him that she could be his friend . . . *but not your girlfriend . . . because do you remember that one guy who was at the party and dancing with me?* But then she laughed. Ethan reached for her head again, then guided her onto her back and leaned over to kiss her as Nathan moved with weak-feeling legs down the stairs.

"Nathan."

"What?"

"Where are you going?"

"Where does it look like I'm going?"

"But what's the point?"

"To let them know that I fucking saw them!" Nathan cried, but even as he spoke he felt his strength draining from him. He did not know what the point would be. He could go over and disrupt them, but he was leaving soon. He couldn't shame or argue Leah into wanting him more. He just didn't know what else to do.

"Leave it," Eldwin said.

Nathan must have spoken more loudly than he'd realized. Thayer, Danielle, Ethan, and Leah were all looking up at him as he stood paralyzed on the boardwalk. Leah turned away and shook her head.

Eldwin said, "C'mon, man. Let it go."

The walk down Oceanside Avenue seemed eternal. On the beach, they could have walked in the lengthening shadows of the coastal homes, but on the road, they were exposed to the burning relentlessness of the sun. The air above the blacktop shimmered with heat, and each time a car passed—a gleaming rush of hot metal—flecks of sand and dirt wafted toward Nathan's eyes.

"You know, sometimes the person you're attracted to isn't the best person for you," Eldwin remarked.

Nathan snorted. "Apparently."

Minutes later, Eldwin asked, "What are you thinking?"

"I'm thinking that you can only do this kind of stuff and have it all turn to shit so many times without it killing something inside you."

Nathan couldn't tell if Eldwin was grimacing in the heat or just smiling indulgently.

"You're still a young man."

"I don't feel young," Nathan said, his weary voice reminding him of his father. "I feel like I want to destroy something, and then maybe take a long nap."

After saying good-bye to Eldwin, with promises of getting together again before Nathan had to leave the Cove, Nathan discovered that Ralph's truck was not in the driveway of Ellen's house. In the kitchen, he found a note written in almost illegibly slanting print.

Nathan,

I was thinking this is probably your last night with Leah and I should probably get out of here anyway. Give me a call when you get back to Cleveland.

Ralph

Nathan mixed a drink then went into the living room and sat down in Ellen's chair. Staring out the French doors, he could hear voices drifting up from Parson's Beach, and for a while he watched the sailboats tack toward the mouth of the bay. He did not want to stay in Brightonfield Cove and he did not want to go home. When he finished his drink, he poured himself another. He wandered upstairs to Ellen's bedroom and stared at the lumpy, grayish-crimson stain in the carpet, the emptied closets, the combs and hairpins on the dresser. Then he walked toward the back bedrooms, where Glen and Ralph had stayed. Glen's bed was tightly made and he had left nothing in the sunny, floral-wallpapered room except for an empty wineglass and a Tony Hillerman paperback on the nightstand. Ralph's room was not as tidy. Nathan straightened out the rumpled throw rug, and while bending over to pick up an embroidered pillow near the foot of the unmade bed, he noticed a torn condom wrapper on the floor. Kneeling down amid the dust bunnies that had accumulated along the baseboards, Nathan warily looked for a used condom but couldn't find one. He sat down on the bed and fingered the faded purple wrapper, setting his drink on the bedside table. Because he'd had sex with Leah not long after meeting her, he wondered how long it would be before Ethan had sex with her, too. Imagining them fucking filled him with erotic anxiety. He alleviated some of this anxiety on the woolen throw rug, then lay panting on his side. Back in his bedroom he grabbed his sketchbook and pencils and took them out onto the porch, where, thumbing through his drawings, he found his portrait of Leah. He'd started it the evening she posed for him in his room, but they had ended up in bed before he'd been able to finish. It was a light sketch, using just a 2H pencil. Suddenly, Nathan had an idea. He would finish the portrait and then leave it for her, along with a poignantly dignified note. Then she would see herself as Nathan saw her, and the recognition of what she had given up would be like a burning lance in her heart. Nathan worked for more than an hour, erasing the eyes several times and puzzling over the right expression for her lips. As his shoulders began to ache, he fetched a comforter from inside and stretched out on the porch floor. At first he drew with excitement and expectation, but after the second hour, he felt disappointed with what he'd accomplished and thought he needed to rest. He lay back on the comforter and closed his eyes.

The sky was a darker blue when Nathan awoke. He turned on his side and, after waiting for his eyes to adjust, stared down at the portrait with mounting impatience and disgust. Her eyes were too narrow and her face seemed somehow bonier than it did in real life. If he gave her the portrait as it was, she might think he was trying to be mean, when what he wanted was to be nice in a way that filled her with gut-wrenching regret. Gazing out at the empty beach, Nathan thought he might cry. He exhaled in sharp, staggered breaths through his nose, but he knew almost immediately that he wouldn't weep, and he felt sick of himself for having tried.

Caffeine might be beneficial for his dazed sluggishness, he thought, and in the kitchen he poured some more Coke into his almost empty glass. More rum was not a good idea, but seeing the bottle on the counter, he thought, A little hair of the dog, et cetera, et cetera, and couldn't resist pouring some in. He sat at the table, paging through his sketchbook and staring out the window. Then he reached for the phone. He dialed Leah's number, but when Eldwin answered, he hung up, his heartbeat loud in his ears.

Holding his head in his hands, he noticed that his skin felt flushed and tender, as if he might have a fever. In the bathroom, while looking for a thermometer, he looked in the mirror and discovered that his face was a mottled pinkish red. He pressed two fingers against his right cheekbone and watched the skin go white, then deep pink again. He had fallen asleep in the sun. In the living room, Nathan contemplated his good fortune in Leah's not having answered the phone. She might have agreed to come over and would have seen his face, which, as if in response to the afternoon's humiliation, was now as red as a crying child's. The sunburn, no doubt, would have made it more difficult to take him seriously.

Shaking the ice cubes in his glass, he wondered if she had ever taken him seriously. It was possible that, when talking about his love of comics or how he felt for her, she'd thought him charming or endearing without really respecting him. Sophie had screamed at him, cursed his name, even told him about her test for STDs and ordered him to leave her apartment, but Nathan never doubted that she respected him. He stared out the window, massaging his forehead, then once more picked up the phone.

When a woman answered, he said, "Hi, Mrs. Hurst. Is Sophie there?"

"No, she isn't. May I ask who's calling?"

The friendly question twisted in his gut because although he was hoping not to have to talk with Sophie's mother, he also thought they enjoyed a special bond. Around the time he and Sophie had broken up, Nathan had run into her mother at a local video store. They had talked for a while about what had happened, and when they hugged, her faintly smoky-smelling hair reminded Nathan of the smell of her house. "I'm sure I'll be seeing you again soon," she'd said, lifting her chin optimistically. And Nathan had thought he knew what she meant: that her daughter loved him too much for them not to get back together, and that soon he would be visiting at their house just as he had in the past.

"It's Nathan."

"Oh, Nathan, I thought it sounded like you. How are you doing?"

"I'm doing okay, how about you?"

"Well, I'm just about to put dinner on the table. Sophie's not here, but I can give you her number."

Nathan hesitated, but said, "Okay."

When she finished giving him the number, Nathan said, "I just got a letter from her a little while ago that said she had moved back home."

"Well, she and Derek had had some sort of fight, so she was here for a little while, but now she's back at their apartment."

Nathan paused, then asked, "Do you know what happened? From what she wrote, it just seemed like she was planning to live at home for a while."

"Well, I don't know all of it. But I guess they're working it out now."

"Hmm," Nathan said. "I guess that's good."

"I'm sorry things didn't turn out better for you two."

"No. Don't be. I'm doing all right. I'm just glad things are turning out well for her. In the letter she sounded distressed, so I was just kind of calling to check up on her."

"Oh, that's very sweet of you, Nathan."

"Well."

She asked, "Do you have their address, in case you think it might be better to write her?"

Nathan closed his eyes as she read the address to him. He listened to the echo of Sophie's voice within her mother's, but did not move, holding his sunburned head in his hand.

That night he poured several more drinks and watched more television in a single sitting than he had in a long time. He searched for programs with beautiful women, and stumbled over to the couch to lie down, tucking one of the pillows beneath his head. The television's soothing radiance filled the room, and long after midnight—when he'd muted the volume—Nathan watched a gorgeous brunette deliver bad news to a man with eyes so full of pathos you could almost see his heart trembling inside him.

"Fuck you," Nathan mumbled. He shook his head and soon fell asleep.

Fifteen

Hope Springs a Little While Longer ~ Final Voyage of the *Little Red Hen* ~ We Are Not Dead

Living room draperies billowed gently over the couch, and behind them Nathan saw the blue and cloudless morning sky. His spirits lifted for an instant. Then he remembered everything that had happened. He suffered a dull, sinus kind of headache that radiated from the front of his head. But only one bottle of aspirin remained in the bathroom cabinets, with an expiration date of December 1992. Nathan opened it to peer inside, then decided to make do without. In the kitchen, he prepared a few pieces of toast and chewed them slowly, paging through yesterday's newspaper. On the far side of the table was his sketchbook, and after a while he pulled it over to look at his unfinished portrait of Leah. The hair wasn't bad—a few dark locks falling down the right side of her face, waiting to be tucked back behind her ear. But her eyes were still too narrow. He puzzled over them a few minutes, then let his attention drift out the window.

A mother and her three children in bathing suits and flip-flops were walking through the yard to Parson's Beach. Nathan watched them for a few moments and then gazed out at Stone Island. He could see the dandelion-speckled grass where he and Leah had enjoyed their late-evening picnic and once made love. Absently caressing the sunburned skin beneath his right eye, Nathan considered drawing a picture for Leah that would be different from the one he'd been laboring over. A picture that would remind her of the evening they had spent together on the island. He wasn't thinking of drawing the two of them on the blanket. That would be too sentimental, and besides, he was tired of trying to draw her accurately. Instead he envisioned drawing the island's view of Brightonfield Cove. From the clearing, he and Leah had been able to see most of the town's coastline, including Ellen's house and the narrow gravel road leading up to where Leah lived. Once she saw the drawing, Leah would recognize the vantage point and remember what significance the place held for them. She might roll it back up and put it away, but Nathan hoped for a night when she would come home from some pretentious party in New York, unroll the drawing, and then, choking back sobs, contact him through the phone number or address he planned to write in small, modest print on the back.

By the time Nathan had gathered his sketchbook and pencils, sunscreen, a blanket, two peanut butter and jelly sandwiches, a bottle of water, a plastic cup, rum, and two cans of Coke, it was already midafternoon. He stuffed his supplies in his canvas backpack and headed out to the shed.

The *Little Red Hen* was as heavy as Nathan remembered, and he half-carried, half-dragged it out onto the grass. Away from the shade, the sun began further branding his already sunburned face. Nathan grabbed a straw hat from the shed before easing the boat onto his back, then staggered halfway down the sloping lawn. When a phone rang, he set the boat down with a hurried thud and ran a few yards toward the house before he realized the sound was coming from a neighbor's window. Bending over beneath the boat again, like a turtle lumbering toward water, Nathan felt the seat dig into the base of his neck. He set the boat down and returned to the shed to pick up the backpack and oars. Laying them on the floor of the boat, he decided to just drag the thing. The dinghy made a few dull, scraping sounds as Nathan pulled it through the tall grass. But when he inspected the bottom, near the shoreline, it appeared no worse for the wear.

A hundred yards or so down the coastline, the blond mother Nathan had seen earlier was now reading in a beach chair while her children labored with colored buckets along the tide's edge. Glancing up at Ellen's house, Nathan hoped to see Leah walking along the porch, searching for him. But except for the drift of draperies, the house was still. He kicked off his tennis shoes and placed them beneath the seat. Then, wincing at the chill of the water, he pushed the boat out a few yards and quickly tumbled aboard.

Because Ellen's straw hat had a plastic sunflower attached to the front, Nathan waited until he was a couple hundred yards out to put it on, and by that time he was already having second thoughts about the trip. The sun pressed hot against his back and reflected off the shimmering water into his sunburned face and eyes. As he rowed, he thought about the intense heat he would be stewing under while sitting on his blanket on the island. There were no trees where he needed to sit, only the lighthouse, and the thought of following a column of lighthouse shade for most of the day did little to relieve his throbbing headache.

Why had he wanted to draw this picture, anyway? In the cool air of Ellen's kitchen, he'd thought it might help make Leah want him, but out in the wobbling boat, already exhausted from the rowing, Nathan began to wonder if there wasn't something pathetic about this quest. It would mean spending the rest of the day beneath a merciless sun while Leah was probably taking tennis lessons with Thayer, or frolicking on the beach with the children and Ethan. If she didn't want to be with Nathan now—while he was living just two doors away—what were the odds that she would pine for him while he was living in Cleveland and she was living it up in New York City? Even if she didn't continue seeing Ethan, there were lots of smart, successful, good-looking young men who would want to date her in New York. Thinking about them made Nathan jealous as well as tired of his jealousy. Squinting, he glanced back and forth between Ellen's house and Stone Island, and his brooding thoughts distracted him from the water seeping through the boat's floor.

At first it was just a small pool near the stern, but when it touched the sides of Nathan's feet he stopped rowing to peer behind him. Yanking his already damp-bottomed backpack to the front, he felt around with his hands in the cold and brackish water, but soon gave up the hope of trying to find the source. He cupped a few handfuls of water over the side, then grabbed the oars. The leak was slow but steady, and by the time Nathan turned the boat around, the water was already lapping against his bare ankles.

He rowed like a skinny, coked-up Viking for several minutes, then pulled the oars inside the boat. Unzipping his backpack, he snatched out the plastic cup and used it to scoop out several gallons of water. The ocean leaked into the boat at about the same rate that Nathan was able to throw it out, and although it might have been possible for him to stay afloat indefinitely in this way, screaming for help until someone rescued him, he was also mortified by the idea that Leah and her friends would learn what had happened. Nathan had suffered enough indignities in this town. He jabbed the oars into the bay and continued rowing against the tide, even as the cold, murky water began to creep up his shins.

He did not want to stop rowing, but the bottom of his backpack was turning dark brown, and he couldn't bear to watch months of sketches—including those of Leah—become soaked. So he brought in an oar and slung the backpack onto his back. For several frantic minutes Nathan hoped—perhaps even believed—that he would be able to row the *Little Red Hen* back to shore. He rowed even after every muscle in his arms screamed for rest. But with each inch the boat sank, the less progress he made. Each labored stroke propelled him only a few feet, and he was still several hundred yards from the beach. As the frigid water inched up his calves, Nathan's concerns about dignity drowned in a rising level of panic.

Glancing over his shoulder, he saw the flapping blue umbrella and the children building something in the sand with their buckets.

"Hey!" Nathan shouted. "Help! My boat is sinking!" The words rang in his ears like the lines of a joke and he was stricken to see neither the woman nor her children stand or even look at him. A quarter-mile to his left, a few yachts were anchored, including Bill McAlister's *Daydreamer,* but Nathan saw nobody on deck.

"Help! Fucking help me!" Nathan screamed. The oars slapped chilled, briny water against his body as he lurched back and forth, half standing, trying to pull the boat through the harbor. He knew he might have to try and swim to shore, but the water sloshing around his legs felt as cold as the water from a refrigerator. If he submerged his body in it, he had no idea what effect it would have on him. He yanked the oars into the boat and frantically cupped water over the side while he continued screaming for help. When the water was more than halfway up his calves, Nathan turned to see the woman crouched down beside her children. He stood and screamed at her again, waving his backpack above his head like a shipwrecked sailor waving a flag. The woman stood but made no sign of having heard him. So Nathan carefully laid the backpack on the seat, pulled on his shoes, then leapt into the harbor.

The biting cold swallowed him, then pushed him up, his muscles suddenly hard and jerky in their movements. He felt a great weight against his chest and took shallow, trembling breaths as he treaded water. His plan was to turn the *Little Red Hen* over, then either climb back into the emptied boat or—if that proved impossible—to use the overturned boat for flotation as he kicked and yelled his way back to shore.

Nathan pulled down on the boat's rim—far enough for it to take on more water, but that was all. He snatched his backpack from the boat and watched with dread as the boat sank beneath the surface of the bay.

On shore, the blue umbrella still rippled in the wind, but there was no one nearby. The woman and her children were moseying up Ellen's lawn. Propelling himself higher out of the water, Nathan screamed. He thought he saw the woman turn, but she only ushered her children in front of her and carried on up the hill.

Nathan shrieked at her to come back, and he flung the already saturated backpack a few yards in her direction, where it sank. There was no time to brood about what he had lost. He had never swum the breast-stroke more than the length of a high school pool, but he was encouraged to discover he was making more progress than he had during those last few minutes on the boat. His neck began to hurt from craning it out of the water, but he swam for roughly forty yards. When he paused to rest, he realized that the tide was carrying him almost back to where he had started. Nathan resumed swimming. But the water seemed to grow denser and denser, until its consistency was like a dark paste he had to pull his arms harder and harder to pass through. He rested, then resumed swimming again, but he did not seem to be moving much farther. He noticed that if he minimized his movements, the water warmed around him a little and he didn't feel quite as cold. The current moved unrelentingly against him, wanting to drag him backward through the harbor and into the deeper emptiness of the Atlantic. Nathan shouted once again for help. But after several more minutes of swimming, it occurred to him that he was probably not going to make it to shore.

Dark thoughts moved slothfully through the shadows of his brain. His mother, already earth cold and worm-eaten, would not suffer by losing him. Nor would Sophie or Leah. The latter two might shed a few obligatory tears, but his death would soon be a footnote in their histories. Eldwin? Nathan did not know how he would respond to his death, but Eldwin would probably think it nobler for him to swim. Nathan swam a few more yards, but he quickly tired, and it was so much warmer just to float. He treaded water and floated while thoughts about his mother and father seemed to pull at him from below. He could see his father receiving the phone call from the police and sitting down at the empty dining room table, sobbing, then overturning the table and hurling his dead wife's miniatures and bric-a-brac into the glass of the antique china cabinet. But was that right? Wouldn't he just lean over the table and bury his bleary face in his hands? Nathan could see him more clearly later, with the blinds closed, weeks of dirty dishes in the kitchen, staring at his bedroom television on Sunday in the same T-shirt and underwear he'd been wearing since Friday morning. But what use was Nathan to him? His father needed something—some lightness of being or inspiration—Nathan did not think it in his dark heart to give.

The water formed a warm cocoon around him. Once in a while he would persuade himself that he had energy enough to swim; but each time, he made so little progress, and he wanted so much to be warm again, that he would stop and tilt his head back, kicking occasionally to stay afloat. The brim of Ellen's hat rubbed against the back of his neck, and he flung it away. His shoes were heavy, and he kicked them off, then immediately wished that he hadn't. They had kept a layer of warmer water around his feet, which soon felt as if they were falling asleep. The tide was carrying him toward the mouth of the harbor, and Nathan slowly digested the fact that there was nothing he could do to fight the current. Bill McAlister's property extended into the mouth of the bay, and it was possible the tide would carry Nathan close enough there to swim to shore. But such thoughts were internal gadfly murmurings he was not really listening to anymore. He just wanted to stay where he was, within the somnolent warmth of his cocoon.

He saw a large, dark-haired man in khaki shorts and white T-shirt appear on Ellen's lawn. Nathan raised his hands and tried to yell. His voice sounded less forceful than it had earlier, but the man hurried down toward the beach anyway, a dark Labrador trotting behind him. It was Eldwin. He lumbered down the lawn with arms raised and flapping, a fat man trying to fly.

So the woman did see me, Nathan thought. She saw me and clambered up the hill with her children and told Eldwin, who was probably out walking his dog. Now she was on the phone with the authorities, who would soon be arranging for a motorboat to speed away from the yacht club and pluck him out of the ocean. The thought of being safe and truly warm again seemed to make him warmer already.

Eldwin hurled himself along the shoreline, stumbling over rocks and washed-up logs while waving one hand excitedly above his head. Nathan waved back and tried to shout that it was okay, it wasn't necessary to run.

Nathan knew they were coming soon to pick him up with the speedboat from the yacht club. But Eldwin did not seem to understand. He sprinted the whole length of the beach—like a lineman struggling to return a fumble—but then stopped near the little dock at the bottom of Mr. McAlister's yard. He pulled off his shirt, which made sense, because then he could wave to the speedboat and maybe point to where Nathan was. But then he did a little mincing motion with his feet in order to take off his shoes.

Nathan cried, "No! They're coming!"

Eldwin trotted off the shore of broken shells, his heavy, flaccid body crashing into the water. Nathan waved his arms above him and shouted, "No! I can hold on! You're going to drown, you stupid motherfucker!" even though he knew his words were being stripped away by the wind. Across the small but rolling waves he could only occasionally see Eldwin's head. Nathan used his arms to propel himself forward as he continued screaming for Eldwin to turn back. The water was cold and his body trembled, but he started swimming harder toward shore.

Sunlight poured through the draperied hospital window and warmed the left side of Nathan's face. The first time he'd awakened, he had not known where he was, and for one irrational instant he feared he had somehow become Ellen. Now he breathed more easily. The ham and eggs the nurse brought in for breakfast allowed him to apply his new sensory awareness to eating. He sucked on the warm meatiness of the ham and with his tongue rolled the rubbery eggs around his mouth. Biting into his toast, Nathan stared out his window at the sunlit courtyard.

I am not dead, he thought.

He was about to say this aloud when he glimpsed through the doorway a nurse slowly pushing a middle-aged woman in a wheelchair down the hall. The woman's dark head was titled at a palsied angle and drool hung pendulously from her lips.

Later in the day, the limp raucousness of the morning game shows echoed through the hallway into his room. A delivery woman brought in a vase of red tulips and handed Nathan a card.

Nathan,

I'm so sorry to hear about your accident. The summer has turned out so awfully for you! I wish we could have hit it off better while you were here, and I hope you know how much all of us appreciate what you did for Aunt Ellen this summer. Lucien and I wish you a speedy recovery.

Sincerely,
Kendra

Nathan slid the card beneath the vase and tilted the vase toward him to smell the tulips, pulling off one of the petals with his mouth before taking it out and laying it on the bedside table. While sitting beside Ellen one afternoon in the hospital, Glen had read her a Jack London story called "Love of Life." In it, a starving man struggles through northern Canadian wilderness until a ship discovers his emaciated figure writhing on shore. Once on the ship, the man eats everything he can find and grows fat, but after a while he eats like normal again.

"You awake?" Eldwin asked.

Nathan opened his eyes and pushed himself up in the bed. Even though he knew he wasn't dying, it was still a relief to see Eldwin wearing jeans and a tan polo shirt instead of pastoral black. In his left hand, he carried a white plastic bag.

"How are you feeling?"

"Alive," Nathan said.

Eldwin took a seat in the chair beside the bed. "You had me worried there for a little while."

"Yeah, well, thanks for bringing me in."

"How much do you remember?"

Nathan said, "I think I remember everything." But he didn't, at least not at first. He remembered swimming toward Eldwin—the big man shouting encouragement to him as both of them fought the frigid waves.

He also remembered that they'd both stumbled, exhausted, out of the harbor and onto the jutting peninsula of Bill McAlister's property. Nathan had wanted to lie on the bed of warm sand and battered seashells, but Eldwin had hustled him up to a neighbor's home, shouting for help. Nathan had trembled so much he could barely walk. In the house, an old couple had dressed Nathan in . . . oh fuck . . . Nathan remembered now that his trembling hands were so useless that Eldwin and the old man had helped him out of his soaked clothes, unbuttoning his shorts and pulling them off with his underwear, then zipping him up into one of the old man's tracksuits. The wife was much heavier than the old man, so Eldwin had had to push himself into a tracksuit of patterned roses and lavender. The couple swaddled the two men in blankets and drove them to Brightonfield Hospital.

Eldwin said, "I was wondering if you were going to have a heart attack on our way over. You would look okay for a little while, and then you would suddenly look like you were about to shake out of your skin."

Nathan recalled moments of the drive, the back of the old man's furry head, the woman's face knotted with worry, and it embarrassed him to remember that he had been sobbing against the window of the car.

"You probably saved my life."

"I didn't. I don't think I even touched you until we got to shore."

"Yeah, but—" Nathan stopped, not wanting to admit to what he'd been thinking while in the water. Instead, he said, "I might have had a heart attack on shore there if you hadn't taken me up to that house."

Eldwin shook his head. "You would have made it." He spoke with such frowning conviction that for an instant Nathan persuaded himself that this was true. Eldwin grabbed the white plastic bag from the floor and said, "I picked you up another sketch pad and some pens. I thought you might want to draw while you were here. I didn't know what kinds of pens you would want, so I just got you some of the different types."

Nathan took the fistful of pens and laid the sketch pad in his lap, briefly flipping through the pages. "Thanks a lot," he said, smiling down at the sketch pad. He must have been weaker than he'd realized, because his voice broke when he added, "I'll pay you for them when I get back to the house."

"They're a gift," Eldwin said. Inspecting the sole of his shoe, he asked, "Have you told anybody what happened?"

Nathan rubbed his nose and shook his head. "No, I've just been sleeping for most of the day."

"You might want to call Glen, and maybe your dad, and let them know you're okay, before they hear the story from someone else."

"Who else knows?"

"Well, the Vogels, the couple who drove us here. Also, Mrs. Trentman. She was the woman who saw you out there and ran and told me. They might have told other people."

"Does Leah know?"

Eldwin nodded. "Yeah, she knows."

For a moment, they sat in silence. Then Nathan said, "Were they trying to get you to stay here, too?"

"Yeah, I was fine, though. I wasn't in the water as long as you were, and I've got a protective layer of blubber you don't have." He pulled a pack of cigarettes from his shirt pocket and then shook his head, murmuring, "Hospital," before putting them back. Nathan worried aloud about the loss of the *Little Red Hen,* but Eldwin told him he thought Glen would just be glad to hear he was okay. When the conversation turned to insurance—Nathan's father had long ago begged him to pay eighty bucks a month for basic health insurance that would help cover some of the expenses he was incurring—Eldwin said, "Probably better to stay one more night like they want." He asked the nurse what time Nathan would be released, and then returned to tell him he'd be back tomorrow morning to take him back to the Cove.

"Don't knock up any candy stripers," Eldwin warned.

Nathan had only a vague idea of what a candy striper was, but a smile remained on his face a few moments after Eldwin had left. He was grateful for Eldwin's gift—for the sentiment, of course, but also because the pens and paper seemed once again like a ragged lifeline being thrown to him. He wasn't sure that it was possible to escape entirely from his sadness, but at least he could try to pull himself through with his drawing. *Follow your bliss!* he'd often heard from well-meaning people, or read on bumper stickers, but the most common interpretation of this advice—that everyone has a passion he or she should pursue—always made Nathan uncomfortable. His parents, and even people he had met in Brightonfield Cove, seemed to have lots of activities that brought them pleasure, and even joy, and Nathan disliked seeing good, otherwise life-loving people grappling with the gloomy uncertainty of what their bliss was, or how to go about finding it. Nathan thought he understood the wisdom the bumper stickers were attempting to impart, but even for him, for whom drawing was beginning to seem as much a part of who he was as his face, bliss seemed too light and carefree a word to describe the exhausted elation he felt—every once in a great while—when staring at something he'd just created.

It seemed more appropriate to think of bliss with regard to romance, but his front-row seat this summer for the romantic flailings of Carl Buchanan, Ellen, and Mr. McAlister, had allowed Nathan to witness how endlessly elusive such bliss could be. His memories of Ellen, friendless at home, aching for Bill's arrival, and of his own similarly focused attempts to win (and hold on to) Sophie and Leah, reminded Nathan that when he returned home to Cleveland he would have no one really to talk with.

He wasn't sure if Eldwin regarded him as a friend or as just a companionable kayak partner / charity case, but Nathan wished he knew more people like him. The man was suffering under the burden of a depressive wife, an unhealthy desire for booze, and any number of parishioners wanting his help to sort through their anguish. Yet, wittingly or not, he had found the means to buoy Nathan in ways the younger man could not help but acknowledge. Already Nathan was considering more seriously Glen's offer to live with Ellen. He saw it as an opportunity to make up for his occasional ineptitude as a caregiver, to complete the graphic novel about his mother (and maybe start one about this summer), and to free up some expenses so he could enroll in classes at the university. He felt like he had been long oppressed by a preoccupation with happiness—*Was he happy? Was he really following his bliss?*—and felt emboldened by the prospect of learning more about Aristotle, and thinking in terms of virtue and bravery.

When the nurse brought a turkey sandwich and tomato soup, Nathan ate with the TV on as he stared out the window. In the courtyard a stone bench sat amidst a colorful garden. Nathan did not know the names of many of the plants, but the spear-length stalks with red, conical blossoms looked familiar. Maybe they could grow in the Midwest. The modest circle of earth was beautifully landscaped and might give his father ideas for his garden. In a little while, Nathan would call him and let him know what had happened. Then maybe he would draw the garden and, when he returned to Cleveland, give his father the illustration. It had been a long time since Nathan had done something like that for him. He mulled the idea over as he finished eating his turkey sandwich. Then he wiped his mouth, cleared the table, and began to sort through his new pens.

ACKNOWLEDGMENTS

I am grateful for the invaluable wisdom of my editor, Lee Boudreaux, as well as for the encouragement and support of JB, Katie Bollmer, Evan Carroll, Martin Edlund, Inga Fairclough, Atieno Fisher, Mya Frazier, Jeff Groh, Steven and Marisa Groh, Jake Halpern, David Hayes, Holly Herr, Kate Isenberg, Rob Jefferson, Amelie Arbour Lasalle, my sharp-eyed agent PJ Mark, Benjamin Soskis, Donna Spivey, Kellie Van Swearingen, Harvey Tharp, and most especially, George and Donita Groh.

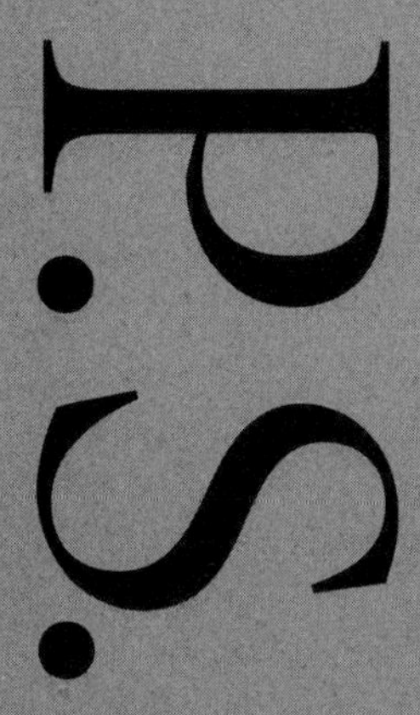

Insights, Interviews & More . . .

About the author

About the book

Read on

About the author

Meet Brian Groh

BRIAN GROH grew up in Ohio and has lived in Great Britain, Costa Rica, and Maine. He has written for *The New Republic*, MTV, and *National Geographic Traveler*. *Summer People* is his first novel.

A Conversation with Brian Groh

How did the idea for this book originate?

I'm not Nathan Empson, the protagonist of my novel, but when I was twenty-two years old, I did, like Nathan, accept a job as a caregiver for an older woman in an exclusive coastal community in southern Maine. It was an extraordinary town, with large, radiantly well-maintained clapboard homes and tree-canopied avenues that always seemed to lead to some breathtaking view of the Atlantic. This was the America I knew from catalogs and romantic comedies, and I had signed on to work there for an entire summer, with apparently very few real duties and lots of time to read and dream of my future while staring out at the ocean. I couldn't believe my good fortune. Yet, soon after my arrival, I realized that my employer's mental health was deteriorating, and that the summer, if I chose to stay, would be one of the strangest of my life.

Did you immediately begin work on the novel?

No—or at least not in the sense that I started putting pen to paper. Very shortly after that summer, I moved to Costa Rica and made a young idealist's promise to myself that I was not going to speak or read or write English any more than absolutely necessary to make money as a teacher until I had mastered Spanish. (This resulted in many near breakdowns, wherein, for example, I nearly wept while waxing nostalgic to a group of third-graders about the pleasure of reading *The Great Gatsby*.) When I returned to the United States, I worked for several years as a freelance writer and as an ▸

“Soon after my arrival, I realized that my employer's mental health was deteriorating, and that the summer, if I chose to stay, would be one of the strangest of my life.”

assistant editor at *The New Republic* before I felt sufficiently distanced from my summer in Maine to begin work on the novel.

Is the woman you lived with in Maine still alive?

No. Unfortunately, she passed away. I liked her very much.

Did you need to do any additional research to write the novel?

Very little. I read about subdural hematomas, and I also talked with nurses and paramedics about emergency procedures. But I drew mostly from the "research" I had already done while living in this community. I had photographs and a hand-drawn map I'd made of the town, and I tacked those to the wall next to my desk so that I could look at them while I worked. I also had notes—painful, often unselfconsciously comic accounts of my experiences that I had scrawled into a journal.

How much of the novel is based on events that actually happened?

This is a difficult question for me to answer because I find memory—and perhaps my own memory, in particular—so often untrustworthy. Years had passed from the time I left Maine to the time I began work on the novel: more than enough time for my desire for things to have been different that summer to influence the way I remembered them. Then I spent another four years molding characters and shifting the chronology of my memories in a way I thought would create a compelling novel. If I were forced, I'm sure I could point out

“I had photographs and a hand-drawn map I'd made of the town, and I tacked those to the wall next to my desk so that I could look at them while I worked.”

a few events that I believe definitely, positively happened (the incident at the yacht club, for instance), but I hope you'll be kind enough not to force me.

Can you tell us a little about the process of writing the book? How long did it take to write?

While working for *The New Republic* magazine in Washington, D.C., I wanted to devote more and more time to the novel. So eventually I quit my job and moved into an old farmhouse my grandmother had left in Indiana.

My plan was to support myself by freelance writing. However, I soon discovered that after working all day on the novel, I dreaded returning to the desk in the evening to write for another four or five hours about subjects that often did not greatly interest me. I wanted to be outside. I wanted to talk with someone besides my mailman. So I took a job working in the evenings as a "home security advisor" for a local home security company. When families expressed an interest in the company's home security system, my job was to drive out to where they lived, survey the outside and inside of their homes, then sit down with them at their kitchen table and kindly, gently, remind them of all the ghastly things that could happen to them if they did not take the proper precautions. I'm not an extrovert, so I didn't always find the job easy, but it got me out of my house and allowed me enough money to live.

During the first year, I wrote the first draft of the novel longhand. I found that when I was writing on the computer—which made it easy to type the first half of a sentence, wonder if it could be made better, then hit ▸

"I wanted to be outside. I wanted to talk with someone besides my mailman. So I took a job working in the evenings as a 'home security advisor' for a local home security company."

A Conversation with Brian Groh *(continued)*

the delete key—my thoughts began to seem like whirling airborne scraps that were not easy to locate and very easy to discard. Writing longhand seemed to slow my thoughts down, making them heavier, more substantive, and therefore easier to apprehend. I worked on the novel for four years.

No backup copies for that first draft, right? Did that concern you?

I was always deeply spooked by the idea of losing the draft. I wrote it on fifty-page bound legal pads. Each time I'd written ten to fifteen pages, I would drive down to a Shell gas station on Route 50, where, although I never saw anyone else use it, they offered a self-service copying machine. Five cents per copy. I'd copy the pages then slide them into an envelope beneath the front seat of my car. I copied the whole first draft this way, and although it did ease my concerns, I still occasionally had nightmares where my house burned down and my car got totaled on the same day.

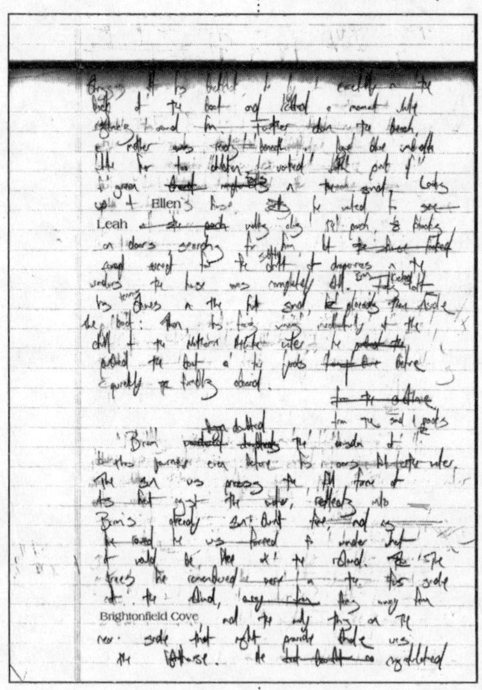

How great of an interest in comic books and graphic novels do you share with the character of Nathan Empson? Did you ever want to be a graphic novelist?

I dreamed of becoming a comic book artist or graphic novelist for a long time. I grew up making weekly pilgrimages to a local comic book store where I would buy the latest issues of Frank Miller's *Daredevil* and *The Uncanny X-Men*. Eventually, I grew to admire graphic novels like Art Spiegelman's *Maus*, Dan Clowes's *Ghost World*, and Lynda Barry's *One Hundred Demons*. But I was never very good at drawing, and I never took any real steps to learn how.

I was mostly drawn to the stories, and I feel a great debt to comic books for this reason. They made me a reader. During all those evenings of my childhood, when it was way past my bedtime and I was trying to read my comics in the wedge of light that fell from the hallway into my room, I think, among other things, I was learning how a story can change you and make you want to write stories of your own.

"I dreamed of becoming a comic book artist or graphic novelist for a long time. I grew up making weekly pilgrimages to a local comic book store where I would buy the latest issues of Frank Miller's *Daredevil* and *The Uncanny X-Men*."

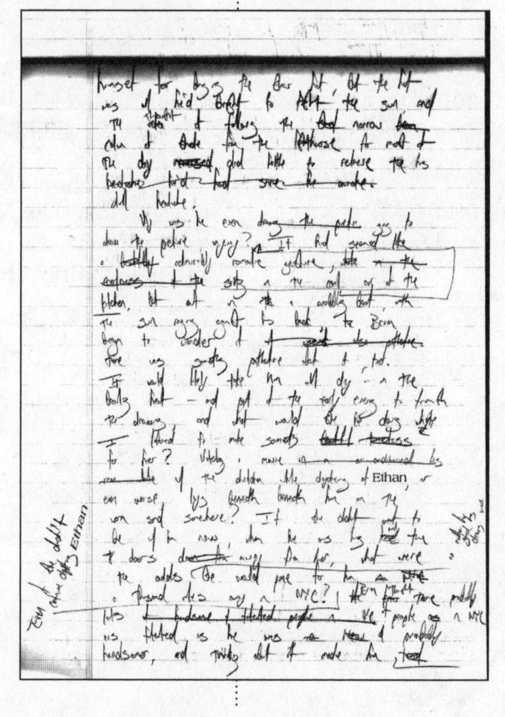

For Nathan and Leah, this is a coming-of-age story, but for Ellen and many of the other residents of Brightonfield Cove, this is a story about aging and various forces in life catching up with you. Which story was harder to write? Which story was more appealing to you?

I probably found it more challenging to write of Ellen and her peers (because I don't yet have a firsthand ▸

understanding of what it's like to be that age), but I've been fortunate enough to have friends who are in their seventies and eighties, and my conversations with them made me more confident when writing about older characters' lives.

I was powerfully interested in every character's life in this book, but writing about the lives of older people, trying to imagine what it would be like to be Ellen or Carl Buchanan, often seemed particularly intriguing to me. I will be their age eventually, and as with most journeys I've taken, I'd like to know as much as possible about where I'm going before I arrive.

What are you working on now?

Four years is a long time to be cooped up in one place, living alone, so I'd like to write another travel article soon. But I'm also at work on something longer. I'm reluctant to talk about the subject because I've found the more I talk about what I'm writing, the more it begins to feel like something I'm obligated to do, and like everyone, I suppose, ideally I want my work to feel like play.

“Four years is a long time to be cooped up in one place, living alone, so I'd like to write another travel article soon.”

Maine Journal
The "Brightonfield Cove" Notebook

Below are excerpts from Brian Groh's notebook, recorded while he was working in Maine. Information in brackets has been added or changed to make things clearer (and, occasionally, vaguer), and names have been changed to protect individuals' privacy.

June 18, 1997

Two days ago [my employer] L asked me to scrape nearly all of her leftover restaurant dinner into her dog's dish. L had eaten very little that evening—as is typical—and there was a large, untouched, rather appetizing quantity of food there that she wanted to give to Max.

"The whole thing?" I asked.

"Yes," she said. But as I began to do it, she cried, "No!"

"What?"

"Save the potato."

"This?" I asked. There were two potatoes on the plate. One very large potato, and one-half of one very small potato. I held up the large one.

"No," she said. "The other one."

"This one?" I was holding the barely quarter-sized piece of potato. "What are we going to do with this?"

"I don't know," she said. "I don't know yet. Wrap it up and stick it in the fridge."

I wanted to pop it in my mouth and be done with it, but instead, while Max dined, I wrapped the tiny potato in cellophane and placed it inside the mostly empty refrigerator.

Yesterday I watched L peer at the books on her mantle until she encountered an ▸

empty, plastic videocassette case that I had left there. Like a child, she picked up the case and rotated it slowly in her hands. After a while, she returned the case to the mantle, apparently resigned to the existence of mysteries in life we cannot answer.

June 19

At the club, there was very little tennis being played, but we sat and drank our half-and-halves. After a while, Tim, a tennis instructor, came to sit with us and watch the lone tennis match being played by two teenage girls on the nearest court.

After a while, I asked him, "Are you going to the club party tonight?"

He glanced at L and then smirked. "No," he said. "I'm not invited. Once the lessons are done, it's 'Get outta here! Get outta here and don't show your face until the next lesson.' "

I laughed, and we watched the young blonde girl double-fault.

Later, a woman, Caroline, (related to L somehow?), came and sat with us. She told me she would let me borrow her dinghy, docked down at the yacht club, if I would like to use it. I said I would.

When Caroline's husband, Devin, came by our table, I asked them where they both lived. "At the fourth cottage on your left after you pass the church," Caroline replied.

Tim snorted. "That always gets me," he said. "People always say *cottage*, and you think of this little one-room thing, you know?" He held his hands in the air and made a square shape with them. "Only once you get there, the cottage is this sprawling monstrosity."

I smiled, but no one spoke.

"Tim [the tennis instructor] snorted. 'That always gets me,' he said. 'People always say *cottage*, and you think of this little one-room thing, you know? . . . Only once you get there, the cottage is this sprawling monstrosity.' "

"I just think that's funny," Tim said, turning again towards the court.

"Hmm," Caroline said.

June 27

This morning was very blustery and there were large whitecaps in the bay. Too windy to watch tennis, so I took L on a long drive to Kennebunkport. Afterward, I read more Herodotus and came down shortly before dinner.

Meeting L in the living room, I held out my hand to her and asked her how she felt.

"Well, I'm upset," she said, folding both hands around mine. Her eyes looked pinkish and a little wet.

"What about?"

"Well, my friend Jane Rogen. She died."

"I'm sorry."

"Did you know her?"

"No."

"Well, she was a very dear friend of mine, and I was just at [a neighbor's], and they told me."

"I'm sorry."

L nodded. She said, "It seems the older I'm getting, I have more friends around me dying."

"I guess that's part of getting older," I agreed.

"Yes, it happens. But it's sad."

June 30

Leisurely day, wherein tensions [between L and I] seem to be waning. I took a walk today to a site where [a seventeenth-century explorer] arrived and spent the winter with the [local] Indians. I returned home and spent most of the late afternoon at the club with L. Saw a photo above the piano in the ▸

clubhouse of the club around the turn of the century. Women playing tennis in long dresses, men in pants and long-sleeve shirts. Returned home and afterward went running and didn't feel well. I began a book by Maugham called *Cakes and Ale*. In it, a character has written a book entitled *The Eye of the Needle*. That would be a good title.

July 3

Two evenings ago, on the porch, Mrs. Kearns [L's nurse] told me the story of an old man she once took care of, who, on the last day she was to work for him, made her promise she would not leave without a hug. Throughout the day, he reminded her, and when she got ready to go and finally hugged him, he reached down and threw back the covers.

"Look what you got excited!" he cried. "Now just look what you got excited!"

Reflecting back on this, Mrs. Kearns, a widow, said, "People are so lonely. It don't matter much who you got sometimes, just so long as you got somebody to talk to."

Later, at dinner, Steven [the student who lives with L in Ohio] was talking about a sign he once saw in the maternity ward of a hospital. Complete with illustrations, the sign detailed the many ways a child might seem afflicted [with some illness] at birth, when in reality their strange appearance is temporary and innocuous.

"Like what?" I asked.

"Well, one of the pictures said that your baby can come out white, like, albino, with this strange milky [layer of] skin that goes away."

"I know what causes that," said Mrs.

“Two evenings ago, on the porch, Mrs. Kearns [L's nurse] told me the story of an old man she once took care of, who, on the last day she was to work with him, made her promise she would not leave without a hug.”

Kearns. "Too much starch. When my second youngest, Elroy, came out, he was all like that, white, and when the doctors came and asked what I'd been eating, I didn't want to tell 'em. But I had to, you know, and so I told 'em I'd been eating starch."

We all stared at her, uncertain.

Steven said, "Like the starch you eat or the starch you…"

"No, no. The kind you use with your laundry," Mrs. Kearns said.

When none of us said anything, she continued, "I couldn't *help* it. It was one of those cravings women have when they're pregnant. I ate a ton of the stuff. I don't know why starch and not something else, but it was starch."

I said, "But the baby was OK?"

"Oh yes. Just white for a little while," Mrs. Kearns laughed.

Steven said, "With no wrinkles?"

July 5

Last night, the fireworks. Bursting large in the waiting dark from three places along the coast. From down below, on the beach, a few pitiful rockets sliced the air—and, after the brief blossoms of light, there was always the clapping and conversation. As I sat on the porch, below me a few children gathered with their parents and began trying to light sparklers despite the wind. Those [who had sparklers that were] lit bounded and swirled across the lawn, little white spheres of youth, shrieking as they faded back into darkness. Later, when several families stood on the lawn watching the fireworks across the bay, I said, "You can all come up here if you want to," but they seemed happy to remain where they were. ▶

"As I sat on the porch, below me a few children gathered with their parents and began trying to light sparklers despite the wind. Those [who had sparklers that were] lit bounded and swirled across the lawn, little white spheres of youth, shrieking as they faded back into darkness."

I was [eventually joined by an older couple named] Fiona and Douglas. Douglas kept talking about the fireworks he'd seen in St. Louis last year.

"Blowing up right over the arches, you see. Beautiful. And I have it on tape. I brought it up here, you know. Found it in a box I'd brought."

When his wife complained about being able to see the fireworks but not hear them very well from where we were sitting, Douglas suggested they go back and watch last year's fireworks in St. Louis.

"No, thank you," she said curtly.

Fiona spoke with condescension when explaining about [Brightonfield Cove]. "The Cove is not open to just anyone," she said.

I said, "Well, anyone with enough money can buy a house here, can't they? And anyone can join the club?"

"Oh, no," she said. "You must have two supporters in order to apply for membership to the club, and then the application is voted upon."

"Her family's been here for over a hundred years," Douglas said. "But when I married her it took almost five years before anyone would speak to me here." He shook his head and laughed, like an old fraternity member fondly remembering the hazing of his youth.

July [?]

This afternoon Loraine [a young woman also working in the community] took her clothes off—or at least some of them, anyway. After hiking with me for a while, she peeled off her shorts and T-shirt and stood wearing only her tennis shoes and a black bikini. The bikini bottoms were more like hot pants and when she walked she sometimes

"She peeled off her shorts and T-shirt and stood wearing only her tennis shoes and a black bikini. The bikini bottoms were more like hot pants, and when she walked she sometimes had to ease her thumb behind her to adjust their fit."

had to ease her thumb behind her to adjust their fit.

We talked a long time. She talked about how much she loved her grandmother—how she almost had had a nervous breakdown when she died. She talked about how mean she had been to boys in her adolescence—how she had often laughed in their faces, taken advantage of their kindness, and generally reduced them to egoless shadows. She talked about a shy boy whose naiveté she and her friends had sometimes exploited, but who, over the years, they grew to like. On his eighteenth birthday, they threw him a surprise party that made him bawl with gratitude before (perhaps due to shame?) he got drunk.

August

[This journal entry is undated. But the color of the ink, and my inability to find the energy to write more than dialogue, makes me think this must have been toward the end of my stay. I remember sitting with L and her nurse, Mrs. Kearns, watching the news on television.]

ME: Whoa. Did you hear that? There's an escaped convict running around in [the neighboring county], not far from here.

L: I'm not a convict.

ME: Neither am I.

MRS. KEARNS: Me neither.

ME: Well, then, I guess we're safe.

MRS. KEARNS: Yep. We're in three. Holy Trinity. Father, Son, Holy Spirit. Ain't nothing gonna touch us.

(L looks at me, confused.)

ME (to L): Mrs. Kearns was just explaining that because there are three of us here, we ►

Maine Journal ***(continued)***

represent the holy trinity and are therefore impervious to anyone who might want to harm us.

(L, looking relieved, eases back in her seat.)

ME: Thank you, Mrs. Kearns.

MRS. KEARNS (wagging a finger in reprimand): No, sir. The Lord. It's the Lord you need to thank.

August

A neighbor, Constance, told L and me yesterday that she saw a man climb out of his truck beside the club and start taking photos of her and her child while they played tennis. Constance walked over to him and asked him to identify himself. He said he was a photographer for *Down East* magazine. Constance firmly told him that the community did not want publicity and that he should go.